# QUERELLE

OTHER WORKS BY JEAN GENET
published by Grove Press

The Balcony
The Blacks: A Clown Show
Funeral Rites
The Maids and Deathwatch
Miracle of the Rose
Our Lady of the Flowers
The Screens
The Thief's Journal

# JEAN GENET

# Querelle

*Translated from the original French
by Anselm Hollo*

*GROVE PRESS* • *New York*

Published by Grove Press, Inc.
920 Broadway
New York, N.Y. 10010

The Library of Congress has cataloged the first printing of this
title as follows:

Genet, Jean, 1910–
        [Querelle de Brest. English]
        Querelle/Jean Genet; translated from the original French by
Anselm Hollo—New York: Grove Press.
        276 p.
        Translation of Querelle de Brest.
        I. Title
PZ3.G2866 Qd 3        843'.9'12        73-17693
[PQ2613.E53]

ISBN 0-394-62368-1  74[8302r83]rev

# QUERELLE

THE NOTION OF MURDER OFTEN BRINGS TO MIND THE NOTION OF sea and sailors. Sea and sailors do not, at first, appear as a definite image—it is rather that "murder" starts up a feeling of *waves*. If one considers that seaports are the scene of frequent crimes, the association seems self-explanatory; but there are numerous stories from which we learn that the murderer was a man of the sea—either a real one, or a fake one—and if the latter is the case, the crime will be even more closely connected to the sea. The man who dons a sailor's outfit does not do so out of prudence only. His disguise relieves him from the necessity of going through all the rigamarole required in the execution of any preconceived murder. Thus we could say that the outfit does the following things for the criminal: it envelops him in clouds; it gives him the appearance of having come from that far-off line of the horizon where sea touches sky; with long, undulating and muscular strides he can walk across the waters, personifying

the Great Bear, the Pole Star or the Southern Cross; it (we are
still discussing this particular disguise, as used by a criminal) it
allows him to assume dark continents where the sun sets and
rises, where the moon sanctions murder under roofs of bamboo
beside motionless rivers teeming with alligators; it gives him the
opportunity to act within the illusion of a mirage, to strike while
one of his feet is still resting upon a beach in Oceania and the
other propelling him across the waters toward Europe; it grants
him oblivion in advance, as sailors always "return from far
away"; it allows him to consider landlubbers as mere vegetation.
It cradles the criminal, it enfolds him—in the tight fit of his
sweater, in the amplitude of his bell-bottoms. It casts a sleep-
spell on the already fascinated victim. We shall talk about the
sailor's mortal flesh. We ourselves have witnessed scenes of seduction. In that very long sentence beginning "it envelops him
in clouds . . . ," we did indulge in facile poeticisms, each one
of the propositions being merely an argument in favor of the
author's personal proclivities. It is, admittedly, under the sign of
a very singular inner feeling that we would set down the ensuing
drama. We would also like to say that it addresses itself to inverts. The notion of love or lust appears as a *natural* corollary to
the notion of Sea and Murder—and it is, moreover, the notion
of *love against nature*. No doubt the sailors who are transported
by ("animated by" would appear more exact, we'll see that later
on) the desire and need to murder, apprenticed themselves first
to the Merchant Navy, thus are veterans of long voyages, nourished on ships' biscuit and the cat-o'-nine-tails, used to leg-irons
for any little mistake, paid off in some obscure port, signed on
again to handle some questionable cargo; and yet, it is difficult,
in a city of fogs and granite, to brush past the huskies of the
Fighting Navy, trained and trimmed by and for deeds we like to
think of as daring, those shoulders, profiles, earrings, those tough
and turbulent rumps, those strong and supple boys, without
imagining them capable of murders that seem entirely justified

by their deigning to commit them with their noble bodies. Whether they descend from heaven or return from a realm where they have consorted with sirens and even more fabulous monsters, on land these sailors inhabit buildings of stone, arsenals, palaces whose solidity is opposed to the nervousness, the feminine irritability of the waters (does not the sailor, in one of his songs, speak of how ". . . the sea's my best girl"?), by jetties loaded with chains, bollards, buoys, maritime paraphernalia to which, even when farthest from the sea, they know themselves anchored. To match their stature they are provided with barracks, forts, disused penitentiaries, magnificent pieces of architecture, all of them. Brest is a hard, solid city, built out of gray Breton granite. Its rocklike quality anchors the port, giving the sailors a sense of security, a launching point when outward bound, a haven of rest after the continuous wave-motion of the sea. If Brest ever seems more lighthearted, it is when a feeble sun gilds the façades which are as noble as those of Venice, or when its narrow streets teem with carefree sailors—or, *then*, even when there is fog and rain. The action of this story starts three days after a despatch-boat, *Le Vengeur*, had anchored in the Roads. Other warships lie round her: *La Panthère, Le Vainqueur, Le Sanglant,* and around these, *Le Richelieu, Le Béarn, Le Dunkerque,* and more. Those names have their counterparts in the past. On the walls of a side chapel in the church of Saint-Yves, in La Rochelle, hang a number of small votive paintings representing ships that have been either lost or saved: *La Mutine, Le Saphir, Le Cyclone, La Fée, La Jeune Aimée.* These ships had had no influence whatsoever on Querelle who had seen them sometimes as a child, yet we must mention their existence. For the ships' crews, Brest will always be the city of La Féria. Far from France, sailors never talk about this brothel without cracking a joke and hooting like owls, the way they talk about ducks in China or weird Annamites, and they evoke the proprietor and his wife in terms like:

"Shoot a game of craps with you—like at Nono's, I mean!"

"That guy, for a piece of ass he'd do anything—he'd even play with Nono."

"Him there, he went to La Féria to *lose*."

While the Madam's name is never mentioned, the names of "La Féria" and "Nono" must have traveled all around the world, in sarcastic asides on the lips of sailors everywhere. On board there never is anybody who would know exactly what La Féria really is, nor do they precisely know the rules of the game which has given it such a reputation, but no one, not even the greenest recruit, dare ask for an explanation; each and every seafarin' man will have it understood that he knows what it is all about. Thus the establishment in Brest appears ever in a fabulous light, and the sailors, as they approach that port, secretly dream of that house of ill repute which they'll mention only as a laughing matter. Georges Querelle, the hero of this book, speaks of it less than anyone. He knows that his own brother is the Madam's lover. Here is the letter, received in Càdiz, informing him of this:

Good Bro.,
I'm writing you these few lines to let you know that I'm back in Brest. I had planned on that dockyard job again, but, nothing doing. So there I was, stuck. And as you know, I'm none too good at finding the jobs, and besides, who wants to work his ass off anyhow. So, to get off the ground again, I went round to Milo's place and right after that the boss lady of La Féria was giving me the old eye. Did my best, we're getting along like a house on fire. The boss doesn't give a shit who goes with his woman, they're just business partners like they say. So, I'm in pretty good shape. Hope you're in good shape too, and when you get some furlough, etc.

(Signed) Robert.

Sometimes it rains in September. The rain makes the light cotton clothes—open shirts and denims—stick to the skin of the muscular men working in port and Arsenal. Again, some evenings the weather is fine when the groups of masons, carpenters, mechanics come out from the shipyards. They are weary. They look heavily burdened, and even when their expressions lighten, their workshoes, their heavy steps seem to shatter the pools of air around them. Slowly, ponderously they traverse the lighter, quicker, more rapid hither-and-thither of sailors on shore leave who have become the pride of this city which will scintillate till dawn with their nautical swagger, the gusts of their laughter, their songs, their merriment, the insults they yell at the girls; with their kisses, their wide collars, the pompons on their hats. The laborers return to their lodgings. All through the day they have toiled (servicemen, soldiers or sailors, never have that feeling of having *toiled*), blending their actions in a network of common endeavor, for the purposes of an achieved work like a visible, tightly drawn knot, and now they are returning. A shadowy friendship—shadowy to them— unites them, and also a quiet hatred. Few of them are married, and the wives of those live some distance away. Toward six o'clock in the evening it is when the workmen pass through the iron gates of the Arsenal and leave the dockyard. They walk up in the direction of the railroad station where the canteens are, or down the road to Recouvrance where they have their furnished rooms in cheap hotels. Most of them are Italians and Spaniards, though there are some North Africans and Frenchmen as well. It is in the midst of such a surfeit of fatigue, heavy muscles, virile lassitude, that Sublieutenant Seblon of the *Vengeur* loves to take his evening walk.

*They used to have this cannon permanently trained upon the penitentiary. Today the same cannon (its barrel only) stands* mounted upright in the middle of the same courtyard where once the convicts were mustered for the galleys. It is astonishing that turning criminals into sailors used to be regarded as a form of punishment.

Went past La Féria. Saw nothing. Never any luck. Over in Recouvrance I caught a glimpse of an accordion—a sight I frequently see on board, yet never tire of watching—folding, unfolding on a sailor's thigh.

Se brester, to brace oneself. Derives, no doubt, from bretteur, fighter: and so, relates to se quereller, to pick a fight.

When I learn—if only from the newspaper—that some scandal is breaking, or when I'm just afraid that it may break upon the world, I make preparations to get away: I always believe that I shall be suspected of being the prime mover. I regard myself as a demon-ridden creature, merely because I have imagined certain subjects for scandal.

As for the hoodlums I hold in my arms, tenderly kissing and caressing their faces before gently covering them up again in my sheets, they are no more than a kind of passing thrill and experiment combined. After having been so overwhelmed by the loneliness to which my inversion condemns me, is it really possible that I may some day hold naked in my arms, and continue to hold, pressed close to my body, those young men whose courage and hardness place them so high in my esteem that I long to throw myself at their feet and grovel before them? I dare hardly believe this, and tears well up in my eyes, to thank God for granting me such happiness. My tears make me feel soft. I melt. My own cheeks still wet with tears, I revel in, and overflow with tenderness for, the flat, hard cheekbones of those boys.


That severe, at times almost suspicious look, a look that seems to pass judgment, with which the pederast appraises every young man he encounters, is really a brief, but intense meditation on his own loneliness. That instant (the duration of the glance) is filled with a concentrated and constant despair, with its own jagged frequency, sheathed in the fear of rebuff. "It would be so great . . . ," he thinks. Or, if he isn't thinking, it expresses itself in his frown, in that black, condemning look.


Whenever some part of his body happens to be naked, He (that is Querelle, whose name the officer never writes down—this not merely for the sake of prudence as regards his fellow officers and superiors, since in their eyes the contents of his diary would be quite sufficient to damn him) starts examining it. He looks for blackheads, split nails, red pimples. Irritated when he can't find any, he invents some. As soon as he has nothing better to do, he becomes engrossed in this game. Tonight he is examining his legs: their black, strong hairs are quite soft in spite of their vigorous growth, and thus they create a kind of mist from foot to groin, which softens the roughness and abruptness, one might almost say, the stoniness of his muscles. It amazes me how such a virile trait can envelop his legs with such great sweetness. He amuses himself by applying a burning cigarette to his hairs and then bends over them to savor the scorched smell. He is not smiling any more than usual. His own body in repose is his great passion—a morose, not an exultant passion. Bent over his body, he sees himself there. He examines it with an imaginary magnifying glass. He observes its minuscule irregularities with the scr ╰

pulous attention of an entomologist studying the habits of insects. But as soon as He moves, what dazzling revenge his entire body takes, in the glory of its motion!

He (Querelle) is never absent-minded, always attentive to what he is doing. Every moment of his life he rejects the dream. He is forever present. He never answers: "I was thinking of something else." And yet the childishness of his obvious preoccupations astonishes me.

Hands in pockets, lazily, I would say to him, "Give me a little shove, just to knock the ash off my cigarette," and he would let fly and punch me on the shoulder. I shrug it off.

I should have been able to keep my sea legs or hang on to the gunwale, the ship wasn't rolling that hard, but quickly, and with pleasure, I took advantage of the ship's motion to sway and to allow myself to be shifted along, always in his direction. I even managed to brush against his elbow.

It is as if a fierce and devoted watchdog, ready to chew up your carotid artery, were following him around, trotting, at times, between the calves of his legs, so that the beast's flanks seem to blend with his thigh muscles, ready to bite, always growling and snarling, so ferocious one expects to see it bite off his balls.

After these few excerpts picked (but not entirely at random) from a private journal which suggested his character to us, we would like you to look upon the sailor Querelle, born from that solitude in which the officer himself remained isolated, as a singular figure comparable to the Angel of the Apocalypse, whose feet rest on the waters of the sea. By meditating on Querelle, by using, in his imagination, his most beautiful traits, his muscles, his rounded parts, his teeth, his guessed-at genitals, Lieutenant Seblon has turned the sailor into an angel (as we shall see, he describes him as "the Angel of Loneliness"), that is to say, into a being less and less human, crystalline, around whom swirl strands of a music based on the opposite of harmony—or rather, a music that is what remains after harmony has been used up, worn out, and in the midst of which this immense angel moves, slowly, unwitnessed, his feet on the water, but his head—or what should be his head—in a dazzle of rays from a supernatural sun.

They themselves tending to deny it, the strangely close resemblance between the two brothers Querelle appeared attractive only to others. They met only in the evenings, as late as possible, in the one bed of a furnished room not far from where their mother had eked out her meager existence. They met again, perhaps, but somewhere so deep down that they could not see anything clearly, in their love for their mother, and certainly in their almost daily arguments. In the morning they parted without a word. They wanted to ignore each other. Already, at the age of fifteen, Querelle had smiled the smile that was to be peculiarly his for the rest of his life. He had chosen a life among thieves and spoke their argot. We'll try to bear this in mind in order to understand Querelle whose mental makeup and very feelings depend upon, and assume the form of, a certain syntax, a particular murky orthography. In his conversation we find turns like "peel him raw!" "boy, am I flying," "oh, beat off!" "he better not show his ass in here again," "he got burnt all right," "get that punk," "see the guy making tracks," "hey, baby, dig my hard-on," "suck me off," etc., expressions which are never pronounced clearly, but muttered in a kind of monotone and as if from within, without the speaker really "seeing" them. They are not projected, and thus Querelle's words never reveal him; they do not really define him at all. On the contrary, they seem to enter through his mouth, to pile up inside him, to settle and to form a thick mud deposit, out of which, at times, a transparent bubble rises, exploding delicately on his lips. What one hears, then, is one of those bits of the argot.

As for the police in port and city, Brest lay under the authority of its Commissariat: in the time of our novel there were two Inspectors, joined together by a singular friendship, by the names of Mario Daugas and Marcellin. The latter was little more than an excrescence to Mario (it is well known that policemen always come in pairs), dull and painstaking enough, yet sometimes a source of great comfort to his colleague. However, there was yet another collaborator whom Mario had chosen, more subtle and more dear—more easily sacrificed, too, should that become necessary: Dédé.

Like every French town, Brest had its Monoprix store, a favorite stamping ground for Dédé and numerous sailors who circulated among the counters, coveting—and sometimes purchasing—pairs of gloves, of all things. To complete the picture, the old-time control by the Admiralty had been replaced by the services of the Préfecture Maritime.

Bought or stolen from a sailor, the blue denim pants belled over his entrancing feet, now motionless and arched after the final table-shaking stamp. He was wearing highly polished black shoes, cracked and crinkled at the point reached by the ripples of blue denim that ran down from the source of his belt. His torso was encased very tightly in a turtleneck jersey of white, slightly soiled wool. Querelle's parted lips slowly began to close. He started to raise the half-smoked cigarette to his mouth, but his hand came to rest halfway up his chest, and the mouth remained half-open: he was gazing at Gil and Roger, who were united by the almost visible thread of their glances, by the freshness of their smiles; and Gil seemed to be singing for the boy, and Roger, like the sovereign at some intimate rite of debauch, to be favoring this young eighteen-year-old mason, so that with his voice he could be the hero of a roadside tavern for a night. The way the sailor was watching the two of them had the effect of isolating them. Once again, Querelle became aware of his mouth hanging half-open. His smile became more pronounced at the corner of his mouth, almost imperceptibly. A tinge of irony began to spread over his features, then over his entire body, giving him and his relaxed posture leaning back against the wall an air of amused sarcasm. Altered by the raising of an eyebrow, to match the crooked smile, his expression became somewhat malicious as he continued his scrutiny of the two young men. The smile vanished from Gil's lips, as if the entire ball of string had been unrolled, and at the same moment expired on Roger's face; but four seconds later, regaining his breath and taking up the song again, Gil, once more on top of the table, resumed his smile, which brought back and sustained, until the very last couplet of the song, the smile on Roger's lips. Not for a second did their eyes stray from the eyes of the other. Gil was singing. Querelle shifted his shoulders against the wall of the bistro. He became aware of himself, felt himself pitting his own living mass, the powerful muscles of his back, against the black and indestructible matter of that wall. Those two shadowy substances struggled in silence. Querelle knew the beauty of his back. We shall see how, a few days later, he was to secretly dedicate it to Lieutenant Seblon. Almost without moving, he let his shoulders ripple against the wall, its stones. He was a strong man. One hand—the other remaining in the pocket of his peacoat—raised a half-smoked cigarette to his lips, still holding the half-smile. Robert and the two other sailors were oblivious to everything but the song. Querelle retained his smile. To use an expression much favored by soldiers, Querelle shone by his absence. After letting a little smoke drift in the direction of his thoughts (as though he wanted to veil them, or show them a touch of insolence), his lips remained slightly drawn apart from his teeth, whose beauty he knew, their whiteness dimmed, now, by the night and the shadow cast by his upper lip. Watching Gil and Roger, now reunited by glance and smile, he could not make up his mind to withdraw, to enclose within himself those teeth and their gentle splendor, which had the same restful effect on his vague thoughts as the blue of the sea has on our eyes. Meanwhile, he was lightly running his tongue over his palate. It was alive. One of the sailors started to go through the motions of buttoning his peacoat, turning up the collar. Querelle was not used to the idea, one that had never really been formulated, that he was a monster. He considered, he observed his past with an ironic smile, frightened and tender at the same time, to the extent that this past became confused with what he himself was. Thus might a young boy whose soul is evident in his eyes, but who has been metamorphosed into an alligator, even if he were not fully conscious of his horrendous head and jaws, consider his scaly body, his solemn, gigantic tail, with which he strikes the water or the beach or brushes against that of other monsters, and which extends him with the same touching, heart-rending and indestructible majesty as the train of a robe, adorned with lace, with crests, with battles, with a thousand crimes, worn by a Child Empress, extends her. He knew the horror of being alone, seized by an immortal enchantment in the midst of the world of the living. Only to him had been accorded the horrendous privilege to perceive his monstrous participation in the realms of the great muddy rivers and the rain forests. And he was apprehensive that some light, emanating from within his body, or from his true consciousness, might not be illuminating him, might not, in some way from inside the scaly carapace, give off a reflection of that true form and make him visible to men, who would then have to hunt him down.

In some places along the ramparts of Brest, trees have been

planted, and these grow in alleys bearing the perhaps derisive name of the "Bois de Boulogne." Here, in the summer, there are a few bistros where one can sit and drink at wooden tables swollen by rain and fog, under the trees or in arbors. The sailors had vanished into the shade of those trees, with a girl; Querelle let them, his buddies, take their turns with her, and then he came up to her as she lay stretched out on the grass. He proceeded to unbutton his fly, but after a brief, charming hesitation expressed in his fingers, he readjusted it again. Querelle felt calm. He had only to give the slightest turn of the head, to left or right, to feel his cheek rub against the stiff, upturned collar of his peacoat. This contact reassured him. By it, he knew himself to be clothed, marvelously clothed.

Later, when he was taking off his shoes, the bistro scene came back to Querelle's mind, who lacked the ability to assign it any precise significance. He could hardly put it into words. He knew only that it had aroused a faint sense of amusement in him. He could not have said why. Knowing the severity, the austerity almost, of his face and its pallor, this irony gave him what is commonly called a sarcastic air. For a moment or two he had remained amazed by the rapport that was established and understood and became almost an object between the eyes of those two: the one up on the table, singing there, his head bent down toward the other, who was sitting and gazing up at him. Querelle pulled off one of his socks. Apart from the material benefits derived from his murders, Querelle was enriched by them in other ways. They deposited in him a kind of slimy sediment, and the stench it gave off served to deepen his despair. From each one of his victims he had preserved something a little dirty: a slip, a bra, shoelaces, a handkerchief—objects sufficient to disprove his alibis and to condemn him. These relics were firsthand evidence of his splendor, of his triumphs. They were the shameful details, upon which all luminous but uncertain appearances rest. In the world of sailors with their striking good looks, virility, and pride, they were the secret counterparts of a greasy, broken-toothed comb at the bottom of a pocket; full-dress gaiters, from a distance impeccable as sails, but, like those, far from true white; a pair of elegant but poorly tailored pants; badly drawn tattoos; a filthy handkerchief; socks with holes in them. What for us is the strongest memory of Querelle's expression can best be described by an image that comes to mind: delicate metal strands, sparsely barbed, easily overcome, grasped by a prisoner's heavy hand, or grazing against sturdy fabric. Almost in spite of himself, quietly, to one of his mates, already stretched out in his hammock, Querelle said:

"Pair of fuckin' faggots, those two."

"Which two?"

"What?"

Querelle raised his head. His buddy, it seemed, didn't get it. And that was the end of the conversation. Querelle pulled off his other sock and turned in. Not that he wanted to sleep, or think over the scene in the bistro. Once he was stretched out, he had at last the leisure to consider his own affairs, and he had to think quick, in spite of his fatigue. The owner of La Féria would take the two kilos of opium, if Querelle only could get them out of the despatch-boat. The customs officials opened all sailors' bags, even the smallest ones. Coming ashore, all but the officers were subjected to a thorough search. Without cracking a smile, Querelle thought of the Lieutenant. The enormity of this idea struck him even while he was thinking what only he himself could have translated into:

"He's been giving me the old eye for some time now. Nervous like a cat on a hot tin roof. I got him hooked, I guess."

Querelle was glad to know that Robert was now living a life of Oriental ease and luxury; to know that he was a brothel Madam's lover as well as a friend to her obliging husband. He closed his eyes. He regained that region in himself where his brother was there with him. He let himself sink into a state where neither could be distinguished from the other. From this state he was able to extract, first, some words, and then, by a fairly elementary process, little by little, a thought—which, as it rose from those depths, again differentiated him from Robert and proposed singular acts, an entire system of solitary operations: quite gently these became his own, completely his, and Vic was there, with him, taking part. And Querelle, whose thoughts had overcome his personal autonomy in order to reach Vic, turned away again, re-entered himself, in the blind search for that inexpressible limbo which is like some inconsistent *pâté* of love. He was hardly touching his curled-up prick. He felt no urge. While still at sea, he had announced to the other sailors that once in Brest, he was sure going to shoot his wad; but tonight he wasn't even thinking about whether he should have kissed that girl.

Querelle was an exact replica of his brother. Robert, perhaps a little more taciturn, the other, a little hotter in temper (nuances by which one could tell them from each other, except if one was a furious girl). It so happens that we ourselves acquired our sense of Querelle's existence on a particular day, we could give the exact date and hour of—when we decided to write this story (and that is a word not to be used to describe some adventure or series of adventures that has already been lived through). Little by little, we saw how Querelle—already contained in our flesh—was beginning to grow in our soul, to feed on what is best in us, above all on our despair at not being in any way inside him, while having him inside of ourselves. After this discovery of Querelle we want him to become the Hero, even to those who may despise him. Following, within ourselves, his destiny, his development, we shall see how he lends himself to this in order to realize himself in a conclusion that appears to be (from then on) in complete accordance with his very own will, his very own fate.

The scene we are about to describe is a transposition of the event which revealed Querelle to us. (We are still referring to that ideal and heroic personage, the fruit of our secret loves.) We must say, of that event, that it was of equal import to the Visitation. No doubt it was only long after it had taken place that we recognized it as being "big" with consequences, yet there and then we may be said to have felt a true Annunciatory thrill. Finally: to become visible to you, to become a character in a novel, Querelle must be shown apart from ourselves. Only then will you get to know the apparent, and real, beauty of his body, his attitudes, his exploits, and their slow disintegration.

The farther you descend toward the port of Brest, the denser the fog seems to grow. It is so thick at Recouvrance, after you cross the Penfeld bridge, that the houses, their walls and roofs appear to be afloat. In the alleys leading down to the quayside you find yourself alone. Here and there you encounter the dim, fringed sun, like a light from a half-open dairy doorway. On you go through that vaporous twilight, until confronted once more by the opaque matter, the dangerous fog that shelters: a drunken sailor reeling home on heavy legs—a docker hunched over a girl—a hoodlum, perhaps armed with a knife—us—you—hearts pounding. The fog brought Gil and Roger closer together. It gave them mutual confidence and friendship. Though they were hardly aware of it as yet, this privacy instilled in them a hesitation, a little fearful, a little tremulous, a charming emotion akin to that in children when they walk along, hands in pockets, touching, stumbling over each other's feet.

"Shit—watch your step! Keep going."

"That must be the quay. Never mind 'em."

"And why not? You got the jitters?"

"No, but sometimes . . ."

Now and again they sensed a woman walking by, saw the steady glow of a cigarette, guessed at the outline of a couple locked in an embrace.

"Howzat . . . ? Sometimes what?"

"Oh come on, Gil, no need to take it out on me. It ain't my fault my sister wasn't able to make it."

And, a little quieter, after two more steps in silence:

"You can't have been thinking too much about Paulette, last night, dancing with that brunette?"

"What the fuck's that to you? Yeah, I danced with her. So what?"

"Well! You weren't just dancing, you took her home, too."

"So what, I'm not hitched to your sister, jack. Look who's talking. All I'm saying is, you could have made sure that she came along." Gil was speaking quite loudly, but none too distinctly, so as to be understood only by Roger. Then he lowered his voice, and a note of anxiety crept into it.

"So, what about it?"

"Gil, you know it, I just couldn't swing it for you. I swear."

They turned to the left, in the direction of the Navy warehouses. A second time they bumped into one another. Automatically, Gil put his hand on the boy's shoulder. It remained there. Roger slackened his pace, hoping that his buddy would stop. Would it happen? He was almost melting, feeling infinitely tender; but at that moment someone passed by—he and Gilbert were not in a place of perfect solitude. Gil let go of his shoulder and put his hand back into his pocket, and Roger thought that he had been rejected. Yet, when he took his hand away, Gil couldn't help bearing down a little harder, just as he let go, as if some kind of regret at taking it away had added to its weight. And now Gil had a hard-on.

"Shit."

He tried to visualize a sharp image of Paulette's face, and was immediately tempted by his erratic mind to concentrate on another point, on what Roger's sister had under her skirt, between her thighs. Needing an easily, immediately accessible physical prop, he said to himself, thinking in the inflections of cynicism:

"Well, here's her brother, right beside me, in the fog!"

It was then that it seemed to him it would be a delight to enter that warmth, that black, fur-fringed, slightly pursèd hole that emits such vague, yet ponderous and fiery odors, even in corpses already cold.

"She gives me the hots, your sister, you know."

Roger smiled, from ear to ear. He turned his radiant face toward Gil.

"Aaahh . . ."

The sound was both gentle and hoarse, seeming to originate in the pit of Gil's stomach, nothing so much as an anguished sigh born at the base of his throbbing rod. He realized that there was a rapid, immediate line connecting the base of his prick to the back of his throat and to that muffled groan. We would like these reflections, these observations, which cannot fully round out nor delineate the characters of the book, to give you permission to act not so much as onlookers as creators of these very characters, who will then slowly disengage themselves from your own preoccupations. Little by little, Gil's prick was getting lively. In his pants pocket his hand had hold of it, flattening it against his belly. Indeed, it had the stature of a tree, a mossy-boled oak with lamenting mandrakes being born among its roots. (Sometimes, when he woke up with a hard-on, Gil would address his prick as "my hanged man.") They walked on, but at a slower pace.

"She gives you the hots, eh?"

The light of Roger's smile came close to illuminating the fog, making the stars sparkle through. It made him happy to hear, right there beside him, how Gil's amorous desire made his mouth water.

"You think that's funny, don'cha."

Teeth clenched, hands still in pockets, Gil turned to face the boy and forced him to retreat into a recess in the stone wall. He kept pushing him with his belly, his chest. Roger kept on smiling, a little less radiantly perhaps, hardly shrinking back from the thrust of the other young man's face. Gil was now leaning against him with his entire vigorous body.

"You think that's a scream, hey?"

Gil took one of his hands out of his pocket. He put it on Roger's shoulder, so close to the collar that the thumb brushed against the cool skin of the kid's neck. His shoulders against the wall, Roger let himself slide down a little, as if wanting to appear smaller. He was still smiling.

"So say something? You think it's funny? Eh?"

Gil advanced like a conqueror, almost like a lover. His mouth was both cruel and soft, like those movie seducers' mouths under their thin black mustaches, and his expression turned suddenly so serious that Roger's smile, by a faint drooping of the corners of his mouth, now seemed a little sad. With his back to the wall, Roger kept on sliding, holding that wistful smile with which he looked to be sinking, submerging in the monstrous wave that Gil was riding, one hand still in pocket, clutching that great spar.

"Aaahh . . ."

Again, Gil voiced that groan, hoarse and remote, that we have had occasion to describe.

"Oh, yeah, I'd like to have her here, all right. And you bet your ass I'd screw her, and good, if I had her here, the way I've got you!"

Roger said nothing. His smile disappeared. His eyes kept on meeting Gil's stare, and the only gentleness he could see there was in Gil's eyebrows, powdered with chalk and cement dust.

"Gil!"

He thought: "This is Gil. It's Gilbert Turko. He's from Poland. He's been working at the Arsenal, on the gantry, with the other masons. He's in a rage."

Close to Gil's ear, under his breath which entered the fog, he murmured:

"Gil!"

"Oh . . .! Oh . . .! I sure could use a piece of her, right now. You, you look alike, you know. You've got that same little mouth of hers."

He moved his hand closer to Roger's neck. Finding himself so the master, in the heart of the light mass of watery air, increased Gil Turko's desire to be tough, sharp and heavy. To rip the fog, to destroy it with a sudden brutal gesture, would perhaps be enough to affirm his virility, which otherwise, on his return to quarters tonight, would suffer mean and powerful humiliation.

"Got her eyes, too. What a shame you ain't her. Hey, what's this? You passing out?"

As if to prevent Roger from "passing out," he pressed his belly closer still to his, pushing him against the wall, while his free hand kept hold of the charming head, holding it above the waves of a powerful and arrogant sea, the sea that was Gil. They remained motionless, one shoring up the other.

"What are you going to tell her?"

"I'll try to get her to come along tomorrow."

Despite his inexperience, Roger understood the extent, if not quite the meaning of his confusion, when he heard the sound of his own voice: it was toneless.

"And the other thing I told you about?"

"I'll try my best about that too. We going back now?"

They pulled apart, quickly. Suddenly they heard the sea. From the very beginning of this scene they had been close to the water's edge. For a moment both of them felt frightened at the thought of having been so close to danger. Gil took out a cigarette and lit it. Roger saw the beauty of his face that looked as if it had been picked, like a flower, by those large hands, thick and covered with powdery dust, their palms illuminated now by a delicate and trembling flame.

o     o     o

They say that the murderer Ménesclou used a spray of lilacs to entice the little girl closer to him so that he could then slit her throat; it is with his hair, with his eyes—with his full smile—that He (Querelle) draws me on. Does this mean that I am going to my death? That those locks, those teeth are lethal? Does it mean that love is a murderer's lair? And could it mean that "He" is leading me on? And "for that"?

At the point of my going under, "in Querelle," will I still be able to reach the alarm siren?

(While the other characters are incapable of lyricism which we are using in order to recreate them more vividly within you, Lieutenant Seblon himself is solely responsible for what flows from his pen.)

I would love it—oh, I deeply wish for it!—if, under his regal garb, "He" were simply a hoodlum! To throw myself at his feet! To kiss his toes!

In order to find "Him" again, and counting on absence and the emotions aroused by returning to give me courage to address "Him" by his first name, I pretended to be leaving on a long furlough. But I wasn't able to resist. I come back. I see "Him" again, and I give "Him" my orders, almost vindictively.

He could get away with anything. Spit me in the face, call me by my first name.
"You're getting overly familiar!" I'd say to "Him."
The blow he would strike me with his fist, right in the mouth,

*would make my ears ring with this oboe murmur: "My vulgarity
is regal, and it accords me every right."*

By giving the ship's barber a curt order to clip his hair very
short, Lieutenant Seblon hoped to achieve a he-mannish appearance—not so much to save face as to be able to move more
freely among the handsome lads. He did not know, then, that
he caused them to shrink back from him. He was a well-built
man, wide-shouldered, but he felt within himself the presence
of his own femininity, sometimes contained in a chickadee's
egg, the size of a pale blue or pink sugared almond, but sometimes brimming over to flood his entire body with its milk. He
knew this so well that he himself believed in this quality of
weakness, this frailty of an enormous, unripe nut, whose pale
white interior consisted of the stuff children call milk. The
Lieutenant knew to his great chagrin that this core of femininity could erupt in an instant and manifest itself in his face,
his eyes, his fingertips, and mark every gesture of his by rendering it too gentle. He took care never to be caught counting the
stitches of any imaginary needlework, scratching his head with
an imaginary knitting needle. Nevertheless he betrayed himself
in the eyes of all men whenever he gave the order to pick up
arms, for he pronounced the word "arms" with such grace that
his whole person seemed to be kneeling at the grave of some
beautiful lover. He never smiled. His fellow officers considered
him stern and somewhat puritanical, but they also believed they
were able to discern a quality of stupendous refinement under-
neath that hard shell, and the belief rested on the way in which,
despite himself, he pronounced certain words.

*The happiness of clasping in my arms a body so beautiful, even
though it is huge and strong! Huger and stronger than mine.*

∘          ∘          ∘

Reverie. *Is this him?* "*He*" *goes ashore every night.* When he comes back, "*His*" *bell-bottom pants—which are wide, and cover his shoes, contrary to regulations—look bespattered, perhaps with jism mixed with the dust of the streets he has been sweeping with their frayed bottoms. His pants, they're the dirtiest sailor's pants I've ever seen. Were I to demand an explanation from* "*Him*," "*He*" *would smile as he chucked his beret behind him:*

"*That, that's just from all the suckers going down on me. While they're giving me a blowjob, they come all over my jeans. That's just their spunk. That's all.*"

"*He*" *would appear to be very proud of it.* "*He*" *wears those stains with a glorious impudence: they are his medals.*


While it is the least elegant of the brothels in Brest, where no men of the Battle Fleet ever go to give it a little of their grace and freshness, La Féria certainly is the most renowned. It is a solemn gold and purple cave providing for the colonials, the boys of the Merchant Navy and the tramp steamers, and the longshoremen. Whereas the sailors visit to have a "piece" or a "short time," the dock workers and others say: "Let's go shoot our wads." At night, La Féria also provides the imagination with the thrills of scintillating criminality. One may always suspect three or four hoodlums lurking in the fog-shrouded *pissoir* erected on the sidewalk across the street. Sometimes the front door stands ajar, and from it issue the airs of a player piano, blue strains, serpentines of music unrolling in the dark shadows, curling round the wrists and necks of the workmen who just happen to be walking past. But daylight allows a more detailed view of the dirty, blind, gray and shame-ravaged shack it is. Seen only by the light of its lantern and its lowered Venetian blinds, it could well be overflowing with the hot luxury of a bounty of boobs and milky thighs under clinging black satin, bursting with bosoms, crystals, mirrors, scents, and champagne, the sailor's dreams as soon as he enters the red-light quarter. It had a most impressive door. This consisted of a thick slab of wood, plated over with iron and armed with long, sharp spikes of shining metal—perhaps steel—pointing outward, into the street. In its mysterious arrogance it was perfectly suited to heighten the turmoil of any amorous heart. For the docker or stevedore the door symbolized the cruelty that attends the rites of love. If the door was designed for protection, it had to be guarding a treasure such as only insensate dragons or invisible genies could hope to gain without being impaled to bleed on those spikes—unless, of course, it did open all by itself, to a word, a gesture from you, docker or soldier, for this night the most fortunate and blameless prince who may inherit the forbidden domains by power of magic. To be so heavily protected, the treasure had to be dangerous to the rest of the world, or, again, of such a fragile nature that it needed to be protected by the means employed in the sheltering of virgins. The longshoreman might smile and joke about the sharp spear-tips pointing at him, but this did not prevent his becoming, for a moment, the man who penetrates—by the charm of his words, his face, or his gestures—a palpitating virginity. And from the very threshold, even though he was far from a true hard-on, the presence of his prick would make itself felt in his pants, still soft perhaps, but reminding him, the conqueror of the door, of his prowess by a slight contraction near the tip that spread slowly to the base and on to the muscles of his buttocks. Within that still flabby prick the docker would be aware of the presence of another, minuscule, rigid prick, something like the "idea" of horniness. And it would be a solemn moment, from the contemplation of the spikes to the sound of bolts slamming shut behind him. For Madame Lysiane the door had other virtues. When closed, it transformed her, the lady of the house, into an oceanic pearl contained in the nacre of an oyster that was able to open its valve, and to close it, at will. Madame Lysiane was blessed with the gentleness of a pearl, a muffled gleam emanating less from her milky complexion than from her innate sense of tranquil happiness illuminated by inner peace. Her contours were rounded, shiny, and rich. Millennia of slow attrition, of numerous gains and numerous losses, a patient economy, had gone into the making of this plenitude. Madame Lysiane was certain that she was sumptuousness personified. The door guaranteed that. The spikes were ferocious guardians, even against the very air. The lady of La Féria passed her life in a leisurely time, in a medieval castle, and she saw it often in her mind's eye. She was happy. Only the most subtle elements of the life outside found their way to her, to anoint her with an exquisite ointment. She was noble, haughty, and superb. Kept away from the sun and the stars, from games and dreams, but nourished by her very own sun, her own stars, her own games and dreams, shod in mules with high Louis Quinze heels, she moved slowly among her girls without so much as touching them, she climbed the stairs, walked along corridors hung with gilt leather, through astounding halls and salons we shall attempt to describe, sparkling with lights and mirrors, upholstered, decorated with artificial flowers in cut-glass vases and with erotic etchings on the walls. Moulded by time, she was beautiful. Robert had now been her lover for six months.

"You pay cash?"
"I told you so already."
Querelle was petrified by Mario's stare. That stare and his general demeanor expressed more than indifference: they were icy. In order to appear to ignore Mario, Querelle deliberately looked only at the brothelkeeper, looked him straight in the eye. His own immobility was making him feel awkward too. He regained a little assurance when he had shifted his weight from one foot to the other; a modicum of suppleness returned to his

body, just as he was thinking: "Me, I'm only a sailor. My pay's all I've got. So I've got to hustle. Nothing wrong with that. It's good shit I'm talking about. He's got nothing on me. And even if that one *is* a cop, I don't give a shit." But he felt that he wasn't able to make a dent in the proprietor's imperturbability: he showed hardly any interest in the merchandise offered, and none at all in the person offering it. The lack of movement and the almost total silence among these three characters was beginning to weigh on each one of them. Querelle went on, in his mind: "I haven't told him that I'm Bob's brother. All the same, he wouldn't dare put the finger on me." At the same time he was appreciating the proprietor's tremendous build and the good looks of the cop. Until now, he had never experienced any real rivalry in the male world, and if he was not all that impressed by what he was confronted with in these two men—or unaware of his feelings in terms of such phraseology—he was at least suffering, for the first time, from the indifference of men toward him. So he said:

"And there's no heat on, is there?"

It had been his intention to demonstrate his contempt for the fellow who kept on staring at him, but he did not care to define that contempt too pointedly. He did not even dare so much as indicate Mario to the boss with his eyes.

"Dealing with me you don't have to worry. You'll get your dough. All you've got to do is bring those five kilos here, and you'll receive your pennies. OK? So get cracking."

With a very slow, almost imperceptible movement of the head the boss nodded toward the counter against which Mario was leaning.

"That's Mario, over there. Don't worry about him, he belongs to the family."

Without one twitch of his face muscles, Mario held out his hand. It was hard, solid, armored rather than ornamented with three gold rings. Querelle's waist was trimmer than Mario's, by an inch or so. He knew that the very moment he set eyes on the

splendid rings: they seemed to be signs of great masculine
strength. He had no doubt that the realm over which this
character lorded it was a terrestrial one. Suddenly, and with a
twinge of melancholy, Querelle was reminded that he possessed,
hidden forr'ard in the soaking despatch-boat out in the Roads,
all it needed to be this man's equal. The thought calmed him
down a little. But was it really possible for a policeman to be so
handsome, so wealthy? And was it possible that he would join
forces with, no, join his beauty to the power of an outlaw
(because that is what Querelle liked to think the brothelkeeper
was)? But that thought, slowly unfolding in Querelle's mind,
did not set it at rest, and his disdain yielded to his admiration.

"Hello."

Mario's voice was large and thick like his hands—except that
it carried no sparkle. It struck Querelle slap in the face. It was a
brutal, callous voice, like a big shovel. Speaking of it, a few days
later, Querelle said to the detective: "Your pound of flesh,
every time you hit me in the face with it . . ." Querelle gave
him a broad smile and held out his hand, but without saying
anything. To the proprietor he said:

"My brother isn't coming, is he?"

"Haven't seen him. Dunno where he is."

Afraid that he might seem tactless and rile the boss, Querelle
did not pursue the question. The main parlor of the brothel was
silent and empty. It seemed to be recording their meeting,
quietly, attentively. It was three o'clock in the afternoon, the
ladies would be having their meal in the "refectory." There was
no one about. On the second floor, in her room, Madame
Lysiane was doing her hair by the light of a single bulb. The
mirrors were vacant, pure, amazingly close to the unreal, having
nobody and nothing to reflect. The boss tilted and drained his
glass. He was a formidably husky man. If he had never been
really handsome, in his youth he had no doubt been a fine
specimen, despite the blackheads, the hair-thin black wrinkles
on his neck, and the pockmarks. His pencil-line mustache,

trimmed "American style," was undoubtedly a souvenir of 1918. Thanks to those doughboys, to the Black Market, and to the traffic in women he had been able to get rich quick and to purchase La Féria. His long boat trips and fishing parties had tanned his skin. His features were hard, the bridge of his nose firm, the eyes small and lively, the pate bald.

"What time d'you think you'll get here?"

"I'll have to get organized. Have to get the bag out of there. No problem, though. I've got it figured out."

With a flicker of suspicion, glass in hand, the boss looked at Querelle. "Yeah? But, make no mistake, you're on your own. It's none of my business."

Mario remained motionless, almost absent: he was leaning against the counter with his back reflected in the mirror behind him. Without a word he removed his elbows from the counter, thus changing his interesting posture, and went to the big mirror next to the proprietor: now it looked as if he were leaning against himself. And now, faced with both men, Querelle experienced a sudden malaise, a sinking of the heart, such as killers know. Mario's calmness and good looks disconcerted him. They were on too grand a scale. The brothelkeeper, Norbert, was far too powerful-looking. So was Mario. The outlines of their two bodies met to form one continuous pattern, and this seemed to blur and blend their muscular bodies as well as their faces. It was impossible, the boss couldn't be an informer; but then it seemed equally out of the question for Mario to be anything but a cop. Within himself, Querelle felt a trembling, a vacillation, almost to the point of losing himself, by vomiting it all out, all that he really was. Seized by vertigo in the presence of these powerful muscles and nerves that he perceived as towering above him—as one might when throwing one's head back to appraise the height of a giant pine tree—that kept on doubling and merging again, crowned by Mario's beauty, but dominated by Norbert's bald head and bullish neck,

Querelle stood there with his mouth half-open, his palate a little dry.

"No, sure, that's all right. I'll take care of all that."

Mario was wearing a very plainly cut double-breasted maroon suit, with a red tie. Like Querelle and Nono (Norbert), he was drinking white wine, but like a true cop he seemed completely disinterested in their conversation. Querelle recognized the authority in the man's thighs and chest, the sobriety of movement that endows a man with total power: this, again, stemming from an undisputed moral authority, a perfect social organization, a gun, and the right to use it. Mario was one of the masters. Once more Querelle held out his hand, and then, turning up the collar of his peacoat, he headed for the back door: it was indeed better to leave through the small yard at the back of the house.

"So long."

Mario's voice, as we have observed, was loud and impassive. On hearing it, Querelle felt reassured in some strange way. As soon as he left the house he compelled himself to be aware of his attire, his sailor's attributes: above all, of the stiff collar of the peacoat, which he felt protected his neck like armor. Within its seemingly massive enclosure he could feel how delicate his neck was, yet strong and proud, and at the base of that neck, the tender bones of the nape, the perfect point of vulnerability. Flexing his knees lightly he could feel them touching the fabric of his pants. Querelle was stepping out like a true sailor who sees himself as one hundred per cent just that, a sailor. Rolling the shoulders, from left to right, but not excessively. He thought of hitching the coat up a bit and putting his hands in the vertical front pockets, but changed his mind and instead raised a finger to his beret and pushed it to the back of his head, almost to the nape of his neck, so that its edge brushed against the upturned collar. Such tangible certainty of being every inch a sailor reassured him and calmed him down.

Nevertheless, he felt sad, and mean. He was not wearing that habitual smile. The fog dampened his nostrils, refreshed his eyelids and his chin. He was walking straight ahead, punching his weighty body through the softness of the fog. The greater the distance he put between himself and La Féria, the more he fortified himself with all the might of the police force, believing himself to be under their friendly protection now, and endowing the idea of "police" with the muscular strength of Nono, and with Mario's good looks. This had been his first encounter with a police officer. So he had met a cop, at last. He had walked up to him. He had shaken hands with him. He had just signed an agreement that would protect both of them against treachery. He had not found his brother there, but instead of him those two monsters of certainty, those two big shots. Nevertheless, while gaining strength from the might of the Police as he drew away from La Féria, he did not for one moment cease to be a sailor. Querelle, in some obscure way, knew that he was coming close to his own point of perfection: clad in his blue garb, cloaked in its prestige, he was no longer a simple murderer, but a seducer as well. He proceeded down the Rue de Siam with giant strides. The fog was chilling. Increasingly the forms of Mario and Nono merged and instilled in him a feeling of submission, and of pride—for deep down the sailor in him strongly opposed the policeman: and so he fortified himself with the full might of the Fighting Navy, as well. Appearing to be running after his own form, ever about to overtake it, yet in pursuit, he walked on fast, sure of himself, with a firm stride. His body armed itself with cannon, with a hull of steel, with torpedoes, with a crew who were agile and strong, bellicose and precise. Querelle became "Le Querelle," a giant destroyer, warlord of the seas, an intelligent and invincible mass of metal.

"Watch your step, you asshole!"

His voice cut through the fog like a siren in the Baltic.

"But it was you who . . ."

Suddenly the young man, polite, buffeted, thrown aside by the wake of Querelle's impassive shoulder, realized that he was being insulted. He said:

"At least you could be civil about it! Or open your eyes!"

If he meant "Keep your eyes open," for Querelle the message was "Light up the course, use your running light." He spun around:

"What about my lights?"

His voice was harsh, decisive, ready for combat. He was carrying a cargo of explosives. He didn't recognize himself any more. He hoped to appeal to Mario and Norbert—no longer to that fantastic compound creature that consisted of the sum of their virtues—but in reality he had placed himself under the protection of that very idol. However, he did not yet admit this to himself, and for the first time in his life he invoked the Navy.

"Lookahere, buddy, I hope you ain't trying to get my goat, or are you? Because, let me tell you, us sailors won't let anybody get away with that kind of shit. Understand?"

"But I'm not trying to do anything, I was just passing . . ."

Querelle looked at him. He felt safe in his uniform. He clenched his fists and immediately knew that every muscle, every nerve was taking up its battle station. He was strong, ready to pounce. His calves and arms were vibrating. His body was flexed for a fight in which he would measure up to an adversary—not this young man intimidated by his nerve—but to the power that had subjugated him in the brothel parlor. Querelle did not know that he wanted to do battle *for* Mario, and *for* Norbert, the way one would do battle for a king's daughter and against the dragons. This fight was a trial.

"Don't you know you can't push us around, not us Navy guys?"

Never before had Querelle applied such a label to himself. Those sailors proud of being sailors, animated by the *esprit de corps*, had always seemed comical to him. In his eyes they were

as ridiculous as the bigheads who played to the gallery and then
got shown up for the braggarts they were. Never had Querelle
said, "Me, I'm one of the guys from the *Vengeur*." Or even,
"Me, I'm a *French* salt . . ." But now, having done so, he felt
no shame; he felt completely at ease.

"OK, scram."

He pronounced these words with a twisted sneer directed
right at the landlubber, and with his face fixed in that expression he waited, hands in pockets, until the young man had
turned and gone. Then, feeling good and even a little tougher
than before, he continued on down the Rue de Siam. Arriving
on board Querelle instantly perceived an opportunity for the
dispensation of rough justice. He was seized by sudden and
violent fury on noticing that one of the sailors on the larboard
deck was wearing his beret the very same way he thought
Querelle alone should wear it. He felt positively robbed, when
he recognized that particular angle, that lock of hair sticking up
like a flame, licking the front of the beret, the whole effect of it
as legendary, now, as the white fur bonnet worn by Vacher, the
killer of shepherds. Querelle walked up, his cruel eyes fixed on
those of the hapless sailor, and told him, in a matter-of-fact
tone:

"Put it on straight."

The other one did not understand. A little taken aback,
vaguely frightened, he stared at Querelle without budging.
With a sweep of his hand Querelle sent the beret flying down
on to the deck, but before the sailor could bend down to pick it
up, Querelle pounded his face with his fists, rapidly, and with a
vengeance.

Querelle loved luxury. It seems obvious that he had a feeling
for the common beliefs, that he did glory in his Frenchness, to
some extent, and in being a Navy man, susceptible like any
male to national and military pride. Yet we have to remember
some facts of his early youth, not because these extend across
the entire psyche of our hero, but in order to make plausible an

attitude that does not boil down to a simple matter of choice. Let us consider his characteristic manner of walking. Querelle grew up among hoodlums, and that is a world of most studied attitudes, round about the age of fifteen—when you roll your shoulders quite ostentatiously, keep your hands thrust deep into your pockets, wear your pants too tight and turned up at the bottoms. Later on he walked with shorter steps, legs tight and the insides of his thighs rubbing against each other, but holding his arms well away from his body, making it appear that this was due to overdeveloped biceps and dorsals. It was only shortly after he committed his first murder that he arrived at a gait and posture peculiar to himself: he stalked slowly, both arms stiffly extended, fists clenched in front of his fly, not touching it; legs well apart.

This search for a posture that would set him, Querelle, apart, and thus prevent him from being mistaken for any other member of the crew, originated in a kind of terrifying dandyism. As a child he had used to amuse himself with solitary competitions with himself, trying to piss ever higher and farther. Querelle smiled, contracting his cheeks. A sad smile. One might have called it ambiguous, intended for the giver rather than the receiver. Sometimes, in thinking about it, the image, the sadness Lieutenant Seblon must have seen in that smile, could be compared to that of watching, in a group of country choirboys, the most virile one, standing firm on sturdy feet, with sturdy thighs and neck, and chanting in a masculine voice the canticles to the Blessed Virgin. He puzzled his shipmates, made them uneasy. First, because of his physical strength, and secondly by the strangeness of his overly vulgar behavior. They watched him approaching, on his face the slight anguish of a sleeper under a mosquito net who hears the complaint of a mosquito held back by the netting and incensed by the impenetrable and invisible resistance. When we read ". . . his whole physiognomy had its changeable aspects: from the ferocious it could turn gentle, often ironic: his walk was a sailor's, and standing up, he always kept his legs well apart. This murderer had traveled a great deal . . .," we know that this description of Campi, beheaded April 30, 1884, fits like a glove. Being an interpretation, it is exact. Yet his mates were able to say of Querelle: "What a funny guy," for he presented them, almost daily, with another disconcerting and scandalous vision of himself. He shone among them with the brightness of a true freak. Sailors of our Fighting Navy exhibit a certain honesty which they owe to the sense of glory that attracts them to the service. If they wanted to go in for smuggling or any other form of trafficking they would not really know how to go about it. Heavily and lazily, because of the boredom inherent in their task, they perform it in a manner that seems to us like an act of faith. But Querelle kept his eye on the main chance. He felt no nostalgia for his time as a petty hoodlum—he had never really outgrown it—but he continued, under the protection of the French flag, his dangerous exploits. All his early teens he had spent in the company of dockers and merchant seamen. He knew their game.

Querelle strode along, his face damp and burning, without thinking about anything in particular. He felt a little uneasy, haunted by the unformulated glimmer of a suspicion that his exploits would gain him no glory in the eyes of Mario and Nono, who themselves were (and were for each other) glory personified. On reaching the Recouvrance bridge he went down the steps to the landing stage. It was then that it occurred to him, while passing the Customs House, that he was letting his six kilos of opium go too cheap. But then again it was important to get business off to a good start. He walked to the quayside to wait for the patrol boat that would come to return seamen and officers to the *Vengeur* which was lying at anchor out in the Roads. He checked his watch: ten of four. The boat would be there in ten minutes. He took a turn up and down to keep warm, but chiefly because the shame he felt forced him to keep on the move. Suddenly he found himself at the foot of the wall supporting the coastal road that circles the port, and from which springs the main arch of the bridge. The fog prevented Querelle from seeing the top of the wall, but judging by its slope and the angle at which it rose from the ground, from the size and quality of its stones—details he was quick to observe—he guessed that it was of considerable height. The same sinking of the heart he had felt in the presence of the two men in the brothel upset his stomach a little and tightened his throat. But even though his obvious, even brutal physical strength appeared subject to one of those weaknesses that cause one to be called "delicate," Querelle would never dare to acknowledge such frailty—by leaning against the wall, for example: but the distressing feeling that he was about to be engulfed did make him slump a little. He walked away from the wall, turned his back on it. The sea lay in front of him, shrouded in fog.

"What a strange guy," he thought, raising his eyebrows.

Stock-still, legs wide apart, he stood and pondered. His lowered gaze traveled over the gray miasma of the fog and came to rest on the black, wet stones of the jetty. Little by little, but at random, he considered Mario's various peculiarities. His hands. The curve—he had been staring at it—from the tip of his thumb to the tip of the index finger. The thickness of his arms. The width of his shoulders. His indifference. His blond hair. His blue eyes. Norbert's mustache. His round and shiny pate. Mario again, one of whose fingernails was completely black, a very beautiful black, as if lacquered. There are no black flowers; yet, at the end of his crushed finger, that black fingernail looked like nothing so much as a flower.

"What are you doing here?"

Querelle jumped to salute the vague figure that had appeared in front of him. First and foremost, he saluted the severe voice that pierced the fog, with all the assurance emanating from a place that was light and warm and real, framed in gold.

"Under orders to report to the Naval Police, Lieutenant."

The officer came closer.

"You're ashore?"

Querelle held himself to attention but contrived to hide, under his sleeve, the wrist on which he was wearing the gold watch.

"You'll take the next boat back. I want you to take an order to the Paymaster's Office."

Lieutenant Seblon scrawled a few words on an envelope and gave it to the seaman. He also gave him, in too dry a tone of voice, a few commonplace instructions. Querelle heard the tension in his voice. His smile flickered over a still trembling upper lip. He felt both uneasy at the officer's unexpectedly early return and pleased about it; pleased, above all, at meeting him there, after emerging from a state of panic—the ship's Lieutenant, whose steward he was.

"Go."

Only this word the Lieutenant pronounced with regret, without that customary harshness, even without the serene authority that a firm mouth ought to have given it. Querelle cracked a cautious smile. He saluted and headed toward the Customs House, then once again ascended the steps to the main road. That the Lieutenant should have caught him unawares, before there was time for recognition, was deeply wounding: it ripped open the opaque envelope which, he liked to believe, hid him from men's view. It then worked its way into the cocoon of daydreams he had been spinning the past few minutes, and out of which he now drew this thread, this visible adventure, conducted in the world of men and objects, already turning into the drama he half suspected, much as a tubercular person tastes the blood in his saliva, rising in his throat. Querelle pulled himself together: he had to, to safeguard the integrity of that domain into which even the highest-ranking officers were not permitted any insight. Querelle rarely responded even to the most distant familiarity. Lieutenant

Seblon never did anything—whether he thought he did, or not—to establish any familiarity with his steward; such were the excessive defenses the officer armored himself with. While making Querelle smile, he left it to him to take any step toward intimacy. As bad luck would have it, such awkward attempts only served to put Querelle out. A few moments ago he had smiled because his Lieutenant's voice had been a reassuring sound. Now a sense of danger made the old Querelle bare his teeth. He had gone off with a gold watch from the Lieutenant's cabin drawer, but it was only because he had believed that the Lieutenant had really departed on a long furlough.

"When he gets back, he'll have forgotten all about it," had been his reasoning. "He'll think he lost it some place."

As he climbed the steps Querelle let his hand drag along the iron guard rail. The image of the two guys at the brothel, Mario and Norbert, suddenly flashed back to his mind. An informer and a cop. The fact that they had not denounced him immediately made it even more terrifying. Perhaps the police forced them to act as double agents. The image of the two grew larger. Grown monstrous, it threatened to devour Querelle. And the Customs? It was impossible to get round the Customs. Again the same nausea that had previously deranged his innards: now it culminated in a hiccough that did not quite reach his mouth. Slowly he regained his calm, and as soon as it spread throughout his body he realized that he was home free. A few more steps, and he would be sitting down up there on the top step, by the side of the road. He might even take a little nap, after such a wonderful brainstorm. From this moment on he forced himself to think in precise terms:

"Boy, that's it! I've got it. What I need is some guy (Vic was the man, he'd already decided), a guy to let down a piece of string from the top of that wall. I get off the boat and hang around on the jetty for a while. Fog's thick enough. Instead of going on, past the Customs, I'll stay at the foot of the wall. And up there, on the road, there's that guy holding the string. Need about ten, twelve meters of it. Then I tie the package to it. The fog'll hide me. My buddy pulls it up, and I walk through Customs, clean as a whistle."

He felt deeply relieved. The emotion was identical with the one he felt as a child at the foot of one of the two massive towers that rise in the port of La Rochelle. It was a feeling of both power and the lack of it: of pride, in the first place, to know that such a tall tower could be the symbol of his own virility, to the extent that when he stood at the base of it, legs apart, taking a piss, he could think of it as his own prick. Coming out from the movies in the evening he would some-times crack jokes with his buddies, standing there, taking a leak in the company of two or three of them:

"Now that's what Georgette needs!"

or:

"With one like that in my pants I could have all the pussy in La Rochelle,"

or:

"You're talking like some old guy! Some old Rochellois!"

But when he was by himself, at night or during the day, opening or buttoning his fly, his fingers felt they were capturing, with the greatest care, the treasure—the very soul—of this giant prick; he imagined that his own virility emanated from the stone phallus, while feeling quietly humble in the presence of the unruffled and incomparable power of that unimaginably huge male. And now Querelle knew he would be able to deliver his burden of opium to that strange ogre with the two magnifi-cent bodies.

"Just need to get another guy to help. Can't do it without him."

Querelle understood, though hazily, that the entire success of the venture depended on this one sailor, and (even more vaguely, in the peace of mind afforded by this very remote and sweet idea, yet as insubstantial as the dawn), in fact, on Vic—

whom he would enroll for the job, and it would be through him that he would be able to reach Mario and Norbert.

Now the boss seemed straight; the other one was too handsome to be a mere cop. Those rings were too nice for that.

"And what about me? And my jewels? If only that sonofabitch could see them!"

Querelle was referring to the treasure hidden away in the despatch-boat, but also to his balls, full and heavy, which he stroked every night, and kept safely tucked away between his hands while he slept. He thought of the stolen watch. He smiled: that was the old Querelle, blooming, lighting up, showing the delicate underside of his petals.


The workmen went and sat down at a bare wooden table in the middle of the dormitory, between the two rows of beds. On it stood two large, steaming bowls of soup. Slowly Gil took his hand off the fur of the cat lying stretched on his knee; then put it back there. Some small part of his shame was flowing out into the animal and being absorbed by her. Thus, she was a comfort to Gil, like a dressing staunching a wound. Gil had not wanted to get into a fight when, on coming back, Theo had started poking fun at him. And that had been obvious from his tone of voice, so surprisingly humble when answering: "There's some words better left unsaid." As his retorts were usually dry and laconic, almost to the point of cruelty, Gil had been all the more conscious of his humiliation when he heard his own voice ingratiate itself, stretch out like a shadow round Theo's feet. To himself, to console his self-regard, Gil had remarked that one does not fight with such assholes, but the spontaneous sweetness of his voice reminded him too strongly that he had, in fact, given in. And his buddies? What the hell did they matter, fuck'em. Theo, that was well known, Theo was a queer. He was tough and nervy all right, but he was a queer. No sooner had

Gil started to work in the shipyard than the mason had showered him with his attentions, favors which sometimes were real masterpieces of subtlety. He also bought Gil glasses of the syrupy white wine in the bistros of Recouvrance. But within that steely hand slapping him on the back in the bar Gil sensed—and trembled at sensing—the presence of another, softer hand. The one wanted to subjugate him, so that the other could then caress him. The last couple of days Theo had been trying to make him angry. It riled him that he had not yet had his way with the younger man. In the shipyard Gil would sometimes look across at him: it was rare not to find Theo's gaze fixed on him. Theo was a scrupulous workman, regarded as exemplary by all his mates. Before placing it in its bed of cement, his hands caressed each stone, turned it over, chose the best-looking surface, and always fitted it so that the best side faced outward. Gil raised his hand, stopped stroking the cat. He put it down gently, next to the stove, on a soft spot covered with shavings. Thus he perhaps made his companions believe that he was a very sweet-tempered man. He even wanted his gentleness to be provoking. Finally, for his own benefit, he had to give the appearance of wishing to distance himself from any excessive reaction induced by Theo's insult. He went to the table, sat down at his place. Theo did not look at him. Gil saw his thick mop of hair and thick neck bent over the white china bowl. He was talking and laughing heartily with one of his friends. The overall sound was one of mouths lapping up spoonfuls of thick soup. Once the meal was finished, Gil was the first one to get up; he took off his sweater and went to work on the dirty dishes. For a few minutes, his shirt open at the neck, sleeves rolled up above elbows, his face reddened and damp from the steam, his bare arms plunging into the greasy dishwater, he looked like a young female kitchen worker in some restaurant. He knew, all of a sudden, that he was no longer just an ordinary workman. For several minutes he felt he had turned into a strange and ambiguous being: a young man who acted as a serving maid to the masons. To prevent any of them coming up to tease her, to smack her on the buttocks with great gusts of laughter, he made sure all his motions were brisk and busy. When he took his hands out of the now revoltingly tepid water, they no longer appeared soft like that at all—you could see the ravages wrought by plaster and cement. He felt some regret at the sight of these workman's hands, their cracked skin, their permanent white frosting, their fingernails crusted with cement. Gil had been storing up too much shame over the last couple of days to even dare think about Paulette at this point. Nor about Roger, either. He was unable to think of them warmly; his feelings had been soiled by shame, by a kind of nauseating vapor that threatened to mingle with all his thoughts in order to corrupt and decompose them. Yet he did think of Roger: with hatred. In that atmosphere, the hatred grew more noxious, grew so forcefully that it chased away the feeling of shame, squeezed it, rammed it into the remotest corner of his consciousness; there, however, it squatted brooding and reminding him of its presence with the heavy insistence of a throbbing abscess. Gil hated Roger for being the cause of his humiliation. He hated Roger's good looks, even, for providing Theo with ammunition for his evil sense of irony. He hated Roger for coming down to the shipyard, the previous day. True, he had smiled at him all through an evening, while singing, on a table top—but that was simply because Roger alone knew that the last song was the one Paulette liked to hum, and thus he was addressing her, through an accomplice

*He was a happy bandit,*
*Nothing did he fear . .*

Some of the masons were playing cards now on the table cleared of the white china bowls and plates. The stove was going great guns. Gil wanted to go and take a leak, but in turning his head he saw Theo walking across the room and opening the door, most probably on his way to the same place. Gil stayed where he was. Theo closed the door behind him. He went out into the night and fog, dressed in a khaki shirt and blue pants patched with various faded bits of blue, very pleasing to look at; Gil had a similar pair, and valued them highly. He began to undress. He peeled off his shirt, revealing an undershirt from which his muscles bulged through the wide armholes. With his pants round his ankles, bending down, he saw his thighs: they were thick and solid, well developed by bicycling and playing soccer, smooth as marble and just as hard. In his thoughts Gil let his eyes travel up from his thighs to his belly, to his muscular back, to his arms. He felt ashamed of his strength. Had he taken up the challenge to fight, "on the level" perhaps (no punching, just wrestling) or "no holds barred" (boot and fist), he could certainly have beaten Theo; but that one had a reputation for extreme vindictiveness. Out of sheer rage Theo would have been capable of getting up at night to pad over to Gil's bed and cut his throat. It was thanks to this reputation that he was able to go on insulting others as blithely as he did. Gil refused to run the risk of having his throat cut. He stepped out of his pants. Standing for a moment in front of his bed in his red shorts and white undershirt, he gently scratched his thighs. He hoped that his buddies would observe his muscles and understand that he had only refused to fight out of generosity, so as not to make an older man look like a fool. He got into bed. His cheek on the bolster, Gil thought of Theo with disgust, that feeling growing more intense as he realized that in days past, as a young man, Theo surely had been a very handsome man. He was still pretty vigorous. Sometimes, at work, he would make awkward, punning references to what he thought was the proverbial virility of the men of the building trade. His face, with its hard, manly, still unspoilt features, was covered as with a net of minuscule wrinkles. His dark eyes, small but brilliant, mostly expressed sarcasm, but on certain days Gil had caught them looking at him, overflowing with an extraordinary tenderness; and that more often than not toward evening, when the gang was getting ready to leave. Theo would be scouring his hands with a little soft sand, and then he would straighten his back to take a good look at the work in progress: at the rising wall, at the discarded trowels, the planks, the wheelbarrows, the buckets. Over all these, and over the workmen, a gray, impalpable dust was settling, turning the yard into a single object, seemingly finished, the result of the day's commotion. The peace of the evening appeared due to this achievement, a deserted yard, powdered a uniform gray. Stiff after their day's work, worn out and silent, the masons would drift off with slow, almost funereal steps. None of them were more than forty years old. Tired, kit bag over left shoulder, right hand in pants pocket, they were leaving the day for the night. Their belts uneasily held up pants made for suspenders; every ten meters they would give them a hitch, tucking the front under the belt while letting the back gape wide, always showing that little triangular flap and its two buttons intended for fastening to a pair of suspenders. In this sluggish calm they would return to their quarters. None of them would be going to the girls or the bistro before Saturday, but, once abed and at peace, they would let their manhood take its rest and under the sheets store up its black forces and white juices; would go to sleep on their side and pass a dreamless night, one bare arm with its powder-dusted hand stretched out over the edge of the bed, showing the delicate pulsation of the blood in bluish veins. Theo would trail along beside Gil. Every evening he offered him a cigarette before setting out to catch up with the others, and sometimes—and then his expression would change —he would give him a great slap on the shoulder.

"Well, buddy? How's it going?"

Gil would reply with his usual, noncommittal shrug. He would barely manage a smile. On the bolster, Gil felt his cheek grow hot. He had lain there with his eyes wide open, and by reason of his ever increasing need to empty his bladder, his anger was aggravated by impatience. The rims of his eyelids were burning. A blow received straightens a man up and makes the body move forward, to return that blow, or a punch—to jump, to get a hard-on, to dance: to be alive. But a blow received may also cause you to bend over, to shake, to fall down, to die. When we see life, we call it beautiful. When we see death, we call it ugly. But it is more beautiful still to see oneself living at great speed, right up to the moment of death. Detectives, poets, domestic servants and priests rely on abjection. From it, they draw their power. It circulates in their veins. It nourishes them.

"Being a cop's just a job like any other."

Giving this answer to the slightly scornful friend of long standing who was asking him why he had joined the police force, Mario knew that he was lying. He did not much care for women, although it was easy for him to get a piece of the action from prostitutes. The fact of Dédé's presence made the hatred he felt all around him in his life as a policeman seem like a heavy burden. Being a cop embarrassed him. He wanted to ignore the fact, but it enveloped him. Worse, it flowed in his veins. He was afraid of being poisoned by it. Slowly at first, then with increasing force, he became involved with Dédé. Dédé could be the antidote. The Police in his veins circulated a little less strongly, grew weaker. He felt a little less guilty. The blood in his veins was then less black, and this made him a target for the scorn of the hoodlums and the vengeance of Tony.

Was it true that the prison of Bougen was filled with beautiful female spies? Mario kept hoping that he would be called in for a case involving a theft of documents concerning national defense matters.

In Dédé's room, Rue Saint-Pierre, Mario was sitting, feet on the floor, on the divan bed covered with a plain fringed blue cotton bedspread pulled over unmade sheets. Dédé jumped on to the bed to kneel beside the immobile profile of Mario's face and torso. The detective didn't say anything. Not a muscle in his face moved. Never before had Dédé seen him look so hard, drawn, and sad; his lips were dry and set in a mean expression.

"And now what? What's going to happen? I'll go down to the port, take a good look around . . . I'll see if he's there. What d'you say?"

Mario's face remained grim. A strange heat seemed to animate it, without heightening its color; it was pale, but the lines were set so hard and so rigidly drawn and patterned that they lit the face up with an infinity of stars. It looked as if Mario's whole life were surging upwards, mounting from his calves, parts, torso, heart, anus, guts, arms, elbows, and neck, right up into the face, where it grew desperate at not being able to escape, to go on, to disappear into the night and come to an end in a shower of sparks. His cheeks were a little hollowed, making the chin look firmer. He wasn't frowning; his eyeballs were slightly protuberant, and his eyelid looked like a small amber rosebud attached to the stem of his nose. In the front of his mouth Mario was rolling around an ever increasing amount of spittle, not daring, not knowing how to swallow it. His fear and his hatred mingled and massed there, at the farthest reaches of himself. His blue eyes looked almost black, under brows which had never appeared so light, so blond. Their very brightness troubled Dédé's peace of mind. (The boy was far more peaceful than his friend was agitated—profoundly agitated, as if he alone had dredged up to the surface all the mud deposited in both of them; and this new force of purpose in the detective made him look both desperate and grave, with a touch of that restrained irritation so typical a trait in accredited heroes. Dédé seemed to have recognized this and could find no better means of displaying his gratitude than by accepting, with elegant simplicity, his purification, his becoming endowed with the vernal grace of April woodlands.) We were saying—that extreme brightness of

Mario's eyebrows troubled the young fellow, as he saw so light
a color casting such shadows, over so dark and stormy an expression. Desolation appears greater when pinpointed by light. And
the whiteness of the brows troubled his peace of mind, the
purity of it: not because he knew that Mario went in fear of
his life because of the return of a certain stevedore he had once
arrested, but because he was watching the detective manifest
unmistakable signs of acute mental struggle—by making him
understand, in some indefinite way, that there was hope of
seeing joy return to his friend's face as long as it still showed
signs of such brightness. That "ray of light" on Mario's face
was, in point of fact, a shadow. Dédé put a bare forearm—his
shirtsleeves were rolled up above the elbow—on Mario's shoulder and gazed attentively at his ear. For a moment he contem-
plated the attractions of Mario's hair, razor-cut from the nape
of the neck to the temples: recently cut, it gave off a delicate,
silky light. He blew gently on the ear, to free it of some blond
hairs, longer ones, that fell from the forehead. None of this
caused Mario's expression to change.

"What a drag, you looking so grouchy! What do you think
they're going to do, those guys?"

For a couple of seconds he was silent, as if reflecting; then he
added:

"And it's really too damn bad you didn't think of having
them arrested. Why didn't you?"

He leant back a little way to get a better view of Mario's
profile, whose face and eyes did not move. Mario was not even
thinking. He was simply allowing his stare to lose itself, to
dissolve, and to let his whole body be carried away in this
dissolution. Only a short while ago Robert had informed him
that five of the most determined characters among the dockers
had sworn they'd "get" him. Tony, whom he had arrested in a
manner these sons of Brest regarded as unfair, had been released from the prison of Bougen the previous evening.

"What would you like me to do?"

Without shifting his knees, Dédé had managed to lean back even farther. He now had the posture of a young female saint at the very moment of a visitation, fallen on her knees at the foot of an oak tree, crushed by the revelation, by the splendor of Grace, then bending over backwards in order to save her face from a vision that is searing her eyelashes, her very eyeballs, blinding her. He smiled. Gently he put his arm round the detective's neck. With little kisses he pecked at, without ever touching them, his forehead, temples, and eyes, the rounded tip of the nose, his lips, yet always without actually touching them; Mario felt like being subjected to a thousand prickly points of flame, darting and flickering to and fro. He thought:

"He's covering me with mimosa blossoms."

Only his eyelids fluttered, no other part of his body moved, nor did his hands, still resting on his knees, nor did his pecker grow lively. He was, nevertheless, touched by the kid's unaccustomed tenderness. It reached him in a thousand small shocks, sad only in their tentativeness, and warm, and he permitted it slowly to swell and lighten his body. But Dédé was pecking at a rock. The intervals between kisses grew longer, the youngster withdrew his face, still smiling, and started to whistle. Imitating the twitter of sparrows on all sides of Mario's rigid and massive head, from eye to mouth, from neck to nostrils, he moved his small mouth, now shaped like a chicken's ass, whistling now like a blackbird, now like an oriole. His eyes were smiling. He was having a good time, sounding like all the birds in a grove. It made him feel quite soft inside to think that he was all these birds, and that at the same time he was offering them up on this burning but immobile head, locked in stone. Dédé tried to delight and fascinate him with these birds. But Mario felt a kind of anguish, being confronted with that terrifying thing: the smile of a bird. Then, again, he thought with some relief:

"He's powdering me with mimosa blossoms."

Thus, to the birdsong was added a light pollen. Mario felt vaguely like being held captive in one of those fine-meshed widows' veils that are dotted with pea-sized black knots. Then he retired into himself to regain that region of flux and innocence that can be called limbo. In his very anguish he escaped from his enemies. He had the right to be a policeman, a copper. He had a right, to let himself slip back into the old complicity that united him with this little sixteen-year-old stoolie. Dédé was hoping that a smile might open that head, to let the birds in: but the rock refused to smile, to flower, to be covered with nests. Mario was closing up. He was aware of the kid's airy whistlings, but he was—that part of him that was ever-watchful Mario—so far gone into himself, trying to face up to fear and to destroy it by examining it, that it would take him a while to return as far as his muscles and to make them move again. He felt that there, behind the severity of his face, his pallor, his immobility, his doors, his walls, he was safe. Around him rose the ramparts of The Police Force, and he was protected by all that only apparent strictness. Dédé kissed him on the corner of his mouth, very quickly, then bounded back to the foot of the bed. Perching in front of Mario, he smiled.

"What's happening, for crissakes? You sick, or in love, or what?"

In spite of his desire, he had never even thought of going to bed with Dédé, nor had he ever made the slightest equivocal gesture in that direction. His chiefs and colleagues knew of his association with the kid, who to them was merely an auxiliary nonentity.

Dédé had no answer for Mario's sarcasm, but his smile faded a little, without disappearing altogether. His face was pink.

"You must be out of your gourd."

"Well I haven't hurt you, have I? I just planted a few friendly kisses on you. You've been sitting there scowling long enough. Just trying to cheer you up."

"So I haven't got a right to sit and think things over, eh?"

"But it's such a drag when you're like that. And anyway, how do you know for sure that that Tony's really out to get you . . ."

Mario made an irritated gesture. His mouth hardened.

"You don't think I'm getting cold feet, do you?"

"I didn't say that."

Dédé sounded angry.

"I didn't say that."

He was standing in front of Mario. His voice was hoarse, a little vulgar, deep, with a slight country accent. It was the kind of voice that knows how to talk to horses. Mario turned his head. He looked at Dédé for a couple of seconds. All he would proceed to say during the ensuing scene would be tight-lipped and stern, as if trying to put the full force of his will into his expression, so that the youngster would realize, once and for all, that he, Mario Lambert, inspector of the mobile squad, assigned to the Commissariat of Brest, went in no fear for his future. For a year now he had been working with Dédé who provided him with information on the secret life of the docks and told him about the thefts, the pilfering of coffee, minerals, other goods. The men on the waterfront paid little attention to the kid.

"Get going."

Planted in front of him, feet apart and looking stockier than before, Dédé gazed at the policeman, somewhat sulkily. Then he swiveled round on one foot, keeping his legs extended like a compass, and, in reaching over to the window where his coat was hanging on the hasp, moved his shoulders and chest with surprising speed and strength, displacing the weight of an invisible vault of heaven. For the first time Mario realized that Dédé was strong, that he had grown up into a young man. He felt ashamed about having given in to fear in his presence, but then very quickly retreated into the shell of The Police, which justifies every kind of behavior. The window opened on to a narrow lane. Facing it, on the other side, was the gray wall of a garage. Dédé put on his coat. When he turned around again, briskly as before, Mario got up and stood in front of him, hands in pockets.

"Now, did you get it straight? No need to go in too close. I've told you, no one suspects that you're in with me, but it's better if you don't let them spot you."

"Don't worry, Mario."

Dédé was getting ready to leave. He wound a red woolen muffler round his neck and put on a small, gray cap, the kind still worn by lads in the villages. He pulled out a cigarette from a number of loose ones in his coat pocket and nimbly popped it into Mario's mouth, then one into his own, without cracking a smile in spite of what it brought to mind. And then, in a suddenly grave, almost solemn fashion, he donned his gloves, the only symbol of his minimal enough affluence. Dédé loved, almost venerated these poor objects and would never just carry them in his hand, but always put them on with great care. He knew that they were the only detail by which he himself, from the depths of his self-imposed—therefore ethical—dereliction, touched upon the world of society and wealth. By these clearly purposeful motions he put himself into his proper place again. It amazed him now that he had dared that kiss, and all the games that had preceded it. Like any other mistake, it made him feel ashamed. Never before had he shown Mario, nor Mario him, any sign of affection. Dédé was serious by nature. In his dealings with the detective, he seriously went about collecting his clues, and reported them as seriously every week in some secluded spot that had been agreed on over the phone. For the first time in his life he had given in to his own imagination.

"Stone cold sober, too," he thought.

In saying that Dédé was a serious person, we do not mean that this was a quality he thought desirable. It was rather that his inherent gravity made it hard for him to ever force himself into a semblance of gaiety. He struck a match and held out the little flame to Mario, with a gravity greater than his ignorance of the rites. Since Mario was the taller, the little fellow offered

up his face at the same time, in all innocence, partly shadowed
by the screen of his hands.

"And what are you going to do?"

"Me . . . ? Nothing. What d'you suppose. I'll just be waiting for you to get back."

Once again Dédé looked at Mario. He gazed at him for a
couple of seconds, his mouth half-open and dry. "I'm scared,"
he thought. He took a pull at his cigarette and said: "All right."
He turned to the mirror to adjust the peak of his cap, to bend it
over a little more to the left. In the mirror he could see the
whole room in which he had now lived for over a year. It was
small, cold, and on the walls there were some photographs of
prize fighters and female movie stars, clipped out of the papers.
The only luxury item was the light fixture above the divan: an
electric bulb in a pale pink glass tulip. He did not despise Mario
for being scared. Quite some time ago he had understood the
nobility of self-acknowledged fear, what he called the jitters, or
cold feet . . .

Often enough he had been forced to take to his heels in order
to escape from some dangerous and armed foe. He hoped that
Mario would accept the challenge to fight, having decided
himself, should a good occasion arise, to knock off the docker
who had just come out of the joint. To save Mario would be to
save himself. And it was natural enough for anyone to be scared
of Tony the Docker. He was a fierce and unscrupulous brute.
On the other hand, it seemed strange to Dédé that a mere
criminal should cause The Police to tremble, and for the first
time he had his doubts that this invisible and ideal force which
he served and behind which he sheltered might just consist of
weak humans. And, as this truth dawned on him, through a
little crack in himself, he felt both weaker and—strangely
enough—stronger. For the first time he was taking thought, and
this frightened him a little.

"What about your chief? Haven't you told him?"

"Don't you worry about that. I've told you your job: now get

on with it." Mario dimly feared the boy might betray him. The
voice in which he answered showed signs of softening, but he
caught himself quickly, even before opening his mouth, and the
words came out tough and dry. Dédé looked at his wristwatch.

"It's getting on for four," he said. "It's dark already. And
there's *some* fog rolling in . . . Visibility five meters."

"Well, what are you waiting for?"

Mario's voice was suddenly more commanding. He was the
boss. Two quick steps had been quite sufficient to take him
across the room and bring him, with the same ease of movement, in front of the mirror, where he combed his hair, and
once more became that powerful shadow, raw-boned and
muscular, cheerful and young, which corresponded to his proper
form, and sometimes to that of Dédé as well. (As he watched
Mario approach their meeting place, Dédé sometimes told him,
with a grin: "I like what I see, and I'd like to be it," but at
other times his pride rebelled against such identification. That,
then, was when he would attempt some timid gesture of revolt,
but a smile or a concise order would put him right back where
he belonged, in Mario's shadow.)

"All right."

He tried to sound tough, but for his own ears only. Stock-still
for a second, to prove his absolute independence to himself, he
let a puff of smoke drift in the direction of the window at
which he was staring; one hand in his pocket he then turned
abruptly toward Mario and, looking him straight in the eye,
extended his other hand, stiffly, at arm's length.

"So long."

He sounded positively funereal. With a more natural calm,
Mario replied:

"So long, buddy. Get back soon as you can."

"And don't you feel too blue. T'ain't worth it."

He stood by the door. He opened it. The few items of clothing hanging from the door hook billowed out, sumptuously,

while the stench from the open latrines on the outside landing
penetrated the room. Mario noticed this sudden magnificent
swirling of materials. With slight embarrassment he heard
himself saying:

"Stop play-acting."

He was moved, but he could not permit himself to be moved.
His sensitivity, carefully hidden and not really aware of formal
and definitive beauty, but very much so of flashes of what we
know only by the name "poetry," sometimes overtook and
stunned him for a few seconds: it might be some docker,
smiling such a smile as he was pocketing a pinch of tea in the
warehouse, under his very eyes, that Mario felt like going on
without a word, caught himself hesitating, almost regretting
that he was the policeman instead of the thief: this hesitation
never lasted long. He had hardly taken a step before the
enormity of his behavior struck him. The law and order whose
servant he was might be overthrown irreparably. A huge breach
had already occurred. They might say he refrained from arresting the thief for purely esthetic reasons. At first his habitual
watchdog temper would be checked by the grace of the docker,
but once Mario became aware of the working of that charm, it
was then obviously out of sheer hatred for the thief's beauty
that he finally arrested him.

Dédé turned his head, signaling a last farewell from the
corner of his eye, but his friend took this to be a wink of
complicity at Dédé's own mirror image. Dédé had scarcely
closed the door when he felt his muscles melt, his extremities
soften as in the execution of a graceful bow. It was the same
feeling he had experienced while playing around Mario's face:
he had been overcome by a weakness, quickly restrained, that
had awakened in him a longing—his neck already bending
forward, languidly—to rest his head on Mario's thick thigh.

"Dédé!"

He opened the door again.

"What is it?"

Mario came toward him, looked him straight in the eye. He said, in a gentle whisper:

"You know I trust you, don't you, buddy?"

Surprise in his eyes, mouth half-open, Dédé looked at the detective without answering, without seeming to understand.

"Come back in for a minute . . ."

Gently Mario drew him into the room and shut the door.

"I know you'll do your best to find out what's going on But, as I said, I trust you. Nobody must get to know that I am here in your room. All right?"

The detective put his large, gold-beringed hand on the little informer's shoulder, then pulled him close to his chest:

"We've been working together for quite some time now, eh, buddy? Now you're on your own. I count on you."

He kissed him on the side of the head and let him go. This was only the second time since they had gotten to know one another that he had called the boy "buddy." Mario considered this fairly low-class language, but it was effective in sealing their friendship. Dédé took off down the stairs. Natural young tough that he was, it did not take him long to shake off his gloom. He stepped out into the street. Mario had listened to his familiar footfall—bouncy, sure and steady—as he descended the wooden staircase of the miserable little hotel. In two strides, for the room was small and Mario a big man, he was by the window. He pulled aside the thick tulle curtain, yellowed by smoke and dirt. Before him were the narrow street and the wall. It was dark. Tony's power was growing. He was turning into every shadow, every patch of the thickening fog into which Dédé was now plunging.

Querelle jumped ashore from the patrol boat. Other sailors came after him, Vic among them. They were coming from *Le Vengeur*. The boat would be there to take them back on board shortly before eleven. The fog was very dense, so substantial that it seemed as if the day itself had taken on material form.

Having conquered the city, it might well decide to last longer than twenty-four hours. Without saying a word to Querelle, Vic walked off toward the Customs shed through which the sailors passed before ascending the steps that lead up to the level of the road, the quayside, as we have mentioned before, being immediately below. Instead of following Vic, Querelle merged into the fog, heading toward the sea wall. A cunning grin on his face, he waited a moment, then started walking along the wall, running his bare palm over its surface. It did not take long before he felt something brush against his fingers. Taking hold of the string, he tied the end of it round the opium package he had been carrying under his peacoat. He gave the string three sharp little tugs, and up it went, over the wall face, slowly, all the way to Vic.

The Admiral in command of the port was quite shaken the next morning when he was told that a young sailor had been found on the ramparts with his throat cut.

Nowhere had Querelle been seen in Vic's company. In the boat they had not spoken to one another, or certainly not at any length. That same evening, in the shadow of a smokestack, Querelle had given Vic a quick briefing. As soon as Querelle reached the road, he took the ball of string and the package back from Vic. Walking by Vic's side, with the sailor's blue coat sleeve, stiff and heavy from the fog's moisture, brushing against his own, Querelle felt the presence of Murder in every cell of his body. At first this came upon him slowly, a little like the mounting of an amorous affect, and, it seemed, through the same channel—or rather, through the *reverse* of that channel. In order to avoid the city and to enhance the bravado of their venture, Querelle decided to follow the rampart wall. Through the fog, his voice reached Vic:

"Get over here."

They continued along this road as far as the Castle (where

Anne of Brittany once resided), then they crossed the Cours Dajot. No one saw them. They were smoking cigarettes. Querelle was smiling.

"You told nobody, right?"

"Hell, no. I'm not crazy."

The tree-lined walk was deserted. Besides, no one would have thought twice about two sailors coming out of the postern-gate of the rampart road and continuing into the trees, now almost obliterated by the fog, through the brambles, the dead foliage, past ditches and mud, along paths meandering toward some dank thicket. Anyone would have thought they were just two young guys chasing a bit of skirt.

"Let's go round the other side. You see? That way we get around the fort."

Querelle went on smiling, smoking. Vic was matching Querelle's long, heavy stride, and as long as he kept pace with him, he was filled with surprising confidence. Querelle's taciturn and powerful presence instilled in Vic a feeling of authority similar to the one he had experienced the times they had pulled stick-up jobs together. Querelle smiled. He let it rise inside him, that emotion he knew so well, which very soon now, at a good spot, there where the trees stood closer together and where the fog was dense, would take full command of him, driving out all conscience, all inhibition, and would make his body go through the perfect, quick and certain motions of the criminal. He said:

"It's my brother who'll take care of the rest. He's our partner."

"Didn't know he was in Brest, your bro."

Querelle was silent. His eyes became fixed, as if to observe even more attentively the rising of that emotion within him. The smile left his face. His lungs filled with air. He burst. Now he was nothing.

"Yeah, he's in Brest all right. At La Féria."

"La Féria? No kidding! What's he do there? La Féria's a
weird kind of joint."

"How so?"

No longer was any part of Querelle present within his body.
It was empty. Facing Vic, there was no one. The murderer was
about to attain his perfection, because here, in the dark of the
night, there now loomed up a group of trees forming a kind of
chamber, or chapel, with the path running through it like an
aisle. Inside the package containing the opium there were also
some pieces of jewelry, once obtained with Vic's assistance.

"Well, you know what they say. You know it as well as I do."

"So what? He's screwing the Madam."

A fraction of Querelle returned to the tips of his fingers, to
his lips: the furtive ghost of Querelle once again saw the face
and overwhelming presence of Mario combined with Norbert.
A wall that had to be dealt with, still, and Querelle paled and
dissolved at the foot of it. It had to be scaled, or climbed, or
broken through, with a heave of the shoulder.

"Me, too, I've got my jewels," he thought.

The rings and the gold bracelets belonged to him alone. They
invested him with sufficient authority to perform a sacred rite.
Querelle was now no more than a tenuous breath suspended
from his lips and free to detach itself from the body, to cling to
the closest and spikiest branch.

"Jewels. That copper, he's covered in jewels. I've got my
jewels, too. And I don't show them off."

He was free to leave his body, that audacious scaffolding for
his balls. *Their* weight and beauty he knew. With one hand,
calmly, he opened the folding knife he had in the pocket of his
peacoat.

"Well then the proprietor must've screwed him first."

"And so? If that's his game."

"Shee-it."

Vic sounded shocked.

"If someone proposed that to you, would you say 'sure, go ahead'?"

"Why not, if I felt like it. I've done worse things than that."

A wan smile appeared on Querelle's face.

"If you saw my brother, you'd fall for him. You'd let him do it."

"They say it hurts."

"You bet'cha."

Querelle stopped.

"Smoke?"

The breath, about to be exhaled, flowed back into him who became Querelle once more. Without moving his hand, with a fixed stare, paradoxically directed inward at himself, he saw himself making the sign of the Cross. After that sign, given to warn the audience that the artiste is about to perform a feat of mortal danger, there was no looking back. He had to remain totally attentive in order to go through the motions of murder: he had to avoid any brutal gesture that might surprise the sailor, because Vic most probably wasn't used to being murdered, yet, and might cry out. The criminal has to contend with life and death, both: once they start shouting, one might stick them anywhere. The last time, in Cádiz, the victim had soiled Querelle's collar. Querelle turned to Vic and offered him a cigarette and lighter, with a seemingly awkward gesture hampered by the parcel he was holding under his arm.

"Go head, light one for me too."

Vic turned his back to keep the wind out.

"Yeah, he'd like you, you're such a sweet little kitten. And if you could suck his prick as hard as you're pulling on the old coffin nail, boy he could really swing with that!"

Vic blew out a puff of smoke. Holding out the lighted cigarette to Querelle, he said:

"Well, yeah, I don't think he'd get a chance."

Querelle sniggered.

"Oh, no? And what about me, I wouldn't get a chance either?"

"Oh, come off it . . ."

Vic wanted to move on, but Querelle held him back, stretching out one leg as if to trip him. Baring his teeth, cigarette clamped between them, he went on:

"Hey? Hey . . . Tell me something, ain't I as good as Mario? Ain't I?"

"What Mario?"

"What Mario? Well . . . It's thanks to you that I got over that wall, right?"

"Yeah, so what? What the hell are you driving at?"

"So you don't want to?"

"Come off it, stop horsing around . . ."

Vic would never add anything to that. Querelle grabbed him by the throat, letting his package fall onto the path. As it fell, he whipped out his knife and severed the sailor's carotid artery. As Vic had the collar of his peacoat turned up, the blood, instead of spurting over Querelle, ran down the inside of his coat and over his jersey. His eyes bulging the dying man staggered, his hand moving in a most delicate gesture, letting go, abandoning himself in an almost voluptuous posture that recalled, even in this land of fog, the dulcet clime of the bedchamber in which the Armenian had been murdered—whose image Vic's gesture now recreated in Querelle's memory. Querelle supported him firmly with his left arm and gently lowered him down onto the grass where he expired.

The murderer straightened his back. He was a thing, in a world where danger does not exist, because one is a thing. Beautiful, immobile, dark thing, within whose cavities, the void becoming vocal, Querelle could hear it surge forth to escape with the sound, to surround him and to protect him. Vic was not dead, he was a youth whom that astonishing thing, sonorous and empty, with a mouth half-open and half-hidden, with sunken, severe eyes, with hair and garments turned to stone, with knees perhaps enveloped in a fleece thick and curled like an Assyrian beard, whom this thing with its unreal fingers, wrapped in fog, had just done to death. The tenuous breath to which Querelle had been reduced was still clinging to the spiky branch of an acacia. Anxiously, it waited. The assassin snorted twice, very quickly, like a prize fighter, and moved his lips so that Querelle might enter, flow into the mouth, rise to the eyes, seep down to the fingers, fill the thing again. Querelle turned his head, gently, not moving his chest. He heard nothing. He bent down to pull out a handful of grass turf to clean the blade of his knife. He thought he was squashing strawberries into freshly whipped cream, wallowing in them. He raised himself up from his crouched position, threw the bunch of bloodstained grass onto the dead man's body, and, after bending down a second time to retrieve his package of opium, resumed his walk under the trees alone. That the criminal at the instant of committing his crime believes that he'll never be caught is a mistaken assumption. He refuses, no doubt, to see the terrible consequences of his act at all clearly, yet he *knows* that the act does condemn him to death. We find the word "analysis" a little embarrassing. There are other ways of uncovering the workings of this self-condemnation. Let us simply call Querelle a happy moral suicide. Unable to know whether he'll be caught or not, the criminal lives in a state of anxiety, which he can only get rid of by negating, that is to say, by expiating his deed. And *that* is to say, by suffering the full penalty (for it would seem that it is the very impossibility of confessing to murders that provokes the panic, the metaphysical or religious terror in the criminal). At the bottom of a dry moat, at the foot of the ramparts, Querelle was leaning against a tree, cut off from the world by fog and night. He had put the knife back in his pocket. His beret he was holding in front of him, with both hands, at the level of his belt, the pompon against his belly. The smile was gone. He was now, in fact, appearing before the

Criminal Court that he made up for himself after every murder. As soon as he had committed the crime, Querelle had felt the hand of an imaginary policeman on his shoulder, and from the site of the slaughter all the way to this desolate place he had walked with a heavy tread, crushed by his appalling fate. After some hundred meters he abandoned the path to plunge in among the trees and brambles and down a slope to the old moat below the battlements girding the city. He had the frightened look and downcast mien of a guilty man under arrest, yet within him the certainty—and this joined him to the policeman, in a shameful yet friendly fashion—that he was a hero. The ground was sloping and covered with thorny shrubs.

"Well, here we go," he thought. And, almost at once: "Yassir, this is it, folks. Back to the worm farm."

When he reached the bottom of the moat, Querelle stopped for a moment. A light wind was stirring the dry, brittle, pointed tips of the grasses, making them rustle quietly. The strange lightness of the sound only made his situation seem more bizarre. He walked on through the fog, still heading away from the scene of the crime. The grass and the wind went on making their gentle noise, soft as the sound of air in an athlete's nostrils, or the step of an acrobat . . . Querelle, now clad in bright blue silk tights, proceeded slowly, his figure moulded by the azure garment, waist accentuated by a steel-studded leather belt. He felt the silent presence of every muscle working in unison with all the others to create the effect of a statue carved out of turbulent silence. Two police officers walked on either side of him, invisible, triumphant and friendly, full of tenderness and cruelty toward their prey. Querelle continued a few more meters, through the fog and the whispering grasses. He was looking for a quiet place, solitary as a cell, sufficiently secluded and dignified to serve as a place of judgment.

"Sure hope they don't pick up my tracks," he thought.

He regretted that he had not simply turned around and walked backwards in his own footsteps, thus raising the grass he had trodden down. But he perceived, quickly, the absurdity of his fear, while hoping his steps would be so light that every blade of grass would be intelligent enough to stand up again of its own accord. But the corpse surely wouldn't be discovered until later on, in the early morning hours. Yes, it would have to wait for the working men on their way to their jobs: *they* are the ones who come across what criminals leave by the roadside. The foggy weather did not trouble him. He noticed the marshy stench prevailing in the area. The outstretched arms of pestilence enfolded him. He kept on going. For a moment he was afraid a couple of lovers might have come down here among the trees, but this time of the year that seemed quite unlikely. Leaves and grass were damp, and the gaps between the branches interlaced with cobwebs moistened his face with their droplets as he passed through them. For a few seconds, to the astonished eyes of the assassin, the forest appeared most enchanted and lovely, vaulted and girded by hanging creeper plants gilded by a mysterious sun hanging in a sky both dim and clear and of an immensely distant blue, the womb of every dawn. Finally Querelle found himself by the trunk of a huge tree. He went up to it, cautiously walked around it, then leant against it, turning his back to the place of murder where the corpse lay waiting. He took off his beret and held it in the way we have described. Above him, he knew, a tangle of black branches and twigs was penetrating and holding the fog. And from within him rose, up to his waking consciousness, all the details of the charges against him. In the hush of an overheated room brimming with eyes and ears and fiery mouths, Querelle clearly heard the deep and droning and by its very banality most vengeful voice of the Presiding Judge:

"You have brutally slaughtered an accomplice of yours. The motives for this deed are only too evident . . ." (Here the Judge's voice and the Judge himself blurred. Querelle refused to see those motives, to disentangle, to find them in himself. He relaxed his attention to the proceedings and pressed himself more closely against the tree. The entire magnificence of the ceremonial appeared in his mind's eye, and he saw the Public Prosecutor rising to his feet.)

"We demand the head of this man! Blood calls for blood!"

Querelle was standing in the box. Braced against the tree he extracted further details of this trial in which his head was at stake. He felt good. Intertwining its branches above him, the tree protected him. From far off, he could hear frogs croaking away, but on the whole everything was so calm that the anguish in court suddenly became enhanced by the anguish of loneliness and silence. As the crime itself was the point of departure (total silence, the silence unto death desired by Querelle), they had spun around him (or, rather, it had issued from himself, this tenuous and immaterial extension of death) a thread of silence, to bind him captive. He concentrated more intensely on his vision. He made it more precise. He was there, yet he was not. He was assisting with the projection of that guilty man into the Criminal Court. He was both watching and directing the show. At times the long and pointed reverie was cut across by some clear and practical thought: "There really aren't any stains on me?" or "Supposing there's someone up there on the road . . .," but then a quick smile appeared on his face and drove his fear away. Yet he was not able to pride himself too much on that smile's power to dissipate the gloom: the smile might also bring on the fear, first to one's teeth bared by receding lips, giving birth to a monster whose snout would take on exactly the shape of one's smile, and then that monster would grow inside one, to envelop and inhabit you, ending up being far more dangerous just because of its very nature of a phantom begotten of a smile in the dark. Querelle wasn't smiling much now. Tree and fog protected him against night and retribution. He returned to the courtroom. Sovereign at the foot of the tree, he made his imaginary double go through the stances of fear, rebellion, confidence and terror, shudders, blenchings. Recollections of what he had read came to his aid. He knew there ought to be an "incident" in the courtroom. His lawyer rose to speak. Querelle wanted to lose consciousness for a moment, to take refuge in the droning in his ears. He felt he ought to delay the closing scene. Finally, the Court reconvened. Querelle felt himself grow pale.

"The Court pronounces the death sentence."

Everything around him disappeared. He himself and the trees shrunk, and he was astonished to find that he was wan and weak with this new turn of events, just as startled as we are when we learn that Weidmann was not a giant who could tower above the tops of cedar trees, but a rather timid young man of waxen and pimply complexion, standing only 1.70 meters tall among the husky police officers. All Querelle was conscious of was his terrible misfortune of being certifiably alive, and of the loud buzzing in his ears.

Querelle shivered. His shoulders were getting a little cold, as were his thighs and feet. He was standing at the base of the tree, beret in hand, packet of opium under his arm, protected by the thick cloth uniform and the stiff collar of his peacoat. He put on his beret. In some indefinite way he sensed that all was not yet finished. He still had to accomplish the last formality: his own execution.

"Gotta do it, I guess!"

Saying "sensed," we intend to convey the kind of premonition one celebrated murderer, a short while after his apparently totally unexpected arrest, meant when he told the judge: "I *sensed* that I was about to be nabbed . . ." Querelle shook himself, walked a few steps straight ahead, and, using his hands, scrambled back up the slope where the grass was singing. Some branches grazed against his cheeks and hands: it was then that he felt a profound sadness, a longing for maternal caresses, because those thorny branches appeared gentle, velvety with the fog adhering to them, and they reminded him of the soft radiance of a woman's breast. A couple of seconds later he was back again on the path, then on the road, and he re-entered the

city by a different gate from the one he had emerged from with
the other sailor. Something seemed to be missing from his side.
"It's dull, with no one to talk to."

He smiled, but very faintly. He was leaving, back there in the
fog, on the grass, a certain object, a small heap of calm and
night emanating from an invisible and gentle dawn, an object,
sacred or damned, waiting at the foot of the outer walls for
permission to enter the city, after expiation, after the proba-
tionary period imposed for purification and humility. The
corpse would have that boring face he knew, all its lines
smoothed away. With long, supple strides, that same free and
easy, slightly rolling gait that made people say "There's a guy
steps like an hombre," Querelle, his soul at peace, took the road
leading to La Féria.


*That* episode we wanted to present in slow motion. Our aim
was not to horrify the reader, but to give the act of murder
something of the quality of an animated cartoon—which in any
case is exactly the art form we would most like to be able to use,
to show the deformations of our protagonist's musculature and
soul. In any case, and in order not to annoy the reader too
much—and trusting him to complete, with his very own malaise, the contradictory and twisted windings of our own vision
of the murder—there is a great deal we have left out. It would
be easy to have the murderer experience a vision of his brother.
Or to have him killed by his brother. Or to make him kill or
condemn his brother. There are a great number of themes on
which one might embroider some revolting tapestry like that.
Nor do we want to go on about the secret and obscene desires
inhabiting the one going to his death. Vic or Querelle, take
your pick. We abandon the reader to this confusion of his
innards. But let us consider this: after committing his first
murder Querelle experienced a feeling of being dead, that is to
say, of existing somewhere in the depths—more exactly, at the

bottom of a coffin; of wandering aimlessly about some trite
tomb in some trite cemetery, and there imagining the quotidian
lives of the living, who appeared to him curiously senseless since
*he* was no longer there to be their pretext, their center, their
generous heart. However, his human form, or "fleshly envelope," went on busying itself on the earth's surface, among all
those senseless people. And Querelle proceeded to arrange
another murder. As no act is perfect to the extent that an alibi
could rid us from our responsibility for it, Querelle saw in each
crime, be it only a theft, *one* detail which (in his eyes only)
became a mistake that might lead to his undoing. To live in the
midst of his mistakes gave him a feeling of lightness, of a cruel
instability, as he seemed to be flitting from one bending reed to
another.

From the time he reached the first lights of the town
Querelle had already resumed his habitual smile. When he
entered the main parlor of the brothel he was just a husky
sailorboy, clear-eyed and looking for some action. He hesitated
for a few seconds in the midst of the music, but one of the
women lost no time in getting to him. She was tall and blonde,
very skinny, wearing a black tulle dress pulled in over the region
of her cunt—and hiding it in order to evoke it better—by a
triangle of black, longhaired fur, probably rabbit, threadbare
and almost worn bald in places. Querelle stroked the fur with a
light finger while looking the girl in the eye, but refused to
accompany her upstairs.

After delivering the package of opium to Nono and receiving
his five thousand francs Querelle knew that the time had come
for him to "execute himself."

This would be capital punishment. If a logical chain of events
had not brought Querelle to La Féria, the murderer would no
doubt have contrived—secretly, within himself—another sacrificial rite. Once more he smiled, looking at the thick nape of
the brothelkeeper's neck as that one bent over, on the divan, to
examine the opium. He looked at his slightly protruding ears,

the bald and shiny top of his head, the powerful arch of his body. When Norbert looked up again, he confronted Querelle with a face both fleshy and bony, heavy-jowled and broken-nosed. Everything about the man, in his forties, gave an impression of brutal vigor. The head belonged to a wrestler's body, hairy, tattooed perhaps, most certainly odorous. "Capital punishment, for sure."

"Now then. What's your game? What do you want with the Madam? Tell me."

Querelle discarded his grin in order to appear to smile expressly at this question and to wrap up his answer in another smile which this question alone could have provoked—and which this smile alone would succeed in rendering inoffensive. And so, he laughed out loud as he replied, with a free and easy shake of the head and in a tone of voice designed to make it impossible for Nono to take umbrage:

"I like her."

From that moment on Norbert found all the details of Querelle's face totally enchanting. This wasn't the first time a well-built lad had asked for the Madam in order to sleep with the brothelkeeper. One thing intrigued him: which one would get to bugger the other?

"All right."

He pulled out a die from his waistcoat pocket.

"You go? I go?"

"Go ahead."

Norbert bent down and threw the die on the floor. He rolled a five. Querelle took the die. He felt certain of his skill. Nono's well-trained eye noticed that Querelle was going to cheat, but before he could intervene the number "two" was sung out by the sailor, almost triumphantly. For a moment Norbert remained undecided. Was he dealing with some kind of joker? At first he had thought that Querelle was really after his own brother's mistress. This fraudulent trick had proved that was not so. Nor did the guy look like a fruit. Perturbed all the same, by the anxiety this beast of prey showed in going to its own perdition, he shrugged lightly as he rose to his feet and chuckled. Querelle, too, stood up. He looked around, amused, smiling the more he relished the inner sensation of marching to the torture chamber. He was doing it with despair in his soul, yet with an unexpressed inner certitude that this execution was necessary for him to go on living. Into what would he be transformed? A fairy. He was terrified at the thought. And what exactly is a fairy? What stuff is it made of? What particular light shows it up? What new monster does one become, and how does one then feel about the monstrosity of oneself? One is said to "like that," when one gives oneself up to the police. That copper's good looks were really at the back of everything. It is sometimes said that the smallest event can transform a life, and this one was of such significance.

"No kissing, that's for sure," he thought. And: "I'll just stick my ass out, that's all." That last expression had for him much the same resonance as "I'll stick my prick out."˙

What new body would be his? To his despair, however, was added the comforting certainty that the execution would wash him clean of the murder, which he now thought of as an ill-digested morsel of food. At last he would have to pay for that somber feast that death-dealing always is. It is always a dirty business: one has to wash oneself afterwards. And wash so thoroughly that nothing of oneself remains. Be reborn. Die, to be reborn. After that he would not be afraid of anybody. Sure, the police could still track him down and have his head cut off: thus it was necessary to take precautions not to give oneself away, but in front of the fantasy court of justice he had created for himself Querelle would no longer have anything to answer for, since he who committed that murder would be dead. The abandoned corpse, would it get past the city gates? Querelle could hear that long, rigid object, always wrapped in its narrow fog shroud, complaining, murmuring some exquisite tune. It was Vic's dead body, bewailing its fate. It desired the honors of funeral rites and interment. Norbert turned the key in the lock of the door. It was a big, shiny key, and it was reflected in the mirror opposite the door.

"Take your pants down."

The brothelkeeper's tone was indifferent. Already he had ceased to have any feelings for a guy who interfered with the laws of chance. Querelle remained standing in the middle of the room, his legs wide apart. The idea of women had never bothered him much. Sometimes, at night, in his hammock, his hand would mechanically seek out his prick, caress it, jack off quietly. He watched Nono unbuttoning. There was a moment's silence, and his gaze became fixed on the boss's finger as he was prying one of the buttons out of its buttonhole.

"Well, have you made up your mind?"

Querelle smiled. He began, desultorily, to undo the flap of his sailor's pants. He said:

"You'll take it easy, you hear? They say you can get hurt."

"Well, hell, it won't be the first time . . ."

Norbert sounded dry, almost mean. A flash of anger ran through Querelle's body: he looked extremely beautiful now, with his head held up, shoulders motionless and tense, buttocks tight, hips very straight (drawn in by the strain in the legs that was raising the buttocks), yet of a slimness that enhanced the overall impression of cruelty. Unbuttoned, his flap fell forward over his thighs, like a child's bib. His eyes were glittering. His face, even his hair seemed to be gleaming with hatred.

"Listen, buddy, I'm telling you it's the first time all right. So don't you try any monkey business."

Norbert, struck by this sudden outburst as by a whiplash, felt his wrestler's muscles tense for action, ready to recoil, and answered right back:

"Don't come on so high and mighty. That don't wash with me. You don't think I'm some kind of hick, do you now? I saw you, man. You cheated."

And, with the force of his bodily mass added to the force of his anger at finding himself defied, he came close enough to Querelle to touch him with the whole of his body, from brow to knee. Querelle stood his ground. In a still deeper voice, Norbert went on, impassively:

"And I think that's enough of that. Don't you? It wasn't me who asked you. Get ready."

That was a command such as Querelle had never before received. It came from no recognized, conventional and detached authority, but from an imperative that had issued from within himself. His own strength and vitality were ordering him to bend over. He felt like punching Norbert in the mouth. The muscles of his body, of his arms, thighs, calves were ready for action, contracted, flexed, taut, almost on tiptoes. Speaking right into Norbert's teeth, into his very breath, Querelle said:

"Man, you're mistaken. It's your old lady I was after."

"And what else is new."

Norbert grabbed him by the shoulders and tried to swing him around. Querelle wanted to push him away, but his pants had started gravitating toward his ankles. To retain them, he opened his legs a bit wider. They glared at each other. The sailor knew he was the stronger one, even in spite of Norbert's athletic build. Nevertheless he yanked up his pants and stepped back a pace. He relaxed his face muscles, raised his eyebrows, frowned a little, then shook his head lightly, to indicate resignation:

"All right," he said.

Both men, still facing each other, relaxed and simultaneously put their hands behind their backs. This perfectly synchronized double gesture surprised both of them. There was an element of understanding, there. Querelle grinned, looking pleased.

"So you've been a sailor."

Norbert snorted, then answered, testily, in a voice still somewhat shaken by anger:

"Zephir."

Querelle was struck by the exceptional quality of the man's voice. It was solid. It was, at one and the same time, a marble column issuing out of his mouth, holding him up, and against which he rested. It was, above all, to this voice that Querelle had submitted.

"What's that?"

"Zephir. The Battalion, if you prefer."

Their hands moved to unfasten their belts, and sailors' belts are, for practical reasons, buckled behind their backs—to avoid, for example, an unsightly pot-belly effect when wearing a tight-fitting rig. Thus, certain adventurous characters for no other motive than their own memories of Navy days, or their submission to the glamor of the naval uniform, retain or adopt that particular eccentricity. Querelle felt a whole lot friendlier. Since the brothelkeeper belonged to the same family as himself, with roots stretching far down into the same shadowy and perfumed lands, this very scene was something like one of those trite little escapades in the tents of the African Battalion—which no one mentions later when meeting again on civvy street. Enough had been said. Now Querelle had to execute himself. That's what he would do.

"Get over there, to the bed."

Like the wind subsides at sea, all anger had subsided. Norbert's voice was flat. Querelle pulled his leather belt out of the loops and held it in his hand. His pants had slipped down over his calves, leaving his knees bare, and, on the red carpet, they looked like a sluggish pool in which he was standing.

"Come on. Turn round. It won't take long."

Querelle faced about. He bent over, supporting himself on clenched fists—one closed round the belt buckle—on the edge of the divan. Norbert felt disheveled and unobserved. With a light and calm touch he liberated his prick from his underpants and held it for a moment, heavy and extended in his hand. He saw his reflection in the mirror in front of him and knew it was repeated twenty times in this room. He was strong. He was The Master. Total silence reigned. Advancing calmly, Norbert rested his hand on his prick as if it were some strong and flexible tree branch—leaning, as it were, on himself. Querelle was waiting, head bowed, blood mounting to his face; Nono looked at the sailor's buttocks: they were small and hard, round, dry, and covered with a thick brown fleece which continued on to the thighs and—but there, more sparsely—up to the small of the back, where the striped undershirt just peeped out from under the raised jersey. The shading on certain drawings of female rumps is achieved by incurving strokes of the brush, not unlike those bands of different colors on old-fashioned stockings: that is how I would like the reader to visualize the bared parts of Querelle's thighs. What gave them a look of indecency was that they could have been reproduced by those incurving strokes, with their emphasis on rounded curves, and the graininess of the skin, the slightly dirty gray of the curling hairs. The monstrousness of male love affairs appears in the uncovering of that part of the body, framed by undershirt and dropped pants.

"That's the way I like you."

Querelle did not reply. The smell of the opium packet lying on the bed disgusted him. And there the rod was already, entering. He recalled the Armenian he had strangled in Beirut, his softness, his lizard- or birdlike gentleness. Querelle asked himself whether he should try to please the executioner with caresses. Having no fear of ridicule now, he might as well try out that sweetness the murdered pederast had exuded.

"He did call me the fanciest names I ever did hear, that's for sure. One of the softest, he was, too," he thought.

But what gestures of affection were appropriate? What caresses? His muscles did not know which way to bend to obtain a curve. Norbert was crushing him. Slowly he penetrated him up to the point where his belly touched Querelle, whom he was holding close, with sudden, fearsome intensity, his hands clasped round the sailor's belly. He was surprised how warm it was inside of Querelle. He pushed in farther, very carefully, the better to savor his pleasure and his strength. Querelle was astonished at suffering so little pain.

"He's not hurting me. Have to admit he knows how to do it."

What he felt was a new *nature* entering into him and establishing itself there, and he was exquisitely aware of his being changed into a catamite.

"What's he going to say to me afterwards? Hope he doesn't want to talk."

In a vague way he felt grateful toward Norbert for protecting him, in thus covering him. A sense of some degree of affection for his executioner occurred to him. He turned his head slightly, hoping, after all, and despite his anxiety, that Norbert might kiss him on the mouth; but he couldn't even manage to see his face. The boss had no tender feelings for him whatsoever, nor would it ever have entered his head that a man could kiss another. Silently, his mouth half-open, Norbert was taking care of it, like of any serious and important business. He was holding Querelle with seemingly the same passion a female animal shows when holding the dead body of her young offspring—the attitude by which we comprehend what love is: consciousness of the division of what previously was one, of what it is to be thus divided, while you yourself are watching yourself. The two men heard nothing but the sound of each other's breathing. Querelle felt like weeping over the skin he had sloughed and abandoned—where? at the foot of the city wall of Brest?—but his eyes, open in one of the deep folds of the velvet bedcover, remained dry.

"Here it comes."

At the first thrust, so strong it almost killed him, Querelle whimpered quietly, then more loudly, until he was moaning without restraint or shame. Such lively expression of pleasure gave Norbert reason to feel certain that this sailor was not really a man, in that he was not able to exercise, at the moment of pleasure, the traditional reserve and restraint of the manly male. The murderer suddenly felt ill at ease, hardly able to formulate the reason for it: "Is that what it's like, being a real

fairy?" he thought. But at once he felt floored by the full
weight of the French Police Force: without really succeeding,
Mario's face was attempting to substitute itself for that of the
man who was screwing him. Querelle ejaculated onto the
velvet. A little higher up on the cover he softly buried his head
with its strangely disordered black curls, untidy and lifeless like
the grass on an upturned clump of turf. Norbert had stopped
moving. His jaws relaxed, letting go of the downy nape of
Querelle's neck which he had been biting. Then the brothelkeeper's massive bulk, very gently and slowly, withdrew from
Querelle. Querelle was still holding his belt.

The discovery of the murdered sailor caused no panic, not
even surprise. Crimes are no more common in Brest than
anywhere else, but by its climate of fog, rain, and thick low
cloud, by the grayness of the granite, the memory of the galley
slaves, by the presence, right next to the city but beyond its
walls—and for that reason all the more stirring—of Bougen
Prison, by the old penitentiary, by the invisible but durable
thread that linked the old salts, admirals, sailors, fishermen, to
the tropical regions, the city's atmosphere is such, heavy yet
luminous, that it seems to us not only conducive, but even
essential to the flowering of a murder. Flowering is the word. It
appears obvious to us that a knife slashing the fog at any con-
ceivable spot, or a revolver bullet boring a hole in it, at the
height of a man, might well burst a bubble full of blood and
cause it to stream along the inside walls of the vaporous edifice.
No matter where the blow falls, small stars of blood appear in
the wounded fog. In whatever direction you extend your hand
(already so far from your body that it no longer belongs to
you), now invisible, solitary and anonymous, the back of it will
brush against—or your fingers grab hold of—the strong, trembling, naked, hot, ready-for-action, rid-of-its-underwear prick of
a docker or sailor who waits there, burning hot and ice cold,

transparent and erect, to project a jet of jism into the froggy fog. (Ah, those knock-out body fluids: blood, sperm, tears!) Your own face is so close to another, invisible face that you can sense the blush of his affect. And all faces are beautiful, softened, purified by their blurriness, velvety with droplets clinging to cheeks and ears, but the bodies grow thicker and heavier and appear enormously powerful. Under their patched and worn blue denim pants (let us add, for our own pleasure, that the men on the waterfront still wear red cloth underwear similar in color to the pants worn by those olden-day galley slaves), the dockers and workmen usually have on another pair which gives the outer pair the heavy look of bronze clothes on statues—and you will perhaps be even more aroused when you realize that the rod in your hand has managed to penetrate so many layers of material, that it needed such care on the part of thick and work-soiled fingers to undo this double row of fly-buttons, to prepare your joy—and this double garment makes a man's lower half appear more massive.

The corpse was taken to the morgue in the Naval Hospital. The autopsy revealed nothing not already known. He was buried two days later. Admiral de D . . . du M . . ., Commander of the Port, ordered the police judge to conduct a serious and secret investigation and to keep him informed of its progress on a daily basis. He hoped to be able to avert any scandal that might besmirch the entire Navy. Armed with flashlights, police inspectors searched woods and thickets and all overgrown ditches. They searched meticulously, turning over every little heap of manure they came across. They passed close to the tree where Querelle had gone to his true condemnation. They discovered nothing: no knife, no footprint, not a shred of clothing, not a single blond hair. Nothing but the cheap cigarette lighter Querelle had handed to the young sailor; it lay in the grass, not far from the dead body. The police said they were unable to determine whether it had belonged to the murderer or to his victim. Nothing was learned in an enquiry as to its

ownership on board the *Vengeur*. Querelle had picked up that
lighter on the eve of the crime, pocketed it, almost automatically, from among the bottles and glasses on the table on which
Gil Turko, its owner, had been singing. Theo had given it to
Gil.

As the crime had been committed in those woods by the
ramparts, the police had a notion that the man they were
looking for might well be a pederast. Knowing with what horror
society recoils from anything even remotely connected with the
idea of homosexuality, it seems surprising that the police should
find it so easy to consider that idea. Once a murder has been
committed, the police habitually put forward the two motives
of robbery or jealousy; but as soon as someone who is or has
been a sailor is involved, they simply say to themselves: sexual
perversion. They cling to that conclusion with almost painful
intensity. To society-at-large, the police are what the dream is to
the quotidian round of events; what it excludes from its own
preoccupations, at least as far as possible, polite society author-
izes its police force to deal with. This may account for the
combined repulsion and attraction with which that force is
regarded. Charged with the drainage of dreams, the police catch
them in their filters. And that explains why policemen bear
such resemblance to those they pursue. It would be a mistake to
believe that it is merely the better to trick, track down, and
vanquish it more effectively, that those inspectors blend so well
with their quarry. Looking closely at Mario's personal life, we
notice first of all his habitual visits to the brothel and his friendship with its proprietor. No doubt he finds Nono an informer
who is in some ways a useful kind of link between law-abiding
society and shady doings, but in talking to him he is also able to
acquire (if he did not know them already) the manners and
idioms of the underworld—tending to overdo them, later, in
moments of danger. Finally, his desire to love Dédé in forbidden ways is an indication: this love alienates him from the

police force whose conduct must always be quite beyond reproach. (Those propositions appear contradictory. We shall see
how that contradiction resolves itself in actuality.) Up to their
necks in work we refuse even to admit, the police live under a
curse, particularly the plainclothes men, who, when seen in the
middle of (and protected by) the dark blue uniforms of the
straight coppers, appear like thin-skinned, translucent lice, small
fragile things easily crushed with a fingernail, whose very bodies
have become blue from feeding off that other, the dark blue.
That curse makes them immerse themselves in their efforts with
a vengeance. Whenever the occasion arises, they then bring up
the notion of pederasty—in itself, and fortunately, a mystery
they are unable to unravel. The inspectors had a vague feeling
that the murder of that sailor over by the ramparts was not
quite run-of-the-mill: what they should have found there was
some "sugar daddy," assassinated, abandoned on the grass,
picked clean of his money and valuables. Instead of which they
had found the body of the most likely type of suspect, with his
money in his pockets. No doubt this anomaly worried them a
little, and interfered with the progress of their ruminations, but
it did not really bother them overmuch. Mario had not been
given any specific orders to participate in the investigation of
this case. Thus, at first, he paid only cursory attention to it,
being more preoccupied with the danger he was in after Tony's
discharge. Had he taken time to interest himself in the case, he
would have been no more able than anyone else to explain it in
terms of homosexual goings-on. Indeed, neither Mario nor any
of the heroes of this book (excepting Lieutenant Seblon, but
then Seblon is not *in* the book) is a pederast; for Mario, those
people were of two kinds—those who wanted to get laid and
paid for it and were known as sugar daddies, and, well, the
others who catered to them. But then, quite suddenly, Mario
became engrossed in the case. He felt a keen desire to unravel
the plot, which he imagined carefully and tightly organized and

of potential danger to himself. Dédé had returned without any precise information, yet Mario was sure of the risk he was running: he started going out again, came out into the open with the crazy notion that by his speed and agility he would outdistance death, and that even if he were killed, death would simply pass through him. His courage was designed to dazzle and blind whatever it was that was threatening him. All the same, secretly, he reserved the right to negotiate with the enemy along lines that will eventually become apparent: Mario was merely waiting for the occasion. In that, too, he demonstrated courage. The police made enquiries among all known "queens." There aren't many of those in Brest. Although it is a big naval base, Brest has remained a small provincial town. The avowed pederasts—self-avowed, that is—manage to remain admirably inconspicuous. They are peaceful citizens of irreproachable outward appearance, even though they may, the long day through, perhaps suffer from a timid itch for a bit of their fun. Nor could any detective have supposed that the murder discovered in the neighborhood of the ramparts might have been the violent and—in terms of time and place—inevitable outcome of a love affair that had developed on board a solid and loyal Navy vessel. No doubt the police knew about the worldwide reputation of La Féria, but the reputation of the boss himself seemed unassailable: they did not know of a single client—docker or other—who had buggered him or whom he had buggered. Yet the notoriety of La Féria was legendary. However, Mario did not consider any of these matters until later, when Nono, in a moment's playful braggadocio, told him about his doings with Querelle. When Querelle emerged from the coal bunkers and came up on deck on the day after that big night, he was black from head to toe. A thick but soft layer of coal dust covered his hair, stiffening it, petrifying every curl, powdering his face and naked torso, the material of his pants, and his bare feet. He crossed the deck to reach his quarters.

"Mustn't worry too much," he was thinking as he walked

along. "There's only one thing to be afraid of, and that's the guillotine. Now even that ain't so terrible. They're not going to execute me every day."

His blackface act served him well. Querelle had begun to realize—and to think, for the first time, about doing something about it—the turmoil within Lieutenant Seblon, betrayed by the officer's frowning mien and overly severe tone of voice. Being just a simple sailor, he could not understand the ways of his Lieutenant who would punish him for the slightest infraction and look for the least little pretext for doing so. But one day the officer had happened to pass too close to the machinery and had soiled his hands with axle grease. He had turned to Querelle, who happened to be standing close by. In a suddenly quite humble manner he asked:

"D'you happen to have a rag I could use?"

Querelle produced a clean handkerchief, still folded, from his pocket and held it out to him. The Lieutenant wiped his hands on it and kept it.

"I'll have it washed. Come by and pick it up sometime."

Some days later the Lieutenant found an opportunity of addressing Querelle and, he hoped, of wounding him. Harshly:

"Don't you know it's against regulations to fix the beret that way?"

He grabbed the red pompon on top of the beret and yanked it off the seaman's head. The sun then shone its rays on such a splendid mop of hair that the officer came close to giving himself away. His arm, his sudden gesture turned leaden. In a changed voice, he went on, holding out the beret to the dumbfounded sailor:

"That's what you like, to look like some ruffian. You deserve . . . (he hesitated, not really knowing whether to say '. . . all the genuflections, all the caresses of seraphim's wings, all the perfume of lilies . . .'). You deserve to be punished."

Querelle looked him in the eye. Simply and so calmly that it was hurtful, he said:

"Have you finished with my handkerchief, sir?"

"That's right. Well, come along and get it."

Querelle followed the officer to his cabin. The latter started looking for the handkerchief, but did not find it. Querelle waited, immobile, strictly at attention. Then Lieutenant Seblon took one of his own, monogrammed, clean handkerchiefs, white cambric, and offered it to the seaman.

"Sorry. Seems I can't find yours. Do you mind if I give you this one?"

Querelle nodded his indifferent-seeming acceptance.

"I'm sure it'll turn up again. I had it laundered. Now, I'm pretty certain you wouldn't have done that yourself. You don't look like that kind of lad to me."

Querelle was taken aback by the officer's "tough" expression as he uttered those words in an aggressive, almost accusing tone. All the same, he smiled.

"That ain't quite so, sir. I know how to take care of things."

That's news to me. You're the kind of guy, it seems to me, takes his washing to some little sixteen-year-old Syrian chick, so she can do it and . . . (here Lieutenant Seblon's voice quavered. He knew he better not say what he perfectly well knew he would say, after three seconds of silence) . . . bring it to you all nicely smoothed and ironed."

"No such luck. I don't know any girls in Beirut. What there is to wash, I do myself."

And then, without understanding why, Querelle noticed a slight relaxation of the officer's rigid attitude. Spontaneously, with the amazing sense for putting their attractions to work for them that young men have, even those to whom any degree of methodical coquetry is quite foreign, he gave his voice a somewhat sly inflection, and his body, relaxing too, became animated from neck to calves—by the almost imperceptible shifting of one foot in front of the other—by a series of short-lived ripples that were truly graceful and reminded Querelle himself of the existence of his buttocks and shoulders. Suddenly he appeared as if drawn in quick, broken lines, and, to the officer, drawn by the very hand of the master.

"Well?"

The Lieutenant looked at him. Querelle was again immobile, yet the grace of his movements remained. He smiled. His eyes were like asterisks.

"Well, in that case . . ."

The Lieutenant spoke in a casual drawl. "Well . . . (and in one breath, managing not to betray too much of his unease) . . . if you're really so good at all that, how would you like to be my steward for a while?"

"I'd like that, sir . . . It's just that I wouldn't be getting any hardship money, then."

It was a straightforward reservation, added on to a straightforward acceptance of the offer. Without knowing that it was love that had inspired them, Querelle was now witnessing, in his mind's eye, the sudden and simultaneous transformation of all potential and actual punishments meted out by the Lieutenant: he saw them lose their primary meaning and take on the nature of "encounters," which, and that for quite some time, were pointing toward a union, an understanding between the two men. They held memories in common. Their relationship, as from that day, had its own past history.

"But why not? I'll take care of that. Don't you worry, you won't stand to lose any pay."

The Lieutenant cherished his belief that he had never revealed his love one little bit, while hoping (at the same time) that he had made it abundantly clear. As soon as the picture became comprehensible to Querelle—the following day, in fact, when he found, in a place where logically it should never have been, in an old croc-skin briefcase, his own handkerchief—stained with axle grease and further starched with some other fluid—he found such games of hide and seek most amusing, being able to see through them perfectly well. And that day, when he emerged from the coal bunkers, he felt certain that his surprisingly black face, looking more massive than usual under its light coating of coal dust, would appear beautiful enough for the Lieutenant to lose his cool. Perhaps he would even have "a confession to make"?

"Well, we'll see. Maybe he hasn't even heard . . ."

Within his body, his anxiety was giving rise to a most exquisite sensation. Querelle called his star: his smile. And the star appeared. Querelle kept on moving forward, planting his wide feet firmly on the deck. He gave a slight roll to his hips, narrow as they were!—to provide a little action there in the midriff region, where an inch of his white underpants showed above the wide, plaited leather belt, buckled at the back. He had of course registered, and not without spite, that the Lieutenant's gaze often dwelt on that region of his physique, and he had a natural awareness of his own seductive points. He thought of them in a serious manner, sometimes with a smile, that habitual, sad smile of his. He also swung his shoulders a little, but the motion, like that of his hips and his arms, was more discreet than usual, closer to himself, more internalized, one might say. He was hugging himself: or one might say, he was playing at being huggable. As he approached the Lieutenant's cabin he was hoping that the officer would have noticed the abortive theft of his watch. He longed to be taken up on that.

"I'll handle it. I'll sock him in the mouth . . ."

But while he was turning the doorknob he realized he was hoping that the watch (which he had returned, as soon as he got back on board, to its place in the drawer—while the Lieutenant wasn't looking) had stopped, of its own accord—broken or run down or—he dared to think it—stopped by virtue of a particular kindness of destiny, or even out of a particular kindness on the part of that already once-seduced watch itself.

"Well, so what. If he says just one word about that, I'll take care of him, but good."

The Lieutenant was waiting for him. From the first moment, the caress of the Lieutenant's quick glance at his body and his face, Querelle was confirmed in his power: it was his body that was emitting the ray that ran through the officer's eyes down to the very pit of his stomach. The handsome blond boy, secretly adored, would very soon appear, naked perhaps, but re-invested with great majesty. The coal dust was not thick enough to quite conceal the brightness of the hair, the eyebrows and the skin, nor the rosy coloration of the lips and ears. It was obviously just a veil, and Querelle raised it now and again by occasionally, coquettishly, one might say artfully blowing on his arms or ruffling a curl of his hair.

"You're a good worker, Querelle. You even go for the rough chores, without even telling me. Who told you to coal?"

The Lieutenant sounded tough and sardonic. He was struggling to suppress his feelings. His eyes were making pitiful and useless efforts not to rest too obviously on Querelle's hips and pelvis. One day when he had offered him a glass of port wine, and Querelle had replied that he couldn't take alcohol on account of a dose of the clap (Querelle had lied: on the spur of the moment, and to whet the Lieutenant's desire, he had pretended to be suffering from a "man's disease," to appear a true "bedroom athlete"), Seblon, ignorant of the nature of this affliction, imagined a festering penis under that blue denim, dripping away like one of those Easter candles inlaid with five grains of incense . . . He was already quite furious with himself for being unable to take his eyes off those muscular and powdered arms, where particles of coal dust clung to hairs still curled and golden. He thought:

"What if it really was Querelle who murdered Vic? But that's impossible. Querelle is too much of a natural beauty to need to assume the beauty of crime. He doesn't need that kind of trimming. One would have to make up all kinds of things about them, secret messages, meetings, embraces, stolen kisses."

Querelle gave him the same answer he had given to the Captain at Arms:

"Well . . ."

That glance, quick as it was, Querelle caught it. His smile broadened, and in shifting his feet, he performed a quick, seductive "bump."

"So you don't really like working here, eh?"

Having found himself unable to resist such a trite explanation and wording, the officer experienced yet another surge of self-loathing and blushed to observe Querelle's black nostrils quiver delicately and the pretty middle part of his upper lip join in with more rapid and more subtle tremors—clearly a most delightful outward sign of great efforts to restrain a smile.

"But no, I do like it. But I was down there to help out a buddy. Colas, in fact."

"He could have picked someone else to replace him. You're in a pretty incredible state. Do you really like breathing coal dust all that much?"

"No, but . . . But then, well, for me . . ."

"What's that? What do you want to say?"

Querelle let his smile shine bright. He said:

"Oh, nothing."

That nailed the officer's feet to the floor. It only needed a word, a simple order, to send Querelle to the showers. For a few moments they remained very ill at ease, both of them in a state of suspense. It was Querelle who brought matters to a close.

"Is that all, sir?"

"Yes, that's all. Why ask?"

"Oh, no reason."

The Lieutenant thought he detected a hint of impertinence in the sailor's question, and in his answer as well, both delivered in the sunshine of a blinding smile. His dignity prompted him to dismiss Querelle on the spot, but he could not muster the strength to do that. If bad luck would have Querelle decide to go back down to the coal bunkers again, he thought, his lover would certainly follow him there . . . The half-naked seaman's presence in his cabin was driving him out of his mind. Already he was heading on down to hell, descending the black marble staircase, almost to those depths into which the news of Vic's murder had plunged him earlier. He wanted to engage Querelle in that sumptuous adventure. He wanted him to play his part in it. What secret thought, what startling confession, what dazzling display of light was concealed under those bell-bottoms, blacker now than any pair ever known to man? What shadowy penis hung there, its stem rooted in pale moss? And what was the substance covering all these things? Well, certainly nothing but a little coal dust—familiar enough, in name and consistency; that simple ordinary stuff, so capable of making a face, a pair of hands, appear coarse and dirty—yet it invested this young blond sailorboy with all the mysterious powers of a faun, of a heathen idol, of a volcano, of a Melanesian archipelago. He was himself, yet he was so no longer. The Lieutenant, standing in front of Querelle, whom he desired but did not dare approach, made an almost imperceptible gesture, nervous, quickly withdrawn. Querelle noted all the waves of uneasiness passing across the eyes fixed firmly on his, without letting one of them escape him—and (as if such a weight had, by squashing Querelle, caused his smile to broaden more and more) he kept on smiling under the gaze and the physical mass of the Lieutenant, both bearing down on him so heavily that he had to tense his muscles against them. He understood nonetheless the gravity of that stare, which at that moment expressed total human despair. But at the same time, in his mind, he was shrugging his shoulders and thinking:

"Faggot!"

He despised the officer. He kept on smiling, allowing himself to be lulled by the monstrous and ill-defined notion of "faggot" sweeping back and forth inside his head.

"Faggot, what's a faggot? One who lets other guys screw him in the ass?" he thought. And gradually, while his smile faded, lines of disdain appeared at the corners of his mouth. Then again, another phrase drifted through his mind, inducing a vague feeling of torpor: "Me, I'm one too." A thought he had difficulty in focusing on, though he did not find it repulsive, but of whose sadness he was aware when he realized that he was pulling his buttocks in so tight (or so it seemed to him) that they no longer touched the seat of his trousers. And this fleeting, yet quite depressing thought generated, up his spine, an immediate and rapid series of vibrations which quickly spread out over the entire surface of his black shoulders and covered them with a shawl woven out of shivers. Querelle raised his arm, to smooth back his hair. The gesture was so beautiful, unveiling, as it did, the armpit as pale and as taut as a trout's belly, that the Lieutenant could not prevent his eyes from betraying how very weary he was of this state of unrequited passion. His eyes cried for mercy. Their expression made him look more humble, even, than if he had fallen on his knees. Querelle felt very strong. If he despised the Lieutenant, he felt no impulse to laugh at him, as on other days. It seemed unnecessary to him to exert his charms, as he had an inkling that his true power was of another kind. It rose from the depths of hell, yet from a certain region in hell where the bodies and the faces are beautiful. Querelle felt the coal dust on his body, as women feel, on their arms and hips, the folds of a material that transforms them into queens. It was a make-up that did not interfere with his nakedness, that turned him into a god. But for the moment he was content to merely turn on his smile again. He was sure, now, that the Lieutenant would never ever raise the matter of the watch.

"So what are you going to do now?"

"Don't know, sir. I'm at your service. But, well, the buddies are a hand short, down below."

The officer engaged in some quick thinking. To send Querelle to the shower would be to destroy the most beautiful object his eyes had ever been given to caress. As the seaman would be back again the next day, to be close beside him, it would be better to leave him covered with that black stuff. And sometime during the day he might find an occasion for going below to the bunkers, and there he might surprise this giant morsel of darkness at its flagrant amorous activities.

"All right, then. Get going."

"Very good, Lieutenant. I'll be back tomorrow."

Querelle saluted and turned on his heel. With the anguish of a shipwrecked man watching island shores recede, and yet delighted with the casual tenor of complicity in Querelle's parting words—tender as the first use of a nickname—the officer saw those ravishingly neat buttocks, that chest, those shoulders and that neck draw away from him, irrevocably, yet not so far that he wouldn't be able to recall them with innumerable and invisible outstretched hands, enfolding those treasures and guarding them with the tenderest solicitude. Querelle went back to his coaling, as was his habit now, after murders. If on the first occasion he had thought that he would thus escape recognition by possible witnesses, at subsequent times he simply remembered the feeling of astounding power and security that that black powder, covering him from head to toe, had given him, and thus he sought it out again. His strength lay in his beauty and in his daring to still add to that beauty the appearance of cruelty inherent in masks; he was strong—and so invisible and calm, crouching in the shadow of his power, in the remotest corner of himself—strong, because he was menacing, yet knew himself to be so gentle; he was strong, a black savage, born into a tribe in which murder ennobled a man.

"And besides, hell, I've got all that jewelry!"

Querelle knew that the possession of certain wealth—gold,

especially—gives one the right to kill. At that level, killing is done in "the interests of the State." He was a black among the whites, and the more mysterious, monstrous, beyond the laws of this world, as he owed this singularity to a hardly intentional blackface act, being covered in mere coal dust—but he himself, Querelle, was proof that there is more to coal dust than meets the eye: that it has the power to transform, just by being sprinkled over his skin, the soul of a man. He gained strength by being a blaze of light to himself, an incarnation of night to the others; he gained strength from working in the farthest depths of the ship. Lastly, he was experiencing the gentleness of funereal things, their light solemnity. He came, in the end, to veil his face and wear black mourning garb for his victim, secretly, in his own fashion. Though he had dared to do so on former occasions, today he could not bring himself to recapitulate the details of the murder. On his way back to the bunkers all he said to himself was:

"He didn't say anything about the watch."

Had the Lieutenant not been trying to involve Querelle in that story he was imagining around Vic's murder, perhaps he would have been more surprised at the way his steward contributed to the strange doings of this day by voluntarily joining the work party in the coal bunkers. But the day was proving too distracting as it was for him to attempt an interpretation of this additional mystery. And when the two police inspectors charged with the inquiry on board came to interrogate him about the men, he did not mention his idea that Querelle might be the suspect. However, he found himself in more kinds of trouble: if, to his fellow officers, the Lieutenant's preciosity of speech and gesture, the sometimes overly sensuous tones of his voice, appeared merely as signs of distinction—accustomed as they were to the smooth and unctuous mannerisms of their blessed families—the inspectors made no mistake and instantly saw what they had here, a faggot. Although he still worked on the contrary impression when dealing with crewmen, either by

stressing the hardness of his metallic voice or by giving exceed-
ingly laconic commands—sometimes in sheer telegraphese—the
police officers shook his self-confidence. Faced with them, their
authority, he immediately felt guilty and slipped into acting like
a distracted girl, giving further indications of his guilt feelings.
Mario decided to open the proceedings:
"I'm sorry to take up your time, Lieutenant . . ."
"And so you should be."
That remark, apparently accidental, certainly inadvertent,
made him appear both cynical and rude. The inspector thought
that he was trying to be funny, and this set him on edge. While
the Lieutenant's embarrassment grew, Mario, who had been
somewhat intimidated at first, started putting his questions
more bluntly. To the fairly obvious
"Did you ever notice any goings-on between Vic and any
particular buddy of his?" Seblon gave the reply—cut in half by
a frog-in-the-throat that did not go unnoticed by the ques-
tioners—:
"How exactly does one recognize such affairs?"
His own, obviously overstated retort made him blush. His
embarrassment grew. To Mario, the strangeness of the officer's
replies was only too apparent. Since the Lieutenant's strength
lay in his speech—his weakness, too—he now tried to regain the
upper hand by this sorely undermined verbal ability. He said:
"How can I keep track of what the boys do in their own
time? Even if that crewman, Vic, got murdered because of
some unsavory involvement, I just wouldn't know about it."
"Of course not, Lieutenant. But, sometimes one happens to
hear something."
"You must be joking. I do not eavesdrop on my men. And
you better realize that even if some of the young fellows did
have dealings with revolting types such as you have in mind,
they wouldn't boast about them. I should imagine their meetings are shrouded in such secrecy . . ."
He realized that he wasn't far from singing the praises of

homosexual affairs. He would have liked to keep his mouth
shut, but being aware that a sudden silence would appear
strange to the inspector, he added, in an offhand manner:
"Those disgusting characters are wonderfully organized . . ."
That was too much. He himself noticed the ambivalence of
the opening statement, with the "wonderfully" striking a note
of joyous defiance. The inspectors felt they had had enough.
Without being able to distinguish exactly what it was that
betrayed him, it seemed to them that his manner of speaking
took pleasure in the manners and morals of precisely those
elements whom he pretended to condemn. Their thoughts
might have been expressed in clichés like: "He talks about them
quite sympathetically, doesn't he?" or "It doesn't sound like
he'd really detest them all that much." In short, he appeared
suspect. Fortunately for him, he had an alibi, for he had been
on board the night of the crime. When the interview was over,
but before the two police officers had left the cabin, the Lieutenant wanted to put on his cloak of navy blue, and then did so
with such coquetry—which he at once, and clumsily, corrected
—that the total effect was not of just "putting it on," that
would have been far too manly, but rather that of "wrapping
himself in it"—which, indeed, was the way he thought of it
himself. Again, he experienced embarrassment, and he made up
his mind (once more) never to touch a piece of material again
in public. Querelle donated ten francs, when they came round
to collect for a wreath for Vic. And now some excerpts, picked
at random, from the private diary.

*This journal can only be a book of prayers.*

*God grant that I may envelop myself in my chilly gestures, in a
chilly fashion, like some very languid Englishman in his traveling
rug, an eccentric lady in her shawl. To confront men with, You
have given me a gilded rapier, chevrons, medals, gestures of com-*

mand: these accessories are my salvation. They allow me to weave about me some invisible lace, of intentionally coarse design. That coarseness exhausts me, even though I find it comforting. When I grow old, I shall take refuge in the last resort, behind the ridiculous façade of rimless steel pince-nez, celluloid collars, a stammer, and starched cuffs.

Querelle told his comrades that he is a "victim" of the recruitment posters! So am I, a victim of those posters, and a victim's victim.

What sudden joy! I am all joy. My hands, mechanically at first, described, in empty space, at the height of my chest— two female breasts, grafting them on as it were. I was happy. Now I repeat the gesture, such bliss. Such great abundance. I am overflowing. I stop: I am her, overflowing. I start over. I caress these two aerial boobs. They are beautiful. They are heavy, my palms support them. It happened when I stood leaning against the rail, at night, looking across, listening to the noises of Alexandria. I caress my breasts, my hips. I feel my buns getting rounder, more voluptuous. Egypt lies behind me now: the sands, the Sphinx, the Pharaohs, the Nile, the Arabs, the Casbah, and the wonderful adventure of being her. I would like them a little pear-shaped.

Once again, I dragged the door curtains in with me, quite unwittingly. I felt how they wanted to envelop me in their folds, and I could not resist making a splendid gesture, to free myself of them. The gesture of a swimmer parting the water.

I come back in. Still thinking about the liveliness of the cigarette between the sailor's fingers. A ready-made cigarette. It burned, it went through its little motions between Querelle's almost immobile fingers, and he had no idea of the life he was imbuing that little tobacco stick with. I was no more able to take my eyes off his fingers than off the object they were animating. Animated by such grace, such elegant, delicate, scintillating movements! Querelle stood listening to one of his buddies talking about the girls in the brothels.

"I have never seen myself." Do I have charms another could fall for? Who else, besides myself, is subject to Querelle's charms? How could I turn into him? Could I bring myself to graft onto my body his best features: his hair, his balls? Even his hands?

To feel more comfortable while jacking off I roll up the sleeves of my pajama top. This simple expedient turns me into a fighter, a tough guy. Thus I then confront the image of Querelle, in front of whom (or which) I brandish my rod like a lion tamer. But then it's all over again, get the towel, wipe it off my belly.

It is not our design to disengage two or several characters—or heroes, as they have been extracted from a fabulous domain, that is to say, they have their origin in fable, fable and limbo—and describe them, methodically, as odious. One should rather consider it to be ourselves, pursuing an adventure unfolding in ourselves, in the deepest, most asocial region of our soul; it is, indeed, because he breathes life into his creatures—and voluntarily assumes the burden of sin of this world he has given birth to—that the creator delivers and saves his creature, and at the same time places himself beyond or above sin. May the reader, too, escape from sin, while he, reading our words, discovers in himself these heroes, who have been in hiding until this time . . .

Querelle! All the Querelles of the Fighting Navy! Beautiful sailors, you taste sweet, like wild oats.

A reception on board. The deck is decorated with green plants, red carpet. Crewmen, all in white, come and go. Querelle looks indifferent. I observe him without his seeing me. He stands there, hands in pockets, leaning back a little, his neck thrust forward like that of the bull (or is it a tiger? a lion?) on the Assyrian bas relief, its flank pierced by an arrow. The festivities mean nothing to him. He's whistling, smiling.

Querelle hauling a heavy launch to the quayside; four crewmen are pulling on the rope, expanding their chests with the effort, the rope passed over their left shoulders, but Querelle faces the other way. He pulls walking backwards. I'm sure he does it to avoid looking like a dray-beast. He noticed that I was looking at him. I had to take my eyes off his.

Beauty of Querelle's feet. His bare feet. He plants them firmly on the deck. His strides are wide and long. Despite his smile, Querelle's face is sad. It makes me think of the sadness of a handsome boy, very strong, very manly, who has been caught like a kid but on a grave charge, and who now sits in the prisoner's booth, crushed by the severity of his sentence. In spite of his smile, his good looks, his insolence, the radiant vigor of his body, his boldness, Querelle seems to be branded with the indescribable brand of some profound humiliation. This morning he appeared quite washed out. His eyes looked tired.

Querelle lay sleeping on the deck in the sun. Stood and looked down at him. My face, it dove down and submerged in his; and then I drew back almost instantly, for fear that he should see me. To those tranquil, assured—and long—moments, perhaps granted us one day, to sleep in each other's arms, I still prefer these instants of discomfort, these rapid moments one has to destroy because the legs grow stiff from bending down, or an arm goes numb, or because a door or an eyelid isn't quite properly closed. I cherish those stolen moments, and Querelle pays no attention to them.

Reception on board, for Admiral A . . . He's a tall and thin old man, with very white hair. He rarely smiles, but I know that behind that severe and even a little haughty exterior he conceals great gentleness, great kindness. He made his appearance up the gangway followed by a Marine, a big bruiser in full battle dress —gaiters, cartridge belt, helmet and all. His bodyguard. The spectacle moved me a great deal, and I enjoy recollecting it. The fragile outline of the old man with his neat gestures, seen against the magnificent bearing of his orderly! One day I, too, shall be an old officer, decorated, gilded, and frail, but framed thus, by the solid muscular body of some twenty-year-old warrior.

We are at sea. There is a storm. If we get shipwrecked, what will Querelle do? Would he try to save me? He does not know that I love him. I would try to save him, but I would rather try to make him save me. In a shipwreck, everybody grabs hold of what is most precious to him: a violin, a manuscript, some photographs . . . Querelle would take me. But I know that he would first of all save his own beauty, even if I should die.

He stood watching another crewman scrubbing the deck. Not having anything else to lean on, Querelle was leaning on his hands, one on top of the other, resting on his belt, above the flap. The whole upper part of his body was leaning forward, and under that weight the belt (and the top of his pants) was sagging, like a stretched-out rope.

No young prick to hold in my hand—I could cry. I howl out my pain, to the sea, to the night, to the stars. I know that there are some marvelous ones, back there in the crew's quarters, but I shall never be permitted to touch them.

The Admiral gives the order, and in the most docile fashion the goon who follows him everywhere enters his cabin, unfastens the flap and presents a rod, fully extended according to regulations, to his lips. I know no couple more elegant or more perfectly matched than that Admiral and his beast.

Querelle has forgotten his jersey in my cabin. It's lying on the floor, just as he left it. I don't dare to touch it. The striped sailor's jersey has the power of a leopard skin. More than that, even. It is the animal itself, hiding there, wrapped up in itself, showing only its outward form. "Someone must have thrown it there." But if I should stretch out my hand to touch it, it would instantly swell up with all the muscles in Querelle's body.

Cádiz. A Negro, dancing, with a rose between his teeth. As soon as the music starts up, he starts shaking. About him, I wrote: he exudes, a powerful fragrance—like horses do. Next to his image that of Querelle loses its brightness.

Querelle, sewing on his buttons. I watch him tense his arm the better to thread the needle. The gesture cannot appear ridiculous: not in one who last night crushed his body against that of a girl, pushing her up against a tree, with a conqueror's smile. When he is drinking coffee, Querelle often shakes the cup to dissolve all the sugar in the last drops with that rotary motion of the right hand, from right to left (that is, counterclockwise), most women use, and five minutes later he'll reverse the motion and swill it the way men do. Thus each one of Querelle's most insignificant actions is charged with the humanity, the gravity, of a nobler action that precedes it.

Under the word "pederast," Larousse entry: "In the quarters of one of them was found a large quantity of artificial flowers, garlands and wreaths, intended, without any doubt, for use as decorations and ornaments in their grand orgies."

Gil was asleep, lying on his belly. Like every Sunday morning, he woke up late. Although they were in the habit of indulging in a long lie-in on that day, some of the other workmen were up and about. The sun was already high in the sky, piercing the fog. In addition to a strong pressure in his bladder Gil immediately felt the anguish of having to face this coming day, its atmosphere thick with his own shame; as if to gulp it all down as fast as possible, he opened his mouth in a huge yawn. He was delaying the moment of getting out of bed. He decided to take the greatest care to remain unnoticed, as he would now have to invent a whole new method in order to start in on a life which would—from now on—be lived under the sign of contempt. Thus, this very morning, he had to create a new relationship with his mates from the shipyard. Stretched out under the sheets, he remained motionless. He didn't intend to go back to sleep, but wanted to think some more about what lay in store for him, to get used to the new situation, to think it through, so that his body would then be ready for it. Slowly, eyes closed as if still asleep, and hoping to look convincing in case all other eyes were attending his awakening, he turned round in his bed. A beam of sunlight from the window shone straight onto his blankets, on which some buzzing flies had settled. Without knowing what it was that attracted them, Gil knew that it had to do with the exposure of some secret. As nonchalantly as possible, he pulled the object—his briefs—down under the sheets, to find that they were a pair slightly soiled with shit and blood at the back: this, in the sunlight, had been attracting the flies. Now they buzzed off with such an infernal drone that the room was filled with the sound of it, revealing Gil's infamy, proclaiming it with the majesty and splendor of an organ voluntary. Gil felt certain that it was Theo's vengeful doing: he had gone through Gil's kit bag, come up with the disgusting item, and placed it on the young mason's bed while he was still asleep. The boys had watched these preparations gravely, silently, not interfering, as they knew Theo to be a violent character, and as that trait of his made them feel more real to themselves. And, well, there was no harm in taking that young guy down a peg or two, was there? The sun and the flies—Theo hadn't even reckoned with them—had added their talents to the show. Without raising it from the pillow, Gil turned his head to the left: he felt something hard under his cheek. Most carefully, slowly, he extended his hand and pulled the object down under the sheets, against his chest. It was a huge eggplant. He held it in his hand; it was quite beautiful, terrifyingly large, violet in color, round. All of Gil's suppressed anger—manifest in the taut muscles under the smooth white skin, in the fixed stare of his green eyes, in his lack of wit, in his mouth ill at ease with his always unfinished smile that refused to disclose any but his front teeth and looked as tight-stretched as a cruel length of elastic that must flip back and hurt you; in his dry, colorless, and rather sparse hair; in his silences; in his clear and frosty voice; in short, in everything which led people to refer to him as a "berserker"—all of that smouldering rancor was now wounded to the quick, and it almost brought tears to his eyes. The others had attacked it so fiercely that it melted, became soft and tepid, pitiful, ready to expire. From his toes to the rims of his dry eyes, Gil's body was shaken by deep sobs, and these destroyed all remaining traces of cruelty. His need to urinate became more and more imperative. It turned all of Gil's attention to his bladder. But in order to reach the latrine he would have to get up and cross the room, the room he imagined was bristling with sneers and jeers. He remained stretched out, thinking only of his violent physical need. Finally he decided to "live with shame." Pushing back the bedsheets he already felt the inadequacy of his gestures. His wrist moved over the folds without his hand clutching them—as it was not permitted to make a fist—looking like some humble Christian brow, a miserable sinner showing only his ashen gray neck, unworthy of any brightness. Humbly Gil raised his head, without looking around, hesitantly gathered up his socks and put them on, taking care not to expose his legs. The door across from him suddenly opened. Gil did not raise his eyes.

" 'Tain't too warm out there, boys."

It was the voice of Theo who had just come in. He went over to the stove where a saucepan full of water was heating.

"Is *this* going to be soup? Not much in it!"

"That's not for soup. That's for shaving," someone told him.

"Oh. I'm sorry, my mistake."

And, with a faint note of resentment in his voice, he went on:

"But it's true, you can't really spoil soup by putting too much in. But I guess we'll have to tighten our belts—dunno why, but there just don't seem to be any vegetables these days."

Gil blushed as he heard the sound of four or five snickers. One of the younger masons took him up:

"That's because you haven't really been lookin'."

"Is that right?" said Theo. "No kidding, you know where to get ahold of some? So it ain't you who takes and hides them up his ass, sometimes?"

Great gusts of laughter, all around. Smiling, the same young mason replied:

"Your mistake, Theo. Not one of my habits."

This dialogue, it seemed, could go on for quite a while. Gil had got his socks on. He raised his head and waited a moment without moving, hunched up in the bed, his eyes fixed straight ahead of him. He saw that life would be unbearable, but it was too late to fight Theo. Now he would have to take on the whole bunch. They had all ganged up on him. They were all excited by that swarm of flies, now dispersed in the sunshine, singing their lively airs. His anger looked for revenge: all the masons would have to die. Gil thought of setting fire to their quarters. That idea did not last long. It was too slow for his rage and rancor. He had to express them in some act, and immediately, even if this might turn against him and ravage his insides. Theo went on:

"Well, hell, you know? There's some who like it. They like taking in things through *that* hole."

Gil's urge to piss grew even stronger. It was now about as powerful as the pressure in a steam engine. He would have to be quick about it. He realized, even if dimly, that all his courage, his audacity, would have to depend on speed and obedience toward a pressing obligation. He was now sitting on his bed with his feet on the floor, and the look in his eye grew more human as he slowly let it come to rest on Theo.

"So you've really made up your mind now, Theo?"

He pursed his lips as he pronounced the name, and gave his head a slight toss:

"Or haven't you? You've been giving me all this shit, and I'm tired of it."

"Oh no I haven't, kiddo. I wish you'd shit a little less, though."

And when the rather shifty laughter this answer had caused to reverberate round each mason's head had died away:

"Because there's times it seems you don't mind taking it, and for my part, I ain't saying I wouldn't enjoy giving it to you."

Gil stood up. He had only his shirt on. In his stockinged feet he went across to Theo and then, turning to face him squarely, pale, icy, terrifying, he said:

"You? Well, let's get on with it, and don't you back out of it now."

And in a continuous movement he swiveled round, pulled up his shirt, bent over and held out his backside. The masons were watching. Only yesterday Gilbert had been a workman like the rest of them, neither more nor less than any of them. They felt no hatred for him, rather a faint sense of friendship. They could not see the desperation in the young man's face. They laughed. Gil straightened up again, looked at each and every one of them and said:

"Having a good time, eh? You've decided to gang up on me. Well, who wants to take a shot at it?"

The words were spoken in a loud, scathing voice. And Gil repeated his performance in front of the masons, aggravating it by spreading his buttocks apart with both hands, and by shouting, in a pained voice directed down at the floor, as if through heavy fumes:

"Come on! As you can see, I've got hemorrhoids! But never mind, get going! Shove it in! Dig into the shit!"

He straightened up again. He was red in the face. One big guy walked up to him.

"Come off it, man. If you've got something going with Theo, that's none of our damn business."

Theo snickered. Gil looked at him and said, coldly:

"I never let you do it to me. And *that*'s what's riling you."

He turned on his heels. Clad in shirt and socks, he went back to the bed and put on the rest of his clothes, in silence. Then he left the room. Close by there was a small wooden shed where the masons kept their bicycles. Gil went in. He walked up to his bike. It had a yellow frame. The nickel plating shone brightly. Gil loved its lightness, the curve of its racing handle bars which obliged him to bend right over them, loved its tires, the wooden rims, the mud guards. Sundays, and sometimes on weekday evenings after work, he would clean and polish it. His hair falling over his eyes, his mouth always half-open, he would loosen the bolts, take off chain and pedals and strip down the bike as it stood upended on saddle and handle bars. Engaged in this, Gil knew his life made sense. Each operation was carried out scrupulously, neatly, whether it required a greasy duster or a monkey wrench. Every action was good to watch. Squatting on his heels or bending over the wheel to set it spinning, Gil was transfigured. Every one of his movements was a radiant instance of precision and skill. So he went straight up to his bicycle, but as soon as he placed his hand on the saddle, the feeling of shame returned. He could not work on it, not today. He was unworthy of being what the bike had made him. He leaned it against the wall and walked out, to the shithouse. After he had wiped himself, Gil put his hand between his buttocks to finger the small excrescence formed by his hemorrhoids. He felt happy to have it, right there, under his fingers: both proof and object of his anger and violence. Once more he touched it, with the tip of his index finger. He was glad and proud to know he had this thing to protect him. It was a treasure he had to revere and cherish, because it permitted him to be himself. Until further notice, his hemorrhoids were himself. Once the sun had disappeared that afternoon, the city became shrouded in fog again. Gil felt sure he would run into Roger on the Esplanade. He wandered up and down there for a few minutes. At four P.M. the shop fronts were lit up. The Rue de Siam glimmered faintly. Gil walked on for a while, on the almost deserted Cours Dajot. He had not decided anything, not yet. He had no very clear idea of what would be happening an hour later, but a feeling of anguish darkened his entire vision of the world. He was walking in a universe where the forms were still larval. To rise to that other, luminous world, where one dared to assume the function of thinking, one would, or so it seemed, have to wield a dagger. Parenthetically, and by your leave: if murder with an implement that is sharp, pointed, or simply heavy enough, seems to give the murderer a measure of solace by bursting a kind of murky wineskin in which he had felt himself imprisoned, poison, on the other hand, cannot provide the same deliverance. Gil was choking. The fog, in conferring invisibility on him, gave him some comfort, but it was not capable of isolating him from the day before nor, certainly not, from the day to come. Given some powers of imagination Gil would have been able to rid himself of what had happened, but as the nature of his resentment was arid, it deprived him of that possibility. The next day, and the days after the next day, he was doomed to live on in shame.

"Why the hell didn't I bust his head back then."

Furiously he repeated this phrase that wasn't a question in any sense. He saw Theo's mean and sarcastic face. In his pockets, his fists clenched, his fingernails biting into the palms. As he was unable to question himself, let alone give answers, he could only pursue his desolate line of thought so thoroughly that when he reached the balustrade in the emptiest corner of the square his spirit had reached down to rock-bottom humiliation. He turned his head toward the sea; in a loud voice, but choking it back, he uttered a raucous cry:

"Aarrghh!"

It was a relief, for a few seconds. After two strides, his dark pain was upon him again.

"Why oh why didn't I sock him in the teeth, that dirty sonofabitch? The others, the hell with them. Let 'em think what they please, fuck'em. But him, I should of . . ."

When Gil had first arrived in the yards, Theo had demonstrated a kind of paternal comradeship. Little by little, accepting a drink now and then, the young man came to accept the mason's authority. Not consciously: simply submitting to the fact that Theo did order, and did pay, for those rounds. Querelle was able to treat his officer with a fair amount of insolence, merely because they did not speak the same language. No doubt the Lieutenant cracked a joke now and again, but with a restraint that indicated the timidity or the haughtiness behind which Querelle guessed at the existence of a violent, unadmitted desire. Querelle knew himself to be the light-hearted and audacious half of the relationship. Even if the officer had not shown any timidity, the crewman would have openly despised him. First because he knew the officer's love placed him at his mercy, and secondly because the officer wanted that love to remain hidden. In Querelle's case, cynicism was possible. But Gil was defenseless, faced with the cynicism of Theo, who spoke the mason's jargon, liked heavy practical jokes, was unafraid of proclaiming his interest in buggery and did not have to fear being given the sack because of it. Though Theo had decided to pay for a drink now and again, Gil sensed very clearly that he would never shell out a sou for his favors. What finally reinforced the mason's power over him was that friendship—however casual—which had developed during the first month. The more clearly he realized that the friendship was not leading anywhere, and that it would never lead to the goal he had envisaged, the more venomous Theo became. He refused to believe that he had been wasting his time and trouble and consoled himself by trying to believe that he had in fact created the association with the very intention of bringing about those tortures Gil was now undergoing. He hated Gil, hated him all the more because he could see no reason for hating him, only reasons for making him suffer. Gil hated Theo for having gained such a strong upper hand. One evening when, on coming out of the bistro, Theo had offhandedly patted his ass, Gil had restrained himself from punching him.

"Well, he just bought me a drink," he thought.

He was content to merely push Theo's hand away, but with a

smile, as if it had been a joke. Over the next few days, almost unconsciously, feeling the mason's desire thickening around him, he let himself go to the extent of some coquettish gestures. He simply exaggerated his natural allure. He was strolling about the yards bared to the waist, he thrust out his chest, he pushed his cap a bit farther back on his head to let more of his hair show, and when he then saw Theo's eyes devouring each one of these pointed routines—he smiled. Not long after, Theo repeated his advances. Without appearing visibly annoyed Gil declared that he did not go for that sort of thing.

"I'd like us to be buddies, for sure. But I won't put up with any of that other shit."

Theo lost his temper. So did Gil, but he didn't dare hit him, because of the drink he had just consumed at the mason's expense. From then on, in the yards, both while at work and during the breaks, and in the living quarters, at table and even sometimes when he was in bed, Theo would crack terrible jokes at the expense of Gil who did not know how to retaliate. Little by little, the gang—from laughing, to start with, at Theo's jokes—ended up laughing at Gil who tried to rid himself of those seductive mannerisms he now saw provided each joke with its point, but he could not destroy his natural beauty; the too green, too vivacious shoots, burgeoning within him and scenting him, refused to wilt and die, since they were permeated with, and drew their nourishment from, the very sap of adolescence. Without their being aware of it, all respect for the young man dwindled away in the minds of the others. Step by step, Gil lost his standing; word by word, his dignity. He became a mere pretext for belly laughs. No longer did he receive any exterior confirmation of his own sense of himself. That sense was now sustained within himself only by the presence of shame, its pale flame rising as if fanned by the wind of revolt. He let himself be run into the ground.

Roger did not show up. What would he have had to say?

That Paulette had not come out with him? He would not be able to see her. She was no longer working as a waitress at the little bistro, it was difficult to get to meet her now. And if she had turned up, by a stroke of bad luck, an even more scorching feeling of shame would have set Gil sizzling. He found himself hoping that Paulette would not appear.

"All this just because I never busted his fucking face."

He was being crushed by an ever more oppressive malaise. Had he been smarter, and less *macho* as well, he would have understood that tears, without making him any softer, would have provided a true relief. But all he knew to do there in the deepening dark was to parade the pallor of young men who have backed out of fights, that crucified countenance of nations who refuse to do battle. He closed his jaws firmly, gritting his teeth.

"Why'n the hell didn't I smash that asshole's face in."

But never for a moment did he think of doing so. It was too late for that. The phrase had a soothing effect on him. He heard himself saying it very calmly. The rage became transformed into a great sorrow, heavy and solemn, emanating from his chest to wrap his entire body and spirit into an infinite sadness that was to be his permanent condition. He walked on a while in the midst of the fog, hands in pockets, always certain of the elegance of his bearing, glad to retain it even in this solitude. There wasn't much of a chance of his meeting Roger. They had not agreed on a meeting. Gil thought of the kid. He saw his face, lit up with that smile that always appeared when he was listening to a song. The face was not quite the same as Paulette's, whose smile was not so clear, but was troubled by her femininity, which destroyed the natural ease in the smiles of Gil and Roger.

" 'Twixt her thighs, oh wow! La Paulette, what hasn't she got there, between her thighs!"

And went on, almost murmuring it out loud:

"Her pussy! Her little pussy! Her cunt!"

He thought of it, imbuing the words with a tenderness that turned them into a desperate incantation.

"Her damp little pussy! Her little thighs."

He continued the line of thought: "Mustn't call them her 'little thighs,' she's got beautiful thighs, Paulette has. She's got nice fat thighs, and up there between them there's that little furry pussy." He had a hard-on. In the midst of his sadness—or shame—and obliterating it, he now recognized the existence of a new, yet already proven certainty. He was discovering himself again. All his being was now running down into his prick, to make it hard. It was just a part of him, but it had this providential vigor that was capable of keeping his shame at bay. By siphoning off the shame which was oozing from his body, into the prick, replenishing its spongy tissues, Gil felt himself growing harder, stronger, prouder again. There could be no doubt that it was a moment to call to his aid all the fluids which bathed his internal organs. Instinctively he looked for the darkest and most out-of-the-way spot on the esplanade. Paulette's smile was alternating with that of her brother. In a state of extreme animation Gil's mind's eye wandered down the thighs, raised the skirt, there were her garters. Above those (his thoughts slowed down a little) there was white skin, suddenly darkened by the presence of a fleece which he just couldn't get a stationary, a fixed image of, under the spotlight of his desire. And in one go, after running up under her dress and lingerie, his prick came out again at just about the level of Paulette's breasts: he would be able to see better with the tip of his prick. Facing the sea Gil leaned against the balustrade. Out in the Roads the lights of the *Dunkerque* glimmered. Gil kept on climbing, from the breasts to the chubby white neck, to the chin, to the smile (Roger's smile, then Paulette's). Gil understood, albeit dimly, that the feminine quality which veiled the girl's smile had its source between the thighs. That smile was of the same nature as—he didn't know what, exactly—but that it was the most remote, the subtlest, yet the most powerful (as it could travel such distances), the most disturbing of all the vibrations emitted by that artful apparatus situated between the thighs.

He imagined that he was pressing up close against her, hugging and kissing her. Quite promptly the image of Theo intervened, and Gil suspended his reverie well on its way to fulfillment in order to fill up on hatred of the mason. As a consequence, his erection wilted a little. He wanted to banish all notions of the mason, whom he now sensed standing right behind him, caressing his buttocks with a huge rod, twice as fat as his own.

"Me, I'm a man," he muttered into the fog. "I shove it up other guys! I'll screw you too!"

In vain he tried to compose an image of a Theo whom he was buggering. He got as far as imagining the mason's dusty, unbuttoned garments, his pants down, his shirt tucked up, but that was all. To make his happiness total, his pleasure certain, he would have had to visualize in detail, and gloating over that detail, Theo's face and buttocks: but, finding it impossible to imagine them anything but (as indeed they were) bearded and hairy, the vision of the face and downy back of another male intervened: it was Roger. When he realized this, Gil knew that he would enjoy a surfeit of pleasure. He held fast to the image of the boy, which had blotted out the mason's. With violence, thinking he would like to address Theo in such terms, and no doubt also enraged and desperate at finding that he was inevitably going to bugger the young one, he cried:

"Come on, stick it out! Let me stuff it right up your ass, you little heifer you! Hurry up, no messing around!"

He was holding Roger from behind. And he heard himself sing, in that jumble of glasses and broken bottles:

"*He was a happy bandit,*
*Nothing did he fear . . .*"

He smiled. He arched his back and his legs. Facing Roger, he knew himself to be a man. His hand let go. He did not come. That great sadness born of shame welled up once more, but Roger's smile was still there, responding to his own.

"Why'n the hell didn't I bust his jaw!"

For a moment Gil dreamt that the power of his thought, being so obstinately aimed at the mason, might bother him, cause him trouble, drive him crazy. Roger would not be coming along now. It was too late. Even if he came, Gil would never see him in this dense fog. Almost sleepwalking, Gil stepped into a bistro.

"Shot of brandy, please."

The sight of the bottles provided diversion. He read the labels.

"Another one."

Drinking only red or white wine as a rule, Gil was not accustomed to hard liquor.

"Another, please."

He knocked back half a dozen in all. Little by little, an arrogant, vigorous lucidity began to dispel his confusion, his sadness, to dissipate the heavy atmosphere in which his brain had been breathing and which he normally took to be that of "clear reasoning." He went outside again. Already he was able to think about his desire for Roger without ambiguity. A couple of times he evoked the pale, matte inner surfaces of Paulette's thighs, but then arrived quickly at the boy's smile. Yet he was still dependent on Theo, the thought of whom became all the more aggravating as its power waned while refusing to be obliterated altogether. "That asshole!"

He was thinking about Roger as he walked on down toward Recouvrance.

"It's that easy," he said to himself, vaguely musing over Theo's diminished stature.

"I can make him disappear, whenever I want to."

Tears were running down his cheeks. And now he saw quite

clearly that the mason *was* interfering with his love for Roger. He also realized that this love rid him of Theo, but not completely. Minuscule as Theo now was, he was still lurking in a corner of his mind. By compressing his love like a gas, Gil hoped to crush, to stifle what remained of the idea of Theo—and that Idea, fading into Theo's physical presence, now grew ever smaller in relation to Gil. Climbing the steps up from the Rue Casse would have sobered him up, most probably, had he not run into the boy right in the middle of the fog. He might well have resumed his lugubrious existence among the other masons. As it was, he uttered a joyful shout, quickly wiping off the tears with the back of his hand.

"Roger, my buddy, let's go have a drink!"

He put his arm round the boy's neck. Roger smiled. He looked at the cold and damp face separated from his own by a thin curtain of fog they were both breathing through.

"You all right, Gil?"

"I'm fine, kiddo. Shipshape. That old fucker, he's out of it now. It won't take much. He better not mess around with me. I wasn't born yesterday, you know. He ain't no man, anyway, he's a faggot! A goddamn faggot! D'you hear me, Roger, a dirty faggot! Or a fairy, if you prefer. But us, we're buddies, we're like brothers. We can do as we damn well please. We have a right, being like brothers-in-law. It's all in the family. But that one, he's just a faggot!"

He talked fast so as not to falter, he walked fast so as not to stumble.

"Listen, Gil, haven't you had a few too many?"

"Don't you worry, kid. Paid for 'em meself. Don't need his shitty dough. But like I said, now we're gonna have a drink. Come on."

Roger smiled. He was happy. His neck felt proud under Gil's calloused and gentle hand.

"No room for him, no more. He's a mosquito. I tell you, that's what he is, just a damn little skeeter. And I'll swat him."

"Who is it you're talking about?"

" 'Bout a dirty shit, if you want to know. Don't you worry. You'll see him. See for yourself. I'm telling you, he won't be no problem to us, no more."

They went down the Rue du Sac and turned into the Rue B . . . Gil was heading for the bistro where he was sure to find Theo. They went in. As they heard the glass door opening, the patrons of the place turned their heads to look at them. As if in a cloud, and very far away from him, Gil saw the mason, alone in front of a glass and a liter bottle of wine, sitting at the table next to the door. Gil dug his hands deep into his pockets and said to Roger:

"You see that one? That's him."

And to Theo:

"Hi there."

He went up to him. Theo was smiling.

"But aren't you going to ask us to join you in a glass, Theo? This here's my buddy."

And, before he had done talking, he grabbed the bottle by the neck and with a motion swift as forked lightning broke it against the table. With the jagged bottleneck, twisting it like a drill, he stabbed the mason through the throat and yelled:

"I told you, there's no longer any room for you!"

By the time the *patronne* and the drinkers, stupefied, stupid, thought to intervene, Gil was outside. He disappeared in the fog. Round about ten P.M. the police came to see Roger at his mother's house. They let him go again the following morning.

A twin escutcheon of France and Brittany is the principal ornament of the majestic façade of the old penitentiary of Brest, whose architectural features derive from the days of sailing ships. Bracketed together, these two oval shields of stone are not flat but convex, protuberant. They imply the presence of a sphere which the sculptor did not carve in its entirety, but which nevertheless lends these fragments the power of perfect form. They are the two halves of a fabulous egg, dropped, perhaps, by Leda after she had known the Swan, containing the germ of a power and wealth both natural and supernatural. No joke, no clumsy decorator's puerile fancy called them into being, but a tangible and terrestrial power resting on armed and moral force, despite all the fleurs-de-lis and the ermine motifs. Had they been flat, they could never have possessed such fecund authority. In the morning, from very early on, they are gilded by the sun. Later on in the day the light slowly glides over the entire front of the building. When the galley convicts clanked out of the prison in their chains, they stopped in this paved courtyard which stretches down to the Arsenal buildings adjoining the Penfeld quays. Symbolically perhaps, and to render the captivity of the inmates more evident, yet making light of it, this yard is bordered by a row of huge stone posts, connected to each other by chains, but chains heavier than any anchor chain, so heavy, in fact, that they look soft. In that space, to the crack of bullwhips, the warders used to lick the gangs into shape, yelling their weirdly phrased commands. The sun descended slowly upon the granite of that harmonious façade, as noble and golden as that of a Venetian *palazzo*, and then it penetrated into the yard, shining on the cobblestones, the dirty and crushed toes, the bruised ankles of the convicts. Looking ahead, at the Penfeld quays, all was still shrouded in a golden and sonorous mist behind which one could vaguely perceive Recouvrance and its low buildings, and beyond that, quite close by, Le Goulet—the Brest Roads, already busy with boats and tall ships. From dawn on the sea was constructing its own architecture of hulks, masts and rigging, under the still sleep-blurred eyes of the men chained together in pairs. The galley convicts stood shivering in their outfits of gray linen (known as "faggot"). They were served a weak and tepid broth, in wooden bowls. They were rubbing their eyes, trying to ungum the lashes sealed by the secretions of sleep. Their hands

were numb and red. They saw the sea, or rather, from out of
the depths of the fog they could hear the shouts of captains,
free sailors, fishermen, the creaking of oars, the oaths rolling
across the water, and then, little by little, they could see the
sails billowing out, with the solemn self-importance of that
double escutcheon of stone. The roosters were crowing. On the
Roads, dawn came, more radiant every day. Barefoot on the
damp cobblestones the galley convicts waited a few moments
longer, in silence or whispering to each other. In a couple of
minutes they would be boarding the galley and start rowing.
Then a captain in silk stockings, ruffed and cuffed with lace,
passed through their ranks, brightening the air. Seated in a
sedan chair suddenly surging out of the fog he appeared as its
god or incarnation, and all the mist vanished on his arrival.
Surely he had remained in it all night, commingling with it,
turning himself into that dense vapor (yet lacking something, a
certain particle of radium which, eight or ten hours later, would
crystallize around itself the most attenuated elements of that
fog and thus obtain that man, hard, violent, gilded, sculpted
and decorated like a frigate). The galley convicts are dead.
They may have died of hope. They have not been replaced. On
the Penfeld wharves today, specialist workmen are constructing
ships of steel. Another hardness—even more ferocious—has
replaced the hardness of faces and hearts that used to make this
such a sorrowful place. There exists a beauty of the fugitive,
revealed and illuminated by fear in a wonderful interior flash;
and then there is the beauty of the conqueror, whose serenity
has been accomplished, whose life has been achieved, and who
now has to remain immobile. On the water, and in the fog, the
presence of metal is cruel. The façade and the front yard are
intact, but within the penitentiary there is nothing but coils of
rope, tarred heaps of rigging, and rats. When the sun rises,
revealing the *Jeanne d'Arc* anchored under the cliffs of Recouvrance, one can see the cub sailors already at it. These
clumsy children are the monstrous, delicate and degenerate

progeny of those chained and coupled convicts. Behind the training ship, up on the cliff, one may distinguish the dull outlines of the Naval Academy. All around us, right and left, are the Arsenal construction yards where they are building the *Richelieu*. One can hear the hammers and the voices. In the Roads one can see the outlines of great steel monsters, huge and hard, now a little softened by the night's waning humidity, the first timid caress of the sun. The Admiral is no longer, as he was in days gone by, the Prince de Rosen, a Lord High Admiral of France; he's just a Port Admiral. The convexity of the double escutcheon no longer carries any significance. It does no longer correspond to the swelling of sails, to the curve of the hull, to the proud breasts of the figureheads, to the groans of the galley slaves, to the magnificence of naval engagements. The interior of the penitentiary, that immense granite edifice, divided into cells open on one side where the convicts lay on straw and stone, is now merely a storehouse for rope. In each room of rough-hewn granite there still are two iron rings, but they contain only those huge bales of tarred rope, abandoned there by the Admiralty, never inspected. The Admiralty knows they are there, preserved by the tar for some centuries to come. Nor is there any reason to open the windows, most of which have lost their glass panes. The main gate, the one opening onto the sloping courtyard we have been describing, is locked several times over, and the enormous key of forged steel hangs on a hook in the office of a petty officer assigned to the Arsenal who never even sees it there. There is another gate that doesn't shut too well, which nobody ever gives a thought as it is obvious that no one would dream of stealing the bales of rope piled up behind it. This gate, equally massive and armed with a huge lock, is to be found at the northern end of the building and opens directly onto a narrow and almost forgotten lane separating the penitentiary from the Navy Hospital. The lane winds its way between the hospital buildings and finally loses itself, grown over with brambles, in the vicinity of the ramparts. Gil knew the lay of the land. Dazzled by the sight of blood, he kept running very fast for a while, only stopping to regain his breath. When he did, he was stone cold sober, made horribly clear-headed by the enormity of his act, and shaking with panic; thus his main concern was to take the darkest and most deserted streets to some gate that would allow him to escape beyond the city walls. He did not dare return to the shipyards. Then he remembered the old abandoned penitentiary and its easily opened gate. He decided to spend the night in one of its rooms of stone. Cowering in a corner, sheltered by great coils of rope, he communed with fear, despair in his thoughts.

A haughty and knowledgeable woman, Madame Lysiane, seated at the cash register, was able to maintain a charming smile while her eyes coolly counted the tricks or silently warned her more nervous lodgers whenever their dresses of pink tulle or silk were in danger of being torn by a table leg or a heel. When she dropped her smile, it was just to pass her tongue more comfortably over her gums behind closed lips. This simple mannerism provided her with a sense of independence, of sovereignty. Sometimes she would raise her heavily beringed hand to her superb blonde hair-do, which was a curly and complicated affair incorporating *postiches*. She felt herself a true child of this abundance of mirrors, lights and dance music, and at the same time that sumptuousness emanated from her in each breath, rising from the warm depths of the breast of a truly opulent woman.

There is a kind of male passivity (at the point where virility might be characterized by negligence, by indifference to flattery, by the detached observation of the body whether it is being offered pleasure or pleasure is being obtained from it) which makes the one who lets himself be sucked less active than the one who is sucking, just as the latter becomes a more passive being when being fucked. That true passive quality we have already encountered in Querelle was equally apparent in his brother Robert who let himself be loved by Madame Lysiane, sinking into the wraps of her tough and tender maternal femininity. He enjoyed floating around in it and was sometimes even tempted to forget himself. As for the Madam, she had at long last found a chance to revolve round an axle and to accomplish a "true marriage of mast and sail." In bed, she worshipped at the blasé altar of her lover's outstretched body by rubbing her face and her heavy boobs all over it. During Robert's languorous arousal, Madame Lysiane enjoyed the foreplay, starting out with a mock version of it: after pecking at the base of her lover's nose, she would suddenly and greedily pop that entire organ into her mouth. Sensitive to all tickling, Robert would then snort, withdraw his nose from the hot wet mouth and wipe off the saliva. As she looked up and saw him come through the parlor door, Querelle's face gave her the same shock she had experienced when she first saw the two brothers together, with their look-alike faces. Quite often since that day a pang of anxiety flashed through the gentle and regular progression of her placid mind, and this made her aware of the undercurrent that would alter the course of her life. So great was Querelle's resemblance to her lover that for a moment she even thought (not really believing it) that it had to be Robert, dressed up as a sailor. Querelle's face, advancing toward her with a smile, both annoyed and completely fascinated her.

"So what? They're brothers, so it's quite natural," she reassured herself. But she became obsessed with the monstrousness of this so perfect resemblance.

*I am a repulsive object. I have loved him too much, and excess of love makes you weak. Too strong a love upsets the organism in all its depths—and what rises up to the surface is merely nauseating.*

o            o            o

Your faces are cymbals that never strike each other, but glide
in silence over each other's waters.

Querelle's murders multiplied his personality, each one cre-
ating a new one that did not forget its predecessors. The last
murderer born of the last murder lived in the company of his
noblest friends, those who had preceded him and whom he now
surpassed. And so he convened them in that ceremony the
bandits of yore called blood marriage: all the participants stuck
their knives into the same victim, a ceremony essentially similar
to the one of which we have this description:

"Rosa said to Nucor:

" 'This is a real man. You may take off your socks and serve
the kirsch.'

"Nucor obeyed. He put the socks on the table and slipped into
one of them a lump of sugar, handed to him by Rosa; then,
after pouring some kirsch into the bottom of a bowl, he picked
up the two socks, held them above the bowl and dipped them
into it, taking care not to let the kirsch moisten anything but the
tips, and then offered them to Dirbel, saying:

" 'Take your pick, suck either one, with sugar or without.
Don't act disgusted. This is the way one joins, to eat and drink
at the same trough. There must be honor among thieves.' "

And the latest Querelle, born in one piece at the age of
twenty-five, arisen, defenseless, from a shadowy region within
ourselves, strong, solid, swung his shoulders round gladly to
greet his self-chosen, smiling, happy brothers, each one of them
both younger and older than himself. And each Querelle regarded him with sympathy. In his dark moments Querelle was

aware of their presence around him. While the fact that they
were creatures of memory made them a little hazy, that very
haze endowed them with a lovable gracefulness, a feminine
quality that gently arched over him. If he had been inventive
enough, he might have called them his "daughters," as Bee-
thoven used to call his symphonies. By dark moments we mean
those instants when the other Querelles crowded closer round
the latest athlete, and when the haze around them was more
like a veil of mourning than one of bridal tulle: when he himself already felt those gentle folds of oblivion descending over
his body.

"Seems they just don't know who it was cut him down."

"Did you know him?"

"Sure. Everybody knew him. But he wasn't no buddy of
mine."

Nono said:

"Well, that mason, he must've been like the other one that
got killed. The same type, most probably."

"What mason?"

Querelle said it slowly, stretching the vowels.

"Haven't you heard?"

Then Querelle and his brother were talking. The brothelkeeper stood leaning his elbows on the counter. He was observing them, especially Querelle, as Robert was telling him about
Gil's ferocious deed. A powerful feeling of hope, the source of
which seemed to be the universe itself, was gradually mounting
in Querelle. An exquisite sense of freshness spread all through
him. More and more he came to see himself as an exceptional
and blessed being. His limbs and their gestures showed greater
strength, greater grace. He was aware of this, gravely recorded
the fact in his mind, all the while retaining the customary smile.


The two brothers had been fighting for five minutes. As they
didn't really know where to strike or grab the other, their tactics

being identical, the fight had started out with a series of ridiculously hesitant attacks. Rather than wanting to fight they seemed to be backing away and avoiding each other with considerable success. Then things changed. Querelle stumbled, slipped and managed to grab hold of Robert's ankle. From that moment on it was an all-out brawl. Dédé jumped to one side, wanting to prove to the full-fledged man within him, still slumbering and germinating there, that nothing can be gained from interfering in a showdown between two men. The street was transformed into a passage from the Bible in which two brothers, guided by two fingers of a single God, insult each other and fight to the death for two reasons which are really but one. For Dédé, the city of Brest did not exist now, only this street. He was waiting for one soul to rise heavenwards from it. The two men fought in silence, their rage increasing in proportion to that very silence: it excited them, being punctuated only by the noise of their punches and counterpunches, their own huffing and puffing; increasing, too, as they felt themselves slowing down, which held the threat they might both go under, both resort to the one final dirty blow, delivered slowly, almost tenderly, that would wipe out the exhausted winner as well. Three dockers stood watching them, smoking. Silently they were placing bets with themselves, first on one, then on the other. It was hard to predict the outcome, the combatants were so equally matched; this impression was enhanced by their close resemblance to each other which made the fight look as balanced and harmonious as a dance. Dédé stood and watched. Though he knew his friend's muscles in repose, he did not dare guess at their efficiency in a brawl—especially not one with Querelle whom he had never seen fight before. Suddenly Querelle bent over and rammed Robert in the stomach with his head, but was instantly knocked flat on his back. When he had decided to strike his brother, Robert had experienced an instant of sheer freedom, a very brief instant, hardly enough for any kind of decision. The sailor's cap fell to one side of the flailing pair,

Robert's to the other. In order to gain the might of right, to justify his actions, Robert took it into his head to proclaim out loud, in the midst of battle, his scorn for his brother and its reasons. The first words that came to mind were:

"You dirty faggot."

They came out as a hoarse, rattling sound. Then an entire confused discourse ran through his head, barely audible under his breath:

"Let a brothel boss screw you, hey! You dirty swine! And so high and mighty, too. How does that make me look, hey, a brother whose asshole's for sale."

For the first time in his life he dared think those obscene words that he had never been able to employ in his speech, had not even liked to hear.

"Dragging me through your shit! And the look on Nono's mug, that asshole, when he told me about it!"

The three dockers shifted their ground. Dédé caught a glimpse of Robert's head, jammed between Querelle's thick thighs, pummeled by both his fists. All of a sudden one of Robert's felt-slippered feet swung up to kick Querelle in the face so that he had to let go. Dédé hesitated for a moment before bending down to pick up the sailor's beret. He held it in his hand for a second and then put it on top of a stone post. If Robert was going to lose, he should not have to suffer the humiliation of seeing his little buddy, looking disconsolate, but wearing that flamboyant beret, blatant as a searchlight—nor would he see the boy holding out that remarkable piece of headgear to the winner, as if crowning him. While he had not hesitated long, the chain of deliberations involved quite amazed Dédé himself. It surprised him, and gave him a feeling that was both painful—there had been a breach—and almost voluptuous. He was astonished to find—having made up his mind on what seemed a trivial matter—that it had become a matter of importance. The importance lay in the revelation to the kid's consciousness that he was a free agent. He thought that over.

The previous evening he had, while kissing Mario, cut across the even flow of an emotion that had begun long ago, and this first act of audacity had given him a glimpse of freedom, intoxicated him and fortified him enough to permit him to make a second attempt. Yet that (successful) attempt had seemed to repulse the man (who, as we've said, lay slumbering) within him, and who really was his own longed-for resemblance both to Mario and, in a greater degree, to Robert. Dédé had known Robert when the latter was still working in the dockyards. Together they had pulled a couple of jobs in the warehouses, and when Robert had graduated from docker to pimp, Dédé had not told him about his relationship with the detective. All the same, because of their old friendship, and out of respect for Robert's success, Dédé never thought of spying on him, but managed to obtain information from him that he could pass on to Mario. Querelle had gotten up again. Dédé watched his buttocks contract. A mocking but appreciative voice yelled:

"Wow, what a piece of ass! Wanna try it?"

Through the denim of Querelle's bell-bottoms Dédé could well imagine the workings of those muscles he knew so well—in Robert. He knew the reactions of those buttocks, thighs, calves; and he could see, despite the thick peacoat material, that tense back, those shoulders and arms. Querelle seemed to be fighting himself. Two women had appeared on the scene. At first they did not say a word. They clutched their shopping nets, filled with provisions, and long thin loaves of fancy bread close to their bodies. After a while they wanted to know why these two were fighting.

No one had any idea. Family affair, most likely. The women were reluctant to continue on their way, as the street was blocked by the action, and they stood hypnotized by this knot of disheveled, sweating manhood. Closer and closer grew the resemblance between the two brothers. The expression on their faces had lost its cruelty. Dédé remained calm. It seemed hardly important to him who won—whatever the outcome, it would be the same face and the same body would pick itself up, dust off its torn and dirty garments, use a hand for a comb, quite carelessly, before putting one or the other of those caps on a still tousled head. Those two faces so exactly alike had just finished a heroic and idealistic struggle—of which this brawl was only a vulgar projection visible to ordinary human eyes—for their very singularity. Rather than trying to destroy one another they seemed to want to become united, to fuse into what would surely be, given these two specimens, an even rarer animal. Their fight was a lovers' quarrel, and no one dared any serious inter-vention. It was apparent that the two combatants would at once join forces against any mediator, who, after all, would intervene only in order to get a piece of the action for himself. Dédé was dimly aware of this. He was equally jealous of both of the brothers. They charged and spun, turned and twisted with the desire to incorporate each other, trying to batter down the resistance of their doubles. Querelle was the stronger one. When he was sure he had gained the upper hand, he whispered in his brother's ear:

"Say it again. Go on, say it."

Robert was panting in Querelle's powerful hold, struggling in the heavy coils of his muscles. He stared down at the ground. He was biting the dust, all right. His conqueror, flames, smoke and lightning issuing from nostrils, mouth and eyes, murmured into the nape of his neck:

"Repeat what you said."

"No, I won't."

Querelle was ashamed. Still retaining his hold, he hit his brother the harder for his own shame at having hit him at all. Not having been satisfied with beating his opponent, but having humiliated him as well, he hurled himself at him to destroy the one who lying in the dust or on his feet still hated him. Treacherously, Robert managed to pull his knife. One of the women screamed, and all the windows in the street flung open. There appeared a number of women with their hair down, in petticoats, their breasts almost showing, leaning, hanging right out over the elbow-rests on the balustrades of their balconies. They did not have the presence of mind to tear themselves away from the spectacle long enough to run to the tap and get a bucketful of water to pour over these males, as one does over a pair of coupling dogs who have become stuck together in their ardor. Dédé himself was afraid now, yet he pulled himself together and told the dockers who were about to intervene in the fight:

"Just leave 'em alone. Hell, they're grown men. And they're brothers, as well. They ought to know their own business."

Querelle let go of Robert. He was in mortal danger. For the first time in his life, the murderer himself was threatened, and within himself he felt the weight of a cramping numbness which he did his best to overcome. He, too, whipped out his knife, and with his back to the wall, ready to pounce, he held it open in his hand.

"Seems they're brothers! Stop them!"

But the people of the street, watching from their balconies, were not able to hear a more moving dialogue:

"I'm crossing a stream covered with lace . . . Help me, I'm approaching your side . . ."

"That'll be hard, dear brother; you resist too much . . ."

"What is it you're saying? I can hardly hear you."

"Jump up, onto my smile. Hang onto it. Forget your pain. Jump."

"Don't lose heart. Try."

The trumpets blared.

"They're going to kill each other!"

"Come on, you men, stop them!"

The women wailed. The brothers watched each other, knives in hand, their bodies very erect, almost peaceful, as if they intended to march toward each other, ceremoniously, to exchange, with raised arm, that Florentine oath which can only be sworn with a dagger in the other hand. Or perhaps they were about to cut each other's flesh, in order to then sew, or graft, themselves together forever. A police patrol appeared at the end of the street.

"The cops! Break it up!"

That was Mario, talking gruffly and rapidly and hurling himself at Querelle who tried to push him aside; but Robert, after taking one look in the direction of the patrol, closed his knife and put it away. He was shaking. A little embarrassed and out of breath, he then turned to Dédé—for a go-between still seemed necessary—and said:

"Tell him to get outta here."

But then, as time was of the essence, getting rid in one stroke of all the tragic protocol required by heroics, like an Emperor who addresses his enemy directly, ignoring the frills of warrior etiquette and the babble of generals and ministers, he spoke directly to his brother. With a matter-of-factness and authority only Querelle was capable of understanding, implying a secret familiarity that excluded all onlookers and bystanders from their conversation, he said:

"Beat it. I'll get ahold of you. We'll settle this another time."

For a moment Robert had thought of confronting the patrol on his own, but now it was approaching at ominous speed. He added:

"All right. Take-off time."

Nothing more was said, they did not even look at each other, but started walking along on the sidewalk with no cops on it. Dédé followed Robert in silence. Now and again he looked at Querelle, whose right hand was smeared with blood.

Talking to Robert, Nono regained his true manliness which he tended to lose a little when he was with Querelle. Not that he took on any homosexual mannerisms, but in the presence of

Querelle he ceased to think of him as a man who loved women
and relaxed into the special atmosphere that a man who loves
men always calls forth. Between them, for them alone, a universe came into being (with its own laws and its secret, invisible
understandings) that totally excluded the idea of woman. At
the moment of pleasure a certain tenderness had disturbed the
relationship between those two—it affected the boss in particular. Tenderness is not quite the right word, but it does serve to
indicate the *mélange* of gratitude toward the body providing
one with pleasure, of the sweetness of the moment of joy, of
physical exhaustion and even disgust drenching, relieving, sinking and raising your spirits, and finally, of sadness; and this poor
touch of tenderness, manifested like a kind of quiet and colorless flash of lightning, then continues to subtly influence and
alter the simple physical relationship between men. Not that
this becomes anything even approaching the true love between
man and women, or between two beings one of whom is
feminine, but it is the absence of woman in this universe that
obliges the two men to call forth a measure of womanliness in
themselves. To invent the woman. It is not the weaker, or the
younger, or the more gentle of the two who succeeds better in
this, but the one who has more experience in it, frequently the
stronger and older man. A complicity unites the two men, but
while it arises from the absence of woman, that complicity calls
forth the woman who joins them together by her very absence.
Thus there need be no fakery in their dealings in that regard,
no need to be anything but what they are: two males, most
virile, perhaps jealous of each other, perhaps even hating, but
never loving each other. Almost inadvertently Nono had told
Robert everything. Nono had never tried to seduce Robert, nor
had Robert, knowing the rules of the game, ever asked him for
the Madam's favors. In fact, when he first came to the brothel
as a client he only noticed Madame Lysiane when she picked
him out herself. Noticing what he thought was Robert's indifference to the idea of his brother's sleeping with him, Nono

was more than pleased. In some obscure way he hoped to establish a friendship with Robert and gain his recognition as a "brother-in-law." Two days later he made a full confession, but started out with care:

"I think I've made it. With your bro, I mean."

"No kidding."

"Honest to God. But don't mention it, not even to him."

"It's none of my business. But are you trying to tell me that you managed to bugger him?"

Nono laughed, looking both embarrassed and triumphant.

"No kidding, you've done that? It does surprise me, you know."

Madame Lysiane was kind and gentle. The tasty gentleness of her pale meat was combined with that kindness of a woman whose most essential function consists in watching over brothel clients, treating them like charming invalids. She told her "girls" to be ministering angels to these gentlemen; to see that the official from Police Headquarters, in love with Carmen, was voluptuously deprived of his candy; to let the old Admiral strut about naked, clucking, with a feather stuck in his anus, pursued round the room by Elyane dressed up as a farmer's wife; to be an angel to Mr. Court Reporter who liked to be rocked to sleep; an angel to the one who was chained to the foot of the bed where he would bark like a dog; to be angels to all those stiff and secretive gentlemen who were stripped bare to their very souls by the warmth of the brothel and Madame Lysiane's ministrations; all of which goes to show that she carried within her the lushness and beauty of a Mediterranean landscape. To herself, with a shrug of her shoulders, Madame Lysiane sometimes used to say:

"Well, my dear girls—it is fortunate that such men exist: it gives the lowly-born a chance to experience love."

She was a kind lady.

o          o          o

Still disbelieving, Robert smiled at Nono.

"Well, that's what happened. But you'll keep it to yourself, right?"

"Sure thing."

As the boss told him all about it, all the details, including Querelle's cheating at dice, Robert began to seem more and more indifferent. Inwardly, he was seething. Shame kept his mouth shut, creased his pale cheeks, and Nono thought he was rather dim-witted and gutless, after all.


Except where it borders on the sea and the Penfeld wharf, the city of Brest is surrounded by its solid old ramparts. These consist of a deep ditch with steep embankments. The embankments—both on the inner side and the outer—have been planted with acacias. On the outer side runs that road off which Vic was slain and abandoned in the dark of the night by Querelle. The ditch is overgrown with brushwood, brambles, and here and there, in marshy places, even rushes. It also serves as the city dump. During the summer all the sailors ashore for the evening, if they miss the last liberty boat (at 2200 hrs), doss down there until the arrival of the morning boat at six o'clock. They lie down on the grass, among the brambles. Ditch and banks are littered with them, sleeping on leaves, often in bizarre positions, having to adjust themselves to roots, trees, terrain, and often in attempts to protect their clean uniforms. Before stretching out or curling up they relieve themselves one way or the other, and then, completely wiped out, crash right next to the spot they have befouled. The ditch is strewn with turds. In the midst of the others the few sober ones prepare some kind of lair for themselves and bed down. And there they lie, snoring under the branches. The freshness of dawn will awaken them. In certain places along the ditch there are some gypsy caravans, a few fires, yells of verminous children, loud arguments. These gypsies travel about the surrounding countryside, where the

Bretons are naïve and the girls vain and easily taken in by a basket full of odds and ends of machine-made lace. The masonry of the old rampart walls is solid. The wall running along the city side is thick and intact save for a few stones that have been dislodged by trees growing in the interstices. On this sloping bank thick with trees, not far from the hospital or the old penitentiary, the buglers of the 28th Regiment of Colonial Infantry hold their practice every day. On the day following the murder, Querelle before going to La Féria took a walk along the old fortifications, taking care not to pass too close to the scene of his crime in case the police had posted a guard. He was looking for a suitable place to hide his jewels. In various spots around the world he had such secret caches, carefully noted down on papers which he kept in his kit bag. China, Syria, Morocco, Belgium. The notebook containing these directions were not unlike a "Register of Massacres" kept by the police.

Shanghai, Maison de la France. Garden. Baobab tree by the gate.

Beirut, Damascus. Lady at the Piano. Wall to left.

Casa, Alphand Bank.

Antwerp, Cathedral. Bell tower.

Querelle retained very clear memories of these storehouses of his treasures. He knew the details and the surroundings with scrupulous precision, using as mnemonic all the circumstances that had led to the discovery and choice of each spot. He was able to recall every crack in the stone, each root, the insects, the smell, the weather, the triangles of shadow or light; and every time he evoked them, these minuscule scenes appeared to him in precise detail, in the light of an exact memory, all of a piece and festively illuminated. Thus, in one flash and all together, the details of each hiding place would leap to mind. Querelle took care to remember his caches, but forced himself to forget their contents, in order to later savor the joys of surprise when he would make a world tour expressly to collect them. This imprecise idea of buried wealth was like a nimbus shining out from each cache, each malevolent fissure gorged with gold, and as those rays slowly extended away from their intense sources, they finally joined and bathed the entire globe in a lovely blond luminescence in which Querelle's soul felt at ease, in which it felt free. Querelle derived much strength from his feeling that he was rich. In Shanghai, under the roots of the baobab tree by the gate, he had concealed the booty from five burglaries and the murder, committed in Indo-China, of a Russian danseuse; in Damascus, in the ruins of the Lady at the Piano, he had buried the profits of a murder committed in Beirut. By that crime hung the memory of twenty years hard labor, awarded to his accomplice. In Casablanca, Querelle had hidden a fortune stolen from the French Consul in Cairo. To the memory of this was attached the death of an English sailor, his accomplice. In Antwerp, in the cathedral bell tower he had hidden a small fortune, the result of several successful burglaries in Spain, linked to the death of a German docker, his accomplice and victim.

Querelle was wandering about amongst the brambles. He could hear the delicate sound of the wind rustling through the tips of the grasses, familiar from the previous evening, after the murder. He felt no fear, no remorse either, and this will be less of a surprise once one realizes that Querelle had already accepted the fact that he carried the crime in him—not that he was part of the crime. This calls for a brief explanation. If Querelle had suddenly found himself, with his habitual responses to normal situations, in a transformed universe, he would have experienced a certain sense of loneliness, a certain fear: the awareness of being an alien. But, as he accepted it, the idea of the murder was more than familiar to him, it was merely an exhalation from his body, and he drenched the whole world with it. His actions were not without an echo. Thus Querelle felt a different sense of loneliness: that of his creative singularity. Let us emphasize, however, that we are describing a mechanism our hero used without being fully aware of it himself. He examined every crack in the stone wall along the ditch. At one spot the brambles grew thicker and closer to the wall. Their roots were caught in the masonry. Querelle looked closer. The place appealed to him. No one had followed him there. No one was behind him, nor was there anyone on top of the wall. He was all alone in the old moat. With his hands thrust deep into his pockets, to protect them from being scratched, he deliberately forced his way through the shrubs. Then, for a moment, he just stood at the foot of the wall, looking at the masonry. He discovered the stone he would have to pry loose in order to create a niche in the wall: a small sailcloth bag, containing some gold, rings, broken bracelets, earrings, and some Italian gold coins, did not need a lot of space. He stared at the wall for a long time. He hypnotized himself. Soon he had induced a form of sleep, of self-forgetfulness, and this allowed him to become part of his surroundings. He saw himself entering the wall, its every detail clearly apparent. His body penetrated it. There were eyes in the tips of his ten fingers; even all his muscles had eyes. Soon he *became* the wall, and remained so for a moment; he felt every detail of its stones alive in him, the cracks like wounds, invisible blood flowing from them, with his soul and his silent cries; he felt a spider tickling the minute cavern between two of his fingers, a leaf gently attaching itself to one of his damp stones. Finally, becoming aware of himself again, flattened against the wall and feeling its damp, rough contours, he made an effort to leave it  gain, to step out of it, but as he did so he was marked by it forever, by this most particular spot near the ramparts, and it would remain in his bodily memory and he would be certain to find it again in five or ten years' time. As he turned to leave he remembered, without giving it much thought, that there had been another murder in Brest. In the morning paper he had seen a photograph of Gil, and he had recognized the smiling singer.

Aboard *Le Vengeur*, Querelle had lost nothing of his sulky arrogance and irritability. Despite his duties as a steward n preserved a redoubtable elegance. Without really appearing to be working, he took care of the Lieutenant's business; Seblon no longer dared to look him in the face, after that unequivocally ironical answer given with the perfect assurance of Querelle's power over one who was in love with him. Querelle dominated his shipmates by his strength, his toughness and his reputation, which increased when they found out that he went to La Féria every evening. However, he only frequented its public parlor, where some of the sailors had seen him shaking hands with the owner and with Madame Lysiane. The reputation of La Féria's owner spanned the seven seas. Sailors spoke of him among themselves (as we have said) as they did of ducks in China, as they did of Crillolla, Bousbir and Bidonville. They were impatient to get to know the joint, but when they first saw, in a dark, dank street, that small dilapidated house, surrounded by a stench of urine, its shutters closed, they were both surprised and uneasy. Many did not find the courage to go through the studded door. Becoming a regular visitor added to Querelle's stature. It was inadmissible to suppose that he had gambled with the boss. Querelle was powerful enough for his reputation to remain unsullied and even to be further enhanced by his association with the place. And if he was never seen with a whore round his neck, that was just further proof that he did not go there as a client, but as a friend or pimp. To have a girlfriend in a brothel made a *man* of him, no longer just a sailor: he had as much authority as the guys with the stripes. Querelle knew himself surrounded by immense respect, and bathing in that glory sometimes made him forget himself. He became arrogant toward the Lieutenant, whose suppressed desire he well knew. Maliciously Querelle tried to exacerbate it; with remarkable natural talent he found the most suggestive poses; he would lean against the doorjamb, one arm raised to show off his armpit; he would sit on the table, flexing his thighs and letting his trouser leg ride up to exhibit his muscular, hairy calves; he would throw in a little "bump" for good measure, or he would respond to the officer's call by swaggering up in an even more outrageous manner, hands in pockets pulling the material of his pants tight over his prick and balls, sticking out his belly. The Lieutenant went almost crazy, not daring to get angry, not daring to complain, nor to burst out into passionate praise of Querelle's attractions. The most striking memory Seblon had of him—and it was one he often recalled—was a time in Alexandria, Egypt, one blazing noon when the crewman showed up at the foot of the ship's gangway. Querelle was smiling, a dazzling, silent smile that showed all his teeth. At that time his face was bronzed, or rather, tanned a golden color, as is mostly the case with blonds. In some Arab garden he had broken off five or six branches of a mandarin tree, laden with fruit, and, as he liked to keep his hands free, to be able to swing his arms and roll his shoulders while walking, he had stuck them into the V-neck of his short white jacket, behind the regulation black satin cravat, their tips now tickling his chin. For the Lieutenant, that visual detail triggered a sudden and intimate revelation of Querelle. The foliage bursting forth from the jacket was, no doubt, what grew on the sailor's wide chest instead of any common hair, and perhaps there were—hanging from each intimate and precious little twig—some radiant balls, hard and gentle at the same time . . . For a second Querelle remained stock-still at the top of the gangway, before setting foot on the metallic and burning hot deck, and then he moved on toward his mates. Most of the ship's crew were still ashore. Those aboard were lounging about in the shade of a tarpaulin. One of them yelled:

"Wow, look at that! What a lazy sonofabitch! Or is it that he wouldn't dare be seen carrying them."

"Well, would you? It would look like I was on my way to my own wedding."

Carefully, Querelle pulled out the branches, which were catching on his striped T-shirt and on the black satin cravat. He kept smiling.

"Where'd you find 'em?"

"In a garden. Just walked in."

Though Querelle's murders surrounded him with a kind of charmed, tall hedge, this sometimes seemed to shrink, down to the dimensions of a low metal wire border round a flower bed. When it happened, it was a horrifying feeling. Deprived of their protection—whose reality then seemed doubtful, beyond his control, or perhaps really reducible to that insignificant form of a few bent wires—he suddenly stood poor and naked among men. But, sure enough, he got hold of himself again. With one clack of the heel on the fierce deck of the *Vengeur* he regained that region of the Elysian Fields were he would find, ranged all about him, the true manifestations of his bygone murders. But always before that his despair at being a "failure" caused him to commit numerous cruelties he thought were caresses. The other crewmen referred to him—among themselves—as a berserker. Having never really experienced either friendship or camaraderie, he made mistakes. He would spring sudden jokes on his mates in order to gain their approval and end up offending them. Being hurt, they lashed out, and as Querelle persisted, he himself tended to fly into a rage. Yet, in a certain sense, true sympathy may be engendered by cruelty and hatred. The others started admiring Querelle's brutal humor while hating him. Now he saw the Lieutenant who was still watching him. He smiled and started walking over to him. Their being far away from France, the freedom granted the men on this day of rest, the crushing heat, and the general air of festivity aboard the ship at anchor in the Roads, all contributed to relax the rigors of discipline between officers and crewmen. Querelle said:

"Lieutenant, would you like a tangerine?"

The officer smiled, took a step in his direction. They went into a kind of *paso doble*, perfectly synchronized: while Querelle raised his hand to detach a tangerine from the branch, the Lieutenant took his hand out of his pocket and extended it slowly toward the crewman, who then, with a smile, deposited his gift in the outstretched palm. More than anything, the very harmony of the two gestures tugged at the Lieutenant's heartstrings. He said:

"Thank you, sailor."

"Don't mention it, sir."

Querelle turned back to his buddies, pulled off a few more tangerines and threw them over to them. The Lieutenant had walked off slowly and stood peeling the fruit with an affectation of carefree absent-mindedness, while telling himself, with great pleasure, that his love relationship with Querelle would surely remain pure, as their first gesture of union had just been accomplished according to the laws of such touching harmony that it could only have been created by their two souls, or even better, by a unique power—love itself—that had but one focus, but two rays . . . He glanced warily to left and right, and then, having now quite turned his back to the group of sailors, and certain that no one could observe him, he popped the whole tangerine into his mouth and held it there for a moment, one cheek bulging.

"Just what us old sea dogs ought to chomp on," he said to himself, "the balls of handsome young men."

Circumspectly, he turned round again. In front of the sprawling sailors, who from this distance looked like one great blob of virility, stood Querelle, his back to the Lieutenant. And Seblon caught just the right moment to see him bending his strong legs in their white ducks, hands resting on buttocks, straining (the Lieutenant envisaged the congested face and the smile of the crewman waiting for deliverance, his eyes bulging out of his head, his smile freezing), straining even harder, and then letting fly—straight at him—a barrage of sonorous, lively, rough-and-tumble farts—so loud that they seemed to rend those glorious white bell-bottoms truly from top to bottom (Querelle did, indeed, refer to them as his "farting-gear")—greeted by a thousand cheers and salutes, the gales of laughter emitted by his buddies. Mortified, the Lieutenant quickly averted his eyes and moved off. Querelle accomplished the most dangerous of his delights without consciously choosing to include a mistake in them, but as soon as he left the scene of a robbery, or even a murder, he immediately perceived the mistakes—at times, the several mistakes—he had, inadvertently, made. Quite often they weren't anything much. Some slight slip in the very act, a shaky hand, a cigarette lighter left behind in the dead man's fingers, a silhouette shadow he had cast on some bright surface that he thought might have remained there permanently; bagatelles, certainly, yet sometimes he even feared that his eyes—having taken in the image—might render his victim visible to others. After each one of his crimes he reviewed it in his mind. That was when he discovered the mistake. His amazing retrospective lucidity uncovered the only one he had made. (There always was at least one.) And then, so as not to be devoured by despair, with a smile on his lips, Querelle offered up this mistake, this error of his, to his guardian star. He convinced himself of the affective equivalent of this thought: "We'll see. I did it *on purpose*. On purpose. And isn't *that* a big joke."

But instead of being down in the mouth with fear, he felt elated by it, living, as he did, in a deep, violent and finally organic belief in his lucky star. His smile was an act of sympathetic magic, directed at that star. He was certain that such a deity, the protector of assassins, was a joyful one—the sadness one could see, and even he could sometimes discern in that smile, rising into his consciousness only in those moments when he felt aware of the absolute loneliness such a most particular destiny imposed on him.

"What would I do if I hadn't got it?"

Which was as much as to say: "What would I *be*, without it? There's no way one could be *just a sailor*; that, that's a function, for others to believe in; but if you want to *be* somebody, you have to be what does not meet the eye." It was the same gratitude Gilbert Turko felt when he thought of his hemorrhoids. When Querelle left one of the gardens of Alexandria, it was too late to throw the broken-off branches into the street and then nervously cower behind some shrub, waiting for the favorable moment to vault across the garden wall. Where was there one could throw them, at all? Any beggar hunkered down in the dust, any Arab street kid would certainly notice a French sailor engaged in the process of getting rid of a whole load of tangerines still on the branch. It appeared best to hide them on his person. Querelle wanted to avoid any bizarre gesture that would call attention to him, and thus he moved in plain view from garden to ship, in uninterrupted motion, simply slipping those branches into the neck opening of his sailor's jacket, letting some leaves and fruit stick out, turning his chest, in honor of his star, into a living repository for them. But back on board he sensed the danger he was still running, would be running for quite a while, although it did not have the insistent quality of fear following a true crime: one foot still on the gangway, the other suspended in air, he addressed a bewitching smile to the deity of his secret night. In his pants pocket he carried the necklace of gold coins and the two hands of Fatmah he had stolen in the villa of that tangerine garden. The gold lent him weight, terrestrial security. When he had distributed the foliage and the fruit to the other crewmen, languorous with heat and boredom, and feeling suddenly pure, he experienced such a powerful sense of his own limpidity, in fact, that he had to watch himself every second while walking along the deck to his quarters, so as not to pull out the stolen treasures from his pocket in plain view of everybody. The same feeling of light-heartedness, confounding his single-minded belief in his star and his certainty of being a lost man, had uplifted him (his heart, light, like a balloon) during his walk on the road along the city ramparts when—flashing into his mind with piercing clarity—a certain fact had become clear to him: the police had discovered a cigarette lighter in the vicinity of the murdered

sailor, and that lighter, so it said in the newspapers, belonged to
Gilbert Turko. This discovery of a dangerous detail exalted him
as if it had suddenly tuned him in to the entire universe. It was
the point of contact permitting him to re-do his deed in reverse—thus, to undo it—but, from that detail on, to cut it into
pieces, with noisy and radiant gestures, so that the entire
unraveled act would only concern God or some other witness
and judge, any longer. In that deed he discerned the presence of
the powers of Hell, and yet, already, mustered against them,
there appeared a patch of dawn, as pure as the corner of heaven
adorned with a blue and naïve Virgin Mary that had appeared,
as the fog parted for a moment, in between the votive ships of
the church in La Rochelle. Querelle knew he would be saved.
Slowly he re-entered himself. He then went on, very far, almost
to the point of getting lost in those secret realms, in order to
meet his brother there. Querelle knew that he would be there.
It was true that he had just fought him in a fight that might
have had a deadly outcome, but the hatred he felt for him on
the surface did not prevent him from finding Robert there, in
the most distant inner reaches of himself. What Madame
Lysiane had suspected, came to pass: their beauty turned into a
snarl, showing its teeth, hatred distorted their faces, their bodies
became locked in the coils of a battle to the death. And no
mistress of either one, had she attempted to intervene in this
battle, would have gotten out of it alive. Even when they were
still little boys fighting, one could not help thinking that somewhere, back of their faces twisted with pain, in a more faraway
region, their resemblances were celebrating their union. It was,
thus, in the shadow of such appearances that Querelle was able
to find his brother again.

When they had arrived at the end of the street, Robert
automatically turned left, toward the brothel, and Querelle

right. He was gnashing his teeth. In the presence of Dédé, his brother, drunk with fury and none too quietly either, had addressed him with:

"You dirty bastard. You let Nono bugger you. Why the hell did that shitty boat of yours ever bring you here, you bloody fucking shit!"

Querelle, pale, stared Robert in the eye:

"I've done worse, buddy. And I do damn well as I please. And you better start making tracks, or I'll show you what shit is and what it tastes like."

The young boy turned rigid. He was waiting for Robert to defend his sullied honor until the blood flowed again. The big men would fight again. Nevertheless Querelle, as he went off to the right, was already thinking of ways to rub his brother's pale face into some of his own medicine, so that, once they were quits in terms of their apparent (*and* real) hatred, he might rejoin him within himself. His head held high, straight, rigid, staring straight ahead, his lips but a narrow line, his elbows held close to the body—his entire bearing stiffer and more martinet-like than usual, he directed his steps toward the city ramparts, more exactly, toward the old wall in which he had hidden his treasure. The closer he got to his destination, the less bitter he felt. He did not, now, exactly remember the deeds of derring-do that had put him in possession of that treasure, but the jewels themselves—their mere proximity—were the effective proof of his courage and of his existence. Arrived on the slope facing the holy wall, invisible in the fog, Querelle stopped and stood still, legs wide apart, hands in the pockets of his peacoat: he knew himself to be very close to one of the hearths he had lit on the surface of the globe, he was enveloped by their sweet radiance. As his wealth, to him, was a refuge where he could feel comforted by his sense of power, Querelle was already making his hated brother the heir to it. Only one thing still bothered and depressed him a little, the fact that Dédé had been present at the brawl. It wasn't shame, rather a vague notion that the kid wasn't to be trusted. Querelle knew that he had achieved a certain notoriety in this city of Brest.

*Night, facing the sea. Neither the sea nor the night can bring me peace of mind. On the contrary. It's enough for the shadow of a sailor to move past . . . In that shadow, and thanks to it, he can't help being anything but beautiful. Between its flanks this ship holds such delicious brutes, clad in white and azure. Whom to choose, from among these males? I could hardly let go of one before desiring another. The only reassuring thought: that there is only one sailor, the sailor. And each individual I see is merely the momentary representation—fragmentary as well,` and diminished in scale—of The Sailor. He has all the characteristics: vigor, toughness, beauty, cruelty, etc.—all but one: multiplicity. Each sailor passing by may thus be compared to Him. Even if all sailors were to appear in front of me, alive and present, all of them—not one of them, separately, could be the sailor they jointly compose, who can only exist in my imagination, who can only live in me, and for me. This idea sets my mind at rest. I have Him, The Sailor.*

*It was with pleasure that I signed the order for Querelle's punishment. In any case, he won't have to appear before the Navy Tribunal. I want him to owe me that, and to know that he owes it to me. He smiled at me. All of a sudden I was struck by the horrible nature of the expression: "He's still alive"—when used apropos a wounded man, say, mortally wounded, agitated by a spasm.*

*Querelle to his mates: "Bit of a breeze!" or: "It's blowin' up a gale!" And then he himself moves forward, full of himself, and sure, like a sailing ship.*

•    ◦    ◦

What glorious workmanship it all is, each curl of his hair, each muscle, the eyes, the ears. From the smallest line in his skin, the smallest shadowy corner of his body spring rays that touch me to the quick; the bend in a finger-joint, the intersection of lines in arm or neck, these plunge me into an affect that makes me fire my cannon, in order to delve ever deeper into the sweetness of his belly, soft and smooth like a forest floor covered with pine needles. Does he know the beauty of all that he consists of? And does he know its power? Through ports and arsenals, throughout the day he carries these loads of shadows, this cargo of darkness, on which a thousand regards come to rest and refresh themselves; at night, his shoulders support a yoke of light, his victorious thighs parting the waves of his native sea, and the ocean cringes, lies down at his feet, and his chest is mere space filled with scents, great scented waves. On this ship, his presence is as astonishing—and as useful, and normal, as well—as would be the presence of a coachman's whip, of a squirrel, of a clump of grass. This morning, passing by me—I don't know if he saw me—holding a lighted cigarette between two fingers, he raised them to push his beret back from his forehead and said, who knows to whom or what, straight out into the sunny air:

"Well that's how it is, when you're hard to please."

His gleaming curls, so perfect in their texture and in the way they fall, light brown and blond, peeped out from under the edge of the beret. I looked at him with disdain. No doubt he was, at that moment, still savoring the grapes grown in sunshine and night stolen from the maritime vineyards tended by the mocking daughters of the sea.

Why am I not a plain sailor! I stand here, in the wind. The cold, and a headache, clamp my forehead in a vise, crown me with a tiara of metal. I grow, yet I shrink.

o     o     o

The Sailor is the one love of my life.


One poster was so wonderful: a Marine, in white uniform. Belt and cartridge case of leather. Leggings. Bayonet in its scabbard. A palm tree. A tent. The face was hard, scornful. Scorning death. At eighteen!

"To gently order these strong, proud boys to advance to their deaths! The torpedoed ship sinking slowly, with only myself—perhaps supported by this one Marine who cannot die without me next to him—standing in the prow, watching these beautiful boys drown!"


In French, the sinking of a ship is sombrer. Somberly.


Are the other officers aware of my state, my emotional turmoil? I'm afraid of some of it seeping through even during my fulfilment of my duties, my contacts with them. This morning, my mind was literally haunted by notions such as young boys have, there were robbers, warriors of savage tribes, tough pimps, grinning and blood-spattered looters, and so forth. I didn't really visualize them so much as sensing them within me. All of a sudden they arranged themselves in tableaux that faded away again very quickly. These were, as I've said, young boys' fantasies, invading my mind for a second or two.


To have him spread his thighs so that I can sit down between them, resting my arms on them as in a comfortable chair!

o     o     o

A Navy Officer. As an adolescent, even as an Ensign, I didn't realize what a perfect alibi a Navy career would give me. Remaining a bachelor seems so perfectly understandable. Women don't ever ask you why you aren't married. They pity you for only knowing those brief affairs, never the durable fire. The sea. The solitude. "A woman in every port." No one bothers to enquire whether I have a fiancée. Not my fellow officers, nor my mother. We are traveling men.

From the time I fell in love with Querelle I have become less of a disciplinarian. My love makes me more pliable. The more I love Querelle, the more the woman in me defines and refines herself and grieves over her lack of fulfilment. Faced with anything that has no bearing on my relationship with Querelle, my own misery, my secret frustrations cause me just to stare at it and say: "What's the use of that?"

Saw Admiral A . . . again. It seems he is a widower, has been so for more than twenty years. The big guy who follows him around (it is his chauffeur, not an orderly) is the glorious resurrection of his flesh.

I come back from a ten-day mission. My meeting with Querelle gave me a shock—I felt it even around me, in the sunny air —a delicately tragic trauma. The entire day revolves, floats around a center of luminous vapor: the gravity of this re-turn. Return for good. Querelle knows that I love him. He knows it from the way I look at him, and I know that he knows from his sly and almost insolent smile. But everything within him proves to him that I am attached to him, and thus everything in him seems to work toward the end of making my attachment grow even stronger. And all the embarrassment we are experiencing helps us to see the exceptional significance of this day even more clearly. Even if it had appeared necessary, I could not have made love to Querelle tonight. Nor to anyone else, for that matter. All my affective powers flow into this joy of return, make me feel crowded with happiness.

Just awoke from a horrible dream. This much I can say about it: We were in a stable (ten or so unknown accomplices). Which one of us would have to kill him (I don't know whom)? One young man accepted the task. The victim did not deserve to die. We watched the murder being done. The voluntary executioner struck the greenish back of the unfortunate man several times with a pitchfork. Above the victim, a mirror suddenly appeared, just in time for us to see our faces go pale. They grew paler and paler as the victim's back grew bloodier. The executioner kept on striking, in despair. (I am sure, now, that this is a faithful description of the dream, because it is not as if I were remembering it: I am reconstructing it, with the help of words.) The victim—innocent—despite his atrocious suffering, helped the murderer. He showed him where to strike. He took part in the drama, despite the desolate expression of reproach in his eyes. I also note the beauty of the murderer, and the sense of his being wrapped in garments of malediction. The whole day has been as if stained with blood by this dream. Almost literally, the day had a bleeding wound.

Querelle's hand was thick and strong, and Mario, though without giving it much thought, had expected it to be effeminate and somewhat fragile. His own hand had not been prepared for such a paw. He scrutinized Querelle. A large fellow, exceptionally handsome despite a day's growth of stubble, with the same face and athletic bearing as Robert; he looked manly, a little brutal, tough. (The curtness of his gestures underlined this appearance of strength and brutality.)

"Nono ain't here?"

"No, he went out."

"So you're in charge of the joint?"

"Well, there's the lady. Surely you know her?"

Having said that, Mario looked Querelle in the eye and curled his lips in a light sneer. But if the mouth expressed mere irony, the eyes were hard and pitiless. But Querelle did not suspect anything.

"Yeah . . ."

He drawled out that affirmative, making it seem a matter so self-evident that it was not worth talking about. At the same time he crossed his legs and took out a cigarette. His whole demeanor seemed an attempt to prove, though it wasn't clear to whom, that the importance of the moment did not lie in his affirmative answer, but in the most trivial gesture.

"Smoke?"

"Why not."

They lit their cigarettes, took a first puff, and Querelle returned his forcefully through the nose, expressing by those tough smoke-spewing nostrils his sense of victory over himself, a well-kept secret that permitted him to deal so familiarly with a cop—after all, something almost like an officer.

The police authorities quickly reached the assumption that both the murders had been committed by Gil. Their belief was confirmed when the other masons saw, and identified, the cigarette lighter found lying in the grass near the assassinated sailor. At first, the police considered a revenge motive; then they thought of the possibility of some love drama; and finally arrived at the notion of sexual aberration plain and simple. All the rooms in the Brest Police Headquarters emanated an effluvium of despair, yet it was of a peculiarly consoling kind. The walls were decorated with some photographs provided by the Department of Criminal Anthropometry, and with a few "Wanted" notices for unapprehended criminals, specifically those who were suspected of having reached some port town. The tables and desks were laden with dossiers containing statements and important memoranda. From the moment he entered the office, Gil felt like sinking in an ocean of gravity. He

knew this feeling from the very moment of his arrest by Mario:
when the detective grabbed hold of his sleeve, Gil disengaged
himself, but as totally prescient of that reaction Mario repeated,
more exactly, simply continued his gesture, squeezing the bicep
with such authority that the young mason had to give in to it. It
was all there, in the brief moment between the two "apprehen-
sions"—the first one repulsed, the second one decisive—: all the
glory of the game, the chase, the irony, the cruelty, the sense of
justice that go into building that specific gravity of the police, of
the soul of a cop, of the total despair of Gil Turko. He pulled
himself together, not to succumb to it, seeing that the Inspector
who was with Mario had a very young face, positively radiating
a *mélange* of choler and pleasure at the kill. Gil said:
"What d'you want from me?"
Shaking a little, he added: ". . . Sir . . ."
The young Inspector provided the answer:
"Don't worry, buddy. We'll show you."
From the arrogance of that Gil realized with amazement that
this young copper was delighted with Mario's decisive action,
that of imprisoning the murderer's hands in a pair of handcuffs.
Now it was easy to walk up to, to insult, or to strike the beast of
prey, free and proud a minute ago, rendered quite inoffensive
now. Gil turned back toward Mario. The childlike aspect of his
soul which had come to his help for an instant was completely
gone now. Yielding to the need to utter at least one lovely
phrase before dying—though sometimes, even silence can be
such an impressive line—that would sum up his life, that would
consummate it regally, well, just express it—he said: "*C'est la
vie.*" When he entered the Police Chief's office he was overcome first by the tremendous heat in the room and felt himself
going soft to the point of thinking he would die of exhaustion,
incapable of any effort to escape the radiator which was already
trembling with expectation, preparing to uncoil like an ana-
conda in order to wrap itself round him and strangle him. He
was suffering from both fear and shame. He reproached himself

for not being as magnificent as he should have been. The walls seemed to hold blood-dripping secrets, more terrible than his own. His physical appearance surprised the Police Chief. He would never have dreamt the murderer looked like this. When he had instructed Mario to put a little more zing into the investigation, he had been unable to resist the temptation to describe the potential suspect in some detail. However, crime is an area where previous experience is virtually useless. He had been sitting there at his desk, toying with a ruler, trying to conjure up the portrait of a homosexual murderer. Mario had listened, without believing a word of it.

"There are precedents. Like Vacher. These are types who get carried away by their vices. Sadists, that's what they are. And these two murders are the handiwork of a sadist."

With similar buoyant assurance the Commissioner had then gone on to discuss the matter with his counterpart in the Navy Police. Both of them ended up struggling to make the notion of a murderer coincide with their notions of what inverts were, what they looked like. They invented monsters. The Police Commissioner persisted in looking for clues in the style of that famous little flask of oil that one notorious criminal had carried about him to facilitate the buggering of his victims, or again, for something like fresh fecal matter at the murder site. Not knowing that the murders had been committed by two separate individuals, he tried to connect them, to splice their motives together. He could not know that every murder obeys, in its execution as well as in its motivation, certain laws that make it into a work of art. Besides the moral solitude of Querelle and Gil there was the solitude of the artist who cannot admit of any authority, not even that of a fellow craftsman. (This was what rendered Querelle doubly lonely.) The masons claimed that Gil was a pederast. They regaled the police with a hundred details to prove that hell, yes, he was a fairy, all right. They did not realize that this meant to describe him, not as if he was, that is to say, a child persecuted by a man in the clutches of his obsession, but exactly the way Theo had wanted them to see the kid, as he himself had wanted to show him. Intimidated by the police inspectors, they drifted into a story that was both crazy and tentative—crazy, because of its fear of being tentative—but appeared more plausible the longer they went on talking. They did of course become aware of the fact that these statements had no basis in fact whatsoever, that they were nothing but a kind of poetry which allowed them to talk, at long last, and seriously, about things they had always used in their obscenities—in their songs, even—but at the same time, this sudden outpouring intoxicated them. They knew that their portrait of Gil was inflated, not unlike the cadaver of a drowned man. Here are some of the traits that the masons said they had found indicative of Gil's queerness: the prettiness of his face, his style of singing, trying to make his voice soft as velvet, his sartorial coquettishness, his laziness and carelessness at work, his fear of Theo, the pallor and smoothness of his skin, etc., a number of such details that they felt were real clinchers, having heard Theo and some other guys they had run across in their lives poke fun at fairies in comments like: "Look at the girlie . . . such a little doll's face he's got . . . he likes to work just about as much as some expensive whore . . . he's made to work with his asshole . . . coos like a turtledove . . . and the way he carries his tool kit, dangling it like a queen swinging her purse on the beat in Marseilles . . ." Those traits, poorly interpreted, combined to create a picture of a faggot such as none of the masons could ever have seen. All they knew about the "autnies" and "fairies" was what they said about them themselves, what Theo used to say, a hysterical babble of catch phrases: "Sure as hell, that's a pederast's pet! . . . You take it straight, sideways, or inbetween? . . . To the highest bidder, eh? . . . Why don't you just fuck off to your sugar daddy, you ain't fit to work here! . . ." While they were able to spout this stuff with the greatest of ease, it did not really represent any reality. As their emotions weren't involved in the subject, no conversation could ever add to their knowledge of it, but they found it engrossing nevertheless. What we want to say is that it was exactly this ignorance that left them in a slightly troubled state, indestructible by its very imprecision and haziness: unknown, finally, for lack of a name, yet visible in a thousand reflections. They were unanimous in suspecting the existence of a universe that was both abominable and marvelous, and they felt themselves hovering on the brink of it. Their distance from that universe was, in fact, the same that separates you from the word you are trying to remember, the one floating around at the back of your mind: "I have it on the tip of my tongue." When they had to talk about Gil, they gave each one of those characteristics of his that reminded them, no matter how superficially, of what they knew about homosexuals, such a caricaturistic treatment that the result turned out to be a horrifyingly naturalistic image of a young male prostitute. They talked about the goings-on between Gil and Theo.

"They were inseparable."

"But then they must have had some sort of argument. Maybe Gil had been doing a number with someone else . . ."

At first they never thought of mentioning Roger. Only when one of the detectives said: "And what about that young boy who was with Gil on the afternoon of the murder?" they came up with their stories about Roger's visits to the building site. It was a great new vein to quarry. In their opinion, "those guys" were an amorphous bunch, not much to choose between them, and thus they considered it quite natural for an eighteen-year-old youngster to blithely disengage himself from the arms of a forty-year-old mason to go and make love to a child of fifteen.

"You never saw him with a sailor?"

Well, they weren't sure, but they supposed they had. It wasn't always so easy to distinguish people in the fog. But there were far too many sailors in the city of Brest for Gil not to have known several. Besides, he used to wear bell-bottom pants, like a sailor.

"You sure about that?"

"But of course. Sailor's bags, the real thing, with a flap and all."

"Well, if you don't believe us, there ain't much use telling you anything."

Being at last able to discuss a certain and verifiable fact, they hastened to abandon their initially timid stance, their fawning humility in front of the police. They turned quite arrogant. They knew what they were talking about. As they were in a position to furnish the police with a proven fact that the authorities had overlooked, this had to elevate their standing. The police had spent a whole night interrogating Roger with merciless insistence. All they found on him was his cheap pocketknife, broken and clumsily repaired.

"What's this for?"

Roger blushed, but the policeman thought this was due to a fleeting sense of shame about the poor condition of the knife. He didn't pursue the matter. He had not realized that the weapon, being practically useless, was the more dangerous for being merely symbolic. In the keen edge of a true blade, in its accuracy and true balance, lies the very beginning of the true act of killing: thus it has to appear frightening to any child already living in a state of fear (the child who invents symbols of fear for himself, using the materials we clumsily refer to as "reality"). On the other hand, the symbolic knife represents no practical danger at all, but as it is employed in a multitude of imaginary inner lives, it becomes a sure sign of its owner's acceptance of crime. The cops were unable to see that the knife was an endorsement of Gil's act of murder even before he had committed it.

"Where did you know him from?"

The boy denied ever having slept with the murderer or with Theo, saying that the day of the latter's death was the first time he had ever seen him. Then he admitted that he had gone to see his sister one night in the bistro where she was working as a waitress at that time. Gil had been standing at the bar, exchanging banter with her. At midnight, she finished work, and Gil walked both sister and brother back to their house. The next day Gil was there again. Roger had found him there on five subsequent occasions, and now and again, when they happened to meet, Gil had bought him a drink.

"He never tried to sleep with you?"

The interrogators were quite taken aback by Roger's wide-eyed, innocent look:

"With me? What for?"

"He never made any advances to you?"

"Advances? Oh, no."

He let his limpid gaze rest on the embarrassed police officers.

"He never touched you, like, down there?"

"Never."

They could get nothing more out of the boy, whose love for Gil had grown more intense. At first, he had fallen in love with him as a child, endowed with a quick and vertiginous imagination. The crime made him advance into a world of violent emotions; the sense of drama attached him to Gil, prime mover of that drama, and he had to be joined to the murderer by the strongest and closest of bonds: that of love. The effort Roger made to deceive the police made his love grow. He needed love to have enough strength, and even though he told himself at first that his effort was necessary to protect his own life, his own dream, he soon realized that opposing the police quite naturally meant siding with Gil. Deliberately, and in order to get closer to Gil whose glory was at its height at the time (due to his murders and to his disappearance), Roger made a great effort to keep up his façade. All that remained to him of Gil was a shadow resting at his feet like a dog. Roger felt like placing one of his feet on its back, gently, to hold it there. He implored it, in his mind, not to run away, but to stay close to him, the messenger or witness of the hidden god; or at least, to hesitate, to stretch, then to stop, then to extend itself all the way from

him to Gil. Very quickly, he discovered all the tricks of love:
but being such a natural at them, he became entangled in the
very love that caused them. The more candid he appeared, the
more cunning he became, the purer—that is to say, the purer
his love became, and his own knowledge of his love for Gil. In
the early morning hours, the police let him go. They had
decided that Gil must be a dangerous sadistic maniac. They
started looking for him all over France, but Gil had escaped his
own loneliness and found refuge in the old convict prison. He
knew he would have dreaded that sense of solitude in a crowd,
hemmed in, almost a monster, inflated in size and gestures to
the point of certain self-betrayal. In the penitentiary, as long as
he did not leave it, his certainty that he would not be discovered there ameliorated his anguish. It had to be a desolate
kind of life, considering all the things he was not able to do, but
he felt he could bear it, whereas a life based on pretense would
have been impossible. Nourishment was the only thing lacking.
He was hungry. He had been in hiding for three days, and he
lived in fear of the crime he had committed. Sleeping and
waking, horrors filled his mind. He was afraid of rats, but he
seriously considered catching one and eating it raw. Having
sobered up almost instantly, the uselessness of the murder had
become clear to him. He even felt some tenderness toward
Theo, thinking of him. He remembered how kind Theo had
been at first, remembered the carafes of white wine they had
enjoyed together. He asked for his forgiveness. Remorse gnawed
at him, made him feel hungrier still. Then he thought of his
parents. Surely the newspapers and the police had informed
them about his deed. What would they do? They, too, were
working folk. The father was a mason. What would he think of
his son killing another mason in a fit of amorous rage? And the
kids he had gone to school with? Gil slept on the stone floor.
He didn't pay any attention to his clothes—shirt, undershirt,
pants—and they seemed to slip off him of their own accord, as
if they wanted to leave Gil who crouched in the dark, passing a

light finger—mechanically, voluptuously, but with no feelings
of an erotic nature—almost caressing that sensitive excrescence
of flesh he thought of as a light pink in color, and which once
before had given him the sense of being a man, making it
impossible for Theo to mount him. Having remained there so
faithfully, his hemorrhoids reminded him of the scene, and
their presence strengthened his sense of being.

"I guess they've buried Theo by now. I'm sure the guys took
the day off. They all chipped in for a wreath."

He curled up again, staying in a corner, clutching his knees in
his arms. Now and again he got up and walked, but always
slowly, fearfully, as if mysteriously anchored to the wall like
Baron Franck, by a complicated network of chains fastened to
his neck, his wrists, his waist, his ankles, and to the stones of
the wall. Carefully he dragged along this load of invisible metal,
being surprised in spite of himself that it was so easy to get out
of his clothes, neither shirt nor trousers being held up by the
shackles. Another reason for moving slowly was his fear of the
ghost he might so easily raise by too heavy a footfall: it would
rise and spread like a sail, given the slightest breath of wind.
The ghost was under his feet. Gil had to flatten it out, crush it,
by planting his steps heavily. The ghost was in his arms, in his
legs. Gil had to smother it by moving slowly. Too quick a turn
might make it unfold, spread a wing, black or white, and its
head would appear next to his own, shapeless and invisible, and
then, into his ear, into Gil's ear it would whisper, in a thunder-
ous murmur, the most terrifying threats. The ghost was within
him, and it was imperative to keep it from rising. Killing Theo
had been useless. A man whom you have killed is more alive
than the living. And more dangerous, by not being one of the
living. Not for one second did Gil think about Roger—who
thought of nothing but him. The circumstances of the tragedy
kept eluding him. He knew that he had killed, killed Theo. But
had it really been Theo? Was he really dead? He should have
asked him first: "It is you, Theo, isn't it?" If he had answered

yes, that would have been immensely reassuring, although, come to think of it, the certainty would not have been any greater. The victim might have said yes out of sheer malice, in order to cause Gil to commit a useless crime. Perhaps Theo had been the kind of guy who had wanted to drive him exactly to that point, who felt a metaphysical hatred for him. Then again Gil told himself that he had clearly recognized the thousand little wrinkles in his victim's face, the thin lines around his mouth. Then again, fear and trembling. He had committed a crime that had no reward whatsoever. Not a sou. It was an empty crime, like a bottomless bucket. It was a mistake. Gil pondered ways of correcting it. First of all, crouched in his corner, fetal among the damp stones, his head hanging low, he tried to destroy his act by dividing it up into a series of gestures, each one of them inoffensive in itself: "You open the door! Man's got a right to open a door. You pick up a bottle. Man's got a right to do that. You break it? Well, that can happen. That's all right. You take the bottleneck and point it at the guy? That's not so terrible. You put it up against his neck. You apply a little pressure. Well, those things happen, you know. You draw a little blood? Well, a man's got a right. He's got a right. A little more blood, and yet a little more . . .?" Thus it was possible to make the crime dwindle right down to that ineffable point where what is permissible turns into what is not, firmly embedded in the sequence of events, not detachable from it, but causing the murder to be committed. Gil exerted himself to scale it down, to make it as tenuous as possible. He forced himself to contemplate that point on the dividing line between "OK" and "too late." But he found himself unable to resolve the question: "Why kill Theo?" The murder remained pointless, it remained a mistake, and one of the kind you could not correct. Gil abandoned this initial method, but not his intention to make the crime disappear. Very quickly, after some detours and false starts, thoughts of other events in his life, his mind latched on to a new notion: all he had to do, to retrieve and erase this useless crime, was to commit a useful one (the same). A crime that would make him rich, and thus render the precedent worthy, as any precedent is that results in a definitive achievement. But who should be the victim? He just didn't know anybody rich. Well, he would have to get out of Brest, take the train, get to Rennes or perhaps even Paris where the people were wealthy, walked about in the streets, patiently or impatiently waiting for a robber to strike them down. This acceptance of their destiny, their voluntary wait for murder, lit up Gil's mind in very bright lights. In the great cities, surely, those capitalists positively yearned for the criminal to arrive, to kill them and to make off with their gold. But here, in this godforsaken little town, in this hide-out, he was doomed to drag along the cumbersome and useless weight of his first murder. Several times he felt the urge to turn himself in to the police. However, he had retained his childhood fear of gendarmes and their funereal uniforms. He was afraid they would immediately stick him under the guillotine and chop his head off. He took pity on his mother. He asked her for her forgiveness. He relived his early youth, his apprenticeship with his father, his first jobs on building sites in the South of France. Every detail of his life now seemed to presage a tragic destiny. It wasn't hard for him to convince himself that the only reason he had become a mason was because he had to accomplish that murder. His fear of what he had done, and of such an uncommon destiny, forced him to meditate, to go into himself; it made him *think*. Despair made him become conscious, conscious of himself. He was thinking, but what he was experiencing was, first of all, this: *he saw himself*, in the penitentiary, looking out to sea, as far removed from the world as if he had suddenly found himself in Greece, crouching on top of a boulder and meditating by the Aegean Sea. As his desolate situation obliged him to consider the outside world and its objects as so many enemies, he finally managed to establish relationships between them and himself. He was thinking. He saw himself, and he saw himself large, very large, opposed and equal to the world. And out there, his main opponent was Mario, whose sleepless nights were assuming the great scale of some musical meditation on the origin and end of time. The impossibility of arresting Gilbert Turko, of finding his hide-out, of discovering the connections he somehow knew to exist between the two murders, created the dull feeling of unease in the detective; in some mysterious fashion, he attributed this to his previous worries about Tony the Docker. When Dédé returned without having learnt anything specific about the latter's doings, Mario fell into the clutches of the fear that made him hesitate on the landing, as he was leaving the boy's room, before going down the stairs. Dédé noticed this very slight hesitation and said:

"In any case, you haven't got anything to worry about. He won't dare do anything."

Mario swallowed a curse. If he chose to go out alone, unaccompanied by his habitual companion (that young police-man who had once said to the admiring Dédé: "What a handsome pair you two are"—and had thus managed to make the boy see both of them together as a mighty sexual entity), he did so to erase the shame of his first fright and to exorcise it by audacity. Mario decided to hit the streets at night, in the fog, the best time and place for a quick murder. He strode along purposefully, hands in pockets of his gaberdine coat, or else smoothing and pulling tight the fingers of his brown leather gloves—a gesture connecting him straight back to the invincible machinery of the police. The first time out he didn't even pack his revolver, hoping, by such extreme candor and innocence, to disarm the hypothetical dockers who were after his ass, but the following day he did take it along; it was, after all, a necessary adjunct to what he himself thought of as his courage—his belief in a system of order symbolized by the gun. When he wanted to arrange a meeting with Dédé, he traced a street name on the steamy windowpane of his office in the police station, and when the street kid (who naïvely persisted in his efforts to ferret out the place where the bad guys were sitting in judgment of the detective) walked past, he could simply read the letters backwards and thus be informed. As for Gil, he was busy rerunning the movie of his life, starting out from the murder and cranking it backwards, in order to justify his deed and make it appear inevitable. By reasoning in this fashion: "If I had never run into Roger . . . if I hadn't come to Brest . . . if . . .," etc., he arrived at the conclusion that although the crime had taken its course through his arm, his body, his life, its true source lay outside of himself.

This method of understanding his deed forced Gil into fatalism, which was a further obstacle to his desire to transcend the crime by sheer, deliberate force of will. At last, one night, he left the penitentiary. He managed to reach Roger's house. The darkness was total, further intensified by the fog. Brest lay sleeping. Without making any mistakes, using a couple of cunning detours, Gil arrived in Recouvrance without having encountered a soul. Standing in front of the house he realized, with some apprehension, that he had not yet thought of a way to make his presence known to Roger. Then, suddenly, eager to know if this trick would work, he smiled for the first time in three days, a quiet smile, and then started whistling, quietly:

*He was a happy bandit,*
*Nothing did he fear,*
*His voice in the maquis*
*Made the gendarmes weep . . .*

Up on the second floor a window opened without a sound. Roger's voice floated down in a whisper:
"Gil."
Very cautiously, Gil moved closer. At the foot of the wall,

raising his head, he whistled the same refrain again, even more quietly than before. The fog was too dense for him to be able to see Roger.

"Gil, is that you . . . ? This is Roger."

"Come on down. I have to talk to you."

With infinite care Roger shut the window again. After a few moments he opened the front door, barefoot, clad only in a shirt. Gil entered without making the least bit of sound.

"Better talk very quietly, sometimes the old lady can't sleep. And that happens to Paulette, too."

"You got anything to eat?"

They were standing in the main room where the mother slept, and they could hear her breathing. In the dark, Roger squeezed Gil's hand and whispered:

"Stay right there, I'll go see."

Very gently he slid open the lid of the bread bin and came back with a piece of bread. Groping for Gil's hand, he put the bread in it. Gil was standing motionless in the middle of the room.

"Listen, Roger, can you come and see me tomorrow?"

"Where?"

Their words were carried on the lightest of breaths, circulating from one mouth to the other.

"In the old naval penitentiary. I'm hiding out there. Use the gate on the Arsenal side. I'll expect you in the evening. But don't let anybody see you."

"Sure, you can count on me, Gil."

"You've had no trouble? Did the cops come and talk to you?"

"Yeah, but I didn't tell them anything."

Roger came closer. He grabbed hold of Gil's arms and whispered:

"I swear, I'll be there."

The little mason pressed the boy close to him, and Roger's

breath on his eyes excited him as much as if he had been kissed on cheek or mouth. He said:

"See you tomorrow then."

Roger opened the street door with the same prudence as before. Gil went out. On the doorstep he held on to Roger and after a second's hesitation asked:

"He croaked?"

"I'll tell you all about it tomorrow."

Their hands separated in the dark, and Gil slunk back to the penitentiary, all the while chewing on the chunk of bread.

Roger came to see him every day, in the evening, at the time the fog was at its thickest. He always managed to bring along a little food, and after a while he even stole some money from his mother in order to buy some bread. He hid the loaf under his shirt and made his way to the old prison, across the fortifications. Gil expected him around six o'clock. Roger told him the news. The newspapers had already discontinued their coverage of the double murder and the murderer who, it was assumed, had left the city. Gil ate, alone. Then he had a cigarette.

"And Paulette, what's happening with her?"

"Nothing. She still hasn't found another job. Stays at home."

"You ever talk with her about me?"

"But I can't do that. You've got no idea. The times they've asked me where you are and threaten to follow me around!"

He was happy to have a pretext to remove his sister from the fabulous relationship he was now having with Gil. Next to his friend in the granite cell, with its smell of tar, he felt amazingly calm. He hunkered down at his side on the cotton dust sheet he had appropriated from the attic, sat there and watched his idol smoking a cigarette. He gazed at his face, its smooth bones, the long growth of beard. He admired him. At the beginning of their encounters in the penitentiary Gil had not stopped talking, talking for hours; to anyone but this child who was determined to see him as a monumental figure, such babble would have been a sure indication of a state of abject, almost pathological fear. Roger regarded it as merely the sublime expression of a tempest raging in Gil's breast. That was how he had to be, this hero brimming with outcries, crimes and turmoil. The three years he had on Roger made Gil appear a *man*. The hardness of his pale face where you could see all the muscles working under the skin (muscles that mentally floored Roger every time he looked at them, as promptly as any prize fighter's punch) made him think of the muscles of his limbs and body, so strong, able to do a man's work on a building site. Roger himself was still wearing short pants, and although his thighs were strong, they did not yet have the definitive firmness of Gil's legs. Stretching out by his side, as close as possible, leaning on one elbow Roger watched the beloved face, pallid and twisted by a hatred of this kind of life. He rested his head on Gil's legs.

"Gotta wait a while, still—or, what d'you think? Guess it's better if I wait a while yet, before taking off."

"I should think so. The gendarmes are still looking for you. They have your picture."

"What about you, they haven't been talking to you any more?"

"Not to me, and they haven't been to the house either. But I must take care not to stay away too long."

And suddenly Gil gave vent to a sigh, terminating in a wild groan:

"Oh! Your sister, boy, could I use her now. She's beautiful, you know! Aarrghh . . ."

"She looks a bit like me."

Gil knew it. Not wanting to let Roger see that, and also with the intention of showing his superiority to the boy, he said:

"A whole lot better, though. You're like an uglier version of her."

Roger was glad that the darkness obscured his blush. Nevertheless he raised his face toward Gil's, smiling wistfully.

"Didn't mean to say you was ugly, that ain't so. As a matter of fact, you do have the same little mug."

He bent over the boy's face and took it in his hands:

"God, if I could be holding her the way I'm holding you now. Boy, I'd be off to a flying start."

Of its own accord, rising from the clamp of Gil's hands, the upturned face of the boy approached Gil's. With a quiet murmuring sound Gil touched Roger's forehead. Then their noses met and played at Eskimo kisses for ten seconds or so. As he had suddenly rediscovered the brother's resemblance to his sister and felt the emotion rising in him, Gil was unable to dissimulate. In one breath, his mouth close to Roger's, he whispered:

"It *is* a pity that you ain't your sister."

Roger smiled:

"Is that right?"

Roger's voice sounded clear, pure, apparently unmoved. Having loved Gil for a long time and hoped for this moment, having prepared himself for it, he did not want to appear moved by anything beyond friendship. The same prudence that had enabled him to deceive the police officers by his limpid look now made him couch his reply to Gil in an impassive tone. Gil's avowal of his feelings, having occurred first, allowed the proud child to demonstrate his own cool. But it's also true that he did not yet know the conventional signals of amorous abandon, didn't know that the voluptuous groans have to be willed a little:

"By God, you're as nice to touch as a girl."

Gil pressed his mouth on the boy's lips. Roger drew back, smiling.

"Are you afraid?"

"Oh, no!"

"Well? What did you think I was going to do?"

Gil felt embarrassed by the misfired kiss. With a sneer in his voice, he said:

"You don't feel too safe, hey, with a guy like me?"

"Why shouldn't I? Sure I feel safe. I wouldn't come here, otherwise."

"That's not what it looks like."

Then, with an abrupt change to serious business, as if the idea to be expressed were so important as to make him brush all the previous nonsense aside:

"Listen, you've got to go and talk to Robert. I've thought it over. There ain't nobody but him, and his buddies, can get me out of this mess."

Naïvely, Gil believed that the local heavies would greet him with open arms and make him a member of their gang. He believed in the existence of such a gang, a dangerous one, another society that was fighting against society itself. That evening Roger left the penitentiary in a very confused state of mind. He was happy that Gil had felt desire for him, for a moment (even though it had been based on a confusion with his sister); he was annoyed with himself for having drawn back from Gil's kiss; he felt proud to know that the greatness of his friend was about to be recognized, and that it was he, Roger, who had been chosen to establish contact with the supreme powers. Now, whenever he had the opportunity, Querelle would go, round about dusk, for a walk, unobtrusively strolling in the direction of his hidden treasure. On these occasions he let sadness appear on his face. He felt himself already garbed in convict uniform, slowly meandering along, a ball and chain round his ankle, in a landscape of monstrous palm trees, a region of dream and death, from which neither morning nor any acquittal granted by men could ever save him again. The certainty of living in a world that is the silent double of the one in which you are actually moving about invested Querelle with a certain kind of disinterest, which endowed him, in its turn, with a spontaneous understanding of things. As a rule indiffer-

ent to plants or objects—but had he ever confronted them?—
now he understood them intuitively. The taste of everything is
isolated by some singularity, first recognized by the eye, then
communicated to the palate: hay is hay primarily because of
that characteristic yellowish-gray powder the sense of taste first
expects and then experiences. It is the same with any vegetable
species. The eye may allow some confusion, but the mouth
won't stand for it, and thus Querelle was slowly proceeding
through a universe of savors, of recognitions within recognitions. One evening he ran into Roger. It didn't take the sailor
long to know who the boy was, and to succeed in penetrating to
Gil's hiding place.

### THE GLORY OF QUERELLE

One ear pressed against the inside of his coffin, Querelle listens
to the drums and pipes performing, for him alone, the offices for
the dead. He wraps himself in prudence, waits for the angel to
strike. Crouching in the midst of the black velvet of grasses,
arums, ferns, in the living night of his own south seas, he keeps
his eyes wide open. Over his face, so gentle, open, offered up like
a precious thing, the desire to murder has passed its soft tongue,
without causing Querelle to shudder. Only his blond curls are in
motion. Sometimes the watchdog, awake between his legs, raises
itself onto its front paws, pressing against its master's body and
finally blending into the muscles of his shoulders, hiding, waking,
growling there. Querelle knows that he is in mortal danger. He
also knows that the beast is protecting him. He says: "With one
bite I'll open up his throat . . . ," without exactly knowing
whether he is speaking of the watchdog's throat, or of the white
throat of a peeing infant.

o     o     o

Entering the old penitentiary Querelle was elated by fear and by the responsibility he was about to assume. Silently walking along beside Roger he felt a budding within himself—soon they would open, those buds, all over his body, and perfume it with their corollae: the budding of a violent adventure. Danger was what he needed in order to bloom. Danger and fear made him high. What would he find in the depths of the abandoned prison? He held on to himself. The least sense of excitement would have been enough to make him fear the place. With a tightness in his chest he thought of all those massive walls converging to crush him, and so he fought against them, fought them off, strained against them as he strained against his own anger, with the same effort, almost the same motions as those of the sergeant of the guard when he closes, using both his hands and all the weight of his body, the giant gates of the citadel. In some shadowy sense he was walking back to meet a former and blessed existence. Not that he seriously thought he had ever been a galley slave, nor did his imagination get involved in such fantasies, but he experienced a wonderful sense of well-being, a presentiment of rest, at the idea of entering, a free man, sovereign, the dark interior of these thick walls, which had throughout the ages contained so much shackled pain, so much physical and moral suffering, so many bodies contorted by torture, worn out by disease, knowing no other joys but the memory of marvelous crimes that stood like a pillar of smoke in the light, or pierced the dark in which they had been committed, with a blazing shaft of light. What could remain of these murders under the stones of this prison, or in its corners, or suspended in the humid air? Even though, for Querelle, these reflections were no clear thoughts, at least the same thing that brings them so easily to pen and paper gave him a heavy, confused feeling of pain and bothered his brain with a smidgen of anguish. What's more, Querelle was on his way, for the first time in his life, to meet another criminal, a brother. He had already entertained vague dreams of meeting a murderer of his own stature, with whom he could talk shop. A guy similar to him, his height, his build—well, his brother, as he sometimes wished, but only for a few seconds: his brother was too much of a mirror image—having to his credit crimes different from those Querelle himself had committed, but equally beautiful, as grave, as reprehensible. He did not exactly know how he could have recognized such a man in the street, by what outward signs, and sometimes his loneliness grew so great that he dreamed (but hardly, and very fleetingly) of giving himself up in order to be sent to prison, where he could meet some of the murderers that had been written up in the newspapers. But he abandoned that notion quickly. Those murderers were of no interest—they had been stripped of their secrets. The yearning for such a miraculous friend was partly due to his close resemblance to his brother. Looking at Robert he asked himself whether he wasn't a criminal, too. He was afraid of that, and he wished it were true. He would have liked to be part of such a miracle in this world. But he feared it because he would then have lost his superiority over Robert.

But now, in the abandoned prison, he was to meet a young fellow who had killed. The thought of it made him feel tender. This assassin was just an awkward kid, a murderer for nothing. An idiot. But thanks to Querelle he would be credited with a true murder as well, because the authorities assumed that the murdered sailor had been robbed as well. Even before seeing Gil again Querelle felt almost paternal toward him. He was going to entrust him with one of his murders. In any case Gil was just a dumb kid, he couldn't be the hoped-for buddy. These thoughts (not in the definitive state we are reporting them in, but surging about formlessly), rapid and shifting, self-destructing, one being reborn out of the other, were milling around in his body and limbs rather than in his head. He was walking along, elevated and buffeted by this gale of shapeless notions, none of which really stuck in his mind but left there a feeling of discomfort, insecurity and fear. But Querelle did not relinquish his smile which kept him down to earth. Now Roger stopped, turned:

"Wait here. I'll be back."

Thus the kid departed on his diplomatic mission from an emperor to his own lord, in order to make sure that all was prepared for this meeting between two great ones. Querelle's musings took a new turn. He had not expected this precautionary measure. He could not see an entrance to any cavern there. The path simply turned and disappeared behind a small mound. The trees were no denser nor less dense than before. Nevertheless, as soon as Roger vanished, he became for Querelle a "mysterious link," more precious than he had realized until then. It was his absence that gave the boy such a rare quality and sudden importance. Querelle smiled, but could not help being worried by the fact that the boy was the go-between of two murderers, and, it seemed, a quick and lively one. He was now running along the imaginary connecting line whose very spirit he was, and he could choose to extend or shorten it, at his pleasure. Roger was, in fact, walking briskly. His separation from Querelle made him feel more solemn than before, because he knew that he was bringing Gil the essence of Querelle, in other words that in Querelle which he vaguely understood to be the motive force that propelled Querelle in Gil's direction. He knew that in him, a mere boy in short pants whose cuffs had been turned up over the solid thighs, now was vested all the pomp and circumstance due to ambassadors—and seeing the child's serious demeanor one could well understand why such delegates are always more heavily decorated than their masters. On his frail person, laden down with a thousand ceremonial chains, converged Gil's almost haggard attention, as he sat there in his lair, and Querelle's patience, as he stood waiting by the gateway to the domain. Querelle took out a cigarette and lit it, then stuck both his hands back in the pockets of his peacoat. He wasn't thinking at all. Nothing stirred in his imagination. His consciousness was attentive, soft and shapeless, though still a little troubled by the sudden importance of the boy he was waiting for.

"It's me. Roger."

Quite close to him Gil's voice came in a whisper:

"Is he here?"

"Yes. I told him to wait for me. You want me to go and get him?"

Sounding somewhat tense, Gil replied:

"Yup. Bring him here. Get going."

When Querelle arrived in front of the den, Roger proclaimed, in a loud and clear voice:

"This is it, we're here. Gil, we're here."

The boy was overwhelmed by misery at the sudden feeling that his life was coming to an end with those very words. He felt himself shrinking, losing his *raison d'être*. All the treasures with which he had been entrusted for a couple of minutes were now melting away, very quickly. He fully knew, now, the vanity of mankind, and how it melteth away like wax. He had labored faithfully to bring about a meeting that would abolish him. His whole life had been involved in this giant task of ten minutes' duration, and now his glory dimmed, almost disappeared, taking with it the high proud sense of joy that had made him swell up: to a size great enough to accommodate Querelle, whom he had described, whose words he had reported, and Gil, whom he had conveyed to Querelle.

"Here, brought you some ciggies."

Those were Querelle's first words. In the dark, he held out a pack of cigarettes to Gil, and their hands met in a groping handshake that enclosed the pack.

"Thanks, buddy. That's good of you. I won't forget it."

"Come on. Don't even mention it."

"And I got you some cold meat and a little bit of *pâté*."

"Put 'em on the crate there."

Querelle took out another pack and lit himself a cigarette
from it. He wanted to be able to see Gil's face. He was surprised when he saw how emaciated, pain-racked and dirty it
was, and covered with a fair, soft growth of beard. Gil's hair was
matted. The face was a moving sight, in the light of the match.
It was a murderer's face. Querelle raised the match to look
around.

"It must be pretty grim, living here."

"You said it, it's no joke. But what could I do? Where else
could I have gone?"

Querelle stuck his hands in his pants pockets, and all three
were silent for a moment or two.

"Aren't you going to eat, Gil?"

Gil certainly was hungry, but he didn't want to show it to
Querelle.

"Go ahead and light the candle, there's no one else around."

Gil sat down on a corner of the crate. He started to eat, in a
casual manner. The boy hunkered down at his feet, and
Querelle stood looking at the two of them, his legs apart,
smoking his ciagarette without touching it with his hands.

"I probably look like hell, don't I?"

Querelle grinned.

"Can't say you're a beaut, but it'll be easy to fix. You're safe
here, in any case?"

"Yeah. Unless someone snitches, that is."

"If that's me you have in mind, you're wrong. I got no truck
with informers. But I can't see how much longer you can make
it here. You've got to get out of here, and that's for sure."

Querelle knew that his expression had suddenly turned cruel,
as on the days of arms drill when it was shielded by the steel
triangle of the bayonet fixed to his rifle. Those times his face,
itself, became as if plated with steel. Sheltering behind it and
representing that bayonet was the true soul of a Querelle otherwise put together out of flesh and cloth. To the officer inspect-

ing the men on deck, the bayonet was exactly in line with
Querelle's left eyebrow and eye, and when he met Querelle's
stare it seemed to him like looking into an entire arms factory.

"With a little dough I could perhaps make it to Spain. I
know some guys in Perpignan; I used to work down there."

Gil went on eating. He and Querelle seemed to have run out
of words already, but Roger perceived that a relationship was
being established between them in which there was no room for
him. It was, now, a matter of two men talking, in all earnest,
about things a boy his age could only daydream about.

"Say, you're Robert's brother, the one who's staying at
Nono's?"

"Yeah. And I know Nono, too."

Not for one minute did Querelle consider the nature of his
relationship with Nono. There was no undertone of irony in his
statement.

"No kidding, you're a buddy of Nono's?"

"You heard me. What about it?"

"D'you think he . . . (Gil was going to say: "could help
me," but realized it would be too much heartbreak to get a
"no" for an answer). He hesitated, then said:

"Do you think he might help me?"

In turning him into an outlaw his crime naturally encouraged
Gil to seek refuge among pimps and prostitutes, as they were
people who lived—or so he thought—at the very borderline of
legality. The murder he had committed would have totally
crushed any laboring man of a riper age. Gil, on the contrary,
was hardened by it, it made him glow from within, conferring,
as it did, a reputation he would not have attained otherwise,
and from the lack of which he had been suffering. Gil was a
mason, but his life had been too short for him to identify himself with his trade. He was still entertaining all sorts of vague
dreams, and these had suddenly become true (what we call
"dreams" are those little peculiarities that may indicate *fan-*

*tasies:* a swagger, expressed in hips or shoulders; snapping your fingers to punctuate your words; blowing out cigarette smoke from one corner of the mouth; adjusting the belt buckle with the flat of your hand . . ., favorite expressions, out-of-the-way accessories: a plaited belt, thin-soled shoes, diagonal trouser pockets, all of them indications of the adolescent's fine awareness of such particulars as they appear in the world of men, more precisely, among the proud members of the criminal culture), but the very splendor inherent in that realization could only terrify someone as young as Gil. It would have been easier to accept even a very fast transition to the status of stick-up artist or pimp, aspired to by every corner boy. But to be a murderer—that was almost too much for his eighteen years. Yet he had to try to benefit from the prestige he had won by that act. He was naïve enough to assume that the real heavies would be glad to receive him into their order. Querelle knew the contrary to be the case. The process which finally brings forth a murderer is in itself so weird that whoever goes through it becomes a kind of hero. He remains free of the negative funkiness of crime. The professionals have a fine nose for this, and there are few killers among them.

"I'll check him out. I have to talk to Nono. We'll see what can be done."

"But what do you think? I mean, I've shown what I can do."

"Yeah. You sure have. Anyhow, you can count on me. I'll keep you posted."

"And Robert? I could work with Robert."

"Do you know who he's working with?"

"With Dédé, I know that. He used to be a buddy of mine. I know that they stick together, even though Mario doesn't like it. But he leaves 'em alone. When you see Robert, why don't you ask him if I could swing things with the two of them. But don't tell him where I am."

Querelle suddenly felt very pleased, not because he found himself in this cave dedicated to evil doings, but because he had in his possession a much deeper secret than the one Gil had just revealed to him.

Querelle's question came in a very casual, offhand tone:
"But why did you snuff that sailorboy? That didn't really make sense to me."

The insinuating sentence began with a "but" so heavy with hypocrisy that Querelle, whose common approach was a brusque one, was instantly reminded of Lieutenant Seblon and his wily ways, his roundabout approaches. Gil felt the blood draining away from his face. His life, his presence within himself, rushed to his eyes and made them burn, escaped through them to lose itself, to disperse among the dark shadows of the dungeon. He had to hesitate before answering, not with the kind of hesitation where time is gained by cold-blooded reasoning for and against, but out of a feeling close to complete prostration, aggravated by the impression that it would be useless to deny anything, and this, too, locked his jaws. The charge was so serious that he had to make an effort to comprehend it at all. He remained mute, tried to lose himself in a fixed stare, and became so self-conscious of it that he could feel the muscles round his eyes twitching. Unblinking, he pressed his lips together, until they became a thin line.

"Well? That sailor. What made you snuff him?"

"He didn't do it."

As if half asleep Gil listened to Querelle's question and Roger's answer. The sound of their voices didn't bother him at all. He had withdrawn totally into the intensity of his stare, while being aware of its fixity.

"Who was it then, if it wasn't him?"

Gil turned his head and looked Querelle in the eye.

"It wasn't me, I swear! I can't tell you who did it, I don't know nothing about it. But I'm telling you, by all that's sacred, I swear I didn't do it."

"The papers said they was sure it was you, all right. I'm willing to believe you, but you'd have some explaining to do if the cops got you. See, they found your cigarette lighter, right by that stiff. Anyhow, you better keep the profile low."

Gil resigned himself to the second murder. When the monstrousness of his deed had first blurred his vision, he had thought of turning himself in. He had thought that once the police had recognized his innocence of the second crime, they would let him go, so that he could go and hide again because of the first one. He thought they would respect the rules of the game. The insanity of this train of thought soon became apparent to him. Thus, little by little, Gil took the murder of the sailor upon himself. He tried to think of reasons for doing it. Sometimes he wondered who the true murderer might be. He interrogated himself to find out how he had managed to lose his cigarette lighter at the scene of the crime.

"I would really like to know who did it. I hadn't even noticed I didn't have that lighter any more."

"I'm telling you, you better stay put. I'll talk to my buddies and see what we can do for you. I'll come and see you as often as I'm able. I'll even give your little buddy here some coins so he can buy you some stuff to eat and some smokes."

"That's damn white of you. Thanks."

But the moment before, in order to lose himself, to concentrate himself into his stare and disperse it among the shadows, Gil had used up too much of his energy to be able to express his gratitude with the full warmth of his being. He was tired. An immense sadness had crept over his face, dragging down the corners of the mouth Querelle recalled seeing in a different state—a little moist, gay, open in song. His body was sagging on the corner of the crate, and his entire gestalt was that of someone who thinks: "What the fucking hell am I going to do now?" He was on the verge of grief, not despair, but the grief of a child, abandoned, if only for an instant, when night is coming on. Strength and conviction were ebbing away. He was not a true murderer. He was afraid.

"You think it's all over for me, if they catch me?"

"Who knows. It's a lottery. But don't start worrying now. They won't get you."

"You're a real buddy. What's your first name?"

"Jo."

"You're a buddy, Jo. I'll never forget it."

At last his soul was filled with joy at the encounter with Querelle who was on his way out and back to normal life, and who was strong, with the strength of a hundred million people.

Sheltering behind the old prison walls, Gil was unable to watch the scenes at dusk and dawn that went on outside, but the sounds of banging, the shouts from the naval shipyards came filtering through the stones and conjured up some pleasant images in Gil's mind. Within the young man imprisoned by those walls, by his guilt, and by his adolescence, almost stifled by anguish and by the all-pervasive smell of tar, the powers of imagination began to unfold with extraordinary vigor. They struggled bravely with all the aforementioned obstacles, and in that battle they grew strong. Listening, Gil could pick out the particular squeak and grind of cranes and pulley blocks. His work gang had not been stationed in Brest for very long, and thus he had not yet become impervious to the vivid scenery of the naval shipyards. He had taken in those clear, incisive noises that corresponded to a sunbeam striking a brass rail, a splinter of glass, to a decorated launch flashing by with its load of very upright, gilded officers, to a sail out in the Roads, to the slow maneuvering of a cruiser, to the naval cadets' businesslike yet puerile rigging drill. In the prisoner, each one of these noises released an image a thousand times more exciting than their actual origin. As the sea is our natural symbol for freedom, any visual image including it is charged with that symbolic power, becomes a metaphor of freedom; and in the captive's soul each one of those images left a wound, made even more painful by the very banality of the real things corresponding to it. The spontaneous apparition of a great steamer in mid-ocean would cause an instant crisis of yearning in any child's mind, but Gil's consciousness was no longer so easily invaded by steamer and ocean; rather, it was the characteristic noise of a chain (and can it be that the screeching of a chain releases the mechanism of yearning? A simple chain, its links rusting away from the inside?) . . . Without being aware of it, Gil was serving a dolorous apprenticeship as a poet. The image of the chain cut across some fibers of his awareness, and then the cut widened and became wide enough to let in that ship, and the ocean, and the world, and on to the final destruction of Gil who had gone out of himself and had found that his only true existense was in this world which had just stabbed him, run him through, annihilated him. Squatting most of the day behind the same big coil of rope he had become really attached to it: it was a kind of friend. It had become his. He loved it. This particular rope coil, and only this one, was the one he had chosen. Even when he left it for a few seconds to walk up to the windows which were either so filthy they were opaque or had no glass in them at all, Gil did not entirely detach himself from it. Miserable, cowering in its shadow, he sat listening to the golden song of the port. Listening and interpreting it. The sea was out there, on the other side of the walls, solemn and familiar, hard and gentle toward people like him, to those who have to suffer "a hard blow." Motionless for long moments Gil stared at the rope end in his hands. He fixed it with his stare. He grew attached to the particular quality of this many-stranded, tarred plait of hemp. A sorry sight, one that stripped the murder of Theo of all its glory, as that act had only led Gil to such minimal activity, to this measly sight, a black, dusty rope end twisting and turning

between his dirty fingers. However, it wasn't always quite as bad
as that. Gil's microscopically precise visual imagination enabled
him to push through those times of despair to a more serene
state of mind. Attempting to pierce the secrets, simple enough,
of the tarred rope, his stare sometimes—out of sheer boredom
with the sight—lost its fixity, and a happy memory flashed on
the screen. Then Gil returned to the rope—although he knew
there was no earthly reason for such interest in it—and interrogated it some more, in silence. There were times when tears
welled up in his eyes. He thought of his parents. Were the cops
still interrogating them? During the day, he often heard the
drum and horn students of the academy playing and practicing
marching tunes, quick and slow. For Gil in his perennial darkness those repetitive sounds were like some monstrous cock-
crow, announcing sunrise throughout the day, a sunrise that
never came. Sometimes Gil would take a walk, avoiding all the
lit-up parts of the building. But mainly he was waiting for the
evening, for food, for Roger's caresses.

"The poor kid. Just hope he doesn't let me down. And that
he doesn't get nabbed! What the hell would I do then?"

With the knife Roger had left with him, Gil tried to engrave
his initials in the granite. He slept often, and a lot. On waking,
he instantly recognized his surroundings—knew that he was a
fugitive from the police authorities of all countries in the world,
because of a murder—or two . . . The horrors of his situation
unfolded; when he had become truly aware of his isolation, Gil
had moved into it, by telling himself:

"Gil, Gilbert Turko, that's me, and I'm all alone. In order to
be the real Gilbert Turko, I have to be all alone, and to be all
alone, I have to be all alone. And that means, out in the cold.
Goddamn! The old folks, well, they make me puke! What the
fuck do I care about the old folks? They're dirty bastards! My
old man shot his wad into that great fat cunt of my mother, and
nine months later I crawled out of it. What the hell's that got
to do with me? He just took it out too late, that's all, and there

it was, I had to be born. They can go to hell for all I care, they're just a couple of old shitheads."

He tried to stay as long as possible in this state of sacrilegious fury, as it provided him with an armor of pride and rebellion, made him throw back his shoulders, raise his chin. He hoped it would become his habitual condition: to hate and despise his parents, so as not to be overwhelmed by sorrow in grieving for them. When he first entered into this experience, he allowed himself a few minutes of daydreaming in which he curled up, chin on his chest and hugging himself, to become the obedient and adored child of his parents again. Thus he undid the murder, fantasizing about a loving and simple life that did not include his crime. And then it was time to get back to the demolition job again.

"I wiped him out, and that was the right thing to do. If it had to be done again, I'd do it again."

He made a great effort, killed (or wanted to kill) all feelings of compassion that were still menacing him.

"Poor guy. He's a big bruiser, he's strong, but what has he ever done? Nothing. Goddamn greenhorn," he thought about Querelle. He was able to poke fun at him verbally, but there was a deep and inchoate feeling in him that caused him to respect the young salt whose calm manner, age, and standing in the "milieu" as well as his intact position in society served Gil as a kind of life-saver that held his head a little above the waves of despair. From his second visit on, Querelle had shown himself in a more relaxed mood. He had cracked jokes about death, and Gil had gained the impression that the death of a man was of little importance to this sailor.

"So you don't really think it was such a horrible thing to do, to snuff that sonofabitch?" (When Roger wasn't there, Gil could let himself go a little. He didn't have to play the role of the man.)

"What, me? Listen, buddy, that's not the kind of thing I lose any sleep over. Just think of it. He was bullying you. He was shitting on your honor, man. And you can't do that, to any-body. That gives you the right to kill the bastard."

"That's what I've been tellin' myself. But them judges, they don't understand that too well."

"They couldn't, not in a million years. They're such goddamn fatheads, and even more so out here in the sticks. And that's why you have to keep on lying low. And that's why you need buddies to help you. If you want to live and be a real tough motherfucker."

In the light of the candle and as if looking through a thin sheet of paper Gil saw the little smile on Querelle's face. It gave him confidence. With all his heart he wished to become a real tough motherfucker. (With all his heart—that is to say, Querelle's smile triggered a whirlwind of enthusiasm, a sense of exaltation that made Gil forget even his own body.) Querelle's presence provided some friendly and effective comfort, moving in its own way, as are helpful hints between athletes—even between competitors, sometimes—during an event: "Take a deeper breath" . . . "don't breathe through your mouth" . . . "flex your calves" . . . which indicate all their secret concern for the overall beauty of the action.

"What have I got to lose now? Nothing. I got no parents, no more. Nothing. I better start taking my life in my own hands." Out loud, he said to Querelle:

"I've got nothing to lose. I can do as I please . . . I'm free, now."

Querelle thought it over. He saw, right there in front of him, the suddenly fleshed-out image of himself as he had been five years before. He had killed a guy in Shanghai, accidentally. His pride as a sailor and as a Frenchman had been the motive. It had been a very quick job: the young Russian had insulted him, Querelle lashed out with his knife, taking out one of the other man's eyes. Aghast at the horrible sight, and in order to get rid of it, he then cut his throat. It all happened at night, in a well-lit street. He had dragged the corpse to a dark spot and had propped him against a wall, in a squatting position. Finally, on an impulse, and to humiliate the dead man so as not to be haunted by him, he took a briar pipe from his pocket and stuck it in his victim's mouth.


Madame Lysiane did not grant her "boarders" the right to use black lace underwear. She approved of salmon pink, of green, certainly of beige, but she knew herself to be so beautiful in her own black outfit that she couldn't permit those young ladies to adorn themselves in a similar manner. It wasn't so much because the black enhanced the milky whiteness of her skin: what she liked about it was that it gave her undergarments a certain formality and super-frivolity—and we shall see why. She was standing in her room, undressing, very slowly. As if nailed to the floor in front of the mirror by her high heels, undoing her dress which opened on her left side, the line of hasps stretching from her neck to her waist, the gestures of her right hand, quick and rounded, and in that quickness and roundness, in the liveliness of her fingers, perfect expressions of all that was sugar sweet, yet distinguished and catlike about her. It was a kind of dance, of Cambodian grace. Madame Lysiane loved these movements of her arms, the precise angle of her elbows, and was in every way certain of her superiority over the whores.

"God, can they be vulgar! Do you think Régine can be brought to understand that fringe hair-dos are out of fashion? Not on your life! All of them, and there isn't one exception, all of them seem to think that the clients like them when they look like whores. But that's where they're wrong, so wrong."

She stared at herself dully, while she talked on. Now and again she cast a glance at Robert's reflection in the mirror. Robert was divesting himself of his clothes.

"Darling, are you listening to me?"

"Can't you see that I am?"

He was listening. He admired her elegance and the fact that she had such distinction, compared to the common run of chippies, but he was not looking at her. Madame Lysiane let the fur-trimmed dress slide off her body, down to her ankles. She was literally shedding it. First, her shoulders appeared, white and divided from her torso by the narrow straps of velvet or satin holding up her slip and her breasts under all that black lace and a pink bra; then Madame Lysiane stepped out of the dress, ready for the joys of the bed. Very upright on her extremely high and pointed Louis Quinze heels she advanced toward the bed on which Robert was already reclining. She gazed at him, not a thought in her head. Suddenly she turned round, exclaiming: "Ah!" and headed for her mahogany dressing table. She took off the four rings she wore on her fingers, and then, with motions equally well-rounded, but even more sweeping than befoe, she undid her hair. As the shivers running through a lion's body make desert or jungle vibrate from ground to sky, so her room shook, from the short-pile rug to the last fold of the window curtains, when Madame Lysiane shook her head, her angry mane, her shoulders white as alabaster (or mother-of-pearl): proudly she set out, every night, to vanquish the already conquered male. She came back to the bubbling brook under the palm trees where Robert went on smoking, oblivious to everything but the physical aspect of the ceiling.

"Won't you let me in?"

Casually, he flicked aside the corner of the sheet, so that his mistress could join him on the bed. Such lack of gallantry hurt Madame Lysiane, yet that hurt was one she delighted in every time, because it showed that there still were realms to conquer. She was a courageous, yet vanquished woman. Her physical splendor, the wealth of her breasts and her hair, the total opulence of her body, as it offered itself to men, was, by its very nature (because all opulence is virginal), easily conquered and enjoyed. It is not beauty we are talking about, in her case

Beauty can be an obstacle more fearsome than barbed wire: it can be pointed and barbed, it can kill at a distance, like a burst of gunfire. The opulence of Madame Lysiane's flesh was the exact form of her innate generosity. Her skin was white and soft. As soon as she had stretched out (Madame Lysiane hated the expression "go to bed," and respecting her sense of propriety we won't use it when discussing her, but hope to say a word or two about the "delicacy" of forbidden words), stretched out, she looked around the room. With a slow, circular glance she took in all its treasures, considering every detail: the bureau, the wardrobe with its door mirror, the dressing table, the two armchairs, the oval paintings in their gilded frames, the crystal vases, the chandelier. It was her oyster and the gentle gleam of mother-of-pearl, surrounding herself, who was the royal pearl: the nacre of blue satin, of well-cut glass, of curtains, of wallpaper, of lamps. And the pearl of her bosom and (while thinking of it with pleasure, she could only evoke the other end by assuming a mischievous air, a roguish smile, her little finger in her mouth) and, well, let us say it, the double pearl of her rump. She was happy, and perfectly in line with the tradition of those women they used to call "ruined," "fallen," feckless, bitches in heat, ravishing dolls, sweet sluts, instant princesses, hot numbers, great lays, succulent morsels, everybody's darlings . . . Every night, in order to abandon herself fully and to exhaustion to love and sunshine, Madame Lysiane had to assure herself of her material wealth. Only then could she feel certain that on waking she would find herself in a wonderful chamber, worthy of the curves of her physique, so lavish in its aspect that it would permit her, the next day, to see love disseminated in the warmest corners of this room. Slowly, as if absent-mindedly, and as if they were a wave of liquid, she let one of her legs slide between Robert's hairy calves. At the foot of the bed, those three living feet—trying so very hard for a moment to be the thoughtful brow of this great composite body whose feet, otherwise, bore the features of separate and hostile sexes—three feet joined together, embracing to the best of their clumsy ability. Robert crushed his cigarette out on the marble top of the night table, turned toward Lysiane, and kissed her; but after the first kiss she raised both her hands to his head, held it between them, pushed it back and gazed at it:

"You know, you're beautiful."

He smiled. As he had nothing to say, he attempted another kiss. He did not know how to look at her, not loving her, and this awkwardness resulted in his looking very severe and manly. At the same time, the tremulous intensity of the lovelorn look in his mistress' eyes—that seemed to shatter as it struck his face—made him feel big and strong.

"He can afford to," Madame Lysiane thought.

By which she meant: he can afford to appear impassive, he is such a fiery one. And Robert remained impassive. The already voluptuous flames lit up in the woman's eyes went on battering against, yet caressing, the hard little stones in her lover's face. (Madame Lysiane had very beautiful eyes.)

"My darling."

She moved in for another kiss. Things began to stir in Robert. Gently, and providing him with the reassurance that all the treasures of the room were still his to use, the temperature rose in his dong. Never again—that is to say, until he came— would anything be able to remind him that he had once been a lazy and skinny docker, bored with his job, and that he might well become one again. Forever now he was a king, a Caesar, well nourished and clad in a coronation robe, in the vestments of power that is calm and certain, thus differing from the conqueror's breeches. He had a hard-on. Feeling the touch of his hard and vibrant member, Lysiane gave her blonde flesh the order to quiver.

"You're so wonderful!"

She was waiting for the preliminaries of the real work, from the moment Robert slipped under the covers and started nuzzling around like a truffle-pig in the rich-smelling, dark and nocturnal earth, parted her short hairs and started tickling her with the tip of his tongue. She always wished for this moment, without particularly wanting to think about it. She wanted to remain pure, to remain above the women she had under her command. Although she encouraged them to work on perversions, she could not admit any indulgence in such on her part. She had to remain normal. Her big and heavy thighs were her moral arbiters. She hated the instability of immorality and licentiousness. The knowledge of having such beautiful thighs and buttocks gave her a feeling of strength. They were her citadel. The word we'll use here did not shock her sensibility any longer, she had repeated it so often to herself, ever since she heard a docker make use of it: her "prose." Her sense of responsibility and her self-confidence were firmly anchored in the depths of her "prose."

She clung to Robert who turned his body toward her a few degrees and gently, simply, without helping it along with his hand, put his prick in. Madame Lysiane sighed. She smiled, offering up the velvety night full of stars that extended throughout all of her insides right up to her mouth, as well as her white and pearly skin with its blue veins. She gave herself as usual, yet she was aware—for several days, but particularly that evening—of the pain that the great similarity of the two brothers had begun to cause her. While this worry prevented her from being a happy lover, she still managed a very beautiful flourish of her arm as she swung it up and outward from under the sheet, to put out the light.


*You are alone in the world, at night, in the solitude of an endless esplanade. Your double statue reflects itself in each one of its halves. You are solitaries, and live in that double solitude of yours.*

o          o          o

She couldn't go on. Madame Lysiane sat up, switched on the light again. Robert looked at her, surprised.

"Listen, I don't care what you say, man . . . (Robert's awkwardness, his basic indifference toward women had prevented him from acquiring an even minimally courteous way of addressing them. To speak tenderly to a woman, to acknowledge her femininity, would have made Robert look ridiculous to himself) . . . you're just being difficult. Jo and me, we're the way we are because that's the way we are, goddammit. Right from the start . . ."

"But it does bother me. And I have no reason to keep it a secret."

She was the boss lady. For a long time now that resemblance had tortured and persecuted her lovely flesh. She was the *patronne*. The brothel was a great piece of property. If Robert was a handsome male—one "who could afford to"—she herself was a strong female, strong by virtue of her money, her authority over the girls, and the solidity of her prose.

"It exhausts me! it exhausts me, to think about how alike you are." She suddenly heard herself, plaintive as any weak little woman.

"Now you just stop that, do you hear me. I'm telling you, there ain't nothing one can do about it."

Robert sounded angry. At the beginning of the scene he had thought, mistakenly, that his mistress was alluding to some very tenuous sentiments that only a woman as distinguished as herself was able to experience, but as she kept on about it, he became annoyed.

"I can't help it, how could I. Back when we were little kids they couldn't tell us apart."

Madame Lysiane drew a deep breath, as if preparing for her very last sigh. Before he opened his mouth and while he was saying what he had just said, Robert knew, although vaguely, that it would hurt her terribly, but while he didn't really want to do that, maliciously, with a clean yet obviously dim conscience, he brought up new details in order to make his mistress suffer while at the same time he strengthened his own position and cut himself off from the world to be with Querelle, whom he became profoundly aware of within himself, for the second time in his life. Madame Lysiane both refused to hear and provoked those further revelations. She *waited* for them. She wanted them to become ever more monstrous. Together (without being fully aware of it), the two lovers knew that a return to health would only be possible once they had managed to extract all the venom, all the pus. Then Robert came up with a terrifying phrase that contained the notion of his and his brother's being merely *one*: ". . . yeah, even when we were little kids, they always mistook us, *one for the other*. We used to wear the same duds, same pants, same shirts. Had the same little mugs. No way of getting around that." He detested his brother—or thought he did—but now he put a great deal of effort into identifying with him, strengthening their relationship—a relationship stretching so far back in time that the mental image was of a blob of molasses, as it were, containing and confusing their two bodies. At the same time Robert was afraid of having Madame Lysiane discover what he, Robert, regarded as his brother's vice: this made him exaggerate the nature of their relationship—make it appear, while retaining the straightest of faces, like a rather demoniacal affair.

"I have it up to here, Robert! I don't want to hear any more about your filthy doings!"

"What filthy doings? There weren't any. We're brothers . . ."

Madame Lysiane was surprised, herself, at having brought up the notion of "filth." Obviously, there was nothing wrong (the way one says "wrong" when meaning "that's not right") in the mere fact that two brothers looked alike; the true evil consisted of that quicker-than-the-eye trick by which two beings were turned into one (a trick that is called love, when it involves two disparate beings), or which, by the magic of a single love, divided a single being into two. Her love—and Madame Lysiane's feelings balked at the word "for": her love for Robert —or for Querelle? For a second, she became confused:

"Yes, your filth. Exactly that, I'm telling you: your filth. You think I was born yesterday? I haven't been running a *maison* all these years for nothing. I'm fed up, that's all."

She directed her final remark to God and even beyond, to life itself, so cruelly hurting the warmth and whiteness of her flesh and soul that had been reared on the milk of human kindness. Now she was sure the brothers loved each other so greatly that they had deemed it necessary to find a third person to disengage them and to provide a diversion. She was overcome by shame at seeing herself as this person, although she did not believe it for a second. At the end of her little speech, her voice turned both accusing and plaintive. She was really praying.

"You only have eyes for one another. I don't exist any more. I just don't exist! What does that make me, tell me? And how could I ever get between you two? Tell me, now, tell me! Well?" She was weeping. It pained her to be shouting so loudly, yet not loudly enough. Her voice had risen to an ever sharper pitch, without turning shrill. Robert lay smiling at her.

"You think that's funny? You, dear sir, you live only in the eyes of that brother of yours. Your Jo. That's his name, isn't it? Jo? That's where your heart is, sir: in your brother."

"Come on, Lysiane, take it easy. That ain't the kind of stuff you want to see in print."

She flung the covers aside and disembarked. Robert became aware of the room, its sweetness and its snarl. All its treasures converged to come to her aid, but then they retreated again, very quickly, as if washed away by a wave of distress. Pale and upright Madame Lysiane stood in the midst of her dwindling *meubles*. Fury lit a glimmer of true intelligence in Robert's head. He searched for and found its causes: his mistress was hateful and ridiculous.

"You finished bitching?"

"Your brother. You live in one another."

Robert's abrupt tone and his suddenly quite inhumanly hard eyes hurt her most cruelly. She hoped he would soon reach a high point in his anger that would allow him to spew out, all over those sheets, all his love for his brother and for their alikeness.

"And of course there's no room for me. You know there's no way I could pass between you two. You just leave me standing there. I can't squeeze through, I'm too fat for that . . . That's right, that's right—I'm too fat!"

Standing there on the carpet, bare feet flat on the floor, her physique appeared no longer as imposing as it had when she was wearing her heels. The width of her hips didn't seem to make any sense now, as it did not sustain and balance the heavy folds of some silken material. Her breasts looked less aggressive than before. She became immediately aware of all this, and also of the fact that anger can only be expressed in the tragic manner, which requires the buskin and unfolds only in a well-supported, not in the least pendulous body. Madame Lysiane regretted the passing of the regal era in women's fashions. She missed those corsets, bustles, whalebones that stiffened the body, making it appear both ferocious and authoritative enough to hold the baser instincts in check. She would have liked to be able to squeeze into a pink corset, bending its hard yet flexible stays, and feel the four garters dangling against her thighs. But she was naked, barefoot on the carpet. She felt monstrously inconsistent, falling apart desolate: "So I'm to be shamed into feeling like some fat frump in carpet slippers? But I am divine . . ." Then her mind became instantly clouded with the vision, clear yet indescribable even to herself, of two sinewy and muscular bodies confronting the soft and crumbling mass of her own, overly corpulent one. She stepped into her shoes and regained a little of her proud bearing.

"Robert . . . Robert . . . but Robert, look at me! I'm your

lover. And I love you. You just don't understand how I *feel*
. . ."

"I've got nothing else to say about that. What do you want,
for crissakes. You're making mountains out of molehills."

"But my sweet cabbagehead, I just want you to be the one
and only. What makes me so unhappy is to see there are two of
you. I'm afraid for you. I'm afraid you'll never be able to be
yourself. Just think about that."

She stood naked under the lighted chandelier. At the corner
of his mouth Robert still retained the last vestige of a smile.
But his eyes were somber, as he stared at Lysiane's knees and
through them at some very distant horizon.

"Why did you say we did filthy things? That 'you were fed
up with our filth'?"

Robert's voice sounded as remote as his gaze, and as calm;
but Lysiane, who had studied her lover's reactions, heard in it a
willingness to embark upon the explication of geometrical
theorems; within that voice was sounded an instrument—or
rather, an organ—whose function it was to *see*. With that voice
went an eye that was determined to pierce the darkness. Lysiane
did not answer.

"Well? That's what you said, dammit. What filth were you
talking about?"

The voice was still calm, and it was a strange feeling for
Robert to discuss such accusations so reasonably. At first, he
found it hard to discern the components. The notion of his
brother was completely invisible, only the idea of those "filthy
doings" was present. Yet Robert wasn't thinking: his stare was
too rigid, his body too motionless for him to be able to think
intelligently. He did not know how to think. But the deliber-
ateness of his speech, its apparent calm (though there were
tremors of some almost imperceptible emotion), and the repeti-
tion of the word "filth" increased his confusion. He lay spellbound, as if by some litany of misery whose refrain echoes

through the most secret reaches of our pain. The idea of filthy doings embarrassed him, offended his family feelings. Mournfully he said to himself: "Well, there goes the family, down the drain!" He did not know how, but he knew he was guilty, and to a considerable degree.

Lysiane said nothing. Suddenly she looked stupid and helpless. Uncomprehending, she looked at her lover talking to her from the bottom of the ocean. She was afraid of losing him. Every time he was alone with himself, and especially when he went on his twilight walks to prowl round the hiding place of his treasure, that docker's exclamation kept rolling round his brain: "Wow, what a piece a ass! Wanna try it?" When he was striding over the grass, under the trees, in the fog, sure-footed and looking impassive, he knew that something inside him kept on worrying those words like a bone. He had been violated. He was a Little Red Riding Hood, and a big bad wolf, much stronger than he, had put his paw into his little basket; he was a sweet flower girl, and a street urchin came and stole his carnations, laughing and kicking the display to pieces, and wanted to make off with his treasure—which he was now coming close to: in his inmost heart, Querelle was afraid. He felt a spasm of anguish in his stomach. Madame Lysiane watched Robert as he was lugubriously digesting his own verbal symbol of hurt, like some pill that would dissolve him. She was afraid of such a dissolution.

"But that's what you said, filthy things."

"So I said it, so what, it doesn't mean anything. Oh, darling, I'm so unhappy."

He looked at her. She had lost her authority of womanhood, of being the lady of the house. She had been declawed. Her face was soft now. She was merely a middle-aged woman, with no make-up on, no glamor, but brimming with tenderness, a bursting reservoir of tenderness that wished for nothing so much as to overflow into the room, over an entranced Robert's feet, in long, hot waves, in which little sly fish would then sport about . . . Lysiane shivered.

"Why don't you get back in."

The scene was over. Robert pushed up close to his mistress. For a moment, he didn't know whether he was her son or her lover. His closed lips were glued to her still-powdered cheek, now wet with tears.

"I love you so, my darling! You are my man."

He whispered: "Switch the light off."

His feet were ice cold. At the end of their reunited bodies, their temperature alone prevented them from immediately plunging into that intoxication whence there is no emerging. He moved even closer to her. Madame Lysiane was glowing like a coal.

"I'm all yours, you know, my darling."

She had made her decision, and to make certain that it was not in vain, Madame Lysiane made her voice as inviting as possible. That evening, a veil was finally torn within her, that had resisted all her years. By sacrificing her modesty at the age of forty-five, she lost her true virginity, and like any virgin, she was at that moment ready to engage in previously unheard-of obscenities.

"Let's do what you want, darling."

And in another sigh, as all offertory phrases are short and a little breathless, she added:

"The way *you* like it best."

Almost imperceptibly, her body began to move farther down under the sheets. In her love for Robert she had realized that if she wanted to join her life to the life of those ridiculously indistinguishable brothers, she herself had to descend back to the caves, in order to return to an undecided, protoplasmic, larval state that would enable her to fit in better between the two others, to finally mingle with them, like the egg white of one egg with the whites of two other eggs. Madame Lysiane's love had to melt her down, to reduce her to zero, destroying that moral armature that made her into everything she was and lent her its authority. At the same time she felt ashai꞉d and wished she could cling to a less monstrous man than this single half of a double statue was, a man who knew how to take care of money, who had no other preoccupations but those arising out of his everyday existence; she felt a vague nostalgia for Nono. But then again, it was a great comfort to be thus conquered and dedicated to slave's work; it gave her a new and truer, more essential life. Her mouth glued to the neck tendon of her lover she whispered:

"My dear cabbage, you know, darling, I'll do what you want."

Robert squeezed her hard, then relaxed his grip a little to allow her to continue her slide down his body. She moved on, slowly, and Robert's body stiffened as it moved up to meet her. Lysiane went on down. Robert rose. Lysiane again, and then Robert, finally decisive, imperious and urgent, took hold of her shoulders and pushed her down. She took his whole cock in her mouth and swallowed the jism. Robert made no sound: he was a man, he didn't "let himself go." By the time her face had reappeared above the covers, the light of dawn came trickling in through the curtains that had not been drawn quite shut. She looked at Robert. He was calm, indifferent. Through the strands of hair falling over her face she smiled at him, such a sad smile that Robert kissed her to console her (she understood that, and it made her feel quite desperate). Then he got up. And then she knew, full force, that everything *had* changed: for the first time in her life, after making love—after making a male happy—she did not hasten to wash herself, to get up with her lover and to use the bidet. The strangeness of such a situation troubled her: there she was, lying on the bed—having the bed all to herself—while Robert went to wash. Besides, what would she have had to wash? To rinse her mouth, to gargle, would have seemed ridiculous, after swallowing the spunk. She felt dirty. She watched Robert performing his ablutions, lathering his cock so its tip vanished from sight, then rinsing it, carefully drying it. A bizarre idea flashed into her mind, but did not amuse her overmuch:

"He's afraid of getting poisoned by my mouth. It's he who spurts venom, and it's me who poisons him."

She felt lonely, old. Robert went on washing himself at the porcelain hand basin. His muscles were in motion, jumping about in his shoulders, arms, calves. The daylight grew brighter. Madame Lysiane tried to visualize Querelle's body; she had only seen him in his sailor's uniform. "It's the same . . . but that isn't possible, surely there's some part . . . maybe his prick is different . . ." (and we shall see the development of that symptom). She was very much alone and tired. Robert turned around, calm, solid, centered in his brother, centered in himself. She said:

"Why don't you open the curtains."

It had been her intention to add the word "darling," but was prevented from it by a kind of humility arising out of her feeling of uncleanliness: she did not want to blemish this man, so radiant, so dear by virtue of the night's revelations and the gentling effect of sexual satisfaction, by any insulting intimacy. Without noticing the omission, Robert pulled the drawstring of the curtains. The pale daylight undid the room, as one says someone's face is "undone" by the signs of a grave disease, by great nausea. She felt the need to die, that is to say, her left arm turned into a huge shark's fin, and she longed to wrap herself in it. Thus Lieutenant Seblon dreamt of wearing a wide black cape, in which he could wrap himself, and under the folds of which he could masturbate. Such a garment would set him apart, give him a hieratic and mysterious appearance. A creature without arms . . . We read, in his diary:

*To wear a pelerine, a cape. To have no arms any longer, hardly any legs. To become a larva again, a pupa, while secretly retain-*

*ing all one's limbs. In such a garment I would feel rolled up inside a wave, carried by it, curled up in its curve. The world and its incidents would cease at my door.*

The murders Querelle had committed, his feeling of security among them, the calm with which he executed them, and his tranquility in the midst of such dark shadows—these had turned him into a serious-minded man. Querelle was so certain of having attained the limits of danger that he had nothing to fear from a revelation of his habits. There was nothing anyone could do about him. No one could have discovered his errors, for example, by finding out the meaning of certain markings on trees along the old ramparts. Sometimes he took his knife and cut a highly stylized design of his initials into the humid bark of an acacia. Thus all around the secret hiding place where his treasure slept—like a dragon—there stretched a net, whose impenetrability was due to the special secret of its fabrication. Querelle kept a double watch on himself. He returned their significance to degenerate rites. The oriflamme, the embroidered altar cloths used to be a continuous offering: the number of points and of threads corresponded to so many thoughts offered up to the Holy Virgin. Around his own altar, Querelle embroidered a protective veil, with his own monogram on it, equivalent to the gold-thread "M" on blue altar cloths.

When Madame Lysiane found herself confronted with Querelle in the flesh, she could not help staring at his crotch. She knew her vision could not pierce that navy cloth, yet her eyes had to reassure themselves of that impossibility. Perhaps, tonight, the material would be of a lesser density, perhaps cock and balls would be outlined clearly, and Madame Lysiane would thus be able to note the profound difference between the two brothers. She also wished that the sailor's member would turn out to be smaller than Robert's; yet there were times when she imagined the reverse, even dared to hope for it.

"But then, what difference would that make? If it's him (Robert) who has the smaller one, that would just be . . ." (she couldn't find the right word, but felt a twinge of maternal tenderness toward a Robert less well-endowed than his brother).

". . . I could mention it to him, to make him mad . . . But then, if his eyes turned sad, and he replied to me, in a light and confident tone: 'Well, it isn't my fault'—if he said that, it would be a very serious business. It would mean that he recognized his infirmity and placed himself under my wing, having broken his own. What would I do then? If I kissed him straightway, and smiled the way he smiled at me, the way he kissed me when I pushed my tousled head up from under the sheets—then he would know how it hurts to be pitied, by a creature one loves. Does he love me? I'd go on loving him, I would—more tenderly, but not so passionately."

Querelle flipped his cigarette into the air. It landed some distance away, yet quite close enough to lie there like a small white stick of dynamite, still smouldering, the fateful sign that war had been declared, that it was "out of his hands," even if its burning a little further would lead to some cataclysm. Querelle did not look at it, but he knew what he had thrown away there. The gravity of his gesture became conscious to him, and it forced him—irresistibly, now that the gauntlet had been thrown—to proceed straight ahead. He put his hands into his pockets, the diagonal ones on his belly, and said, staring at Mario with a fixed and malicious frown, taking care to pronounce his words very clearly:

"What are you trying to say? Yeah, you. What is it you're trying to tell me? Asking me if you could take Nono's place."

The sailor's calmness frightened Mario. If he went along with

the course of action he had initiated, he would lose his special
standing as a cop. All Querelle saw in him was a cop trying to
spy on him. With a shrewdness he wasn't quite conscious of,
Querelle decided to counter any suspicions of smuggling, or
even theft (the only ones this cop might have come up with
while visiting La Féria, maybe one of the girls had been gossip-
ing), by piling on the most tragic elements. He had to make the
most out of this one simple opportunity, in order to hide the
murder—the idea of which, however fleetingly, always is on a
cop's mind. He had to provoke the detective in the lower
regions, then to defend himself with bravura. Thus Querelle
started out by appearing vulnerable in a certain way. He
engaged Mario's attention by a thousand pyrotechnics: in the
tone of his voice, the clenching of his jaws, his dark look, the
furrows on his face.

"Well . . . Would you explain that?"

Mario could have restored peace by simply saying something
along the lines of "I just wanted to know if you had any goodies
for me," but the strength he sensed in Querelle communicated
itself to him and gave him, if no greater degree of physical
vigor, more courage and a greater sense of purpose. Querelle's
attitude, frightening in its unexpectedness, his resolute "cool"
bespoke a manliness Mario welcomed, and fervently, as it prevented him from just fading away on some noncommittal note
of retreat. *Querelle reinforced the cop in him.* Looking Querelle
straight in the eye, the sparks flying off his voice to mingle with
those that had issued out of Querelle's mouth and still hung in
the air (as it were), Mario gave an answer:

"I said what I said."

There was no immediate reaction to that from Querelle.
Tight-lipped he stood there, breathing heavily through his nose,
making the nostrils quiver. Mario thought how wonderful it
would be to stick one's prick into such an angry tiger. Querelle
allowed himself a few seconds to scrutinize Mario, to hate him
a little more, and to limber up his physical and moral muscles

before the real fight. It was necessary, he knew, to concentrate all his energy on this incident, caused by a suspicion that he was a thief or a smuggler, so that any idea of his being a real criminal would expire of its own accord, for lack of sustenance, the other one's energy having been used up on those other, boring ideas. He parted his lips and the wind rushed in with torrential strength, with the plenitude and cylindrical exactitude of a nice large-caliber prick.

"Is that so."

"Yeah."

Querelle's stare poked Mario in the eyes like the spoke of an umbrella:

"If that's all right with you, maybe you can step outside. I've got to talk to you."

"Sure, let's go."

Mario strove to sound as much as possible like the tough guys with whom he liked to associate. They went outside. Querelle turned in the direction away from the city and walked a few steps in silence. It was dark. Beside him, perhaps half a step behind, Mario walked hands in pockets, his left clutching a crumpled handkerchief.

"How far we going?"

Querelle stopped, looked at him.

"What is it you want from me?"

"As if you didn't know."

"What proof have you got?"

"Nono told me about it, what more do I need? And if you let Nono screw you, why should I act all coy about it?"

Querelle felt the blood rush to his heart, from the very points of his fingertips. In the dark, he turned so pale he looked almost transparent: this cop was no cop. Querelle himself was neither a murderer nor a thief: there was no danger. He opened his mouth to burst into laughter. He restrained himself. An enormous sigh rose from his innards, up into his throat, to shut his mouth like a wad of cotton. He wanted to kiss Mario, give himself to him, sing and shout: and he did all those things, but within himself, and in one second.

"Oh, I see."

He sounded hoarse. To himself, he sounded raucous. He turned away from Mario and took a few steps. He didn't want to be heard clearing his throat. He felt that the detective's excitement had to be good for something; it might provoke the unfolding of another drama just as necessary—perhaps even more so—as the one that had not taken place. It had to be the solemn musical accompaniment to the thunderstorm. Mario had appeared so determined, under such severe stress: and all the while had been thinking about a totally different matter. That meant that his true preoccupation with Querelle involved considerable tension.

"No need to turn this into an expedition to the North Pole. If there are games you don't like to play, you just have to say so."

"Yeah, that's right . . ."

Querelle scored a humdinger on Mario's chin. Happy to be fighting (with his bare hands), he knew for certain that he would not have to get the better of anything but what could be beaten to submission by fists and feet. Mario blocked the next blow and replied by socking Querelle in the mouth. Querelle retreated. For an instant he hesitated, then pounced. For a few minutes the men fought without a sound. Coming out of their clinches they knew they could have withdrawn to outer limits that would have put a stop to the fight, but they remained at a distance of two meters, watched each other, and then suddenly flew at each other again. Querelle was pleased to be fighting a cop, and he knew already that this fight, in which, due to his youth and good condition, he was doing very well, was comparable to the coquetries of a reputable young girl who went on protesting right up to the moment of penetration. He made himself go through the most courageous, the toughest, the manliest motions—not in the hopes of disgusting Mario, nor to

make Mario believe he had been mistaken—but in order to
make him realize that he would have to vanquish a real man, to
tire him out slowly, to take him, then, with care, to slowly *pluck*
away his male attributes. They went on fighting. The nobility of
Querelle's stance inspired Mario to comparable fairness. At first,
seeing that he didn't cut as dashing a figure as the sailor, the
detective had cursed the other man's style, that very nobility, so
that he wouldn't have to despise himself for not having it. He
wanted to prove to himself that *that* was precisely what he was
fighting against, so as to be better able to beat it down, exalting
and pitting against it his own commonness and heaviness. Thus
Mario took on a new beauty. They were still slugging away at
each other. Querelle was faster on his feet and hit harder.
Mario thought of pulling his revolver and including Querelle's
death in his service record: self-defense, while attempting to
arrest the suspect. Suddenly a marvelous, heaven-scented flower,
buzzing with golden bees, sprang up inside him: outwardly he
was still scrapping, ridiculously hunched-up, looking dark and
gloomy, his mouth twisted, his chest heaving, slow and awkward on his feet . . . He pulled his knife. Querelle guessed at
it before he even saw it in the detective's hand. In the suddenly
changed gestures of the cop—they were now more calculating,
more hidden, feline—in the increasingly tragic stance that
Mario had taken, Querelle discerned an irrevocable and hard-
won decision, a willingness to kill. He did not stop to think
about its underlying reasons, nor even about its gravity, but it
had such significance that the enemy, now armed with a folding
knife instead of the copper's natural weapon, the 6-35 milli-
meter gun, took on a ferocious and human aspect (a hellish
kind of ferocity, totally unrelated to the fight itself, to any idea
of vengeance for the insults they had been hurling at each
other). Querelle was gripped by fear. It was at that very
moment that he actually *saw* the sharp and mortal presence of a
blade, in there among Mario's palpitating and slightly blurred
outline. Only the blade, even when it was invisible, could lend

the clenched fist, the bent arm such sudden lightness, make the enemy appear almost careless and certain of himself, his body like an accordion deflated without visible motion—and not inflated again—to sustain the last long note, in his eyes a look of irrevocably desperate calm. Querelle could not see the knife, yet he saw nothing else, it became a weapon of monumental proportions, by virtue of its invisibility and its potential for the outcome of the fight (which would be two men dead). The knife was not dangerous by virtue of its sharpness: it was the harbinger of nocturnal death. The blade was white, milky, of a somewhat fluid consistency. Its very existence signified murder, and thus it horrified Querelle. Thus, he was frightened by the *idea* of that knife. He opened his mouth and experienced the wonderful, redeeming shame of hearing himself stammer:

"Y-you don't want to cut me with that . . ."

Mario didn't budge. Querelle neither. The thought of blood that was contained in his words, and the hope contained in them, made his own blood circulate a little freer again. He was hesitant to make a move. He feared, so closely linked he felt himself to Mario by a great number of threads, that a single movement (and the gentlest one might release the most fatal mechanism, as it is clear that all fatality depends on a most tenuous equilibrium) might set Mario off. They now stood in the middle of a low cloud of fog in which the knife nestled, invisible but certain. Querelle was completely unarmed. With a voice suddenly gentle, deep, and of a profoundly moving quality, he said to the Prince of the Night and the nearby Trees:

"Listen, Mario, I'm here all alone with you. I can't defend myself . . ."

He had spoken Mario's name in a loud voice, and already Querelle felt himself to be bound to him in great gentleness, by an emotion comparable to the one we may experience on hearing the excited voice of a young boy penetrate the thin partition of a hotel room at night, saying: "You dirty bastard, listen, I'm only seventeen!" He put all his hopes in Mario. At first his words were only a musical phrase, timid, hardly breaking through the silence and the fog, merely a lovely vibration in those two elements; but then it grew stronger, without losing its clarity and simplicity of a catch phrase invented by some ingenious orator trying to bewitch Death itself. Querelle repeated it:

". . . can't defend myself. No way."

One. Two. Three. Four. Four seconds floating down the river of silence.

"You can do what you want, I don't have a blade. If you get me with that, it's all over. Nothing I can do . . ."

Mario didn't move. He felt like a master of fear and of life, it was up to him, to allow it to go on, or to cut it. He was on top of his policeman's calling. He took no great pleasure in his power, for he never paid much attention to what went on inside him and had no desire to explore it. He didn't move because he did not know what move to make. Above all, he was spellbound by this instant of victory, which he would have to destroy for, and by, some other moment, perhaps one that would be of a lesser intensity, would provide him with less pleasure, but would be irreversible as well. Once that came to pass, there would no longer be any choice. Within himself, Mario felt choice hanging in the balance. At last he stood in the center of freedom. He was ready to . . . except that he couldn't remain in this position for long. To shift his weight, to stretch this or that muscle would already be to make a choice, that is to say, to limit himself again. Therefore he had to retain his present state s long as his muscles did not tire too quickly.

"I just wanted you to explain what you meant, I never wanted to . . ."

The voice was beautiful. Querelle found himself in the same spot, that center of freedom, and he realized the danger in Mario's hesitation. It communicated itself to him and gave him the necessary stage fright that inspired his performance, made it look perilous and risky, but also made him invincible. The stage fright could well tumble him down from the flying trapeze which he was hanging onto with cut-glass claws, right above the cage full of panthers. What bizarre spirit-force, represented by a cop in a light blue jersey, tensed to spring, had emanated from Querelle's own body to confront him thus? Querelle had been able to contain this poison without danger to himself as long as it remained within him, or as long as he merely spouted it into the wall of fog. But tonight, his own venom had appeared to threaten him. Querelle was afraid, and his fear reflected the pallor of death, whose workings he knew so well, and he was doubly afraid of having been abandoned by death. Mario folded the blade back into its handle. Querelle sighed, defeated. The weapon created by intelligence had made short shrift of the nobility of the body, of the warrior's heroism. Mario straightened himself and put both hands in his pockets. Facing him, Querelle did the same, but with a slowness he owed himself because of his recent humiliation. They took a step or two toward each other and looked at each other with some embarrassment.

"I never wanted to hurt you. It was your idea to start a fight. I don't give a shit if you're lovers with Nono. It's none of my fucking business. You can do what you please with your asshole, but that's no reason to fly off the handle . . ."

"Listen, Mario, so maybe I am buddies with Nono. And it is my business, right. So there was no call for you to give me that shit back there in the old bagnio."

"I wasn't giving you shit. Just kidding, asking you if we could pretend I was Nono. So what does that mean, I ask you? And there wasn't anybody there, to hear what we were saying."

"So OK, there wasn't anybody there. But you got to realize it ain't no pleasure to listen to cracks like that. Like you said, I have the right to do what I please. That is nobody else's business, and I am big enough to take care of myself. You better get this thing straight, Mario. If you hadn't whipped out that blade, there's no way you could have beaten me."

°     •     •

They walked off into the fog, side by side like brothers, isolated by the mist and by their low, almost confidential voices. They turned left, in the direction of the ramparts. Not only had Querelle lost his fear, but little by little Death, having so strangely abandoned him, returned to his body and strengthened it again with a flexible and unbreakable armor.

"Hell, come on, don't you bear a grudge now. What I said, I meant it to be a joke. Didn't mean no offense. Besides, I didn't fight as dirty as you may think. I did pull that blade, but I could have shot you with my six-thirty-five. I had the right. I could have covered it up. But I didn't want to do it."

Once again Querelle knew it was a copper walking at his side.

He felt very peaceful.

"And Nono, don't you think I know that old sonofabitch? You ask him, some time. When I go to La Féria, I go there as a buddy, not as a cop. Make no mistake, I'm straight. Ain't no one going to tell you otherwise. If they do, don't believe 'em. Myself, I've never been up to any monkey business with boys, never, you hear me. Well, not that that's saying much. You're a Navy guy, old buddy, and we've seen what they can be up to! But I'm telling you, they're real tough guys nevertheless."

"Sure enough. And besides, it ain't all true what they say about Nono, either."

Mario laughed, sounding very delighted, very young. He took a pack of cigarettes from his pocket and without saying anything offered one to Querelle.

"Oh, come on . . . no need to kid me . . ."

Querelle, too, laughed:

"Honest, I'm not trying to kid you . . ."

"I told you, you're free to do whatever you feel like doing. I've been around, you don't have to pretend with me. Your brother, now, that's a different story. He's into the girls, he doesn't put up with the other stuff. You see I know the scene. But let's not talk about it any more."

They had arrived almost at the level of the fortifications, without meeting anybody on their way. Querelle stopped. With the hand holding the cigarette he touched the detective's shoulder:

"Mario."

Staring into his eyes, Querelle went on, in a serious tone:

"I've lain with Nono, I won't deny that. I just don't want you to get any wrong ideas. I'm not a faggot. I like girls. D'you understand what I'm saying?"

"I've got nothing to argue with that. But Nono, or so he says, Nono screwed you in the ass. You can't deny that."

"All right, so he buggered me, but . . ."

"But it ain't worth wasting your breath about it. I can figure things out for myself. You don't have to go on and on telling me what an hombre you are. I know that for a fact. If you were some mincing faggot, you would've lost your nerve when we had that fight. But you're not the kind of guy who loses his nerve."

He put his hand on Querelle's shoulder and gave him a little shove to start walking again. He was smiling, and so was Querelle.

"Listen man, we're old enough to talk. You had your scene with Nono, and that's no crime. The main thing, the way I see it, is that you had a good time, too. Don't tell me you didn't."

Querelle wanted to go on defending himself, but his smile betrayed him.

"Sure, I came. But I don't think there's a guy in the world who wouldn't have."

"See, that's it. You had a good time, and no harm done. I bet Nono spunked like a walrus, too—he's such a hot-blooded guy, and you're damn good-looking."

"Nothing special about my looks."

"Oh, come on, you and your brother . . . I beg your pardon! But Nono, is he a good lover?"

"Come on, Mario, let's change the subject . . ."

But he said that with a smile. The detective kept his hand on Querelle's shoulder, as if leading him to the gallows, gently but irresistibly.

"But why not tell me? Or isn't he too good at it?"

"Why d'you ask me? Is this how you get your kicks? Or are you planning on trying it yourself?"

"And why shouldn't I, if it's good fun? Come on, tell me. How does he go about it?"

"He's pretty good at it. So there. Come on, Mario, you're not trying to get a rise out of me, are you?"

"Hell no, we're just talking. Ain't no one here to listen. Did it feel good, to you?"

"Why don't you try it!"

He laughed, but this time with some embarrassment. He felt nervous, what with the copper's paw on his shoulder and all. Querelle still did not understand that Mario had a crush on him, but his emotions were stirred by those questions, precise as those in an interrogation, by their urgency, by the insinuating tone of voice, by the method that seemed to be pushing for a confession, never mind what it would be. Querelle was aware of the strangeness of the surroundings and of the density of fog and night, further uniting the cop and his victim, together in this solitude that seemed to create a feeling of complicity.

"I can't stand talking about it too much, it gives me a hard-on."

"Wow! No kidding."

Querelle realized that this exclamation (as well as his previous admission that "it didn't disgust him") was only one more move in an entire game that would inevitably lead to an act he had begun to suspect and that would put an end to his sense of freedom. He did not regret that he had agreed to tread this narrow path, but he was amazed at his own cunning, in going along with it, yet being so successful in concealing his own secret desire.

At least he felt a slight sense of shame at performing with a real he-man, without recourse to the pretext of superior strength, an act which he might have dared to try out with, or on, a pederast without letting himself down, or with any man— but then only with the aid of some irresistible pretext.

"So you don't believe me?"

Now Querelle could have simply replied "Yes, I do," thus stopping the game right there. He smiled:

"Horseshit! Tell that to the Marines."

"I swear, it's true."

"You're nuts. I don't believe you. It's too cold."

"Why don't you see for yourself. Put your hand there."

"No . . . I'm telling you, no. You don't even have one, it must've frozen off."

They had stopped again. They looked at each other, smiling, defying their smiles. Mario raised his eyebrows in an exaggerated fashion, wrinkling his forehead, attempting the expression of a young boy totally astonished by the fact of having an erection at such an hour, in such a spot, and for so little reason.

"Touch it, you'll see . . ."

Querelle did not move. By slowly relaxing his smile, which made his upper lip tremble, he caused it to appear more subtle, more mocking than before.

"No, I won't. I'm telling you, it's impossible."

Querelle stretched out his hand, extended his fingers and hesitantly touche  Mario's crotch, but only the material of his trousers. (That hesitation made both of them shiver with anticipation.)

Although both of them knew the game they were playing, they still kept it within the bounds of innocence. They were afraid of abandoning themselves to the truth too precipitately, to rend its veil too soon. Slowly, still smiling, to allow Mario to go on believing in his false naïveté (while knowing Mario didn't believe in it for one minute)—to uphold the pretense that this was merely a joke, child's play, and looking the copper straight in the eye, Querelle undid the buttons: one, two, three. In a voice that he wanted to sound clear but that was vaguely excited he said:

"You were right. Not bad."

"You like it."

Querelle withdrew his hand. Still smiling.

"I told you, I'm not interested in pricks. No matter what size they are."

With one hand still on the sailor's shoulder, Mario thrust his other hand into his pocket and flipped his rod out into the open air. He stood there, legs apart, confronting the sailor who was looking at him and smiling. Querelle whispered:

"Not here. Isn't there some other place?"


Close to his ear, Querelle heard the quiet noise the saliva was making in the detective's mouth. His moist lips were parting, perhaps in readiness for a kiss, the tongue ready to dart into an ear and to flicker about there. They heard the steam whistle of a night train. Querelle listened to its rumbling, almost breathing approach. The two men had arrived at the railroad embankment. It was dark, but the cop's face had to be very close to his own. Again he heard that sharp little noise, now a little hissing and amplified by the freely flowing spittle. It seemed to him like the mysterious preparation for an amorous debauch the likes of which he had never even imagined. He felt a little disquieted by his ability to distinguish such an intimate manifestation of Mario's, to thus perceive his innermost secrets. Even though he had moved his lips, and his tongue inside his mouth, in a completely natural fashion, it appeared to Querelle as if he were smacking his lips at the thought of the ensuing orgy. That quiet spittle-noise in Querelle's ear was enough to isolate the sailor in his own universe of silence that even the vast noise of the train could not penetrate. It rushed past them with a terrifying roar. Querelle was overwhelmed by such a strong feeling of abandonment that he let Mario do what he wanted. The train disappeared into the night, with desperate speed. It was rushing to some unknown destination, some place serene, tranquil, terrestrial—unlike any place the sailor had known for a long time. Only the sleeping passengers might have been witnesses to his making love to a cop: but they just left him and the cop behind like two lepers or beggars on a river bank.

"Hey, now."

But Mario couldn't come. Querelle turned around, abruptly, and squatted down on the ground. As if ordained by fate, the detective's prick plunged into his mouth, just as the train plunged into the tunnel leading to the station.

It was the first time Querelle kissed a man on the mouth. It seemed to him he was pressing his face against a mirror reflecting his own image while letting his tongue run over the harsh surfaces inside a head hewn out of granite. Nevertheless, as it was an act of love, and of forbidden love, he knew that he was committing evil. His erection hardened. Their mouths remained soldered together, their tongues lolling round each other or pricking each other with their tips; neither one of them dared to move on to the rough cheeks, where a kiss would have been a sign of tenderness. Their open eyes met and mirrored expressions of gentle sarcasm. The detective's tongue was very hard.

Querelle's work as a steward neither humiliated him nor lowered his prestige in the eyes of his comrades. Performing all the details of his task with a simplicity that is the true nobility, he could be seen on deck in the mornings, squatting on his haunches, polishing the Lieutenant's shoes. His neck bent, his hair falling over his eyes, he would sometimes look up, the brush in one hand, a shoe in the other: he was smiling. Then he would get up, in one quick motion, return all his utensils to their box with a juggler's speed and go back to the cabin. He walked with quick, limber steps, a steady joy in his body.

"Here you are, sir."

"Very good. But don't forget to put my clothes away."

The officer was too timid to smile. Faced with his joy and this power, he did not dare to show his own happiness, for he was certain that one single moment of abandon would leave him completely at the mercy of the beautiful beast. He was afraid of Querelle. No matter how severe he was, he never succeeded in casting a blight over that body, that smile. Yet he knew his own strength. He was even a little taller than the crewman, but he was aware of a certain weakness lurking in the depths of his own body. It was something almost tangible, and it was sending waves of fear through all the muscles of his body.

"Did you go ashore, yesterday?"

"Yessir. It was starboard watch ashore."

"You could have reminded me of that. I needed you. Next time let me know before you go."

"Aye-aye, sir."

The Lieutenant watched him dusting the desk and folding away clothes. He was looking for a pretext for a chilling remark that would forestall any burgeoning of intimacy. The evening before he had gone to the forward sleeping quarters, ostensibly looking for Querelle to send him on some errand. He was hoping to see him come in or go out in his blue bell-bottoms and peacoat. There were only five men in the quarters, and they rose to their feet as he entered.

"My steward isn't here?"

"No, sir. He's ashore."

"Where does he sleep?"

They pointed out his hammock, and like a wind-up toy Seblon walked stiffly over to it, as if to leave a letter or a note; mechanically, he fluffed up the pillow, as if wanting to take care of the dear absent creature's resting place. With that gesture, as unobtrusive and light as a dandelion seed in the wind, his tender feelings evaporated, and he went out again, feeling more upset than before. So that was where he used to sleep, who was never to lie by his side. He ascended to the bridge and leant on the railing. Surrounded by the fog, facing the city, he was alone here and able to indulge in a reverie about Querelle on his evening out, drunk, laughing, singing with the girls, with other boys—colonial troops or dock workers he had met a quarter of an hour ago. Now and again he maybe walked out of the smoke-filled café and went up to the old fortifications. That was where he soiled the bottoms of his trousers. In his imagination, the Lieutenant witnessed the scene. One day in passing a bunch of crewmen, one of whom was pointing out those stains to Querelle, the Lieutenant had heard him counter that remark by saying, with a devil-may-care air: "Those, those are my medals!" "His medals," indeed, presumably his spew. Querelle's face and body faded away. He disappeared, walking with long strides, proud of his frayed bell-bottoms with their stains at calf-height, gloriously impudent. He went back into the café, drank some more red wine, sang a couple of songs, laughed and shouted and went out again. Several times, at other ports of call as well as at Brest, the Lieutenant had gone ashore to prowl about the districts frequented by sailors, in hopes of somehow participating in the mysteries of shore leave, of catching a glimpse, somewhere in that noisy smoky crowd, of Querelle's shining face. But he owed it to his braid to walk along very quickly, and not to linger and look around except with the quickest of glances. Thus, he saw nothing; the bar and café windows were steamed up to the point of opaqueness, but what he guessed to be going on behind them was all the more exciting.

o        o        o

Insolence is simply an expression of our confidence in our
wit, our speech. Lieutenant Seblon's innate cowardice was
merely due to his physical recoil from any strong male, and to
his certainty that he would be defeated: thus he had to com-
pensate for it by an insolent attitude. At the time of the
decisive scene (which, according to the habitual rules of narrative logic, we ought to have put at the end of this book), his
encounter with Gil at Police Headquarters, he approached the
Police Commissioner in a manner that was high and mighty at
first and then switched to the openly insulting. It was only too
evident that he had recognized Gil as his attacker. He denied
this only out of his adherence to a kind of "freethinking" that
had taken hold of him ever since he had gotten to know
Querelle. It had developed in him, slowly at first, but then
picking up speed, quite vertiginously and devastatingly. The
Lieutenant was more of a freethinker than all the Querelles in
the Navy, he was the purest of the pure. He was able to sustain
his newfound convictions to such a rigorous degree exactly
because they did not involve his body, only his mind. When he
saw Gil sitting on the bench, leaning against a radiator, Seblon
immediately realized what they wanted him to do: incriminate
and thus stamp out this boy. But within himself, a very light
breeze began to blow, down among the grasses ("a breeze,
hardly a zephyr," it said in the diary): it grew stronger, it
inflated him, and finally emerged in generous gusts through his
vibrant mouth—or voice—in a torrent of words.

"Well, do you recognize this man?"

"No, sir, I do not."

"By your leave, Lieutenant—I do understand the reasons you
probably have for saying that, but this is a matter of criminal
justice. Besides, I won't be too hard on him, in my report."

The fact that the cop had recognized his generosity spurred
the Lieutenant on to further sacrifices. It elated him.

"I don't understand what you're trying to tell me there. My deposition is equally based on my concern for justice. How could I accuse an innocent man?"

Standing in front of the desk Gil hardly heard any of this. His body and his spirit disappeared in a kind of gray mist of dawn, which was what he felt himself turning into.

"Do you really think I would not be able to recognize him? The fog wasn't all that dense, and his face was so close to mine . . ."

And that was enough said. A needle shot through the three men's heads, uniting them with the strong white thread of sudden comprehension. Gil turned his head. The mention of his face close to that officer's illuminated his own memory. As for the Commissioner, a quick tremor of intuition revealed the truth to him when he heard Seblon's tone of voice change on the words "his face . . ." For a couple of seconds (if that) a tight sense of complicity united the three men. Nevertheless— nor will this seem strange to any but those readers who have never experienced similar instants of revelation—the police officer tried to suppress this recognition, as if it had been a potential danger. Let us say that he surmounted it. He also buried it, under the thick skin of his mode of thought. In the Lieutenant, the interior theatricals continued, and, so it seemed to him, with ever-increasing success. Now he felt sure that everything would turn out just right. He became more and more attached to the young mason, in a mystical and specific way—the more he *appeared* to be distancing himself from him, not only by denying his identity as the attacker, but then by defending himself against the assumption that he was protect- ing Gil out of a generous impulse. When he negated his generosity, the Lieutenant destroyed it within himself, and all he allowed to remain was a feeling of indulgence for the criminal plus the conviction that he now was a moral partici- pant in the crime. It was this sense of culpability that was to betray him, in the end. Lieutenant Seblon proceeded to insult

the Commissioner. He so to speak slapped him in the face. He
knew that the creation of grave beauty that characterizes a true
work of art often begins in the most despicable kind of ham-
acting. He caught up with Gil, surpassed him. The same
mechanism that had made it possible for Lieutenant Seblon to
say it wasn't Gil who attacked him, had formerly caused him to
appear cowardly and mean in regard to Querelle.

"Come on, buddy! Cough it up, or I'll strangle you! Jewish
combat. Five against one."

He particularly liked that last expression. It fit in perfectly
with his present state of mind. He felt proud of not fearing
anything, of standing there, so safe from reprisals, in his gold-
braided uniform. Such cowardice is a great force. But only a
slight twist is needed for it to turn around to find another
adversary, then finding it in the coward himself. The way he
punished or maltreated Querelle without reason was no doubt
cowardly, but even while he was committing such acts, he was
aware of the presence of a will, or strength—his strength: and it
was this force (discovered, then cultivated, in the center of his
cowardice) that enabled him to insult the police officer. Finally,
carried away on his own generous breath and sustained by the
luminous presence of the actual criminal, he ended up by accusing himself for the theft of the money in question. When he
heard the Commissioner give the detective the order to arrest
him, Seblon hoped they would recognize his prestige as an
officer, but as soon as he found himself in the lockup, feeling
certain that there would be an incredible scandal, he was happy.

Ever since he slew the Armenian, Querelle had always
cleaned out the corpses. It is rare not to find the idea of robbery
following the idea and the act of murder (and of those two, the
act often is the less despicable one). When a young tough hits
a homosexual who has accosted him, he as often as not gets his

wallet as well. It's not that he hits him in order to get his wallet, but he gets his wallet *because he has hit him.*

"Too damn bad you didn't get his dough, I mean that mason. You could have used it now."

Querelle stopped, hesitated. The last words had been said with slight apprehension, noticeable only to himself.

"But how could I? The bistro was packed. I didn't even think of it."

"Well, yeah, that's true. But what about the other one, that sailorboy. You had enough time there."

"But I swear, Jo, that wasn't me. I swear."

"Listen, Gil, I don't give a shit. I didn't come here to give you a bad time. You've got your reasons for keeping things to yourself. That only proves that you're a real tough kid. And when you say so, I believe you. All I was saying was that it don't really make sense to snuff out guys without having *some* benefit from it. So what you want to do, you want to become a real tough sonofabitch, that way too. I'm telling you, kiddo."

"D'you think I could really make it out there?"

"We'll see."

Querelle was still afraid. He thought it best to appear noncommittal. Looking at Gil one was reminded of a young Hindu whose beauty alone prevents his immediate ascension to heaven. His fetching smile, his lascivious look provoked voluptuous ideas in him as well as in others. Like Querelle, Gil had become a murderer by accident—by bad luck—and it would have pleased the sailor to turn the boy into a replica of himself.

"That would be a scream, wouldn't it, to leave a little Querelle here to go on prowling through the fogs of Brest," he thought.

He had to bring Gil to admit a murder he had not wanted to commit, as well as another one, which he was completely innocent of. In such fertile soil he would plant a seed of Querelle, and it would come up and grow. The sailor was aware of his *power*, not over, but *in Gil.* Gil had to see what a murder was. He had to get used to it. And he had to come out of hiding. Querelle got up and said:

"Don't worry, kid. You're doin' all right. In fact, you're doing pretty well, for a beginner, like. Just have to keep on going. I'll tell you what I'll do. I'll go and talk to Nono."

"What, you haven't told him anything yet?"

"Don't worry. You don't think I could just take you to La Féria, or do you? Too many cops around. And you never know with those girls, either. But we'll see what can be done. The thing is not to get too big-headed, you know. Don't think that the big guys will be falling over themselves to meet you, just because you snuffed somebody. You have to get a reputation as a real stick-up artist. What you did was just like a joy-killing. But don't you worry. I'll take care of things. Well, I've got to run now. See you later, kid."

They shook hands, and, as he was leaving, Querelle turned around once more and said:

"What about that little friend of yours, has he been to see you?"

"I'm sure he'll show up any minute now."

Querelle smiled.

"Tell me, he's got a crush on you, that bambino—or am I wrong?"

Gil blushed. He thought that the sailor was pulling his leg, reminding him of the official motive for his killing Theo. It wasn't funny at all. His chest constricted, in a flat voice he replied:

"You're crazy. See, I had a go at his sister once. That's the story. You're nuts, Jo. Don't believe everything they tell you. Cunts is what I like."

"Hell, there ain't nothin' wrong with the kid having eyes for you. I'm a sailorboy, you know, I know what that's like. Well, bye again, Gil. Take it easy."

o     o     o

Returning home, Roger looked at his sister with a feeling compounded of respect and irony. Knowing that it was she whom Gil wanted to find again in him, he tried, maliciously yet naïvely, to imitate her manners, her girlish habits—even gestures like sweeping her hair back over her shoulders, or the way she smoothed her dress when she sat down. He regarded her with irony because he felt happy to intercept Gil's homage to her with his own body, but with respect because she was the repository of those secrets that stirred Gil's soul. In the eyes of his mother, Roger had suddenly grown up, by the mere fact of having been so intimately and directly involved with a crime that had a *vice* motivation. She was afraid to question him, in case she might hear, from her son's lips, some fantastic story in which he had been acting the part of "first lover." She wasn't sure that Roger hadn't, at the age of fifteen, already explored the mysteries of love, perhaps even those of forbidden love, of which she herself was ignorant.

Madame Lysiane was too opulent a lady for Querelle to consider her as his sister-in-law. His imagination rejected the idea of his brother sleeping with such a grand lady. In his eyes Robert was still a smart little kid with a talent for finding soft spots for himself. That part of it didn't surprise Querelle. As for Madame Lysiane, she tried her best to deal with him in a straightforward manner. She was gentle and polite. She knew that he was having an affair with Norbert. Caught in the enchantment of her strange jealousy she gave in to her overriding preoccupation with the essential differences between Querelle and Robert. One evening she was deeply moved by one of Querelle's bursts of laughter: it sounded so fresh and boyish, quite unlike anything Robert could ever utter. Her gaze attached itself to the corner of Querelle's mouth, open wide, disclosing his brilliant teeth, and watched the play of the lines around it, after he had stopped laughing. She knew for certain that this was a happy young man, and it gave her an almost imperceptible shock—caused a little crack to open, through which the incredible *mélange* of her sentiments now flowed freely. Unbeknownst to the women who only saw her calm face, her beautiful eyes, who were always impressed by the melancholy majesty of her bearing, supported as it was by her heavy, ample, in the best sense of the word, hospitable haunches (initially destined for motherhood)—in her, whose bosom appeared so deep and calm, there was a constant swirling, twisting and untangling, for some mysterious reason, of these long and wide black veils, consisting of a soft and opaque material, mourning silks with shadowy folds: there was nothing else going on inside her but this at times rapid, at times languorous to-and-fro motion of those sheets of black, and she could neither pull them out through her mouth to expose them to the sunlight, nor could she blow them out her asshole, like a solitary worm.

"It's ridiculous to arrive at such a state, at my age, and I can't afford to make any mistakes. Not me. Nobody's going to fool Josephine. Just to think of it, in five years I'll turn fifty. Above all, I mustn't throw myself at the mercy of some notion. And it is a crazy notion, of my own making. When I say that *they* resemble one another, to the point where they are just one, in reality 'they' are two. There's Robert, on one side, and Jo on the other."

These tranquilizing daydreams which she indulged in in the daytime and during the moments of respite she granted herself while watching over the transactions in the parlor, were continuously interrupted by everyday concerns. Thus, slowly, Madame Lysiane began to regard her own life, with its thousands of incidents, as something completely stupid and trivial compared to the dimensions of the phenomenon whose witness and stage she had become.

"Two dirty pillow covers? And so what about them? Get them washed. What on earth do they want me to do, do it myself?"

Quickly she abandoned that degrading idea, to return to observing the spellbinding choreography of her black veils.

"Two brothers who love each other so much that they look alike . . . there's one of those veils. There it is. It's moving, gently, unfurled by two naked arms with closed fists, clenched tight inside me. And now it is like a coil. It is sliding. Another one comes to meet it, and it is black too, but of a different texture. And this new veil means: two brothers who look so alike that they love each other . . . And it, too, slides down into the vat, covers the other one . . . No, it is the same one, only turned over . . . Another piece of material, of another shade of black. And it means: I love one of the brothers, only one . . . Another veil: If I love one of the brothers, I love the other one, too . . . I have to go into all this, I have to put my finger on it. But it's impossible to get them out. Do I love Robert? I certainly do, or we wouldn't have stayed together these six months. But that, evidently, doesn't mean a thing. I love Robert. I don't love Jo. Why not? Perhaps I do. They adore each other. Nothing I can do about that. They adore each other: does that mean they make love, as well? But where? Where? They're never together. But that's just it, they take care not to be seen. Where then? In other regions . . . And they've both had that boy . . . That kid, he's their love-boy . . . I'm an idiot, what does one of those dresses matter compared to my veils—but I better give Germaine a piece of my mind for sweeping the floor with her dress. It is a matter of principle. How is it that a woman like me never gets to experience a little peace and quiet?"

Madame Lysiane had waited for love a long time. Males had never excited her a great deal. Only after she had turned forty she developed an appetite for muscular young men. But exactly at a time when she could have achieved happiness, she began to be consumed by a jealousy she was unable to demonstrate to anyone. No one would have understood her. She loved Robert. When she thought of his hair, the nape of his neck, his thighs, her nipples hardened as they were moving forward to their reunion with the evoked image, and all day long, in the feverish joy of an only barely restrained desire, Madame Lysiane prepared herself for nights of love. Her man! Robert was her man. The first one, the true one. Now, if they really loved each other, did they, too, make love? Like pederasts. Pederasts were shameful. To mention them in this brothel was comparable to the evocation of Satan in the choir of a basilica. Madame Lysiane despised them. No one of them ever crossed her doorstep. She only admitted certain clients with bizarre tastes who demanded things one did not otherwise expect women to do, and no doubt these were tainted with a touch of queerness: but it was women they went upstairs with, and so one could assume that it was women they liked. In their own way. But homosexuals—never.

"But what am I trying to do there? Robert's no faggot . . ."

In her mind's eye she saw her lover's regular, tough, composed features—but with incredible speed these faded into an image of the sailor's face, and this again became Robert's, changing into Querelle's, and Querelle, again, into Robert . . . A composite face with an unchanging expression: hard eyes, mouth severe and calm, the chin solid, and over all that, a peculiar air of innocence in regard to the unceasing confusion.

Querelle never dared mention Mario's name. Sometimes he wondered if anyone knew about his escapade with the detective. But why would he brag about it. It didn't look as if Madame Lysiane had heard anything about it. Having met her that first day he walked into La Féria, he had ignored her ever since. But little by little, with her habitual authority, she imposed herself on him and took possession of him, swathing him into gestures and lines of motion whose curves were very wide and beautiful. Those harmonious masses of flesh, that dignified bearing exuded a heat, almost a kind of steam, be-clouding Querelle's senses before he was aware of the witchcraft being worked upon him. Casually he glanced at the golden chain on her breasts, the bracelets on her wrists, and, always vaguely, he felt himself swaddled in opulence. Sometimes he mused, looking at her from a distance, that the brothelkeeper had a beautiful wife, his brother a beautiful mistress; but when she came closer to him, Madame Lysiane was merely a source of warm, amazingly fecund, but almost unreal radiation.

"You wouldn't have a match, Madame Lysiane?"

"Certainly, my dear, I'll get you a light."

She refused the cigarette the sailor offered her, with a smile.

"But why don't you have one? I've never seen you smoking. It's a Craven, you know."

"I never smoke in here. I allow the girls to do it, because it would make a bad impression to be so severe, but I never do, myself. It just wouldn't be class, to have the *patronne* sit there, puffing away."

She did not sound offended at all. She spoke directly, explaining what was self-evident and not open to further discussion. She held out the small flame, to the tip of his cigarette, and she saw Querelle gazing at her. It embarrassed her a little, and without thinking she repeated the phrase she had hit upon from the start, and which had remained in her mouth, stuck to her palate:

"My dear, there you are."

"Thank you, Madame Lysiane."

Neither Robert nor Querelle was sufficiently interested in love-making to experiment with new positions. Yet they did not regard it as a mere occasion of physical satisfaction. In his games with Querelle, Nono saw signs of a violent and some- what flashy lewdness that he recognized in himself. This sailor sprawling on the carpet who presented him his muscular and hairy buttocks, right there in the midst of all the velvet upholstery, performed an act with him that would not have looked out of place in one of those orgiastic convents where the nuns let themselves be fucked by billygoats. It was fun and games, but it sure made a man feel like a man. Looking at the black anus surrounded by brushy hair, so frankly offered up between the long, slightly tanned, heavy thighs emerging from the tangle of pulled-down pants, Norbert opened up his own trousers, raised the bottom of his shirt a little, to really look the devil of a fellow, and stood there for a few seconds and contem- plated himself in this posture, comparable, in his mind, to that of a triumphant hunter or warrior. He knew he was not taking any risks, as no trace of sentimentality marred the purity of his game. No passion, no sir.

"Smells rich," he would say, or "Let's slip it to you," or "What a pretty one."

It was just a game, no problems. Two strapping fellows with smiles on their faces, and one of them—without any drama, no fuss—offered his asshole to the other one.

"Having a good time."

Then there was the added pleasure of cheating the girls. "If they knew what the buddies are doing, spunking around, boy would they start bitching. This sailorboy here, he'll never make a fuss about it. Getting screwed in the ass is what he likes. Nothing wrong with that."

There was also an element of compassion in Norbert's mak- ing love to Querelle. It seemed to him, not that the sailor had fallen in love with him, but that he needed these sessions in order to go on living. Norbert had a certain respect for him— first of all because he had shown himself to be a shrewd dealer when he sold that package of opium, and also because he was a strong man. He could not help admiring the sailor's young and supple musculature.

Querelle felt no affection for Nono, but became aware of something else developing between them, joining him to Nono. Was it because Nono was older? He refused to admit that Nono dominated him by buggering him, although that could be part of it. After all, it is hardly possible to engage, every day, in a game one regards as only that, an amorous game, without ending up being attached to it. But there was some other factor involved in the creation of this new feeling—which was really an atmosphere of relaxed complicity: it consisted of the forms, the gestures, the jewels, the looks of Madame Lysiane, and it included those words she had said twice that very same evening: "My dear." However, after having been wiped out, in every sense, by the detective, Querelle had lost his taste for his games with Norbert. He had given himself one more time, out of habit, almost by accident, but—and Nono's pleasure, which had become too obvious in its manifestations, contributed to this change—he began to detest it. Nevertheless, as it seemed impossible to him to entirely extricate himself, he thought of secretly gaining some advantage of the situation and, first of all, of making Nono pay him for his favors. The *patronne's* smile and gestures seemed to indicate another, dimly perceived possibility. The first idea Querelle abandoned fairly quickly. Norbert was not the kind of guy one could intimidate. We shall see how Querelle did not, however, completely forget the idea itself, and how he applied it to bring about Lieutenant Seblon's downfall.

The newspapers were still discussing the Gil Turko case, "the double murder of Brest," and the police went on looking for the assassin whom the articles presented as a frightful monster whose cunning would enable him to evade justice for a long time yet. Gil's reputation became as hideous as that of Gilles de Rais. As he could not be found, the population of Brest began to think of him as an invisible man: and was that only because of the fog, or was there another and more fantastic reason?

Querelle went through all the papers, and whenever he found one of these stories, he showed it to Gil. The young mason experienced a strange sensation when he saw his own name in headline-size letters, for the first time in his life. On the front page, too. At first it seemed that those words dealt with some-one else as well as himself. He blushed and smiled. His excite-ment turned the smile into sustained, silent laughter, which seemed almost macabre even to himself. That printed name, composed in big fat type, was the name of a murderer, and the murderer to whom it belonged was no more fiction. He existed, in real life. Right next to Mussolini and Mr. Eden. Right above Marlene Dietrich. The papers were talking about a murderer named Gilbert Turko. Gil let the newspaper sink and raised his eyes from the page for a moment in order to see, in himself, in the privacy of his own consciousness, the image of that name. He wanted to get used to the idea, to establish, once and for all, that the name would be written, printed, and read in this fashion for a long time to come. He had to remember it, he had to see it again. Gil made his name (which was a new one, belonging to someone else), and its new and irrevocably defini-tive form, run through the entire night of his memory. He let it roam to the darkest corners, across the roughest terrain, scintil-lating with all its lights, carry its sparkling facets into the most intimate retreats he had within himself, and only then did he look at the newspaper page again. He experienced a new shock at seeing his name there, in such *real* print. And again, a shiver of delightful shame goose-pimpled his body, which now felt quite naked. His name exposed him, it stripped him naked. It was fame, and it was both terrifying and shameful to have entered it through the gate of scorn. Gill had never been altogether used to his own name. Now Gilbert Turko was a person who would forever be grist to the newspapers' mill. But when those articles ceased to be poems, they clearly described a danger that Gil became aware of, even savored, letting himself become totally preoccupied by it, at times; it was then he experienced not only a sharper, almost painful consciousness of being alive, but also a kind of forgetfulness, self-abandon, loss of faith, similar to what he felt when fingering the (no doubt pink) flesh of his hemorrhoids, or when, as a child, he had squatted by the side of the road and written his name in the dust, with his fingers—deriving a curious delight from it, no doubt provoked by the soft feel of the dust and by the rounded shape of the letters; it was then he had forgotten himself to the point of fainting, feeling his heart turn over, wanting to lie down right there on top of his name and fall asleep, never mind the risk of getting run over by a car: but all he had done then was to erase the letters, demolishing their fragile ramparts of dust, gently sweeping the ground with his ten outstretched fingers.

"But anyhow, those judges, they ought to see . . ."

"See what? And what judges? Listen, you're not going to turn yourself in now. That would be one hell of a stupid thing to do. First of all, you've been hiding from them much too long for them not to think that you're guilty. And secondly, you can see what it says in the paper—that you killed one guy who was queer, and another one, a sailor. Not so easy to explain that away."

Gil let himself be won over by Querelle's arguments. He wanted to be won over. No longer did he feel that he was in great danger: on the contrary, he had been saved *by having become permanent*. Part of him would remain because his name, his printed name would remain, escaping justice, being bound for glory. Yet there was a bitter aftertaste. Gil knew he was doomed: his name would always and everywhere be accompanied by the word "murders."

"Well, here's a plan, old buddy. You go out and get yourself a little hard cash, and then you take off to Spain. Or America. I'm a sailor, I can get you aboard a ship. I'll take care of that."

Gil dearly wanted to believe in Querelle. Surely a sailor had to be well connected to all the sailors of the world, to be in secret communication with the most mysterious crews, with the sea itself. This notion pleased Gil. He snuggled up in it, it comforted him, and as he derived a sense of security from it, he was not about to analyze it at all.

"So what have you got to lose? If you pull a stick-up job, and they catch you at it, that won't make any difference at all. What's a stick-up compared to murder?"

Querelle no longer mentioned the murder of the sailor so as not to call forth Gil's denials, not to rouse that sense of true justice that lives in everyone and that might cause him to go and give himself up. Coming from the outside world as he did, calm and collected, Querelle knew that the young mason clung to him with anguished intensity. His anxiety betrayed Gil, betrayed the slightest inner tremor and amplified it, played it out loud, like the needle passing over the grooves of a record. Querelle was able to register all these shifts and fluctuations and made use of them.

"If I wasn't just a sailor . . . but, that's what I am, and there's little I can do to help you. But there's one thing, I can give you some advice. And I believe you can do it."

Gil listened, in silence. By this time it had become clear to him that the sailor would never bring him anything else but a chunk of bread, a can of sardines, a pack of cigarettes, but never any money. Hanging his head, his mouth bitter, he fell to pondering the notion of those two murders. An enormous weariness forced him to resign himself to them, to admit them, to admit that he would henceforth travel the high road to hell. Toward Querelle he felt great anger and at the same time he had absolute confidence in him, though this was strangely intermingled with a fear that Querelle might "turn him in."

"Soon as you got some dough and some new clothes you'll be ready to take the trip."

It looked like a great adventure, and one that the murders had led up to. Thanks to them, Gil would have to dress smartly, more so than he had ever done in his life, not even on Sundays. Buenos Aires, here I come.

"I can certainly hear what you're saying. I sure would like to pull a job, make some dough. But where? Do you know?"

"Right now, here in Brest, I know only one place, a simple breaking and entering scene. There's better ones elsewhere, but here in Brest that's the only thing I'm hep to. I'll go case the joint, and then, if you're ready, we can go do the job together. No sweat. I'll be right there with you."

"I couldn't do it by myself? Perhaps that would be better?"

"You crazy? Forget it. I want to go with you. First time out, you need a buddy."


Querelle was a night-tamer. He had familiarized himself with all the expressions of darkness, he had peopled the dark shadows with the most dangerous monsters he carried within himself. Then he had vanquished them by drawing deep breaths through his nostrils. Thus the night, although it did not entirely belong to him, obeyed his commands. He had become used to living in the repugnant company of his murders; he kept a kind of miniature logbook, a catalogue of blood baths, calling it (only to himself) "my bouquet of mortuary flowers." The log contained maps of the scenes of the crimes. The sketches were primitive. Whenever he found himself unable to draw something, Querelle simply wrote in the word for it, and the spelling was fairly shaky. He was an uneducated man.

· · ·

When he left the old prison for the second time (the first one was his visit to Roger's house), Gil thought that the night and the very vegetation were lurking right in front of the gate, ready to extrude hands that would clamp down on his shoulder and arrest him. He was frightened. Querelle walked ahead of him. They took the narrow path leading toward the Navy Hospital that runs along the walls and ends in the city. Gil tried his best to conceal his fear from Querelle. The night was dark, but that did not really reassure him, because if the night concealed them, it could also conceal other dangers, of a law-enforcement character . . . Querelle felt happy but took care not to show it. As always he held his head very straight in the middle of the upturned, stiff and cold collar of his peacoat. Gil's teeth were chattering. They went into the narrow alleyway joining the prison walls to the esplanade overlooking Brest, close to the Guépin Barracks. At the end of the road lay the city, and Gil knew it. Flush against the great wall of one of the old Arsenal buildings, which were an extension of the old prison, stood a small two-story house. On the ground floor of this building there was a café, the front of which opened up to a street that was at right angles to the one Querelle and Gil were on. Querelle stopped, whispered into Gil's ear:

"See, that's the bistro. The entrance is on the street side. They've got iron shutters. And there's the apartment, up above on the second floor. Just like I told you. It's an easy job. I'm going in."

"What about the door?"

"It's never locked. We'll both go into the hallway. 'Cause there's a hallway, and a staircase. You sneak up the stairs, very quiet, all the way to the top. I'll go into the joint. If anything happens, if the owner opens the door at the top of the stairs, down you come, and fast. I'll take off at the same time, heading back toward the Hospital. But if everything goes right, I'll call you, soon as I've finished. Got it?"

"Sure!"

Gil had never stolen anything. It surprised him how difficult yet easy it was. After looking up and down the fog-shrouded street Querelle, without a sound, opened the door and went into the hallway. Gil followed him. Querelle took his hand and put it on the staircase banister. "Go," he whispered in his ear, then turned away and quickly slid into the space below the stairs. When he estimated that Gil had reached the second-floor landing he began to make a series of very quiet scratching noises. Gil was listening. What he heard was the rumbling of a stagecoach he and the other guys were getting ready to hold up. A shot rang out in the lonely forest, an axletree broke, young girls were raising their veils, and Marie Taglioni went off dancing under the rain-soaked trees, on carpets unrolled by the happy bandits. He pricked up his ears. He heard a hissing whistle in the dark. He understood the message: "Gil, come on, Gil." Slowly, his heart beating loudly, he descended the staircase. Querelle shut the door quietly behind them. Returning the way they had come they walked along in silence. Gil was anxious to know and finally whispered:

"Did you get it?"

"Yup. Let's keep goin'."

They passed through the same masses of fog and darkness. Gil felt the old prison drawing closer, the sense of security returning, calming him down. In his cave they lit the candle and Querelle pulled the loot out of his pocket Two thousand six-hundred francs. He handed half of it over to Gil.

"It ain't no fortune, but what can you do? It's the day's takings."

"But listen, that ain't bad at all! I can get by on that."

"Boy, are you nuts. Where would that get you? You don't even have any threads. No, kiddo, there's more work to do."

"Well, all right. Count on me. But the next time I want to be the one does the job. No use your getting messed up because of me."

"We'll see. Now why don't you just stash that dough."

It broke Querelle's heart to see Gil pocket the money. That pang of pain would serve to justify the double-cross he was preparing for Gil. It wasn't the money he had pretended to steal from a house he well knew to be uninhabited—it would only take him a couple of days to get back a hundred times as much—but it did give him a pain to see Gil go for it hook, line and sinker. Then, every day, Querelle brought him some items of clothing. Within three days he had outfitted Gil in sailor's bells, jersey, peacoat and beret. Roger helped haul each bundle over the sea wall, by the same method employed in getting the opium past customs. One evening Querelle gave him his briefing.

"It's all set. You're not backing out, are you? You better tell me, if you get cold feet at the last moment . . ."

"You can trust me."

Gil was to walk into Brest in broad daylight. The uniform would render him invisible. The police would hardly expect the murderer to take a stroll in the city disguised as a sailor.

"You sure that Lieutenant's an easy one?"

"I told you, he's a little old lady. He looks military and all that, but he ain't no fighter."

The sailor's outfit transformed Gil and gave him a new, strange personality. He didn't recognize himself. In the dark, all by himself, he dressed with the greatest of care. Striving for elegance, he put on the beret, then pushed it back a little, most coquettishly. The charming and forceful soul of the most elegant branch of the armed services entered into him. He became a member of that fighting Navy whose purpose is to grace the shores of France rather than to defend them: it embroiders and strings out a festive garland along the seaboard, from Dunkirk to Villefranche, with here and there a couple of thicker knots in it to mark the naval ports. The Navy is a wonderfully constructed organization consisting of young men who are given an entire education in how to make themselves appear desirable. When he was still working at his trade, Gil used to meet sailors in the bars. He mingled with them, while never daring to hope that he could become one of their company, but he respected them for their membership in that gallant organization. But that night, secretly, to himself only, he was one of them. In the morning he left. The fog was extremely dense. He headed for the railroad station. He held his head low, hoping to conceal his face in the tall collar of the peacoat. It was unlikely that any laborer, one of his old buddies, would cross his path, or that he would be recognized even then, in this disguise. Having arrived in the vicinity of the station Gil turned onto the road that goes down to the docks. The train was due at ten after six. Gil was carrying the revolver Querelle had given him. Would he shoot if the officer yelled for help? He went into the small one-patron *pissoir* that stood next to the guard rails above the sea. If anyone passed by, all he would see was the back of a sailor taking a leak. Gil did not have to fear either officers or policemen. Querelle had arranged everything perfectly. All Gil had to do now was to wait for the train: the Lieutenant would certainly come this way. Would Gil recognize him? He recapitulated all the details of the plan of action. Suddenly he stopped to consider whether he should address the officer familiarly or with the customary respect. "Talk tough, to get the message across." But it would be strange for a sailor to address a superior thus. Gil decided to flaunt formality, but felt some regret that he wouldn't, even on the morning he had donned it for the very first time, be able to know all the pleasures and consolations of his uniform, consisting largely of one's being able to forget oneself in the profound security hierarchy and ritual provide. Hands in the pockets of his peacoat, Gil stood and waited. The fog dampened and cooled his face, softened his wish to be brutal. Querelle was probably still sleeping in his hammock. Gil heard the train whistle, clatter across the iron bridge, pull into the station. A few minutes later occasional silhouettes flitted by: women and children. His heart was thumping. The Lieutenant appeared in the fog, all alone. Gil stepped out of the *pissoir*, holding the gun pointed at the ground at his side. He caught up with the Lieutenant, stopped him.

"*No noise.* Give me that satchel or I'll shoot."

Immediately the Lieutenant understood that he was here given the opportunity to act in a heroic manner, and he even regretted the fact that he would not have any witnesses to report back to his men, above all, to Querelle. While understanding also that such an act would be useless, he saw himself dishonored forever if he didn't accomplish it, and realized by looking at the eyes and the pale, pinched beauty, by considering his tone of voice, that there really was no way out. (Whatever happened, the sailor would get the money.) He hoped for the intervention by some other passenger, but did not really believe, even feared that possibility. All this flashed into his mind in one piece. He said:

"Don't shoot."

Maybe he would be able to wrap the sailor in the folds of a tight dialectic, truss him up verbally and then slowly turn him into a friend. He was excited. The boy was so young, so audacious

"Don't move. And shut up. Hand it over!"

In the still center of his fear Gil was calm, very calm. It was his fear that gave him the courage to talk in this tough and brutal fashion. It, too, had given him the insight that sticking to such short exclamations he would avoid any attempts to "talk it over."

The Lieutenant did not budge.

"The money—or I'll blast your guts!"

"Go ahead."

Gil shot him in the shoulder, hoping that would make him drop the satchel. The gun made a terrifying lot of noise in the small, luminous cavern their bodies carved out of the fog. With his left, Gil grabbed the carrying strap of the satchel and pulled at it, pointing the gun's muzzle straight at the officer's eye:

"Let go, or I'll kill you."

The Lieutenant relinquished his grip and Gil, satchel in hand, staggered a step back, turned round and was off to a flying start. He disappeared in the fog. Fifteen minutes later he was back in his hiding place. The police did not regard him as a possible suspect. They made enquiries among the sailors but found out nothing. Querelle did not have to worry one minute.

As Querelle became more and more important, Roger sadly watched Gil drifting away from him. When he went to see him, Gil no longer had any caresses for him. Gil simply shook his hand. Roger had the feeling that everything was now happening above his head, above his youth. Without hating him he was jealous of Querelle. It had pleased him to have his own small degree of importance, in such a dramatic sequence of events. Finally, having fallen in love with the *Doppelgänger* beauty of the two brothers, he himself withdrew from Gil. He was caught in some kind of complex system of transmission belts, and the faces of Querelle and Robert became necessities for the fulfilment of his happiness. He lived in the anticipation of another miracle that would bring him into the presence of both those young men, in a situation where he would be loved by both of them. Every evening he went long stretches out of his way to pass by the vicinity of La Féria—which to him truly seemed like a chapel; the day he had gone to see Gil at work he had heard one of the masons say:

"Me, I go to Mass at that chapel in the Rue du Sac."

Roger remembered the mason's great horselaugh, his big white hand holding a trowel, plunging it into a trough filled with mortar with sharp, regular movements. Roger had not cared to ask himself what rites the big tough bruiser might practice in that chapel of his: Roger knew the brothel by location and reputation, but now the sight of La Féria excited him because he knew it to be the temple of that god (that bicephalous monster on his mind, although he had no name for it) consisting of two persons, a bizarre object of veneration exercising its spells on his young soul with devastating force; and no doubt the masons went there, too, to render homage to it, not carrying flowers, but their own fears and hopes. Roger also remembered that after this joke had been uttered (he did not know this, but it hadn't been merely a joke), one of the other masons shrugged his shoulders. At first Roger had been surprised by the fact that a one-liner referring to the brothels could offend the sensibilities of a laborer whose shirt, open to the waist, displayed a large, hairy chest, whose hair was stiff and covered with chalk, dust and sunlight, whose chalk-powdered arms looked strong and hard—who was, in short, such an hombre. That shrugging response to the joke and the laughter was now a disturbing element in the otherwise certain affirmation of the existence of that secret cult. It introduced the sign of doubt into the faith, doubt and scorn, perennial fellow travelers of all religious belief.

Roger went to see Gil every day. He brought him bread, butter, cheese, things he bought in a distant dairy close to the church of Saint-Martin, in a quarter where nobody knew him. Gil became more and more demanding. He knew that he was wealthy. His fortune, hidden close by, gave him sufficient authority to tyrannize Roger. He had finally become accustomed to his recluse existence, made himself comfortable in it, moved within its limits with total confidence. The day after his attack on the Lieutenant he tried to find out from Roger what the newspapers were saying. Querelle, however, had told him not to tell the young kid anything about these jobs. Not being able to tell him, nor to get anything out of him, Gil grew furious with Roger. Then he realized that the boy was withdrawing from him.

"I've got to go now."

"Sure, sure. Now you're just dropping me!"

"I am not dropping you, Gil. I come here every single day. But my old lady gives me a rough time whenever I come home late. It wouldn't be so great if she decided to lock me up in the house."

"Yeah, yeah, that's just bullshit. You know what I have to say about all that . . . But get me a liter of red wine tomorrow, all right?"

"All right, I'll try."

"I wasn't telling you to try. I told you to bring me a liter of the red."

Roger did not feel in the least hurt by all this bullying. Like the pestiferous air in the cave, the bad temper emanating from Gil grew thicker every day, so that Roger was unable to distinguish the progression of its density. Had he still been in love, he would no doubt have found a vantage point from which to assess the changes in his friend's attitude, but now he just arrived there every evening like an automaton, obeying some kind of rite whose profound and imperious meaning has been forgotten. He did not even think of breaking out of this drudgery, he only thought about Robert's and Querelle's double countenance. He lived in the hope of one day encountering the brothers together.

"I've seen Jo. He tells you not to worry. He said everything's hunky-dory. He'll come and see you the next two or three days."

"Where did you meet him?"

"He was coming out of La Féria."

"What the hell are you hanging out there for?"

"I wasn't, I was just passing by . . ."

"You've got no business there, it ain't even on your way. Maybe you're thinking of getting in with the tough guys, eh? That's no place for a little shitter like you, La Féria ain't."

"I told you I just happened to walk past it, Gil."

"Tell that to the Marines."

Gil realized that he no longer meant the world to Roger: once the kid was out of the old prison, he lived a life in which there was no room for Gil at all. He was afraid that that life might turn out to be more exciting than his own. In any case, not being attached to Gil any longer, Roger could move about unscathed and participate in festivities from which he, Gil, was excluded, in the rooms of the brothel where the two brothers came and went, from one room to another (whose arrangement and furnishings he mistakenly visualized as corresponding to the dilapidated façade of the building), looking for each other, finding each other (and their meeting would give rise to a command) only to part again, to lose themselves and look for each other in the great to-and-fro of women dressed in veils and lace. Gil managed to see the two brothers standing there, holding hands and smiling at the boy. They had the same smile. They extended an arm to reach for the boy, who came along willingly, and held him between themselves for a moment. At home, Roger could never mention the two brothers, couldn't talk about a pimp and a thief. One word about such people and his sister would have reported it to his mother. His infatuation, however, created such violent pressure inside him that he was running the risk of giving himself away at any moment. In any case, he thought about them in such awkward and childlike terms; one day he exclaimed:

"The Gallant Knights!"

But he found it hard to imagine himself involved in numerous deeds of derring-do in their company. Only certain images formed in his mind, and in these he saw himself offering the reunited brothers something—he did not know what it was, only that it belonged to the most precious part of himself. He even had the notion of transmitting a double image of his own face and body to Jo and Robert, on a mission to make them accept this friendship the unique and essential person, who remained in his room all the while, was offering them. Querelle returned one evening when he knew Roger would not be there.

"Well, old hoss, we're all set. Everything's ready. I got you a ticket to Bordeaux. The only thing is, you have to catch that train at Quimper."

"But what about my clothes? I still haven't got any."

"That's just it, you'll get some in Quimper. You can't buy anything here anyway. But now you've got money, you'll get by. Five thousand, for godssakes. You can take it easy for a while."

"I've been lucky to have you on my side, you know, Jo?"

"That's for sure. But now you've got to watch out so's you won't get caught. And I guess I can count on you not to spill the beans even if that should happen."

"Come on, you won't have to worry about that for a moment. I'll take care of myself, the cops will never get to know anything about you. I never met you. Well, is it tonight I'm leaving?"

"Yeah, it's time for you to get going. Makes me feel a little sick, to see you leaving. Really got to like you, kid."

"Me too. You've been a real friend. But we'll meet again. I won't forget you."

"That's what you're saying now, but it won't take you long to chuck me overboard."

"No, man. Don't say that. I'm not like that."

"Is that right? You won't forget me?"

With these last words Querelle put his hand on Gil's shoulder. Gil looked at him and replied:

"You heard what I said."

Querelle smiled and put his arm round Gil's neck.

"So it's true, we really got to be very close, right?"

"I liked the cut of your jib the moment I saw you."

They stood facing each other, looking into each other's eyes.

"I sure wish everything goes all right for you."

Querelle pulled Gil up against his shoulder. There was no resistance.

"You goddamn kid, get going."

He kissed him, and Gil kissed him back, but Querelle still held him tight, and whispered·

"It's a pity."

In a similar whisper, Gil asked

"What? What is a pity?"

"Eh? Oh, I don't know. I just said that, I don't know why. It's a pity I have to lose you."

"But you know, you're not losing me. We'll meet again. I'll keep you posted on what happens. And once you've done your time in the Navy you can come and stay with me."

"Is that true, you'll still remember me?"

"I swear I will, Jo. You're my buddy for life."

All these exchanges were uttered in whispers growing quieter and quieter. Querelle felt a true feeling of friendship beginning to unfold inside him. The entire length of his body touched Gil's abandoned body. Querelle kissed him once more, and again Gil returned the kiss.

"Here we are, pecking away at each other like lovers."

Gil smiled. Querelle kissed him again, more fervently and very quickly, a fusillade of kisses, working his way up to the ear and covering that with a long kiss. Then he put his cheek against his friend's. Gil hugged him.

"Goddamn kid. I really like you, you know."

Querelle held Gil's head in the crook of his arm and kissed him again. He pressed Gil closer to himself, pushed a leg between his legs.

"So we're really buddies?"

"Yes, Jo. You are my one true friend."

They remained a long time in their embrace, Querelle caressing Gil's hair and showering him with further and warmer kisses. He now felt a physical desire for Gil.

"You're really great, you know?"

"What's so great about me?"

"You let me peck away at you like this, not saying anything, not complaining or anything."

"Why should I? I tell you, you're my best buddy. Ain't nothing wrong with it, is there?"

Gratefully Querelle gave him a fast and violent buss on the ear and then let his mouth slide down to Gil's. When he had found it, and they stood there lip against lip, he whispered, in a breath:

"So it's really true, it doesn't make you want to puke?"

Breathing back, Gil answered:

"No."

Their tongues touched.

"Gil?"

"Yes, what?"

"You have to be my best buddy for real. Forever. Do you understand?"

"Yes."

"D'you want to?"

"Yes."

Querelle's feeling of friendship toward Gil grew toward the limits of love. He regarded him with the tenderness of an elder brother. Like himself, Gil, too, had killed. He was a small Querelle, but one that would not be allowed to develop, who would not go any further; looking at him Querelle felt respect and curiosity, as if he had been admitted into the presence of himself as a fetus. He wanted to make love, because he thought that this would strengthen the tenderness inside him and would join him closer to Gil, by joining Gil closer to himself. But he did not know how to go about it.

"My little buddy . . ."

His hand on Gil's back slid down until it reached the trembling buttocks. Querelle squeezed them, with his large and solid hand. He took possession of them with a newly born authority. Then he stuck his fingers between the belt and the shirt. He loved Gil. He forced himself to love him.

"It is a pity we can't stay together all the time, just the two of us . . ."

"Yes, but we'll get together again . . ."

Now Gil's voice was a little troubled, anguished even.

"I would have liked us to live together, to stay just like this . . ."

The vision of the solitude in which their love might have grown enhanced his feelings for Gil; he knew that Gil existed only for him, was his only friend, his only family.

"I've never loved another guy, you know. You're the first one."

"Is that true?"

"I give you my word."

He pressed his friend's head against his cheek.

"I like you, you know. I really love you."

"I love you too."

When they parted, Querelle had really fallen in love with Gil . . .

Querelle had absolute confidence in his star. That star owed its existence to the very confidence the sailor had in it—it was, in a sense, the point at which his confidence pierced his dark night: his confidence in, exactly, nothing but his own confidence; for the star to retain its greatness and its brilliance, that is to say, its efficacy, Querelle had to retain his confidence in it—which was his belief in himself—and first of all, his smile, so that not even the lightest cloud could come between his star and him, so that its rays did not lose any of their energy, so that not even the most vaporous little wisp of doubt could ever tarnish his star. He remained suspended from it while re-creating it every second of his life. Thus it afforded him effective protection. The thought of seeing it snuffed out created a kind of vertigo in Querelle. He lived at top speed. His attention, always directed toward the nourishment of his star, forced him to a precision of movements that a softer life would not have called forth in him (nor would it have been necessary there). Always alert, he saw all obstacles more clearly and instantly knew what action to take to surmount them. Only when he was exhausted, if he ever was, fear could take hold of him. His certainty that he had a star arose out of a complex of circumstances (what we call good luck), equally random as it was structured, and in such a beautiful, rose-windowlike way, that it is tempting to look for some metaphysical reason for it. Long before he had enlisted in the Navy Querelle had heard the song called "The Star of Love."

*All the sailors have a star*
*Protecting them in Heaven above.*
*When nothing hides it from their sight*
*Ill-luck has no power over them.*

On drunken nights the dock workers would have one of their good voices perform it. The man in question would play hard to get, would ask for drinks, but would then get to his feet and up onto the table and stand there, surrounded by his mates, and let the words of the dream flow out of his gap-toothed mouth to enchant them:

*It is you, Nina, I have chosen*
*From among all the other stars of the night*
*And you are, without knowing it*
*The Star of my life . . .*

Then a bloody nocturnal tragedy would unroll, the somber story of the shipwreck of a brightly-lit ship, symbolizing the shipwreck of love. The dock workers, the fishermen, and the sailors would applaud. Leaning on one elbow against the zinc-topped bar, his legs crossed, Querelle would hardly look at them. He did not envy them their muscles or their pleasures. He did not want to become one of them. His joining the Navy had undoubtedly been due to that recruitment poster, but only because it had suddenly revealed to him the possibility of an easy life. We shall have more to say about posters.

Just as he was about to get on the train to Nantes, from the track side, the detectives grabbed Gil Turko. They had been tipped off by a phone call from one of the pay telephones in the station. An individual resembling the murderer of the sailor and the mason, though in disguise, would try to get on that train. It was Dédé who made the call. The detectives found only a minimal amount of money on Gil's person. They took the young man down to the station, where they interrogated him on his doings during the time elapsed between the second murder and the moment of his arrest. Gil claimed to have been sleeping here and there, in the dockyards, out by the ramparts. Querelle experienced a feeling of pain when the papers informed him of Gil's arrest and subsequent transfer to the prison in Rennes.

The movement of this book has to be speeded up. It will be necessary to pare down the narrative to its bare bones. However, mere notes won't be sufficient. Let us give some explanations: if the reader feels surprised (we say surprised rather than moved or indignant, in order to stress the fact that this novel deals with exhibits) by the pain Querelle felt upon learning of Gil's arrest which he himself had engineered the day before, we would like him to review the development of Querelle's career. Querelle is a killer for gain. Once the murder has been committed, the theft does not become justified by the murder (in terms of justification, it would rather be the other way round: the theft justifying the blood), but *sanctified* by it. It appears that it was a mere accident which made Querelle aware of the moral strength to be gained from a theft or robbery when it was dignified (and thus obliterated) by murder. While the act of stealing, when enhanced and magnified by blood, seems to lose its importance to the point of sometimes being completely obscured by the pomp and glory of murder (yet not withering away altogether but by its nauseating exhalations corroding the purity of the killing), it strengthens the willpower of the criminal, when the victim is a friend. The danger he exposes himself to (his own head at stake) is in itself enough to establish a sense of fittingness in him against which few arguments remain. However, the friendship linking him to the victim—turning the latter into an extension of the murderer's own personality—gives rise to a magical phenomenon we'll try to express in the following terms: I have just been engaged in an enterprise that involved a part of myself (my affection for the victim). Now I know how to enter into a kind of (nonverbal) pact with the Devil in which I do not give Him my soul, or an arm, but something equally precious: I give him a friend of mine. The death of this friend sanctifies my thieving. It is not a matter of formal arrangement (there are reasons stronger than the provisions of any law, inherent in tears, grief, death, blood, in gestures, objects, matter itself), but an act of true magic that makes me the only true possessor of the object for which a friend has been *voluntarily* bartered. I say voluntarily because my victim, in being a friend, was (and my grief confirms this) a greening leaf somewhere close to the tip of one of my branches, nourished by my own sap. Querelle knew that no one on this earth, without committing a sacrilege Querelle himself would try to prevent by fighting against it to his very last breath, would ever succeed in taking certain stolen jewels away from him, as his accomplice (and friend) whom he had delivered into the hands of the police in order to escape more quickly himself, had been sentenced to five years' solitary confinement. It did not exactly cause him grief to find himself the true owner of those stolen goods, but he regarded them with a feeling we have to call more noble, and not in the least tainted by affection, a kind of manly faithfulness to a wounded companion. Not that our hero had the idea that he was holding the booty for his accomplice, in order to share it with him later; the main thing, for him, was to keep the loot intact and out of reach of human justice. Every time he stole or robbed again, Querelle immediately felt the need to establish a mystical connection between the stolen objects and himself. "The right of conquest" became a phrase that meant something. Querelle metamorphosed his friends into bracelets, necklaces, gold watches, earrings. Thus turning one of his feelings—friendship—into cash with some success, he put himself without the pale of any man's judgment. That transmutation concerned only himself. Anyone who tried to make him "cough up the stuff again" would commit an act of grave-desecration. Thus Gil's arrest caused Querelle considerable grief, but at the same time he was keenly aware of becoming almost physically encrusted with all the imaginary jewels and gold that symbolized the money acquired with Gil's help. It is our contention that the mechanism we have just described is a very common one in our time. It is one that can be seen functioning in everybody's consciousness, not only in those who have attained an awareness of their complexity. Nevertheless it should be pointed out that Querelle who needed to have all his resources at his disposal any given moment was thus obliged to rely more or less constantly on extracting them from his own inner contradictions.

When Dédé had told him about the fight between the two brothers, gleefully dwelling on the insults Robert had been hurling at Querelle, Mario at once experienced a feeling of tremendous deliverance while not yet knowing from what it was he had been saved. It originated in a sudden and as yet hazy notion that Querelle had had something to do with the murder of the sailor called Vic. It was hazy, because the dominant feeling was one of relief, sweetness and light. Mario felt himself saved, by this single, far from lucid idea. Slowly, and taking this sense of salvation for his point of departure, he then established effective connections between that murder and what he thought he knew about homosexuals: if it were true that Nono had buggered him, then Querelle had to be a "queer." And that immediately made him a very plausible candidate for the murderer of that or any sailor. Mario's fantasies about Querelle were inaccurate, no doubt, yet they enabled him to discover the truth. Continuing his musings about Querelle and the murder, he immediately came up against the idea regarded as quite certain by the police authorities—that Gil had committed both murders; for fear of betraying himself, he could not contradict it openly. Then he proceeded to establish his own conclusions, by methodical guesswork, and finally decided to give in to the lovely dance of hypotheses. He thought of Querelle in love with Vic, then killing him in a fit of jealous rage; or vice versa, Vic, overwhelmed by similar emotion, trying to kill Querelle and becoming his victim. Mario spent an entire day juggling these ideas, none of which were verifiable, but slowly becoming more and more certain of Querelle's guilt. Mario conjured up Querelle's face, pale despite its sailor's tan, pale and so similar to his brother's. That resemblance provoked a kind of charming confusion in Mario's mind, a witches' cauldron of thoughts that were not to Querelle's advantage. One evening, down by the old moat, the appearance of the two brothers made him feel ill at ease in a way not dissimilar to Madame Lysiane's experience. Mario found he could take every one of Querelle's traits and effortlessly recombine them into a mental image of Robert's face. Slowly this image filled out and took the place of the face Mario was looking at. In the dark of the night, under the trees, Mario remained motionless for a few seconds. He was torn between the actual face he saw and the superimposed image. He frowned, wrinkled his brow. Querelle's face, present and impassive, interfered with Robert's image. The two mugs fused, became muddled, fought, became identical again. That evening there was nothing to differentiate them, not even the smile that turned Querelle into his brother's shadow (Querelle's smile spread rippling over his whole body, like a veil in motion, trembling, very thin with shadowy folds, and thus enhancing the charm of his devil-may-care, supple and fully alive body, while Robert's glumness consisted of a passion for himself: instead of darkening him, this self-love became a hearth without warmth, a light that seemed stifling because his body was so rigid, moved so heavily and deliberately). Then the spell of enchantment was over. The detective returned from the stupefying whirlpool.

"Which one of them?" he thought.

But there seemed to be no doubt to him that Querelle was the murderer.

"What are you thinking about?"

"Oh, nothing."

He refused to be deceived by this great resemblance, although it had a tremendous effect on him. His feelings for Querelle expressed themselves in a slightly scornful thought: "I can see you're trying to stack the deck, buddy, but that won't work with me." He decided, deliberately, to ignore this further complication as being beyond his realm of investigation. It had not been created for him, Mario, to throw himself into it and come out as the winner. In other words, it wasn't really any of his business. Yet he heard himself saying:

"You're a strange guy."

"Why d'you say that?"

"I don't know, no reason. I just said it."

When Mario experienced that sense of great relief, this was also due to a "flash" he had that the sailor's guilt might serve him in another context. Without knowing the reason for it, without even formulating the thought to himself, he simply knew that he had to keep his discovery to himself forever. He swore himself to a vow of silence. If he protected the murderer and became a willing accessory to the crime, perhaps this would earn him absolution from his treachery toward Tony the Docker. It wasn't so much that Mario went in fear of that old buddy's or even the collective dock workers' taking bloody revenge: a general sense of scorn, directed against him, was what he was most afraid of. Although we hardly feel qualified to discuss the psychology of the police, we would like to demonstrate how the development and the use made of certain stock reactions—cultivated by them—fosters the growth of that astonishing plant some find so delightful: the cop. Mario's favorite gesture was to keep turning his golden signet ring round his middle finger; the signet was so large that its edges caused a slight irritation of the adjoining fingers. The tic was particularly evident when Mario was sitting behind his desk and grilling someone caught pilfering at the docks or in the warehouses. He shared an office with a colleague, but they both had desks of their own. Mario was quite an elegant man (there was no question about it, he had excellent taste). He liked to appear well-dressed. We might further note the good, plain cut of his clothes, the austere manner in which he wore them, the predominantly impassive expression on his face, finally, the sobriety and assurance of his gestures. The very fact that he had a desk in an office lent Mario, in the eyes of the delinquents he interrogated, the air of someone of indisputable intellectual superiority. Sometimes he got up, leaving the desk without, it seemed, a second thought, the way one may part from something one knows to be in good hands. That was mostly when he went to consult one of his numerous files. This added further to his prestige: it showed him as the possessor of the secrets of several thousand people. When he went outside, his face instantly turned into a mask. Under no circumstances must anyone suspect, in the cafés or elsewhere, that they were plying a policeman with confidences. But behind that mask—as there always has to be a face behind such a thing, to support it— Mario composed his features into a policeman's face. For a number of hours, every day, he had to be the one who uncovers the weaknesses of mortal men, their sins, the slightest clues whereby they then could be led, with maximum expediency, and even if they had seemed beyond all suspicion, to a most terrible atonement. A sublime profession, and he would have been a fool to degrade it to the level of eavesdropping or peeping through keyholes. Mario felt no curiosity whatsoever about these people, always wanted to remain at the correct distance from them: but as soon as he thought he had discovered that slight indication of guilt, he proceeded in a manner similar to that of a child blowing soap bubbles, picking out of the froth, with the end of its straw, the one little conglomeration of suds that can be worked into a lovely iridescent bubble. Proceeding from one discovery to the next, Mario experienced an exquisite feeling of elation: he was breathing into it, and the crime started swelling, then inflating some more, finally to detach itself from him and rise up into the sky. No doubt Mario told himself on more than one occasion that his profession was a useful and a perfectly ethical one. For over a year now his young friend Dédé had organized his life around two principles: the principle of stealing, and the one of denouncing thieves to the police. A truly remarkable achievement, the more so as Mario, in order to reinforce him in his aspect of paid informer, often said to him:

"You're useful, you know. You're helping *us* apprehend those scoundrels."

As the boy lived in perfect harmony with himself, the argument seemed quite commonplace to him, except for that *us*, which made him feel that he was taking part in a wonderful adventure. He sold the scoundrels and he went on stealing with them, there was nothing to it.

"Gilbert Turko—did you know him, Dédé?"

"Yes. Can't say we were buddies, but I used to know him."

"Where is he now?"

"I have no idea."

"Come on . . ."

"But Mario, I swear. I don't know anything about it. If I did, I'd tell you."

As a matter of fact, Dédé had conducted his own investigation even before the detective asked him about it, but he had not been able to find out anything. Without having really managed to interpret Gil's amorous passes at Roger, he had, at least, an intuitive understanding of what their smiles and their meetings really meant; but Roger's ingenuousness made him in many ways impervious to what we call cunning.

"You better go and look for him."

In his troubled mind Mario had the obscure notion that he could halt that tidal wave of universal scorn we mentioned—and he thought he could already feel its spray on his face—by finding the murderer, finding him out and then turning his body into a mausoleum that would contain the great scorn forever.

"I'll try some more. But I do think he's left Brest."

"There are no indications that he has. And if he's gone, he can't have gone very far. He's a wanted man. You get out there and fucking well keep your mouth shut and your eyes open, and get the wax out of your ears, kid. Like you gotta *do* it."

Somewhat taken aback, Dédé stared at the detective, who was now blushing violently. Mario suddenly felt unworthy of using such speech, whose function, primarily, was the transmission of practical detail, but whose real beauty lay in its ability to convey, from speaker to listener, an otherwise inexpressible and almost instant feeling of membership in a secret and enigmatic brotherhood—not of blood, or language, but of the incredible range of that speech, its conflicting yet interweaving strains of monstrous obscenity and great modesty. Having tried to use the argot while not being in a state of grace, Mario had ended up saying nothing, in so many basically stilted words. Now he was just a copper again, but lacking a counterpart (or adversary) he felt diminished. He could only be a true policeman at his own outer limits, which was where he carried on his war against the criminal world. He was unable to create, within himself, the sense of consistency and profound unity that *is* the internal battle of contrary desires. Although he was most definitely a policeman, Mario knew that he carried in himself a delinquent, perhaps even a criminal—in any case, the shady character he would have become, had he not chosen to be a policeman—but his betrayal of Tony had cut him off from the criminal world, had made it impossible for him to refer himself to it. Now he had to stand outside and be the judge. No longer

could he enter into it as if it were a sympathetic and malleable
element. That love every artist feels for his material, in his case
the material did not reciprocate. Thus he could only wait and
worry. In that one glimmer of hope of salvation he somehow
connected the revenge of the dockers with the glaring evidence
for Querelle's guilt. During the day he talked and cracked jokes
with his colleagues whom he had never told about the threats
that had been addressed to him. Almost every evening he met
Querelle by the railroad embankment. It had not occurred to
him that the discovery of the cigarette lighter lying next to Vic's
dead body could indicate complicity between Gil and the sailor;
thus he hadn't thought of putting Querelle under surveillance.
On his way back from the old prison Querelle came by the
embankment. He felt no friendly emotion toward the detective,
but kept meeting him out of a habit that was based on his being
at Mario's mercy. He also believed that the relationship
afforded him some protection. He felt the roots growing. In the
dark of one evening he whispered:

"If you caught me swiping something, would you put me in
the cooler?"

Taken literally, the expression "you could have knocked him
down with a feather" isn't exactly true, yet the state of fragility
to which it reduces the person who provokes it obliges us to use
it: "you could have knocked" Mario "down with a feather." His
reply, though, was foxy enough:

"Sure, why not? I'd be doing my duty."

"So it would be your duty to have me put away? That's not
very funny!"

"That's the way it is, though. And if you killed someone, I'd
send you on your way to the old chopper."

"I see."

Back on his feet again after what neither he nor the detective
would have gone so far as to call an act of love, Querelle
became a man again, facing another man. He had a little smile
on his face as he stood there, buttoning up, closing the buckle

of the wide leather strap he used as a belt, behind his back: he
seemed to be implying that their doings were just good clean
fun. Since this scene took place close to the beginning of
Madame Lysiane's affair with Querelle, and as Querelle was
unable to figure out the exact intertwining relationships between Nono, the cop Mario, and his brother, he came close to
suspecting some kind of conspiracy. It scared him. The following evening he told Gil to take off. As soon as he entered the
old penitentiary, he methodically went into the routine he had
planned the night before and which was designed to ensure his
own safety. The first thing was to get the revolver back from
Gil, by starting out with the cunning question:

"You still got the heater?"

"Sure. I've got it hidden in here."

"Can I see it?"

"Why? What's the matter?"

Gil was afraid to ask whether the time had come to use it,
but feared this might be the case. Querelle had spoken in very
gentle tones. He knew that he had to proceed very carefully so
as not to arouse any suspicions in Gil's mind. He was doing a
great acting job. Holding back the explanation while making it
impossible for Gil to refuse or even hesitate, he did not say
"Just give it to me," but "Let's see it, I'll tell you what it's
about . . ." Gil watched Querelle watching him, and both of
them were bewildered by the gentleness of their own voices—in
the dark, they sounded almost tender. The shadows and this
gentleness plunged both of them, naked, flayed alive, into the
same vat of sweet balm. Querelle truly felt friendship, more
than that, love for Gil, and Gil reciprocated. We do not want
to imply that Gil *already* suspected what Querelle was leading
him to (that sacrificial and necessary end), we only want to
point out the universality contained in a particular occasion. It
was not a case of forebodings—not that we don't believe in
such, it is only that they belong to a realm of scientific study
that no longer is art—because the work of art is *free*. Reading,

apropos of a painting that is an attempt to represent Jesus as a child, "in his eyes, in his smile, one can already foretell the sadness and despair of the Crucifixion," we say that that is a truly abominable instance of bad literary writing. However, in order to succeed in giving the reader the truth about Gil's and Querelle's relations, he or she will have to allow us to use this detestable literary cliché we ourselves condemn, give us permission to write that Gil suddenly had a presentiment of Querelle's treachery and of his own immolation. It isn't just that this commonplace expediently speeds up the definition of the respective roles of these two heroes: one is a redeemer, the other one quite beyond redemption: there is more to it, as we shall, both of *us*, see. Gil made a movement which to some extent freed him from the all-pervasive tenderness that joined him to his murderer. (It is appropriate to point out, in this context, that it surely is not hate, but another kind of feeling that can cause a father to engage in friendly conversation with the murderer of his son, oblivious to the astonished and appalled stares of the public—directing his quiet questions to the witness of the beloved creature's last moments.) Gil went into the darker part of the cave, and Querelle sauntered after him.

"You have it?"

Gil raised his head. He was on his knees, looking for the gun under a heap of coiled rope.

"What?"

Then he laughed, a little shrilly.

"I must be crazy!" he added.

"Let's see it."

Gently he asked for the revolver, and gently he took it from Gil. Salvation beckoned. Gil had gotten up again.

"What are you going to do?"

Querelle hesitated. He turned his back to Gil, walked back to the corner where Gil usually stayed. Then he said:

"It's time for you to go. Things are hotting up."

"No kidding?"

The length of that remark was just about right for Gil's capability at that moment. His voice was in danger of breaking. The fear of the guillotine, dormant for a long time, suddenly caused a strange phenomenon: it made all the blood in his body run back to his heart.

"Yup. They're looking for you again. But don't get the jitters. And don't think I'll leave you in the lurch."

Gil tried to understand, but vaguely and inconclusively, what all the business about the revolver was about, and then he saw Querelle putting it in the pocket of his peacoat. The notion that an act of treachery was being consummated flashed into his mind, while at the same time he felt profoundly relieved to be rid of an object that would force him to act, probably even to murder. Stretching out his hand he said:

"Will you let me keep it?"

"Look, it's this way. Let me explain. Don't get me wrong now, I'm not saying that they'll get you, I'm sure they won't. But you never know. And if they did, it would be better for you, if you weren't carrying a gun."

Querelle's private reasoning went as follows: if he starts shooting at the cops, the cops'll shoot right back. They'll either kill him, or they'll take him alive. If they arrest him, they'll find out, either from a Gil weakened by his wounds, or by conducting an intensive investigation, that this revolver used to belong to Lieutenant Seblon, and then what else could that poor sod do but put the finger on his steward. In trying to follow the movements in our protagonists' souls, we are also trying to cast some light on our own. Feel free to notice that the attitude we would have liked to adopt—with a view to, or perhaps, with a foreknowledge of the desired end of the story—has led us to the discovery of a given psychological world that supports the idea of freedom of choice; but as soon as the progression of the story requires one or the other of its main characters to pronounce a judgment, to take thought, we are immediately confronted by the arbitrary: the character escapes from its author, becoming its own, singular being. Thus we have to admit that the author is able to reveal certain traits of this character only after the fact. Now in the case of Querelle, if an explanation is needed, let us try this one, no better, no more despicable than any other: his lack of imagination being of the same order as his lack of feelings, he misjudged the officer. Seblon's diary bears witness to the fact that rather than denounce Querelle he would have taken the blame on himself. It is true that in one entry the Lieutenant expressed a desire to point out Querelle as the murderer, but we shall see what sublime use he then made of this desire.

Gil thought he was losing his mind. He could not for the life of him comprehend his friend's intentions. He heard himself say:

"So that's it, I'll have to go out there naked, stark naked."

Querelle had just collected the sailor clothes. He couldn't afford to leave Gil anything that might incriminate him.

"Shut up, you little runt, you won't have to go naked."

That particularly wounding remark subjugated Gil, who had, gradually incited to it by Querelle's gentle yet a little remote behavior, reached the point of rebellion. Querelle knew admirably well that he could still show who was the boss, and thus he dared to treat the one person who could have brought about his own downfall with such supreme scorn. With great nerve and cunning he raised the stakes of the game to a degree where the least mistake would be enough to send the player to his death. Scenting (the word seems most accurate) the success he was having at it, he decided to play it all the way.

"You don't want to piss me off now, do you? Don't start acting the tough guy. Now's the time to listen to my advice."

Having adopted this stance and tone, he came close to running such grave danger (one lucid moment, and Gil might give in to his mounting desperation) that he realized with even greater speed, clarity and presence of mind all the thousand little details still required to bring about, by Gil's death and his silence, Querelle's own salvation. Alert, quick, a winner already, he toned down his scorn and haughtiness, knowing that these might crack or upset the balance now weighted in his favor and indicating that he would gain and keep his freedom. (Let us note that Querelle was able to discern the ways and means he had to employ in order to succeed because he was, and knew himself to be, utterly *free*; thus he saw he could afford to temper his scorn and arrogance with a little buddy-talk.) With a little, crooked smile—thus, in his own mind, showing Gil the irony and basic insignificance of the entire situation—he said:

"Hell, come on. You're not the guy who would break down at a time like this. You just have to listen what I tell you to do. D'you understand?"

He put his hand on Gil's shoulder, whom he was now addressing like a sick man, someone bound to die, giving his final advice that concerned Gil's soul more than his body.

"You get into an empty compartment. Then, first of all, you hide your dough. Just stick it under one of the seat cushions. Just keep some change on you. You see what I mean. You have to take care not to have too much money on you."

"And what about the clothes?"

Gil had thought of saying "So you want me to go in these old rags," but as it indicated too great a degree of intimacy and emotional attachment between the two of them (and he was already ashamed of this), he realized that such a way of putting it might irritate Querelle. He said:

"They'll recognize me in these."

"Hell, no. Don't you worry about that. The cops can't remember what you were wearing then."

Querelle went on in the same, simultaneously imperious and tender manner. As luck would have it (this kind of luck being a kind of affection or disease, caused by the humors circulating in the vascular system of events), there was one more most appropriate slip of the tongue. Holding Gil by the shoulders with both hands, Querelle said:

"Take it easy, old hoss. We'll get some more."

He was talking about their jobs, and Gil understood it that way, but the emotion those words called forth in him, due to a secret *double-entendre* that made them refer to children, made Gil fully aware of his own attachment and created a wonderful confusion in his heart, between the accomplice and the lover. For Gil, it was a revelation. Then, however, error crept in, and we have to record it: it was exactly the same mistake survivors habitually commit when they urge those about to die to have faith and courage. As he thought, most carefully, in fact begging Gil not to betray him even if the police should happen to catch him, he went on:

"It wouldn't really make any difference, you know. Whatever happens, you're not running any risk." And like a babe at the breast of Innocence, Gil asked:

"No risk? What do you mean?"

"Well, you know. You have a death sentence hanging over you already."

Gil felt his stomach turning, becoming quite empty, knotting itself up; then it unfolded again, and the weight of the entire globe entered into it. He leaned against Querelle who took him in his arms. Let us mention, at this point, that Gil never said a word about Querelle to the police. Before Gil was sent on to Rennes, Mario contrived to be present at every one of his interrogations, being slightly afraid that he might bring up Querelle's name. Mario was convinced that the young mason had committed one of the murders, but that he was innocent of the other one. From the moment of his arrest Gil had forgotten Querelle, and he never mentioned his name for the simple reason that no one ever brought it up. No need to labor the point: the reader will easily understand why neither Gil nor the detectives (with the exception of Mario) ever could really understand the connection between the murder of the sailor and the soon truly subterranean existence of a man who had murdered a mason. As for Mario, his part in the sequence of events became quite curious. In order to assign to him his definitive and perhaps final meanings, we have to resort to a couple of flashbacks. Dédé was—or thought he was—informed of all the young boys' sentimental involvements in Brest. In order to serve better—serve Mario, no doubt, and beyond him, the police authorities, but, primarily, to *serve*—he distinguished himself (and this, again, seemed to originate in his physical and ethical agility, in his quick eye) by his speedy powers of observation. Before he acquired a sense of his own consciousness (and with it, anxiety), Dédé was a marvelous recording device. (His admiration for Robert may be regarded the exception to the rule.) The mission Mario had given him, to keep an eye on Querelle, was primarily designed to create a new, sympathetic relationship between those hoodlums the detective had double-crossed and the detective himself. Dédé never dared to remind Robert of the fight between the two brothers that he had been witness to, but he regarded it as a solid item of information that Roger was Gil's lover-boy. Yet he never thought to watch his movements or follow him. One day he said to Mario:

"That's little Roger, Turko's buddy."

Round about the same time Gil said to Querelle who did not pay much attention to it:

"Sometimes I think, if I get arrested, maybe I could make some sort of deal with Mario."

"How?"

"What? Well, you know . . ."

"What kind of deal?"

"You never know. He's a homo. He's buddies with Dédé."


Gil's musings reflect a common enough notion: from the very moment of his arrest, the adolescent thinks about turning the fact of homosexuality to his advantage. Since we are talking about a general reaction, something beyond ourselves, we'll attempt merely a cursory and controversial explanation: is it that the child wishes to sacrifice what is most precious to him; or is it that the danger throws him at the mercy of his most secret desires; is he hoping to appease fate by such immolation; does he suddenly recognize the entire, powerful fraternity of pederasts and put his faith in it; does he believe in the power of love? To know the answers, we would merely have to dip into the inner workings of Gil, but we do not have enough time left to do so. Nor faith. This book goes on for too many pages, and it bores us. But let us simply record the profound hope that fills the young suspects' hearts when they hear that the judge or the lawyer appointed to defend them is a homo.

"Who's Dédé?"

"Dédé? Oh, I'm sure you've seen him with Mario. He's a kid. He spends a lot of time with that cop. But I don't think there's any other reason. What I mean is, I don't think Dédé is an informer."

"What's he look like?"

Gil described him. When Querelle met him one evening, just as he was about to part from Mario, Querelle felt a deep wound reopening within himself. He recognized the boy who had witnessed his dispute with Robert, and his own rival for Mario's favors. Nevertheless, he held out his hand. He felt there was something like a cunning sneer in Dédé's behavior, in his smile, in his voice. When the boy had walked away from them, Querelle asked, with a smile:

"Who's that, now? Is that your little lover?"

Responding with an equal, slightly mocking smile in his voice, Mario said:

"What's it to you? He's a sweet little kid. You aren't jealous or anything?"

Querelle laughed and had the audacity to say:

"What if I am? Why not?"

"Oh, come on . . ."

But then he went on, in an excited, broken voice: "Come on, suck me!" Querelle, too, was in a highly excited mood. Furiously, desperately, he kissed Mario on the mouth. Then, with greater ardor than was customary and with great dedication, he tried his damnedest to really *feel* the detective's prick penetrating his mouth and throat. Mario noticed his desperate mood. To the fleeting but repeating fear that the wild sailor might chomp off his member in one fell swoop, the detective added the spices of excited lovers' hiccoughs and dangerous confessions, expressing the latter in the form of groans or prayers. Certain that his lover rejoiced in cowering on his knees in front of a cop, Mario exhaled all his own ignominy. Teeth clenched, face turned up into the fog, he murmured:

"Yes, I'm a cop! Yes, I'm a dirty bastard! I've screwed a lot of guys! And they're all in the joint now, doing time! I love that, you know, it's my job . . ."

The more he described his abject desires, the harder his muscles grew and imposed on Querelle an imperious, dominant, invincible and beneficial presence. When they were face to face again, standing, buttoning up, retransformed into men, neither one of them dared to mention their delirious state of a moment ago; in order to disperse the disquiet that separated them from one another, Querelle smiled and said:

"Well, you still haven't told me if that kid's your piece of ass?"

"You really want to know?"

Suddenly Querelle was frightened, but he kept his voice calm:

"Yes. Well, then?"

"He's my informer."

"No kidding!"

Now they could go on, talk shop. In low voices, trying, nevertheless, to keep them calm and clear, so as not to show any signs of how bizarre and possibly shameful they felt the subject to be,

they went on talking, and at one point Querelle made this
statement:

"You know, I could fix it so you'd get to arrest that Turko."

Mario took it in his stride.

"Is that right?" he said.

"It is, too. But only if I have your word that you won't
mention me."

Mario gave his word. Already he had abandoned his precautions, forgotten the plan to effect a mystical reconciliation
with the underworld: *he could not resist the chance to act as a
policeman.* He decided not to interrogate Querelle about the
source of his information or about its reliability. He trusted the
sailor. Very rapidly they decided what measures had to be taken
to keep Querelle's name out of it forever.

"Get that kid of yours on his track. But see that he doesn't
suspect anything."

One hour later Mario gave Dédé orders to go to the railroad
station and keep a watch on all departing trains. He was to
notify Police Headquarters as soon as he caught sight of Turko.
He sold Gil. By that act Dédé detached himself from the world
of his fellow beings. That was the beginning of his ascension,
the meaning of which the reader has already been informed
about.


On board *Le Vengeur* Querelle went on serving the officer,
but the latter seemed to despise him, and this caused Querelle
some degree of pain. Having been the target of armed aggres-
sion, the Lieutenant felt proud enough to develop a taste for
adventure. In his diary we find the following statement:


*I feel in no way inferior to this young and marvelous hoodlum.
I resisted. I was ready to die.*

°     °     °

To reward him for his assistance in Gil's arrest, the Police Commissioner entrusted him with special, almost official, assignments. It became his task to watch for youthful shoplifters, sailors and soldiers, in the Monoprix department store.

As Dédé rode the escalator, putting on his yellow leather gloves, he had the feeling of truly being "on his way up." He was an agent now. Everything was there to carry, to transport him. He was sure of himself. Getting off at the summit of his apotheosis, the store floor on which he was to begin his new career, he knew that he had arrived. He had his gloves on, the floor was horizontal, Dédé was master of his domain, free to be either magnanimous or a swine.

To those who are unable to pursue a life of adventure on their own, the Navy (as all armed forces) offers them one on a platter: all they do is sign up, and it will take its methodical course, finally underlined with the thin red ribbon of the Legion of Honor. However, right in the middle of his official adventure, Lieutenant Seblon was chosen for another one which turned out to be far more serious. Not that he went so far as to regard himself a hero, but he became keenly aware of his direct and intimate experience of the most despised, disgusting, and most noble of social activities: armed robbery. He had been the victim of a hold-up in broad daylight. The robber had a charming face. Though it would have been even more marvelous to *be* this robber, it was exciting enough to have been the victim. He made no attempt to disentangle himself from the masses of daydreams that gave him such delicious little jolts. He felt certain that no part of his secret adventure (where he was completely alone with the robber) would ever come to light. "None of that can ever transpire" was the expression he used in his mind. He was able to shelter behind his severe countenance. "My ravisher! he's my ravisher! trotting out of the fog like a wolf, to kill me. For I did defend the money in the face of death." After a couple of days in the infirmary he spent his days at his desk. Carrying his arm in a sling he took walks on deck, then rested, stretched out in his cabin.

"Would you like me to get you some tea, sir?"

"Yes, why not."

He regretted that his ravisher had not been Querelle.


*How happy I should have been to struggle with him over my satchel! He would, at long last, have given me a chance to demonstrate my courage. But then, would I have charged him? Strange question that leads me to discover—what?—in myself. Let us remember the detectives' visit to my cabin and my dizziness then.*

*I came very close to handing Querelle over to them. I still ask myself whether my attitude and my responses did not, after all, point him out to the police. I hate the police, yet I came very close to doing their dirty work. It would be madness to believe that Querelle murdered Vic, except in that dream. I would like him to have done it, but that is only because I can then construct a daydream around a tragedy of love. To offer Querelle my entire devotion! When he would come, at the end of his tether with remorse and torment, his temples throbbing, his hair damp with sweat, hounded by his deed, to confide in me! Then I could be his confessor and give him absolution, hold him in my arms and console him, and finally go to prison with him! If only I could have made myself believe a little more in his being the murderer, then I could have denounced him, thus immediately gaining the opportunity to console him and to share his punishment! Without knowing it, Querelle stood on the brink of incredible peril. I came so very close to delivering him up into the hands of the cops!*

The Lieutenant had never worried about Querelle's ever blackmailing him for money. True, the crewman was a sarcastic fellow, but he seemed devoid of that kind of cynicism. No more was Seblon able to replace the gun-toting false sailor's image with Querelle's, much as he would have loved it. He would have met him and joined him in a battle, and in the midst of the struggle, in the time it takes to take hold and then let go again, they would have reached an understanding that would have enabled them to be better adversaries in the future. In moments of solitude the Lieutenant constructed a heroic dialogue they might have spoken then: it would have conveyed his inmost beauty to Querelle, made it visible to the young man's dazzled eyes. It was a short, harsh exchange, reduced to essentials. *Sovereign* calm in his voice, the officer would have said:

"Geo, you are mad. Put the revolver away. I won't tell anyone about this."

"Just hand over the dough and you'll be all right."

"No."

"I'll shoot you."

"Go ahead."

Nights, the Lieutenant took long solitary walks on deck, avoiding his fellow officers, haunted by this dialogue and by his inability to continue and finish it. "Cowed by me, he throws the gun away. But then my heroism remains unknown. Or, still cowed, nevertheless he fires the gun, exactly out of respect for me, and trying to match my stature. But if he kills me, I just die a stupid death by the roadside." After mulling it over for a long time, the Lieutenant chose this ending: "Querelle pulls the trigger, but in his excitement he misses, only wounding me." He would then return to the ship, but would not provide a description of Querelle (as he had given one of Gil). Thus he would have shown his superior strength to Querelle, and Querelle would have loved him for it.

"May I put in a request for forty-eight hours' leave, Lieutenant?"

To ask this question, pausing in the act of pouring the tea, Querelle raised his head and directed his smile at the Lieutenant's reflection in the mirror, but Seblon beat a quick retreat into himself. He replied, curtly:

"Sure, I'll sign it for you."

A few days earlier he would have reacted differently. He would have asked Querelle a number of insidious questions, describing ever-narrowing circles round what was most essential, to the point of actually touching that center or even revealing parts, but never all of it. Querelle was getting on his nerves. His face, present, did not manage to dispel the image of that audacious gunman who had disappeared into the morning fog. "He was just a boy, but he had nerve." Sometimes he thought, feeling a little ashamed, that it didn't need all that much to attack a fairy. Querelle had been insolent enough to say to his face, with a somewhat artificial undertone of threat directed against the unknown robber: "Those guys, do they know who they tangle with?" Well, it was clear that the "ravisher" had known the inconsistent nature of his victim. He hadn't been afraid. In every respect, Querelle felt the officer putting a distance between them, at the very moment he himself, if slowly and with a thousand reservations, would have been ready to let himself be taken in by the profound and generous tenderness only a homo was able to offer. As to the officer, his adventure generated some reflections and new attitudes we shall account for, and out of these he gained sufficient force to make it possible for him to conquer Querelle.

*Loved by Querelle, I would be loved by all the sailors of France. My lover is a compendium of all their manly and naïve virtues.*

○   ○   ○

A galley crew used to call their captain "Our Man." His gentleness and his toughness. But I know that he could not be otherwise, he had to be both cruel and gentle; that is to say, he did not have men tortured with just a little smile on his lips, but only with an interior smile, something to soothe his hidden organs (the liver, the lungs, the stomach, the heart). That peacefulness became manifest even in his voice, giving the orders to torture gently, with a gentle gesture, a gentle look in his eye. Undoubtedly I am drawing an idealized and overly perfect picture of this captain, illustrating my own desire—yet its origin, in me, does not make it an arbitrary one. It corresponds to the reality of the captain as seen by the galley convicts. This image of gentleness, superimposed on the atrocious features of a commonplace man, is in the eye of the beholder, the galley slave—it comes from farther still, from his heart. When he ordered those notorious punishments, the captain was cruel. He inflicted profound damage on their bodies, lacerating them, putting out eyes, tearing out fingernails (or ordered all these things to be done, to be exact), thus obeying his own instructions and maintaining the fear, the terror without which he could not have remained captain. With the authority invested in him by his rank (which is also mine!), he ordered men to be tortured, but he did so without feeling any hatred for them—how could he help loving, in a distorted fashion, the element to which he owed his very existence? True enough, he worked cruelly and hard on that flesh, delivered to him by the Royal Courts, but he did it with a kind of grave, smiling, yet sad joy. Once again: the galley slaves saw a captain who was both cruel and kind.

"Illustrating my own desire," I wrote. If it is my desire to possess such authority, such admirable form, to evoke the loving fear that the historical figure of the captain is able to attract—and with such violence—I have to arouse it in the hearts of the crew-men. If only they would love me thus! I want to be their father, and hurt them. I want to brand them: they will hate me. Impassively I shall watch their being tortured, not twitching a single nerve. Little by little, a feeling of extreme power will enter into me and fill me. I shall be strong, having overcome pity. I shall be sad as well, while watching my own pitiful comedy: that little smile, the soft voice, illuminating my commands.

I, too, am a victim of recruitment posters. Of one in particular, depicting a Marine rifleman in white leggings, standing guard at the frontiers of the French Empire. A wind rose under his heel, a red thistle above his head.

I know that I'll never abandon Querelle. I shall devote my whole life to him. One day I fixed my stare on him and told him:
"Do you have a slight cast in one eye?"
Instead of getting angry or impertinent, that splendid boy answered, in a voice that was suddenly sad and revealed a small but incurable sorrow:
"It's not my fault."
I understood instantly that there was an opening here, into which I could pour my tenderness. Once his arrogance cracks its armor, Querelle is no longer such pure marble, but human flesh. And it is in this way that Madame Lysiane expressed her kindness and took care of her unfortunate clients.

When I am suffering, I find myself unable to believe in God. I am, then, too keenly aware of my own impotence to address my complaints about a Being—and to Him—that is impossible to attain. In pain, I have recourse only to myself. When I am unhappy, I know I have someone to thank for it.

• • •

Querelle appears so beautiful and so pure—but this appearance is real and sufficient—that I enjoy attributing all manner of crimes to him. Then again, I worry, not knowing whether I want to degrade and soil him, or if it is my desire to destroy what is evil, render it vain and inefficient, and in so doing compromise the human appearance by the very symbol of purity?

The galley convicts' chains were called "the branches." What fruit did they bear!

What is it he involves himself in when he goes ashore? Of what sort are his adventures? It pleases as well as upsets me to think that he may provide pleasure to any passer-by, any stray wanderer in the fog. After some strange gestures of hesitation one of these asks him if he might walk along with him for a while. Querelle, not surprised, smiles and accepts his company. As soon as they discover a suitable shelter, some corner of the city wall, Querelle, still smiling, still silent, proceeds to unbutton himself. The man gets down on his knees. When he rises again, he puts a hundred francs into Querelle's indifferent palm, and then he is gone. Querelle returns on board or goes to the brothel.

Thinking over what I have just written, it strikes me that such a servile function, letting himself be used as a smiling object, does not really fit Querelle. He is too strong, and to see him thus is to add to his strength, is to turn him into some haughty machine capable of crushing me without even noticing.

I have said before that I have sometimes wished him to be an impostor; in that sober and boyish sailor's outfit he hides an agile and violent body, and in that body, the soul of a bandit: Querelle is one, I am sure of that.

°    °    °

When I became an officer, it wasn't so much in order to be a warrior, but rather to be a very precious object, guarded by soldiers. Which they would protect with their lives until they died for me, or I offered up my life in the same manner to save them.

It is thanks to Jesus that we can praise humility, for he made it into the very characteristic of divinity. An interior kind of divinity (how can one deny the powers given one on earth?), opposed to those powers, and it has to be strong in order to overcome them. Humility can only be born out of humiliation. Any other kind is a vain simulacrum.

That last entry refers to an incident the officer does not relate. Having made a rather audacious pass at a young dock worker, he took him to one of those thickets in the old city moat: as we had occasion to mention before, these were perennially littered with turds. The Lieutenant let his pants down, stretched himself out on the slope—and as ill-luck would have it, placed his belly right over a solid portion of shit. Both men were instantly enveloped in its fresh odor. Without further ado, the young fellow disappeared, and there was the Lieutenant, all by himself. With a handful of dry grass—though it was mercifully a little moistened by the dew—he tried to clean his coat. Shame went right to work on him. He watched his beautiful white hands—although humiliated, they still were that to him—energetically, if maladroitly, do what they had to do. In the mist, now enveloping the desolate scenery once and for all, he still glimpsed the gold of the braid on his cuffs. As pride is humiliation's child, the officer now felt prouder than ever. He was acquiring a taste for his own endurance. When he got on his way again, avoiding any populous area in the manner of an old-time leper, all open places onto which the wind wafted his stench, he began to understand that any birth in a manger is a miraculous sign. His thoughts of Querelle (which had rendered the labor of cleaning so painful: in their vagueness and sullenness they had taken on the odor emanating from his midriff) became clearer now. The feelings of shame they caused became like a vast magnet, bringing his life back to him from its farthest borders and beaches, and once that had happened, he was again able to think of the sailor without any inhibitions. He walked into a light gust of wind. He thought, or rather, a deep voice said from somewhere inside him: "I stink! I corrupt the world!" From this particular spot in Brest, in the middle of the fog, on the road overlooking the sea and the docks, a light breeze, gentler and lovelier than the petals of Saadi's roses, spread the humility of Lieutenant Seblon over the whole world.

Querelle had become Madame Lysiane's lover. The turmoil she found herself in when contemplating the identity of the two brothers—which began to appear ever more indistinguishable and unified—reached such a dimension that she finally gave in to it.

Here are the facts. Gil, worried because he had not seen Querelle for some time, told Roger to go and investigate. The boy hesitated for a long time, walking back and forth in front of the spiky door, then finally walked into La Féria. Querelle was in the parlor. Intimidated by all the lights, the women in states of undress, Roger approached him looking anything but assured. Still imperial in her bearing, but already corroded by her disease, Madame Lysiane observed the encounter. She was not very conscious of registering and interpreting Roger's embarrassed smile and Querelle's surprise and worried look, but her soul recorded all the signs. A second later Robert walked into the parlor and went over to his brother and the boy, and that was enough for her to recognize, within herself, what was not yet a thought, but then became one and acquired this formulation:

"There he is, their boy."

Never—nor at this moment—had the Madam imagined that the brothers in their love for each other had accomplished the miracle of true offspring, but their physical resemblance that created such an enormous obstacle for her feelings could not be anything less than love. Besides, this love—she saw only its earthly manifestation—had troubled her for such a long time that the least incident could give it substance. She was not far from expecting it to emanate from herself, from her body, her entrails, where it had been deposited like radioactive matter. Now, all of a sudden, two steps and yet very far away from her, the brothers reunited by an unknown youngster who naturally became the personification of that brotherly love her anguish labored over. But as soon as she had admitted this to herself she felt that she was being ridiculous. She wanted to turn her attention to the clients and whores, but was unable to forget the brothers, to whom she was now turning her back. She hesitated, then chose the pretext of talking to Robert about an expected delivery of liquor, to go over and take a look at the kid. He was adorable. He was worthy of the two lovers. She sized him up.

". . . and when the Cinzano man comes, tell him to wait for me."

She made as if to leave the parlor, but turning back immediately, smiling, she pointed at Roger:

And, smiling even more:

"You know, this could get me into trouble. And I'm not joking."

Robert, trying to look indifferent, asked Querelle:

"Who is he?"

"He's the kid brother of a girl I know. A little chickie I'm after."

Quite ignorant of the love between men, Robert thought that the boy had to be another one of his brother's fairy lovers.

He didn't dare look at him. Madame Lysiane was in the ladies' room, masturbating. Like her, Roger was very excited by it all, and when he left La Féria and went on to the old prison, he was in such a vulnerable frame of mind that (to use a hideous but appropriate expression) Gil had no difficulty in breaking him in. If Querelle, as she had said to him a little sadly, didn't have such great powers of erection, his rod at least was no disappointment, it had been worth dreaming about. It was a heavy, thick, rather massive cock, not elegant, but potentially vigorous. At long last Madame Lysiane found a little peace of mind, in that Querelle's member really was different from Robert's. There, at least, one could tell one from the other. At first Querelle accepted the *patronne's* advances rather nonchalantly, but as soon as he discovered that this could be a way of taking revenge on his brother for the humiliation he had caused him, he decided to speed up the affair. The first time, while he was taking off his clothes, his fury—revenge drawing near!—made him move with such alacrity that Madame Lysiane imagined him to be in the clutches of wild desire. In reality, Querelle was entering this bout with his body on the defensive. His amorous submission to a real cop had liberated him. He was at peace. Whenever he met Nono with whom he no longer wished to enter into secret frolics, he was not surprised to find that Nono seemed in no hurry to remind him of them, either. It so happened that Mario had not told Querelle that he had taken care to tell Nono all about the new developments. Thus, all Querelle had to do was to satisfy his lust for revenge. Madame Lysiane undressed more slowly. The sailor's apparent ardor thrilled her. She was even naïve enough to believe that she herself was its object. She was hoping that even before she was quite naked, the impatient, already glittering faun would charge out of the shrubbery to tumble her over on her back in a flurry of torn lace. Querelle lay down close beside her. At last he had an occasion to affirm his virility and to make his brother appear ridiculous. And Madame Lysiane had the painful experi-

ence of realizing that it was thanks to Querelle that she, like
Mario and like Norbert, had emerged from her solitude, into
which his departure would again plunge all of them. He had
appeared among them with the suddenness and elegance of the
joker in a pack. He scrambled the pattern, yet gave it meaning.
As for Querelle, he experienced a strange sensation as he left
Madame Lysiane's room: he was sorry to leave her. While he
was putting on his clothes again, slowly, a little sadly, his gaze
came to rest on the photograph of Nono that hung in a frame
on the wall. One after another he saw his friends' faces pass:
Nono, Robert, Mario, Gil. He felt a kind of melancholy, a
hardly conscious fear that they would not grow much older
without him; vaguely, and lulled almost to the point of sicken-
ing by Madame Lysiane's sighs as she stood dressing herself
with those overemphatic gestures he could observe in the mirror
on the wardrobe door, he wished he were able to drag them all
down into murder, to fix them there, so that they would never-
more experience love elsewhere or otherwise, only through him.
When he went over to her, Madame Lysiane had cried herself
dry. Strands of her disheveled hair were glued to her face by
tears, and the rouge on her lips was running a little. Querelle
hugged her, pressed her against his own body, already hard in
its navy-blue armor, and kissed her on the cheeks. This may
throw some light on Querelle's later treatment of the Lieutenant, first, and Mario, second. The *Vengeur*'s stay in Brest
was drawing to a close. The crew was aware that they would be
ready to leave in a few days' time. The idea of departure gave
rise to a confused anguish in Querelle. He would be rid of the
dry land with all its tangled and dangerous adventures, but he
would also lose all its joys. Every moment that turned him into
more of a stranger in the city attached him more strongly to life
on the ship. Querelle had a foreboding of the exceptional
importance of that enormous steel construction. The idea that
it was preparing for a cruise to the Baltic, or perhaps even
farther, to the White Sea, made him feel uneasy. Without

accounting for it to himself in any precise manner, Querelle was already arranging the elements of his future. It was on the second day of his liaison with Madame Lysiane that the incident occurred which we have seen mentioned in the Lieutenant's diary. It was Querelle's custom, when walking down the street, to have his own kind of fun with any girls he met. Pretending to grab them, in order to kiss them, he pushed them away if they acquiesced. Sometimes he did kiss them, but the general idea was to mock them, making faces or wisecracks. His vanity yearned for that kind of recognition of his powers as a seducer. He rarely spent more than seconds with any girl he had managed to catch, but kept on rolling along, with his slow and bouncy gait. But that evening things were different. Happy to have escaped, thanks to Madame Lysiane, from the aridity of his affairs with Nono and then Mario, feeling like a winner, proud of having deceived his brother and of having made love to a woman, he was walking down the Rue de Siam. He felt elated, a little drunk. The liquor warmed his chest, lit up his vision. He was smiling.

"Hey, baby!"

He had his arm round the girl's shoulders. She half turned and let herself be carried along by the powerful strides of this big brute. Querelle didn't even wait until they got out of the well-lit part of the street. In a patch of shadow between two shop fronts he pushed her up against the wall. Excited, hardly worried about being seen, the girl put her arms round his neck and held on to him. Querelle breathed into her hair, kissed her face, murmured obscenities into her ear which made her laugh, nervously. He wound his legs around hers. From time to time, he withdrew his face for a moment and glanced up and down the street. When he saw how busy it was, he grew even prouder. His triumph was a public one. That was the moment at which he saw, between two officers from another ship, Lieutenant Seblon come walking down the street. Querelle went on smiling at the girl. When the officers passed the shadowy area,

Querelle hugged her harder and kissed her on the mouth, pushing his tongue into it: but first of all, and retaining an interior smile, he imbued his back, his shoulders, his buttocks, with the entire significance of the moment—his entire powers of seduction directed themselves to that side of his body, and it became his true face, his sailor face. He tried to make it smile, to excite. Querelle wished for this so fervently that an imperceptible shudder ran the length of his spine, from neck to tailbone. He dedicated his most precious parts to the officer. He was sure he had been recognized. The Lieutenant's first impulse was to challenge Querelle in order to punish him for making such an indecent exhibition of himself in public. His respect for discipline was closely connected with his taste for pomp and circumstance—and with his conviction that he owed his actuality to the rigors of an order without which neither his rank nor his authority was able to function—: thus, to betray this order, even just a little, meant self-destruction. Yet he didn't budge. He would not have acted even without the presence of his fellow officers; while he knew the inner need to enforce discipline, to infringe it, or to tolerate an infraction, could make him feel the pleasure of freedom and even complicity with the culprit. In fact, it seemed quite elegant and "really rich" (those were the words in his mind) to show a smiling indulgence toward such a ravishing couple of young lovers. Querelle let the girl go, but as he did not dare to walk on in the direction of the port, where the officers were heading, he slowly retraced his steps. He felt both happy and discontented. Soon after he had turned around, a young girl detached herself from a group of friends and came running toward him, a big smile on her face. In no time she had reached him. She stretched out her arm to touch the pompon on the sailor's beret—for good luck!—who struck her in the face, hard, with the flat of his hand. Her face turning purple from shame and pain, the young girl stood as if petrified by Querelle's furious stare. Stammering, she said:

"I didn't do anything to you."

Now he was the center of attraction for a gathering of young men, all of them ready to smash his face in. Without moving his feet, Querelle made a slow turn. He understood the dangerous mood the boys were obviously in. For a moment he thought of calling some sailors to his aid, but there were none in sight. The men were insulting, menacing him. One of them pushed him: "You goddamn swine! To hit a girl like that! If you've got any balls . . ."

"Take care, you guys, he's got a knife."

Querelle looked at them. The alcohol in his blood dramatized his self-image, magnified the danger he was running. The crowd hesitated. There wasn't one woman in it who did not wish such a beautiful monster to be struck to the ground by the fist of one of the men, then torn and trampled to pieces, thus wreaking vengeance on her behalf, because she couldn't be his well-beloved mistress, protected by his arms, his body; yet she knew that he had to be the winner, after all, being so simply protected by his beauty. Querelle knew that his stare was positively fiery. Small flecks of frothy spittle appeared at the corners of his mouth. Through the enormous and transparent face of Lieutenant Seblon—who had returned, having parted from his companion—he saw dawn-light appearing on one spot on the globe, then saw it fade, rejoin other auroras, each one born in the spot where he had hidden part of the fruits of his murders and his thefts; yet he was still watching out for any threatening or fearful reactions from the crowd.

"Don't be an idiot. Come along."

The Lieutenant had pushed his way through the crowd and put his hand on Querelle's arm—gently, like a friend. Nevertheless he thought he would have to punish the sailor for getting so drunk. Not that he believed himself responsible for the good conduct of the Navy—in a situation like this, he thought, right conduct consisted in facing up to a fight—but he wanted to make evident the spiritual power of his gold braid, this desire reinforced by a fear that order (and thus, truth itself) had been

violated. With astonishing insight he knew that he must not
touch the knife arm, and his white fingers were resting on
Querelle's left. Now, at last, he was free to be brave in every
way. For the first time he addressed Querelle familiarly, and in
the circumstances that seemed the only normal thing to do. In
his private diary, the Lieutenant had said that for him, the most
important thing in becoming an officer was not so much to
become a master, feared or not, as a kind of master spirit,
animating those muscular masses, those big displays of sinewy
flesh. We can thus understand his anxiety at that moment. He
did not know yet whether this powerful body, every nerve alive,
charged and inflated with rage and hatred, would let itself be
calmed down by him, or—better still—allow all that swirling
energy to be directed according to his wishes . . . Seblon felt
quite prepared to accept the homage and the envy of all the
women in the crowd, when he would walk off, right in front of
their noses, with this, the handsomest of all brutes on his arm,
charmed and made docile by his orphic song.

"Get back on board. I don't want you to get messed up. And
give me that thing."

And that was when he held out his hand, to take the knife:
but Querelle, while accepting the officer's intervention, refused
to have his weapon confiscated. He snapped it shut by pressing
the back of the blade against his thigh and put it in his pocket.
Without a word he stepped forward and pushed his way
through the crowd, which gave way with a growl. When the
Lieutenant met him again, in the vicinity of the jetty, Querelle
was stone drunk. A little unsteady on his feet, he came up to
the officer, planted a heavy hand on his shoulder and said:

"You're a buddy! Those were goddamn asshole landlubbers.
But you, you're a real buddy."

Overcome by all the drink, he sat down on a mooring bollard.

"You can get anything you want from me."

He started to fall off his seat. To hold him, the Lieutenant
grabbed his shoulders and said, gently:

"Calm down, now. If an officer should happen to . . ."

"Fuck that! There ain't no one here but you!"

"Pipe down, I'm telling you. I don't want you to get locked up."

Seblon was glad he hadn't succumbed to the desire to punish Querelle. The time had come for him to say goodbye to the world of policemen, to turn away from an order he had respected overmuch. And then—the gesture seemed spontaneous, but was most deliberate—then he put his hand on Querelle's beret, keeping it there lightly at first, then pressing it down and touching the sailor's hair. Querelle was still swaying back and forth. Grateful for the opportunity, the officer pulled the sailor's head toward him, and Querelle rested his cheek on Seblon's thigh.

"Wouldn't like to see you in jail, you know."

"Is that right? Come on, you're just saying that. You're an officer, what the hell do you care!"

It was then that Lieutenant Seblon dared to stroke the other cheek and say:

"You know very well that I do care."

Querelle put an arm round his waist, forced him to bend down and kissed him, hard, on the mouth. Then he got up, throwing his arms round the officer's neck, and there was such a sense of abandon and languor in his movements that for the first time, riding the crest of a wave of femininity from god knows where, this gesture became a masterpiece of manly grace: the muscular arms formed a flower-basket, holding a human head more lovely than any flower, and they had dared to forget their usual function and taken on another one, expressing their most essential nature. Querelle smiled at the thought of drawing so close to that shame from which there is no return, and in which one might well discover peace. He felt so weak, so overcome, that this phrase formed in his mind, saddening in all that it evoked of autumn, of stains, of delicate and mortal wounds:

"Here's the one who will follow in my footsteps."

As we have related, the police arrested the Lieutenant the following day.

*I shall not know peace until he makes love to me, but only when he enters me and then lets me stretch out on my side across his thighs, holding me the way the dead Jesus is held in a Pietà.*

Motionless at her cash-desk, facing the empty and dazzling room, she observed the unfolding of events she wanted to remain in control of, to define down to the least detail. At the same time she was continuously excited by the rhythm of her ever more urgent thoughts. Having no idea how she would justify her crime to the judges, she decided to set fire to the brothel. But that fire, too, would have to be explained; she realized that death was the only way out for her, after the fire. Well, she would hang herself. She was breathing so hard that her chest, in expanding, seemed to raise her entire body upward, and she looked like someone about to begin her Ascension. Dry-eyed, behind burning eyelids, she stared at the terrifying void of mirrors and lights, while following, in her mind, the circular movement of these themes of despair: "Even when they are apart, they'll call for each other, from one end of the world to the other . . ." "If his brother goes to sea, Robert's face will always be turned to the west. I'll be married to a sunflower .       " "The smiles and the insults fly back and forth between them, wind themselves around them, tie them together. No one will ever know which one is the stronger. And their boy just passes through all that, not making any difference . . ." In the precious palace of her white body of flesh like ivory and mother-of-pearl, Madame Lysiane watched ne unrolling of great streamers of watered silk, on which those sumptuous phrases had been embroidered, and she deciphered them with fear and awe. She witnessed the secret history of the inseparable lovers. Their fights were riddled with smiles, their games adorned with insults. Laughter and insults became interchangeable. They hurt each other, laughing. And to this very door, to Madame Lysiane's threshold they keep on weaving themselves together in their rites. They have their feasts, to which they invite only themselves. Every minute they celebrate their nuptials. The thought of setting fire to the building came back, clearer than before. To concentrate on it, to decide where she would pour the gasoline, Madame Lysiane let her body slump into a state of self-oblivion; but as soon as she had made her decision, she pulled herself together again. With both hands she examined the edges of her corset, through the material of her dress. She got up.

"Have to look good and straighten up."

As soon as the thought crossed her mind, she felt deeply ashamed. Then, numbly, Madame Lysiane saw her own words written out in front of her, in her own inimitable grammar. Thinking of her lovers:

"They is singing." Looking at Querelle, Madame Lysiane no longer felt what fencing masters call the hunger of the rapier. She was alone.

# Selected Grove Press Paperbacks

62334-7 ACKER, KATHY / Blood and Guts in High School / $7.95

62480-7 ACKER, KATHY / Great Expectations: A Novel / $6.95

62192-1 ALIFANO, ROBERTO / Twenty-four Conversations with Borges, 1980-1983 / $8.95

17458-5 ALLEN, DONALD & BUTTERICK, GEORGE F., eds. / The Postmoderns: The New American Poetry Revised 1945-1960 / $9.95

17801-7 ALLEN, DONALD M., & TALLMAN, WARREN, eds. / Poetics of the New American Poetry / $12.50

17061-X ARDEN, JOHN / Arden: Plays One (Sergeant Musgrave's Dance, The Workhouse Donkey, Armstrong's Last Goodnight) / $4.95

17657-X ARSAN, EMMANUELLE / Emmanuelle / $3.95

17213-2 ARTAUD, ANTONIN / The Theater and Its Double / $6.95

62433-5 BARASH, D. and LIPTON, J. / Stop Nuclear War! A Handbook / $7.95

62056-9 BARRY, TOM, WOOD, BETH & PREUSCH, DEB / The Other Side of Paradise: Foreign Control in the Caribbean / $9.95

17087-3 BARNES, JOHN / Evita—First Lady: A Biography of Eva Peron / $4.95

17928-5 BECKETT, SAMUEL / Company / $3.95

62489-0 BECKETT, SAMUEL / Disjecta: Miscellaneous Writings and a Dramatic Fragment, ed. Cohn, Ruby / $5.95

17208-6 BECKETT, SAMUEL / Endgame / $3.50

17953-6 BECKETT, SAMUEL / Ill Seen Ill Said / $4.95

62061-5 BECKETT, SAMUEL / Ohio Impromptu, Catastrophe, and What Where: Three Plays / $4.95

17924-2 BECKETT, SAMUEL / Rockababy and Other Short Pieces / $3.95

17299-X BECKETT, SAMUEL / Three Novels: Molloy, Malone Dies and The Unnamable / $6.95

17204-3 BECKETT, SAMUEL / Waiting for Godot / $3.50

62418-1 BERLIN, NORMAND / Eugene O'Neill / $9.95

17237-X BIELY, ANDREW / St. Petersburg / $12.50

17252-3 BIRCH, CYRIL & KEENE, DONALD, eds. / Anthology of Chinese Literature, Vvol. I: From Early Times to the 14th Century / $17.50

17766-5 BIRCH, CYRIL, ed. / Anthology of Chinese Literature, Vol. II: From the 14th Century to the Present / $12.95

62104-2 BLOCH, DOROTHY / "So the Witch Won't Eat Me," Fantasy and the Child's Fear of Infanticide / $7.95

17244-2 BORGES, JORGE LUIS / Ficciones / $6.95

17270-1 BORGES, JORGE LUIS / A Personal Anthology / $6.95

17258-2  BRECHT, BERTOLT / The Caucasian Chalk Circle / $4.95
17109-8  BRECHT, BERTOLT / The Good Woman of Setzuan / $3.95
17112-8  BRECHT, BERTOLT / Galileo / $3.95
17065-2  BRECHT, BERTOLT / The Mother / $2.95
17106-3  BRECHT, BERTOLT / Mother Courage and Her Children / $2.95
17472-0  BRECHT, BERTOLT / Threepenny Opera / $2.45
17393-7  BRETON ANDRE / Nadja / $6.95
17439-9  BULGAKOV, MIKHAIL / The Master and Margarita / $5.95
17108-X  BURROUGHS, WILLIAM S. / Naked Lunch / $4.95
17749-5  BURROUGHS, WILLIAM S. / The Soft Machine, Nova Express,
         The Wild Boys: Three Novels / $5.95
62488-2  CLARK, AL, ed. / The Film Year Book 1984 / $12.95
17038-5  CLEARY, THOMAS / The Original Face: An Anthology of Rinzai
         Zen / $4.95
17735-5  CLEVE, JOHN / The Crusader Books I and II / $4.95
17411-9  CLURMAN, HAROLD (Ed.) / Nine Plays of the Modern Theater
         (Waiting for Godot by Samuel Beckett, The Visit by Friedrich
         Durrenmatt, Tango by Slawomir Mrozek, The Caucasian Chalk
         Circle by Bertolt Brecht, The Balcony by Jean Genet, Rhinoceros
         by Eugene Ionesco, American Buffalo by David Mamet, The Birth-
         day Party by Harold Pinter, Rosencrantz and Guildenstern Are
         Dead by Tom Stoppard) / $14.95
17962-5  COHN, RUBY / New American Dramatists: 1960-1980 / $7.95
17971-4  COOVER, ROBERT / Spanking the Maid / $4.95
17535-2  COWARD, NOEL / Three Plays by Noel Coward (Private Lives,
         Hay Fever, Blithe Spirit) / $7.95
17740-1  CRAFTS, KATHY & HAUTHER, BRENDA / How To Beat the
         System: The Student's Guide to Good Grades / $3.95
17219-1  CUMMINGS, E.E. / 100 Selected Poems / $3.95
17329-5  DOOLITTLE, HILDA / Selected Poems of H.D. / $8.95
17863-7  DOSS, MARGOT PATTERSON / San Francisco at Your Feet
         (Second Revised Edition) / $8.95
17398-8  DOYLE, RODGER, & REDDING, JAMES / The Complete Food
         Handbook (revised any updated edition) / $3.50
17219-1  DURAS, MARGUERITE / Four Novels: The Afternoon of Mr.
         Andesmas; 10:30 on a Summer Night; Moderato Cantabile; The
         Square) / $9.95
17246-9  DURRENMATT, FRIEDRICH / The Physicists / $6.95
17239-6  DURRENMATT, FRIEDRICH / The Visit / $4.95
17990-0  FANON, FRANZ / Black Skin, White Masks / $8.95
17327-9  FANON, FRANZ / The Wretched of the Earth / $4.95
17754-1  FAWCETT, ANTHONY / John Lennon: One Day At A Time, A
         Personal Biography (Revised Edition) / $8.95
17902-1  FEUERSTEIN, GEORG / The Essence of Yoga / $3.95

| 17278-7 | KEROUAC, JACK / Dr. Sax / $5.95 |
| 17171-3 | KEROUAC, JACK / Lonesome Traveler / $5.95 |
| 17287-6 | KEROUAC, JACK / Mexico City Blues / $9.95 |
| 17437-2 | KEROUAC, JACK / Satori in Paris / $4.95 |
| 17035-0 | KERR, CARMEN / Sex for Women Who Want to Have Fun and Loving Relationships With Equals / $9.95 |
| 17981-1 | KINGSLEY, PHILIP / The Complete Hair Book: The Ultimate Guide to Your Hair's Health and Beauty / $10.95 |
| 62424-6 | LAWRENCE, D.H. / Lady Chatterley's Lover / $3.95 |
| 17178-0 | LESTER, JULIUS / Black Folktales / $4.95 |
| 17481-X | LEWIS, MATTHEW / The Monk / $8.95 |
| 17391-0 | LINSSEN, ROBERT / Living Zen / $12.50 |
| 17114-4 | MALCOLM X (Breitman., ed.) / Malcolm X Speaks / $5.95 |
| 17023-7 | MALRAUX, ANDRE/The Conquerors/$3.95 |
| 17068-7 | MALRAUX, ANDRE/Lazarus/$2.95 |
| 17093-8 | MALRAUX, ANDRE / Man's Hope / $12.50 |
| 17016-4 | MAMET, DAVID / American Buffalo / $4.95 |
| 62049-6 | MAMET, DAVID / Glengarry Glenn Ross / $6.95 |
| 17040-7 | MAMET, DAVID / A Life in the Theatre / $6.95 |
| 17043-1 | MAMET, DAVID / Sexual Perversity in Chicago & The Duck Variations / $6.95 |
| 17471-2 | MILLER, HENRY / Black Spring / $4.95 |
| 17760-6 | MILLER, HENRY / Tropic of Cancer / $4.95 |
| 17295-7 | MILLER, HENRY / Tropic of Capricorn / $3.95 |
| 17933-1 | MROZEK, SLAWOMIR / Three Plays: Striptease, Tango, Vatzlav / $12.50 |
| 17869-6 | NERUDA, PABLO / Five Decades: Poems 1925-1970. bilingual ed. / $12.50 |
| 62243-X | NICOSIA, GERALD / Memory Babe: A Critical Biography of Jack Kerouac |
| 17092-X | ODETS, CLIFFORD / Six Plays (Waiting for Lefty, Awake and Sing, Golden Boy, Rocket to the Moon, Till the Day I Die, Paradise Lost) / $7.95 |
| 17650-2 | OE, KENZABURO / A Personal Matter / $6.95 |
| 17002-4 | OE, KENZABURO / Teach Us To Outgrow Our Madness (The Day He Himself Shall Wipe My Tears Away; Prize Stock; Teach Us to Outgrow Our Madness; Aghwee The Sky Monster) / $4.95 |
| 17242-6 | PAZ, OCTAVIO / The Labyrinth of Solitude / $9.95 |
| 17084-9 | PINTER, HAROLD / Betrayal / $6.95 |
| 17232-9 | PINTER, HAROLD / The Birthday Party & The Room / $6.95 |
| 17251-5 | PINTER, HAROLD / The Homecoming / $5.95 |
| 17539-5 | POMERANCE / The Elephant Man / $5.95 |
| 62013-5 | PORTWOOD, DORIS / Common Sense Suicide: The Final Right / $8.00 |

| | |
|---|---|
| 17658-8 | REAGE, PAULINE / The Story of O, Part II; Return to the Chateau / $3.95 |
| 62169-7 | RECHY, JOHN / City of Night / $4.50 |
| 62171-9 | RECHY, JOHN / Numbers / $8.95 |
| 17983-8 | ROBBE-GRILLET, ALAIN / Djinn / $4.95 |
| 62423-8 | ROBBE—GRILLET, ALAIN / For a New Novel: Essays on Fiction / $9.95 |
| 17119-5 | ROBBE-GRILLET, ALAIN / The Voyeur / 4.95 |
| 17490-9 | ROSSET, BARNEY, ed. / Evergreen Review Reader: 1962-1967 / $12.50 |
| 62498-X | ROSSET, PETER and VANDERMEER, JOHN / The Nicaragua Reader: Documents of a Revolution under Fire / $9.95 |
| 17446-1 | RULFO, JUAN / Pedro Paramo / $3.95 |
| 17123-3 | SADE, MARQUIS DE / Justine; Philosophy in the Bedroom; Eugenie de Franval; and Other Writings / $12.50 |
| 17979-X | SANTINI, ROSEMARIE / The Secret Fire: How Women Live Their Sexual Fantasies / $3.95 |
| 62495-5 | SCHEFFLER, LINDA / Help Thy Neighbor: How Counseling Works and When It Doesn't / $7.95 |
| 62438-6 | SCHNEEBAUM, TOBIAS / Keep the River on Your Right / $12.50 |
| 17467-4 | SELBY, HUBERT, JR. / Last Exit to Brooklyn / $3.95 |
| 17948-X | SHAWN, WALLACE, & GREGORY, ANDRE / My Dinner with Andre / $6.95 |
| 62496-3 | SIEGAL AND SIEGAL / AIDS: The Medical Mystery / $7.95 |
| 17887-4 | SINGH, KHUSHWANT / Train to Pakistan / $4.50 |
| 17797-5 | SNOW, EDGAR / Red Star Over China / $9.95 |
| 17939-0 | SRI NISARGADATA MAHARAJ / Seeds of Consciousness / $9.95 |
| 17923-4 | STEINER, CLAUDE / Healing Alcoholism / $6.95 |
| 17926-9 | STEINER, CLAUDE / The Other Side of Power / $6.95 |
| 17866-1 | STOPPARD, TOM / Jumpers / $4.95 |
| 17260-4 | STOPPARD, TOM / Rosencrantz and Guildenstern Are Dead / $3.95 |
| 17884-X | STOPPARD, TOM / Travesties / $3.95 |
| 17912-9 | STRYK, LUCIEN, ed. / The Crane's Bill: Zen Poems of China and Japan / $4.95 |
| 17474-7 | SUZUKI, D.T. / Introduction to Zen Buddhism / $3.95 |
| 17224-8 | SUZUKI, D.T. / Manual of Zen Buddhism / $7.95 |
| 17599-9 | THELWELL, MICHAEL / The Harder They Come: A Novel about Jamaica / $7.95 |
| 17969-2 | TOOLE, JOHN KENNEDY / A Confederacy of Dunces / $4.50 |
| 17403-8 | TROCCHI, ALEXANDER / Cain's Book / $3.50 |
| 62168-9 | TUTUOLA, AMOS / The Palm-Wine Drinkard / $4.50 |
| 62189-1 | UNGERER, TOMI / Far Out Isn't Far Enough (Illus.) / $12.95 |
| 17560-3 | VITHOULKAS, GEORGE / The Science of Homeopathy / $12.50 |

17331-7  WALEY, ARTHUR / The Book of Songs / $9.95
17211-6  WALEY, ARTHUR / Monkey / $8.95
17207-8  WALEY, ARTHUR / The Way and Its Power: A Study of the Tao Te Ching and Its Place in Chinese Thought / $8.95
17418-6  WATTS, ALAN W. / The Spirit of Zen / $3.95
62031-3  WORTH, KATHERINE / Oscar Wilde / $8.95
17739-8  WYCKOFF, HOGIE / Solving Problems Together / $7.95

GROVE PRESS, INC., 920 Broadway, New York, N.Y. 10010